The Place to
KNOW BETTER

ST. LOUIS
PUBLIC
LIBRARY

This book

is given by

Irwin Fredman

in honor of

Avery Fredman

THE
ROAD TO ROME

BEN KANE

ST. MARTIN'S PRESS ⚘ NEW YORK

THE ROAD TO ROME. Copyright © 2010 by Ben Kane. All rights reserved.
Printed in the United States of America. For information, address St. Martin's Press,
175 Fifth Avenue, New York, N.Y. 10010.

Map copyright © 2008 by Jeffrey L. Ward.

www.stmartins.com

Library of Congress Cataloging-in-Publication Data

Kane, Ben.
    The road to Rome : a novel of the forgotten legion / Ben Kane. — 1st U.S. ed.
        p. cm.
    ISBN 978-0-312-53673-2
    1. Brothers and sisters—Fiction.   2. Twins—Fiction.   3. Slaves—Rome—
Fiction.   4. Gladiators—Rome—Fiction.   5. Rome—History—Republic,
265–30 B.C.—Fiction.   I. Title.
    PR6111.A536R63 2011
    823'.92—dc22

                                                              2010042049

First published in the United Kingdom by Preface Books, The Random House Group Limited

First U.S. Edition: April 2011

10 9 8 7 6 5 4 3 2 1

TO KYRAN AND HELEN KANE,
MY WONDERFUL PARENTS,
WITH MUCH LOVE AND THANKS

BRITANNIA

GAUL

Alesia

Massilia

HISPANIA

ITALIA

Ravenna

Rome

DACIA

Dyrrachium

Brundisium

Pharsalus

GREECE

ASIA
MINOR

Mare Internum

AFRICA

Alexandria

N

EGYPT

R. Nilus

0 Miles   200   400

0 Kilometers   400

© 2008 Jeffrey L. Ward

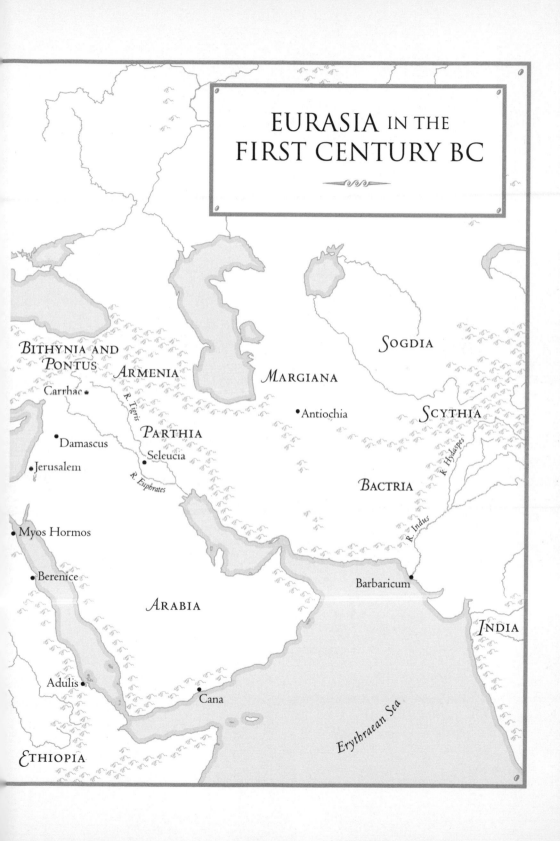

EURASIA IN THE
FIRST CENTURY BC

BITHYNIA AND
PONTUS

ARMENIA

Carrhae

R. Tigris

Damascus

PARTHIA

Seleucia

Jerusalem

R. Euphrates

MARGIANA

Antiochia

SOGDIA

SCYTHIA

R. Hydaspes

BACTRIA

R. Indus

Myos Hormos

Berenice

ARABIA

Barbaricum

INDIA

Adulis

Cana

ETHIOPIA

Erythraean Sea

THE
ROAD TO ROME

I

EGYPT

Get a move on, damn you," cried the *optio*, swiping the flat of his blade at the nearest legionaries' backs. "Caesar needs us!"

His squad of ten men needed little encouragement. Their night picket was positioned on the Heptastadion, the narrow, man-made causeway that ran from the docks to a long, thin island, separating the harbor into two parts. With water on both sides, it was an isolated position. Given what was happening, that was not a healthy place to be.

The yellow glow from the Pharos, the city's huge lighthouse, had been greatly augmented by the burning ships along the quay. Started by Caesar's men, the fire on the vessels had spread fast, reaching out to the nearby warehouses and library buildings to form a conflagration that lit up the scene as bright as day. After regrouping with their comrades who had been driven back into the darkened side streets, thousands of Egyptian troops were re-emerging to slam into Caesar's lines. These were less than a hundred paces away from the Heptastadion, the natural point to hold against an enemy.

Romulus and Tarquinius ran willingly alongside the legionaries.

If the screaming mass of Egyptian soldiers broke through their lines, they would all be killed. Even if the Egyptians didn't succeed initially, the odds of surviving were poor. The legionaries were vastly outnumbered, and had no secure avenue of retreat. The whole city was swarming with unfriendly natives, and the causeway led to an island from which there was no escape. There were only the Roman ships, but thanks to the swarming enemy troops, embarking safely was not possible.

Grimacing, Romulus threw a longing glance at the one trireme that had got away. It was nearing the western harbor entrance, with Fabiola, his twin sister, on board. After nigh on nine years of separation, they had glimpsed each other a few moments previously. Fabiola was headed out to sea, escaping the danger, and there was nothing Romulus could do about it. Oddly, he was not devastated. He recognized why. Just knowing that Fabiola was alive, and safe, made his heart thrum with an unquenchable joy. With Mithras' help, she would have heard him yell that he was in the Twenty-Eighth Legion, and could thus find him one day. After all his prayers about his long-lost sister, the gods had answered.

Now, though, as so often before, he was about to fight for his life.

Press-ganged into the legions, he and Tarquinius were part of Caesar's small task force in Alexandria: a force under imminent threat of being overwhelmed. Romulus took some solace from his new and precarious position, however. If Elysium was waiting for him, then he would not enter it as a slave, nor a gladiator. Not as a mercenary, and not as a captive. Romulus squared his shoulders.

No, he thought fiercely, *I am a Roman legionary. At last. My fate is my own, and Tarquinius will no longer control me.* Not an hour past, his blond-haired friend had revealed that he was responsible for the killing which had originally forced Romulus to flee Rome. The shock of it was still sweeping through Romulus. Disbelief, anger and hurt swirled together in a toxic mix that made his head spin. He shoved the pain away, burying it for another time.

Breathing heavily, the group reached the back of Caesar's formation, which was only six ranks deep. Shouted orders, the metallic clash of arms and the screams of the wounded were suddenly very close. The *optio* conferred with the nearest officer, a nervous-looking *tesserarius*. Wearing a transverse-crested helmet and scale armor similar to the *optio's*, he bore a long staff to keep the legionaries in line. While he and other subordinates stayed at the rear to prevent anyone retreating, the centurions would be at, or near, the front. In a battle as desperate as this, these veteran career soldiers stiffened the resolve of all.

At length the *optio* turned to his men. "Our cohort is right here."

"Trust our luck," muttered one soldier. "Right in the middle of the damn line."

The *optio* smiled thinly in acknowledgment. This was where most casualties would fall. "You've got it easy for the moment. Be grateful," he said. "Spread out, two deep. Reinforce this century."

Grumbling, they did as he said.

With four others, Romulus and Tarquinius found themselves at the front of their two small files. They did not protest at this. As the new recruits, it was to be expected. Romulus was taller than most, and could see over men's heads and past the upright horsehair crests on their bronze-bowl helmets. Here and there a century standard jutted up into the air, and over on the right flank was the silver eagle, the emotive talisman of the legion. His heart raced at the sight of it, the greatest symbol of Rome, and one that he had grown to love dearly. More than anything, the eagle had helped Romulus to remember that he was a Roman. Imperious, proud and aloof, it cared nothing for men's status, recognizing only their bravery and valor in battle.

Beyond it, though, was a sea of snarling faces and glinting weapons, sweeping toward them in great rolling waves.

"They're carrying *scuta*," Romulus cried in confusion. "Are they Roman?"

"Once," spat the legionary to his left. "But the bastards have gone native."

"Gabinius' men then, I would say," said Tarquinius, receiving a gruff nod in response. There were curious stares, especially from those who could see the left side of his face. A prolonged torture session by Vahram, the *primus pilus* of the Forgotten Legion, had left a shiny red cicatrice on the haruspex' cheek in the shape of a knife blade.

Thanks to Tarquinius, Romulus was familiar with the story of Ptolemy XII, the father of the current rulers of Egypt, who had been deposed more than a decade before. Desperate, Ptolemy had turned to Rome, offering incredible sums in gold to restore him to the throne. Eventually, Gabinius, the proconsul of Syria, seized the opportunity. That had been at the same time that Romulus, Brennus, his Gaulish friend, and Tarquinius were traveling in Crassus' army.

"Aye," muttered the legionary. "They stayed here after Gabinius returned in disgrace to Rome."

"How many are left?" asked Romulus.

"A few thousand," came the answer. "But they've got plenty of help. Nubian skirmishers and Judaean mercenaries mostly, and Cretan slingers and archers. All tough bastards."

"There are infantry as well," said another man. "Escaped slaves from our provinces."

An angry growl met his words.

Romulus and Tarquinius exchanged a look. It was imperative their status, particularly that of Romulus, remained secret. Slaves were not allowed to fight in the regular army. To join the legions, which Romulus' press-ganging had effectively done for him, carried the death penalty.

"Those treacherous whoresons won't stand against us," the first legionary proclaimed. "We'll knock seven shades of shit out of them."

It was the right thing to say. Pleased grins cracked across worried faces.

Romulus held back his instinctive retort. Spartacus' followers, slaves all, had bettered the legions on numerous occasions. He himself was the match of any three ordinary legionaries. With a new homeland to defend, the enemy slaves could prove tough to defeat. This was not the time, nor the place, to mention such matters, though. When was? Romulus wondered with a tinge of bitterness. Never.

With ready weapons, they waited as the clash became more desperate. Showers of enemy javelins and stones flew into their lines, cutting down men here and there. Lacking shields, Romulus and Tarquinius could only duck down and pray as death whistled overhead. It was most disconcerting. As the casualties grew heavier, spare equipment became available. A stocky soldier in the rank ahead went down with a spear through the neck. Quickly Romulus pulled off the twitching man's helmet, feeling little remorse. The needs of the living were greater than those of the dead. Even the sweat-soaked felt liner that he jammed on his head first felt like some kind of protection. Tarquinius took the corpse's *scutum*, and it wasn't long before Romulus had his own one too, from another victim.

The *optio* grunted in approval. The two ragged wanderers did not just possess good weapons, they also knew their way around military equipment.

"This is more like it," said Romulus, lifting his elongated oval shield by its horizontal grip. Not since the Forgotten Legion's last battle four years before had they both been fully equipped. He scowled. It was still hard not to feel guilty about Brennus, who had died so that he and Tarquinius might escape.

"Seen combat before?" demanded the legionary.

Before Romulus could reply, a shield boss hit him in the back.

"Forward!" shouted the *optio*, who had shoved in behind them. "The line in front is weakening."

Pushing against the rows in front, they shuffled toward the enemy. Dozens of *gladii*, the Roman short stabbing swords, were raised in preparation. Shields were lifted until the only part of men's faces that could be seen was their flickering eyes under their helmet rims. They moved shoulder to shoulder, each protected by his comrades. Tarquinius was to Romulus' right and the talkative legionary was on his left. Both were responsible for his safety as he was for theirs. It was one of the beauties of the shield wall. Although Romulus was furious with Tarquinius, he did not think that the haruspex would fail in this duty.

He had not appreciated how thin their ranks had become. Suddenly the soldier in front slumped to his knees, and a screaming enemy warrior jumped into the gap, taking Romulus by surprise. He was wearing a blunt-peaked Phrygian helmet and a rough-spun tunic, with no armor. An oval spined shield and a *rhomphaia*, a strange sword with a long, curved blade, were his only weapons. This was a Thracian peltast, Romulus thought, shocked twice over.

Without thinking, he jumped forward, smashing his *scutum* boss at the other's face. The move failed as the Thracian met the attack with his own shield. They traded blows for a few moments, each trying to gain an advantage. There was none to be had and Romulus fast developed a healthy respect for his enemy's angled sword. Thanks to its shape, it could hook over the top of his *scutum* and around the sides to cause serious injury. In the space of a dozen heartbeats, he nearly lost an eye and then barely avoided a nasty injury to his left biceps.

In return, Romulus had sliced a shallow cut across the Thracian's sword arm. He grimaced with satisfaction. While the gash did not disable, it reduced the other's ability to fight. Blood oozed from the wound, running down onto the peltast's sword hilt. The man spat a curse as they cut and thrust at one another repeatedly, neither able to get past his opponent's shield. Soon Romulus saw that the

Thracian could not lift his weapon without wincing. It was a little window of opportunity, and one he was not about to let slip.

Shoving his left leg and his *scutum* forward, Romulus swung his *gladius* over in a powerful, arcing blow that threatened to decapitate. The peltast had to meet it, or lose the right side of his face. Sending up a clash of sparks, the two iron blades met. Romulus' swept the other's down, toward the ground. A groan escaped the Thracian's lips and Romulus knew he had him. It was time to finish it, while his enemy's pain was all-consuming. Using his forward momentum, Romulus lunged forward, putting all his body weight behind the shield.

His power was too much for the peltast, who lost his footing and tumbled backward, losing his shield in the fall. In an instant Romulus was crouched over him, his right arm drawn back and ready. They exchanged the briefest of looks, similar to that which an executioner gives his intended victim; there is no response other than the widening of pupils. A quick downward thrust of Romulus' *gladius* and the Thracian was dead.

Jerking upright, Romulus lifted his *scutum* just in time. His enemy had already been replaced by an unshaven, long-haired man in Roman military dress. Another one of Gabinius' men.

"Traitor," hissed Romulus. "Fighting your own kind now?"

"I'm fighting for my homeland," growled the enemy soldier. His Latin proved Romulus' theory. "What the fuck are you doing here?"

Stung, he had no answer.

"Following Caesar," snarled the talkative legionary. "The best general in the world."

This was met with a sneer, and Romulus took his chance. He stabbed forward, thrusting his sword over the top of his distracted foe's mail shirt and deep into his neck. With a scream, the man dropped from sight, allowing Romulus to see the enemy lines briefly. He wished he hadn't. There were Egyptian soldiers as far as the eye could see and they were all moving determinedly forward.

"How many cohorts have we here?" asked Romulus. "Four?"

"Yes." The legionary closed up with him again. Thanks to their heavy casualties, they were now part of the front rank. With Tarquinius and the others, they prepared to meet the next onslaught, a combined wave of legionaries and lightly armed Nubians. "They're all under strength, though."

Their new enemies were clad only in loincloths; many wore a single long feather in their hair. The black-skinned warriors carried large oval hide shields and broad-bladed spears. Some, the more wealthy among them, wore decorated headbands and gold arm rings. These individuals also wore short swords tucked into their fabric belts and carried longbows. A quiver poked over each man's left shoulder. Knowing the limited range of the Roman javelin, they stopped fifty paces away and calmly fitted arrows to their strings. Their comrades waited patiently.

Romulus was relieved to see that the Nubians weren't using compound weapons, as the Parthians did. The shafts from those could penetrate a *scutum* with ease. It wasn't much consolation. "How weak are we, exactly?" he demanded.

"With the fifth cohort that's guarding our triremes, we number about fifteen hundred." The legionary saw Romulus' surprise. "What do you expect?" he snarled. "Many of us have been campaigning for seven years. Gaul, Britannia, Gaul again."

Romulus looked at Tarquinius grimly. These men were hardbitten veterans, but they were badly outnumbered. All he got was an apologetic shrug. He ground his teeth. They were only here because Tarquinius had ignored his advice, insistent on checking out the dock and the library. Still, he had seen Fabiola. If he died in this skirmish, it would be in the knowledge that his sister was alive and well.

The first volley of Nubian arrows shot up into the air, hissing down in a graceful, deadly shower.

"Shields up!" shouted the officers.

An instant later, the stream of enemy missiles struck their raised *scuta* with familiar thumping sounds. To Romulus' relief, almost none had the power to drive through, so few men were hit. His pulse increased, though, as he noticed some of the stone and iron arrowheads were smeared with a thick, dark paste. Poison! The last time he had seen that was when fighting the Scythians in Margiana. Even a tiny scratch from one of their barbed tips caused a man to die in screaming agony. Romulus felt even more glad of the *scutum* in his fist.

Another volley followed before the Nubians began trotting toward Caesar's lines. Unencumbered by heavy equipment such as the rogue legionaries were carrying, they quickly picked up pace. Screaming ferocious battle cries, the enemy warriors soon reached a sprint. They were followed by Gabinius' former soldiers, who would deliver the hammer blow. Romulus gritted his teeth and wished that Brennus were still with them. The enemy formation was at least ten ranks deep, while Caesar's lines now were barely half that.

Right on cue, the trumpets blew a short series of blasts. From the rear came the shouted order, "Retreat to the ships!" The voice was calm and measured, quite at odds with the urgency of the situation.

"That's Caesar," explained the legionary with a proud grin. "Never panics."

At once their lines began edging sideways, toward the western harbor. It was only a short distance, but they could not let down their guard at all. Seeing this attempt to escape, the Nubians yelled with anger and sprang forward again.

"Keep going," cried the centurion nearest Romulus. "Stop just before they hit. Stay in formation and drive them back. Then move on."

Romulus eyed the triremes, which numbered about twenty. There would be room on board for all—but where would they go?

As ever, Tarquinius butted in with the answer. "To the Pharos." He pointed at the lighthouse. "Over there, the Heptastadion is only fifty or sixty paces across."

His confidence restored, Romulus grinned. "We can defend that until doomsday."

Yet the ships were still out of reach and, a heartbeat later, the Nubians struck the Roman formation with such force that the front ranks were driven back several steps. Screams filled the night air and soldiers cursed the bad luck sent them by the gods. Romulus saw a legionary to his left take a spear through one calf and go down thrashing. Horrendously, another had a blade pierce both cheeks to emerge on the other side of his face. Blood jetted from the wounds as the weapon was withdrawn. Dropping his *scutum* and sword, the soldier raised both hands to his ruined face and let out a thin, piercing cry. Romulus lost sight of both injured men as a mass of Nubians slammed up against his section.

Angry red mouths shouted insults in a foreign tongue. Hide shields smacked off *scuta* and broad spear blades flickered back and forth, searching for Roman flesh. Romulus' nostrils were filled with the black warriors' musty body odor. Quickly he killed the first man within reach, sliding his *gladius* under the man's sternum in one easy move. His next opponent was no harder to dispatch; he practically ran on to Romulus' sword. The Nubian was dead before he'd even realized it.

On Romulus' right, Tarquinius was also dispatching warriors with ease, but to his left, the talkative legionary was struggling. Beset by two hulking Nubians, he soon took a spear through his right shoulder, which crippled him. He had no chance as one of his enemies pulled down his shield while the other stabbed him through the throat. It was the last thing the first Nubian did. Romulus lopped off his right hand, the one holding the spear, and with the backstroke opened the warrior's flesh from his groin to his shoulder. A legionary from the rank behind moved forward to fill the gap and together they killed the second warrior.

The dead were replaced immediately.

We need cavalry, thought Romulus as he fought on. *Or some catapults.* A different tactic to help their cause, which was growing desperate. Small numbers of legionaries had reached the triremes and were swarming aboard, but the majority remained trapped in a fight that they could not win. Panic flared in men's hearts and instinctively they moved backward. Centurions roared at them to stand fast, and the standard-bearers shook their poles, trying to restore confidence, but it was no good. More ground was given away. Scenting blood, the enemy redoubled their efforts.

Romulus did not like it. He could see the situation unraveling fast.

"Keep moving!" cried a voice from behind him. "Hold your formation. Take heart, comrades. Caesar is here!"

Romulus risked a look over his shoulder.

A lithe figure in gilded breastplate and red general's cloak was pushing through to join them. His horsehair-crested helmet was especially well wrought, with silver and gold filigree worked into the cheek pieces. Caesar was carrying a *gladius* with an ornate ivory hilt and an ordinary *scutum*. Romulus took in a narrow face with high cheekbones, an aquiline nose and piercing, dark eyes. Caesar's features reminded him of someone, but he had no time to dwell on the thought. He took heart from Caesar's calm manner, however. Like the centurions, he was prepared to put his life on the line, and where a leader like Caesar stood, soldiers would not run.

Struck, Tarquinius looked from the general to Romulus and back again.

Romulus was oblivious.

The news rippled through the ranks. At once the atmosphere changed, the panic dissipating like early morning mist. Disobeying orders, the reinvigorated legionaries surged forward again, catching the enemy unawares. Soon the lost ground had been regained, and there was a brief respite. With the ground between the lines littered with bloody bodies, writhing casualties and discarded weapons, both sides stood watching each other warily. Clouds of breath steamed the air and sweat ran freely from the felt liners under bronze helmets.

It was Caesar's moment.

"Remember our battle against the Nervii, comrades?" he asked loudly. "We won then, eh?"

The legionaries roared with approval. Their victory against the valiant tribe had been one of the hardest fought in the entire Gaulish campaign.

"And Alesia?" Caesar went on. "The Gauls were swarming over us like clouds of flies there. But we still beat them!"

Another shout went up.

"Even at Pharsalus, when no one gave us a chance in Hades," Caesar said dramatically, encompassing them all with his arms, "you, my comrades, gained victory."

Romulus saw real pride appear in men's faces; he felt their resolve stiffen. Caesar was one of them. A soldier. Romulus felt his own respect growing. This was a remarkable leader.

"Cae-sar!" bellowed a grizzled veteran. "Cae-sar!"

Everyone took up the cry, including Romulus.

Even Tarquinius joined in.

Caesar let his men cheer for a moment, and then began urging them toward the triremes once more.

They nearly made it. Intimidated by the Romans' counterattack and Caesar's bold words, the Egyptian troops held back for twenty heartbeats. Soon the edge of the dock was only a stone's throw away. Guided by sailors, hundreds more legionaries had embarked, and a good number of the low-slung ships had pushed out into the harbor. The three banks of oars on each dug down, pulling them into deeper water. Finally, furious that their foes were escaping, the enemy officers acted. Exhorting their men to finish what had been started, they charged forward, followed quickly by a roiling mass of soldiers that threatened only one thing. Annihilation.

"Spread out!" Caesar ordered. "Form a line in front of the triremes."

His men hurried to obey.

It was all too slow, thought Romulus with a thrill of dread. Maneuvers like this could not be done properly with an enemy host closing in from thirty paces away.

Tarquinius' gaze lifted to the starlit sky, searching for a sign. Where was the wind coming from? Was it about to change? He needed to know, but he was afforded no time.

An instant later, the Egyptians reached them. Attacking a force on the point of retreat was one of the best ways to win a battle, and they sensed it instinctively. Spears reached out, delivering the bloody kiss of death to legionaries who were turning to run. *Gladii* wielded by Gabinius' former soldiers stabbed through weakened links of mail, or into vulnerable armpits; they hammered the shields from their hands. Bronze helmets were smashed into bent pieces of metal and men's skulls cracked open. Humming overhead came sheets of arrows and showers of stones. Seeing the lethal pieces of rock, Romulus felt his heart sink. With enemy slingers in range, their casualties would soar.

Fear now distorted most legionaries' faces. Others threw terrified glances at the heavens and prayed aloud. Caesar's rallying shouts were in vain. There simply weren't enough of them to hold the Egyptians back. The fight became a frantic effort not to fold completely. Still Romulus hacked and slashed, holding his own. With an agility belying his years, Tarquinius was doing the same. The soldier who had joined Romulus on his left side was a skilled fighter too. Together they made a fearsome trio—yet it made little difference to the greater situation.

As the Roman lines moved backward, men died in growing numbers, which weakened the shield wall. At last it disintegrated, and screaming Nubians battered their way in. With their distinctive red cloaks and gilded breastplates, the centurions were targeted first, and their deaths further lowered morale. Despite Caesar's best efforts, the battle would soon become a rout. Sensing this, the general retreated toward the dock. Instantly fear mushroomed throughout his cohorts. Men were knocked over and trampled as their comrades ran for the perceived safety of the triremes. Others were knocked off the quay and into the dark water, where their heavy armor carried them under in the blink of an eye.

"We're not going to make it," shouted Tarquinius.

Romulus took a look over his shoulder. Only a few ships could be boarded at a time, and with the panicked legionaries unprepared to wait, the nearest ones were in real danger of being overloaded. "The fools," he said. "They'll sink." He refused to panic. "What can we do?"

"Swim for it," the haruspex replied. "To the Pharos."

Romulus shivered, recalling a previous time that they had escaped by water. Left behind on the bank of the River Hydaspes, Brennus had died alone. The shame of deserting his comrade had never quite gone away. Romulus forced himself to be practical. *That was then, this is now*, he thought. "Coming?" he asked the legionary to his left.

There was a terse nod.

As one, they shouldered their way past the confused and terrified soldiers surrounding them. In the confusion that now dominated, it was easy enough to break out of the battered Roman formation and make for the water's edge. They had to take extreme care. Slick with blood, the large stone slabs were festooned with body parts and discarded equipment. Leaving the burning warehouses farther behind, the trio were soon moving through semi-darkness. Thankfully, the area was empty. The fighting was confined to the area around the triremes and the Egyptian commanders had not thought to send men west along the dock to prevent an escape.

Their oversight did not matter, thought Romulus, staring back at the slaughter. Wild panic had now replaced Caesar's men's earlier courage. Disregarding their officers' orders, they fought and scrambled to escape. He pointed at a trireme in the second rank from the quay. "That one is going to sink."

Raising a hand to his eyes, the legionary swore. "Caesar's on it!" he cried. "Damn the filthy Egyptians to Hades."

Romulus squinted into the light, finally seeing the general amid the throng. Despite the shouts of the trierarch—the captain—and his sailors, more and more soldiers were climbing aboard.

"Who'll lead us if he drowns?" cried their companion.

"Worry about him later. Let's survive ourselves first," replied Romulus tersely, stripping down to his ragged military tunic. At once he buckled his belt back on, thus retaining his sheathed *gladius* and his *pugio*, the dagger that served both as a weapon and a utensil.

Tarquinius did likewise.

The legionary looked from one to the other. Then, muttering dire imprecations, he copied them. "I'm not the best swimmer," he revealed.

Romulus grinned. "You can hold on to me."

"A man should know who's going to save his skin. I'm Faventius Petronius," he said, sticking out his right arm.

"Romulus." They gripped forearms. "He's Tarquinius."

There was no time for further niceties. Romulus jumped in, feet first, the haruspex behind him. Petronius shrugged his shoulders and followed. Their distance from the battle meant the three splashes went unnoticed. At once Tarquinius beat a diagonal path out into the harbor. They needed some light to see, but had to stay far enough out to avoid the enemy missiles. With Petronius holding on for dear life, Romulus took up the rear.

How good it would be to catch Fabiola's ship, he thought. It was long gone into the night, though, no doubt headed for Italy. The same destination he had been trying to reach for the last age. Despite his own predicament, Romulus did not give up all hope. Time and again, Tarquinius had said there was a road back to Rome for him. That dream was what kept him swimming. With each stroke, Romulus imagined arriving home and being reunited with Fabiola. It would feel like reaching Elysium. After that, there was unfinished business to be done. According to Tarquinius, their mother was long dead, but she still had to be avenged. Killing the merchant Gemellus, their former owner, was the way to do that.

A flurry of splashes, accompanied by shouts and cries, dragged Romulus' attention back to the present. Scores of legionaries were jumping off the outermost trireme, which was foundering under the weight of too many men. Their fate in the water was no better than on board. Most were immediately dragged under by their armor, while those who could swim were targeted by enemy slingers and archers already positioned on the Heptastadion.

Romulus winced at their plight, but there was little he could do.

Petronius' gaze was also fixed on the unfolding drama. A moment later, his grip tightened.

"Easy," Romulus snapped. "Trying to choke me?"

"Sorry," Petronius replied, relaxing his hold. "Look, though! Caesar's about to jump ship."

Romulus turned his head. Lit from behind by the blaze from along the eastern harbor, could be seen the agile figure that had rallied the legionaries earlier. No longer was he attempting to control his men. Caesar had to flee now too. Off came his transverse-crested helmet and red cloak, and then his gilded breastplate. Surrounded by a group of legionaries, Caesar waited until all were ready. Then, clutching a handful of parchments, he stepped off the side rail and into the sea. His men landed around him, sending fountains of water into the air. With a protective cordon established,

Caesar began swimming toward the Pharos, keeping one hand upraised to keep his paperwork dry.

"Mithras, he's got balls," Romulus commented.

Petronius chuckled. "Caesar is scared of nothing."

A flurry of arrows and stones splashed down nearby, reminding them that this was no place to linger. While the majority of the Egyptian soldiers continued to assail the cohorts stuck on the dock, others were hurrying onto the Heptastadion. From there they could send unanswered volleys at the helpless legionaries in the water.

Romulus was horrified by the slingers' accuracy. The light cast onto the calm surface of the harbor was not that bright. Since the swimmers were lower than the docks, and obscured to some extent by the Heptastadion, he had thought their journey would be reasonably safe. Not so. Fitting stones half the size of a hen's egg into their weapons, the slingers whirled them around their heads once or twice before letting fly. Perhaps two or three heartbeats went by before another shower was released. A third and a fourth followed in quick succession. Soon the air was filled with the missiles; jets and spouts of water rose up as they landed. Again and again, Romulus saw legionaries being struck on the head. He cringed at the final-sounding impacts. Either they killed on the spot or knocked the victims unconscious, whereupon they drowned. That was if an arrow didn't take them through the cheek or in the eye.

Soon the enemy slingers and archers needed more targets. Because of their decision to swim farther out, Caesar's group was still unscathed, like themselves. The status quo would not last, though. Thanks to the lack of Caesarean troops on the Heptastadion, the Egyptians could pursue them on a parallel course, raining death down with impunity.

"Faster," urged Tarquinius.

Splash, splash, splash. A torrent of missiles and rocks hit the water not twenty paces away, increasing Romulus' pulse. Petronius' breath grew ragged on his neck. They had been seen. He increased the speed of his strokes, trying not to look sideways.

"Those slingers can hit a bundle of straw at six hundred paces," muttered Petronius.

More stones landed, closer this time. Romulus' gaze was drawn inexorably to the sharply outlined enemy figures, reloading their slings. Laughter carried through the air as leather straps swung hypnotically around their heads and then released—again.

Thankfully, the island was at last drawing near. Caesar had emerged onto the shore and was already screaming orders, guiding his men to defend their end of the Heptastadion. Romulus breathed a tiny sigh of relief. Safety was beckoning, and doubtless there would be some respite once they threw the Egyptians back. When that happened, he would force Tarquinius to tell him everything about the fight outside the brothel.

Still in the lead, the haruspex turned to say something. His eyes met with those of Romulus, which were flinty and full of resolve. Tarquinius' voice died in his throat and they simply stared at each other. The silent exchange spoke volumes, and set off a host of warring emotions in Romulus' heart. *I owe him so much,* he thought, *yet he's the damn reason I had to flee Rome. But for him, I would have had a different life.* Remembering the plain wooden sword owned by Cotta, his old trainer in the *ludus,* Romulus scowled. *A rudis like that could have been mine by now.*

Tarquinius stood up. He had reached the shallows.

Shouts rang out from the frustrated slingers. Reloading their weapons, they redoubled their efforts to bring down the trio. Hastily released stones pattered down harmlessly behind them.

Romulus pushed his *caligae* downward, feeling mud squelch underfoot. Petronius let out a great sigh of relief. Two more strokes and he too was able to stand. The veteran released his grip and thumped Romulus across the shoulders. "My thanks, lad. I owe you one."

Romulus indicated the main force of Egyptians, which was massing for a full frontal attack along the Heptastadion. "There'll be plenty of opportunity to repay me."

"Get over here!" screamed a centurion, right on cue. "Every sword matters."

"Best do as he said," advised Tarquinius.

They were the last words he spoke.

With a hypnotic whirring sound, a rock flashed through the air between Romulus and Petronius. It smashed into the left side of Tarquinius' face, audibly breaking his cheekbone. His mouth opened in a silent scream of agony and, spun to one side by the force of the impact, he dropped backward into the waist-deep water. Half-conscious, he sank immediately.

II

JOVINA

F abiola!" Brutus' voice broke the silence. "We'll be there soon."
Docilosa lifted the fabric side so that her mistress could look
out of the litter. Dawn was fast approaching, but the party had
already been on the road for more than two hours. Neither woman
had complained at having to rise so early. They were both keen to
reach Rome, their destination. So was Decimus Brutus, Fabiola's lover.
He was on an urgent mission from his master Julius Caesar to confer
with Marcus Antonius, the Master of the Horse. More troops were
required in Egypt, to lift the blockade from which Fabiola and Brutus
had only recently broken free. The enemy barricade still held Caesar
and his few thousand soldiers captive within Alexandria.

Between the tall cypress trees that lined the road, Fabiola could
make out plentiful brick-built tombs. Her pulse quickened at the
sight. Only those who could afford it built such cenotaphs on the
approaches to Rome. They were prominent sites that could not be
missed by passersby, thereby preserving the otherwise fragile memory of the dead. Brutus was correct: they were very close. The Via
Appia, the road to the south, had the most mausoleums, mile after

mile of them, but all routes into the capital were dotted with them. This, the road from Ostia, Rome's port, was no different. Decorated with painted statues of the gods and the ancestors of the deceased, the tombs were the dwelling places of cut-throats and cheap whores. Few dared to pass them at night. Even the dim predawn light did not reduce the threat from the whispering trees and looming structures. Fabiola was glad of their heavy escort: a half century of crack legionaries, and Sextus, her faithful bodyguard.

"You'll be able to have that bath at last," said Brutus, riding closer.

"Thank the gods," replied Fabiola. Her traveling clothes felt sticky against her skin.

"The messenger I sent ahead yesterday will ensure that everything is ready in the *domus*."

"You're so thoughtful, my love." She bestowed a beaming smile on Brutus.

Looking suitably pleased, he urged his horse into a trot and headed to the front of the column. Like Caesar, Brutus was not a man to lead from the rear.

Fabiola recoiled as the unmistakable reek of human waste carried to her nostrils. Thick and unpleasant, it was as familiar, but far less appealing, as that of freshly baked bread. It was Rome's predominant aroma, though, one that she had grown up smelling, and it had reappeared the instant their party had come within a mile of the walls. It was because countless thousands of plebeians in this teeming metropolis had no access to sewerage. The contrast with the cleanliness of Alexandria could not be more stark. She had not missed this aspect of life in the capital. While the light morning breeze made the odor less objectionable than during the sultry days of summer, it was already omnipresent.

At first Fabiola had been delighted about returning. Four years away from the city of her birth was a long time. The most recent of her temporary homes—Egypt—was an alien place, whose people hated their Roman would-be masters. Her resentment had vanished at the unexpected sight of Romulus on the battle-torn docks the very night she had left Alexandria. Naturally, Fabiola had wanted to stay and help him. Her twin was alive, and in the Roman army! To her immense consternation, Brutus had refused to delay their departure. The situation had been too desperate. In the face of Fabiola's distress, he was apologetic but resolute. She had had little choice but to defer to his judgment. The gods had seen fit to preserve Romulus' life this far, and with their help, she would meet him again one day. If only she'd understood his shouted words. His cry had been lost in the pandemonium of the trireme's departure; she could only assume he had been trying to tell her which unit he was serving in. Despite this, the encounter had given Fabiola a powerful new zest for life.

Now, after more than a week of hard travel, their journey was nearly over and, despite the thick fabric covering the litter, the air inside already smelled of shit.

Fabiola's stomach churned at the memory of the filth-encrusted bucket she and the other slaves had had to use in Gemellus' house. *Never again,* she thought proudly. *How far I have come since that day.* Even the brothel into which the merchant had sold her had possessed reasonably clean toilets. Yet this small improvement hardly counted against the degradation of strangers using her body for sex. The harsh reality of life in the Lupanar broke most women's spirit, but not Fabiola's. *I survived because I had to,* she reflected. Bent on revenge against Gemellus, and discovering the identity of her and Romulus' father, she had determined to escape her new career—somehow.

The list of rich men who frequented the whorehouse had been its most redeeming feature. Advised by a friendly whore to win over a suitable noble, Fabiola had cast her net far and wide, using her considerable charms to ensnare a number of unsuspecting candidates.

She lifted the heavy fabric and peered surreptitiously at Brutus, who was riding alongside the litter once more. Sextus too was within arm's reach; it was virtually his permanent position during daylight hours. At night, he slept right outside her door. Fabiola inclined her head, glad as always to have her bodyguard nearby. Then Brutus noticed her; a broad grin immediately split his face. Fabiola blew him a kiss. A career soldier and loyal follower of Caesar, Brutus was courageous and likable. After a number of visits to the Lupanar, he had fallen utterly into her thrall. Not that she had decided on him for that reason, of course.

It was Brutus' close links to Caesar that had helped Fabiola to make the final decision. Had it been her gut instinct? To this day, Fabiola was not sure. Thankfully, her gamble on Brutus as the best candidate had paid off richly. Five years before, he had bought her from the brothel, establishing her as the mistress of his new *latifundium*, or estate, near Pompeii.

The property's former owner had been no less than Gemellus! Fabiola's lips curved upward in triumph. To this day, knowing he'd been ruined felt like sweet revenge. Not that she'd pass up an opportunity to kill the whoreson if she got a chance. Several attempts to locate him had failed miserably and, like much of Fabiola's past, Gemellus had faded into obscurity. She still had vivid memories of her short stay on his former *latifundium*, though. Fabiola's guts twisted with fear, and she looked up and down the road.

This close to the city, other travelers were plentiful, moving in both directions. Traders pulled along mules laden with goods; farmers headed for the busy markets. There were children herding goats and sheep to pasture, lepers hobbling on home-made crutches and demobbed veterans marching home together. An irritable-looking priest with a gaggle of shaven-headed acolytes in tow stalked past, lecturing on some religious point. A line of slaves in neck chains miserably followed a muscular figure wearing a leather jerkin and carrying a long-handled whip. Armed guards paced either side of the column, security against the captives' flight. The sight was unremarkable; after all, the need for slaves in Rome was huge. Nonetheless, Fabiola shrank back into the litter as it passed the shuffling, downcast men and women. Bile rose in her throat. More than four years later, the thought of Scaevola—a vicious slave-catcher whom she had run afoul of—still terrified her.

She would not let it stop her, though.

Until she had seen Romulus in Alexandria, Fabiola's greatest discovery had been that Caesar was their father. Just once, she had been left alone with the general, who bore a striking resemblance to her brother. Seizing the opportunity, he had tried to rape her. It was not just the lustful look in Caesar's eyes that had convinced Fabiola of his guilt. His harsh words—"Be quiet or I'll hurt you"—reverberated through her yet. Somehow, on hearing them, she had known he had used them before. With proof in her heart, she had waited and watched since. Her opportunity for revenge would come one day.

While Caesar might currently face the direst of threats in Alexandria, Fabiola did not want him to meet his end there. His dying at the hands of a foreign mob would frustrate her desire for an orchestrated revenge. Yet once Caesar was free to leave Egypt, more wars beckoned. In Africa and Hispania, Republican forces were still strong. Returning to Rome at this time provided Fabiola with the perfect opportunity to plot; to recruit the men who would kill Caesar if he returned. She would unearth plenty of conspirators by telling them, as she had told Brutus, how the general planned to become the new king of Rome.

The very idea of this was anathema to every living citizen. Brutus' *domus* was not the place to scheme, however; smiling, Fabiola trusted in the gods to help her find a better base.

†

Many weeks passed before Fabiola felt confident enough to venture out unaccompanied by Brutus. Entering Rome had brought back her fear of Scaevola with a vengeance. Sheer panic engulfed Fabiola if she went out alone. Consequently, she found herself content to stay in the *domus*. There was plenty to do: keeping the household in order; hosting feasts for Brutus' friends; and doing the lessons set her by the Greek tutor she had employed. Fabiola also learned to read and write, which boosted her confidence enormously. She devoured every manuscript she could lay her hands on. It was easy to understand why Jovina had kept her prostitutes illiterate, she realized. Ignorance kept them more malleable. Returning home exhausted every day, Brutus was impressed by her probing questions about politics, philosophy and history.

Since delivering the news of Caesar's predicament to Marcus Antonius, Caesar's official deputy, Brutus had been engaged in running the Republic with Antonius and other main supporters of the dictator. There was to be no letup either: Rome was more troubled than ever. Unsettled by the lack of information about Caesar—until Brutus' reappearance, his whereabouts had been unknown for more than three months—the populace had been demonstrating. Encouraged by a few power-hungry politicians, unhappy nobles who were heavily in debt were demanding total recompense from Caesar, making a mockery of his earlier law to partially abolish their liabilities. Dissatisfied, some had even declared for the Republicans. To make matters even worse, hundreds of veterans from Caesar's favorite legion, the Tenth, had been sent back to Italy and were adding to the unrest. Infuriated by the delay in providing their retirement settlements of money and land, they were demonstrating on a regular basis.

Marcus Antonius' response had been typically heavy-handed: Troops were brought in to disperse the first sets of troublemakers, and soon after blood had been spilled on the streets. The treatment was reminiscent of that meted out to rebellious Gauls rather than to Roman citizens, Brutus ranted to Fabiola. While the issue of rebellion by Pompeian supporters had subsided, Antonius had done little to reassure the veterans. His token attempt at placation had backfired badly. More diplomatic by nature than the fiery Master of the Horse, Brutus had been to meet the Tenth's ringleaders, and had appeased them for the time being. Yet much remained to be done before the situation was stabilized.

By early summer, Fabiola was content that Brutus was occupied with other matters, and that there had been no sign of Scaevola. An outrageous idea had come to mind and she finally decided to visit the Lupanar, the brothel that had been her home during her prostitution. Brutus was to be left in the dark, though. For the moment, the less her lover knew, the better. Unfortunately, keeping her destination secret meant that none of Brutus' legionaries could escort her. Fear bubbled in Fabiola's throat at the thought of walking the streets accompanied only by Sextus, but she managed to quell it. She could not remain confined behind the house's thick walls forever, nor did she wish always to rely on squads of soldiers to go out in the world.

Secrecy was paramount.

So, ignoring her servant Docilosa's pursed lips and the muttered complaints of the *optio* in charge of Brutus' men, she and Sextus headed out into the Palatine. The suburb was mostly inhabited by the wealthy but, as in all parts of Rome, there were plenty of *insulae*, the tall wooden tenement apartments in which the vast majority of the population lived. With open-fronted shops occupying the ground floors, the *insulae* were three, four and even five stories high. Poorly lit, rat-infested, without sanitation and heated only by braziers, they were death traps. Disease lurked within them, flaring into frequent outbreaks of cholera, dysentery or smallpox. It was commonplace too for *insulae* to collapse, or to go up in flames, burning to death all the inhabitants. Their close proximity to each other meant that little light penetrated down to the narrow, crowded and muddy streets. Only the largest thoroughfares in the capital were surfaced; even fewer were more than ten steps wide. All were thronged daily by citizens, traders, slaves and thieves, adding to the claustrophobic atmosphere.

A city-dweller from birth, Fabiola had grown to love the open spaces around her *latifundium*. She had assumed that she was still used to crowds—until she and Sextus had left the *domus* a hundred paces behind them. They were hemmed in on all sides, and an image of Scaevola instantly came to mind. Try as she might, Fabiola could not throw it off. Her feet began to drag and she fell behind.

Seeing her pinched face, Sextus laid a hand on his *gladius*. "What is it, Mistress?"

"I'm fine," she said, pulling the hood of her cloak closer. "It's just bad memories."

He reached up to touch his empty eye socket, his own memento of Scaevola's ambush. "I know, Mistress," he growled. "Best to keep moving, though. Avoid attention."

Determined not to let dread rule her any longer, Fabiola followed him. It was midmorning after all, the safest time of the day, when ordinary people got their business done. Women and slaves shopped for food among the bakers, butchers and vegetable merchants. Wine-sellers boasted and lied about the quality of their produce, offering a taste to anyone who would listen. Blacksmiths toiled over their anvils while neighboring carpenters and potters exchanged idle banter over a cup of *acetum*. The stink from the nearby tanneries and fullers' workshops laced the air. Money changers sat at low tables, glaring at the cripples who were greedily eyeing their neat piles of coins. Snot-nosed urchins ran through the crowds, chasing each other and stealing what they could. Nothing looked different to any other day in Rome.

Except for the plentiful numbers of Antonius' legionaries, of course, thought Fabiola. The old law denying entry to the city to soldiers had been set aside by Caesar himself. With the threat of rioting constant, there were more of them about than ever. The knowledge gave her strength. In addition to Sextus' presence, they would ensure nothing happened to her. Fabiola stuck out her chin. The Lupanar wasn't far. "Come on," she declared.

Sextus grinned, used to her determination.

A short while later, they had reached a street that Fabiola knew better than any in Rome. Close to the Forum, it was home to the Lupanar. Again her feet slowed, but this time her fear was under better control. Today, she was no terrified thirteen-year-old dragged here to be sold. Soon Fabiola's nervousness had been replaced by excitement. She began to outstrip Sextus.

"Mistress!"

She ignored his cry. The crowds finally parted a few steps from the entrance and Fabiola's mouth fell open. Nothing had changed. A brightly painted, erect stone penis still jutted forth on either side of the arched doorway, graphic evidence of the business's nature. Outside stood a shaven-headed hulk, clutching a metal-studded club. "Vettius," she said, her voice cracking with emotion.

The huge man did not react.

Throwing back the hood of her cloak, Fabiola moved closer. "Vettius."

The doorman's brow wrinkled at being called by name and he glanced around.

"Don't you recognize me?" she asked. "Have I changed that much?"

"Fabiola?" he stuttered. "Is it you?"

With tears of happiness filling her eyes, she nodded. Here was one of the most loyal friends she had ever had. When Brutus had bought Fabiola's freedom, she had been desperate for him to free the two doormen also. Wily to the last, however, Jovina had refused all offers. The pair were simply too valuable to her business. Leaving them behind had torn a deep wound in Fabiola's heart.

Vettius rushed to give her a hug, but stopped short.

Sextus had shot in front of Fabiola. Dwarfed by the other, he nonetheless drew his sword. "Stay back," he snarled.

In a heartbeat, Vettius' face went from surprised to angry, but before he could respond Fabiola had laid a hand on Sextus' arm. "He's a friend," she explained, ignoring her bodyguard's confused expression. With a scowl, Sextus stood aside, allowing Fabiola and Vettius to gaze at each other. "It's been too long," she said warmly.

Conscious of his low status, the lantern-jawed doorman did not try to hug her again, instead making an awkward bow. "Jupiter, it's good to see you, Fabiola," he said, half choking. "The gods must have answered my prayers."

Fabiola picked out the concern in his voice at once. Sudden terror filled her. "Is Benignus all right?"

"Of course!" A lopsided smile split Vettius' unshaven face. "The big fool is inside. Snoring his head off, no doubt. He was on the late shift last night."

"Thank Mithras," she breathed. "What is it then?"

He looked around uneasily.

Jovina, thought Fabiola, remembering her own caution when she lived here. Nothing wrong with the old witch's hearing yet then.

Vettius stooped low to her ear. "Morale has been terrible for months," he whispered. "We've lost most of our customers too."

Fabiola was shocked. In her time, the Lupanar had been busy every day. "Why?"

The doorman had no time to answer.

"Vettius!"

Fabiola felt an instant wave of nausea. For nearly four years, that shrewish voice had called her out to be inspected by prospective customers.

"Vettius!" This time Jovina sounded irritated. "Get in here."

With an apologetic grimace at Fabiola, the doorman obeyed.

She and Sextus were one step behind him.

The mosaic-floored reception area within was just as garish as Fabiola remembered it. Its walls were covered from top to bottom in richly colored paintings of forests, rivers and mountains. Fat little cupids, satyrs and various deities were dotted throughout, peeking coyly at the viewer. The most prominent of the gods was Priapus, with his massive erect penis. One wall was covered with images of sexual positions; each was numbered so that clients could easily ask for their favorite. In the center of the floor was a large painted statue of a naked girl entwined with a swan. The whole room had a faintly disheveled air, as if it needed a good clean, and Vettius' words began to make some sense.

To one side stood a little sparrow of a woman in a low-cut *stola*. Fabiola's heart skipped a beat at her first sight of Jovina in five years. At first glance it seemed as if not much had changed. Plenty of the madam's sagging flesh was still on view; beady eyes flashed from a lined face covered in lead, ocher, and antimony. Her lips were painted a gaudy red. Jewelry glittered around her neck, wrists and fingers—gold, silver and precious stones. Jovina was famed for her discretion, and these gifts from her rich clients proved it. "Go and wake that fool Benignus," she snapped at Vettius. "I need him to go out for me."

"Mistress," Vettius muttered. He moved toward the passage that led to the back of the building.

Fabiola, who had been hidden behind him, was revealed. "Jovina."

For once, the crone was unable to conceal her amazement. A wrinkled hand rose to her gash of a mouth, and fell away. "Fabiola . . . ?"

Sextus' eyebrows rose in shock. Here was startling evidence of his mistress's previous life.

"I've come back," Fabiola said simply.

"Welcome, welcome," Jovina gushed, her public persona taking over again. "Can I offer you a drink? Some food? A girl?" She cackled at her own joke, setting off a paroxysm of coughing.

"How kind. Some wine, thank you." Fabiola smiled. Inwardly, she was shocked at Jovina's haggard appearance. The madam had already been old when Fabiola arrived in the Lupanar. Today she looked positively ancient, and ill. There had never been much to her, but now Jovina's bones jutted everywhere from under her wrinkled skin, turning her into a walking skeleton. Fabiola almost expected to see Orcus, the god of the underworld, waiting in the corner.

The madam scuttled to her desk, which was positioned by the corridor. A red and black clay jug sat there with four fine blue glasses, along with small dishes containing olives and bread. This was refreshment for those clients Jovina deemed suitable.

Returning with two filled goblets, Jovina stumbled and nearly fell. A brittle smile spread across her face. "Excuse my clumsiness," she muttered.

The crone is really sick, thought Fabiola.

"Here we are," purred Jovina. "Just like old times."

"Not quite," she replied archly. "I'm a citizen now."

"And the lover of no less a man than Decimus Brutus," said Jovina, probing. "He paid a lot of money for you."

"Thank the gods," Fabiola answered. "I show him my appreciation of it every day."

"That's wonderful," said the madam, beaming falsely. "A happy ending!"

Making polite small talk, they both sipped their wine. Each studied the other, Jovina wondering what her former slave's purpose was, and Fabiola trying to assess the situation in the brothel. Neither gained a single crumb of information. Inevitably perhaps, their conversation turned to the civil war and Caesar's accession to power. Whatever her opinion, Jovina was careful to shower praise on Brutus' general. "Rumor has it that he is trapped in Alexandria," she said at last. "That cannot be true, surely?"

"It is. He and his men are badly outnumbered by the Egyptians," Fabiola answered. "Brutus and I escaped with great difficulty."

Jovina gasped. "Caesar is such a canny general. What has happened?"

Fabiola wasn't going to go into the details. Caesar's rapid pursuit of Pompey after the battle of Pharsalus, with only a small part of his army, was characteristic of the man. The tactic—moving so fast that an enemy was unprepared—normally worked well. This time, it hadn't. The Egyptians' reaction to his presence had been violent, causing him no end of problems. "Help was already on the way from Pergamum and Judaea when we left," she revealed. "And Marcus Antonius dispatched a legion from Ostia yesterday. The blockade will soon be lifted."

"Jupiter be thanked," said Jovina, raising her glass. "Fortuna too."

"Indeed," replied Fabiola, dark thoughts of revenge filling her mind. *When he has won the civil war, Caesar will return to Rome, where I'll be waiting.*

The noise of sandals slapping down the corridor preceded the arrival of Vettius and Benignus. Both hulks were beaming. "Fabiola!" cried Benignus. He rushed to clutch at the hem of her dress like a supplicant to a queen.

Jovina made a show of pleasure, but beneath it she was clearly displeased.

"Get up," Fabiola ordered fondly, taking hold of Benignus' arms. "It's wonderful to see you." Noticing that the thick gold bands that had encircled his wrists were gone, she frowned. Only their outline remained, yet they had been Benignus' prize possessions. Jovina must indeed be in dire straits.

Oblivious, the madam was fussing and bothering over a document on her desk. Sealing it with wax, she handed it to Benignus. "You know where to take this," she said.

He looked a bit confused. "The usual moneylenders? By the Forum?"

"Yes, of course," snapped Jovina, waving her arms. "Get moving."

Bobbing his head, Benignus headed for the door. He threw a grin at Fabiola, which she returned, and was gone. Vettius followed him, resuming his post on the street. Sextus moved to stand just inside the entrance, from where he could keep a watchful eye on the goings-on.

Fabiola's mind was racing. Jovina clearly didn't like her hearing that Benignus was visiting a moneylender on her behalf. Her crazy idea suddenly seemed possible. "How's business?" she inquired brightly.

At once Jovina's expression became cagey. "Good as ever," she replied. Another heavy bout of coughing shook her tiny frame, increasing Fabiola's suspicions. "Why do you ask?" Jovina wheezed eventually.

Fabiola looked sympathetic. "Running this place on your own must be such hard work," she murmured. "You look wrung out."

The madam forced a smile, but the decaying teeth and reddened gums it revealed provided little in the way of reassurance. "I'm fine," she muttered. "Although trade is a little slack."

Sensing a chink in the other's armor, Fabiola stepped closer. "Really?"

Jovina's face sagged. "Very poor, in fact," she admitted, allowing Fabiola to help her sit down. "About a year ago, a new brothel opened up three streets over. The madam is young and beautiful. And her business partner is bad news." Bitterness twisted Jovina's lined, painted face. "They've got good contacts at the slave market too. Get the best lookers before they even go on sale. I haven't been able to buy a decent replacement in months. How can anyone compete with that? It's a vicious circle; with the usual wear and tear, I'm down to twenty girls."

Fabiola was all solicitousness. "What about Benignus and Vettius? They're well capable of roughing someone up."

A spark of life reappeared in Jovina's tired eyes. "They are, but a dozen heavies with knives and swords is too much, even for them."

It was Fabiola's turn to be surprised. Prostitution had turned even dirtier since she'd left it behind. "Get them to buy more men then," she advised, surprised at how angered she felt by the new business's effect on the Lupanar. "Or hire some gladiators. That's not difficult."

Another sigh. "I'm tired, Fabiola. My health isn't what it was. The idea of a turf war now . . ." Jovina stopped, looking beaten.

With a struggle, Fabiola concealed her amazement. This was the woman who had for decades run the best whorehouse in Rome. The same person who had bought her from Gemellus, tested her virginal status in the most personal of ways, and then offered up her first sexual experience to the brothel's customers for a fortune. Sharp as a blade, Jovina had ruled the Lupanar with an iron fist. It was unsurprising that she should grow frail and weak eventually, Fabiola reflected, yet the sight of her, sick and shrunken, was still shocking. But this wasn't the time or place for sympathy, she told herself. She owed Jovina nothing.

There was silence for a moment, and Fabiola realized that not a single man had ventured inside since she had arrived. She would have expected a few by now. "How bad is the trade exactly?"

Jovina had given up fighting. "Fortuna is smiling on us if we see more than half a dozen clients a day," she whispered.

Aghast at this paltry number, Fabiola again let her face reveal nothing. "That few?"

"I've tried everything," said the madam. "Special offers, discounts, boys. I even forced the girls to offer more 'specialized' services."

Fabiola winced, but did not ask more.

"Nothing seems to work. All of them head to that bitch down the road." Jovina pursed her lips in a brief revival of her former spirit. "A lifetime of work, and it comes to this," she exclaimed.

"Something else can be done, surely?" asked Fabiola.

"I've been to all the temples, made plenty of generous offerings. What else is there?" asked Jovina, weariness oozing from her again.

A surge of adrenaline hit Fabiola. *Seize the moment,* she thought. *Take control of the situation.* But still she hesitated, suddenly unsure. Whatever she said had to be phrased in just the right way, or Jovina would reject it. Her former owner was not completely on her knees. Equally, her plan must not just fall flat on its face. The Lupanar could prove vital to her preparations for Caesar's downfall. Fabiola was inspired; her lips gave the tiniest twitch. "Have you ever thought of . . . retiring?" she asked delicately. "Taking it easy?"

Jovina snorted; then her beady eyes fixed on Fabiola's, like an eagle on its prey. But this bird had no power left. "Who would run the place? You, I suppose?"

"It's only a thought," Fabiola answered smoothly. "I'd pay a good price, of course. Ignore the state of the books right now and go on last year's figures." She made an airy gesture. "If you wished, you could stay on—to oversee the transition period." Jovina's input would be useful until she got the hang of day-to-day affairs.

The madam looked shocked. "What's this about?" she demanded. "After all you went through here, why would you want to take it over?"

Fabiola studied her manicured fingernails. "I'm bored," she declared. It wasn't so far from the truth. "I need something to occupy my time, and this is a job I know well."

"What about Brutus?"

"He lets me do what I want. I've spent years on campaign with him already and now the damn civil war looks as if it might drag on for a while," Fabiola complained. "Greece and Egypt were bad enough. I'm not trailing around Africa and Spain after him as well."

Jovina fiddled with a thick gold bracelet on one wrist. "And the price?"

Fabiola had been doing mental arithmetic since the madam had revealed how few clients remained. "I think a hundred and fifty thousand *denarii* would suffice." She let the amount sink in for a moment. "Five thousand for each girl, and fifty thousand for the building. Any outstanding debts would have to be honored by you."

Jovina's eyes nearly popped out of her head. The sum was more than generous. "You have access to that kind of money?"

Fabiola's smile was serene. "Brutus is wealthier than you can imagine. He'll pay anything to keep me happy."

Jovina sat very still, considering her options.

There was a lengthy silence, during which Fabiola watched the madam from the corner of her eye. Jovina's wiliness was not all gone. When her expression suddenly became more calculating, it was time for the killer blow. "I couldn't pay an *as* more," Fabiola said, her tone no longer friendly. "And I only make a good offer once."

Jovina sank back in her seat. "Give me some time," she whispered. "A few days."

She had the old madam now, thought Fabiola jubilantly. "I don't think so. Two hours should suffice."

Jovina nodded reluctantly. "Very well."

Draining the last of her wine, Fabiola stalked to the door. "I'll be back by *hora sexta*." Triumph filled her. *Finally everything is going my way. Romulus is in the army, so he will return to Rome one day and we will be reunited. Brutus might be one of Caesar's right-hand men, but he is utterly faithful to me. The Lupanar will be mine in two hours, and with the women here, I can win more of his comrades over to my cause. To kill Caesar.* Fabiola was so absorbed in her thoughts that she did not react to Sextus' hiss of alarm. It was only when he prevented her from leaving that it sank in.

She could see his face was worried. "What is it?"

"Trouble," he muttered, pulling his *gladius* from the scabbard.

Fabiola tried to peer outside, but Sextus would not even let her do this.

Loud voices suddenly carried in from the street. One of them belonged to Vettius. "Fuck off," he bellowed.

"We're coming in, whether you like it or not," a man snarled in response. "My master wants to talk to the old bitch right now."

"Over my dead body," Vettius answered.

A burst of laughter rang out, and Fabiola knew that the doorman must be badly outnumbered. Next she heard the distinctive sound of weapons being unsheathed. She cursed. They couldn't just stand by and let this happen. Where was Benignus? She looked at Jovina, who had gone gray under her makeup. "Who are they?"

"Thugs from the new brothel," Jovina managed.

"We'll give you one more chance, fool," said Vettius' adversary. "Stand aside."

"Go fuck yourself," came the loud response. "I'll kill you all."

Fabiola's heart swelled with pride. Part of Vettius' refusal to move would be because she was inside. Terror also filled her at what was about to happen.

Shouts of anger rang out and they heard men swarming forward.

"Vettius!" Somehow Jovina's voice carried over the commotion. "Let them in."

Silence fell outside.

With bated breath, they waited.

A shadow filled the doorway, and Fabiola found herself shrinking behind Sextus, who ushered her against the wall. A cloaked figure entered, followed by five muscle-bound men with drawn swords. Vettius bustled in next, his club raised. Seeing Fabiola unharmed, he also moved to stand in front of her. For the moment, none of the newcomers had seen her or Sextus. Beads of sweat ran down Fabiola's neck, but her feet were rooted to the spot.

The leader's gaze fell first on Jovina. The old madam visibly quailed. "What do you want?" she asked in a shrill tone. "Isn't it enough to take all my business?"

"Jovina," said the man, acting hurt. "We only wanted to ask after your health. Word has it that you're not well."

"Damn your insolence," snapped the madam. "I'm fine."

"Excellent." There was a mocking bow, and Fabiola's heart hammered in her chest. The gesture was familiar to her. So were the man's thick silver wristbands and powerful build. Before she could gather her thoughts, though, the stocky figure went on, "We're worried about you nonetheless. It would be an excellent idea if you left the Lupanar. Took a vacation. Soon."

Jovina's outburst had drained what little energy she had. "It's my business," she said in a low voice. "What would happen to it? To my girls?"

"We'll look after everything. The building, the doormen, and especially the whores," said the man, leering at his companions. "Won't we, lads?"

They laughed unpleasantly.

Fabiola felt the bitter taste of bile in her mouth, and she struggled not to vomit. She knew exactly who this was. Scaevola, the *fugitivarius*. A choking cough left her throat.

At the sound, he spun around to face her. The *fugitivarius* took in Vettius and Sextus with a contemptuous glance, but his eyes widened at the sight of Fabiola. A cruel smile creased his face. "By all the gods," he breathed. "Who would have believed it?"

Suddenly light-headed, Fabiola had to place a hand on Sextus' shoulder. Otherwise she would have fallen.

III

PHARNACES

Undoing his chinstrap with one hand, Romulus lifted his helmet and felt liner a fraction and wiped his brow clean of sweat. It made a difference, but for only a few heartbeats. He was marching while carrying a fascine, a heavy bundle of brushwood; following Caesar's orders, every soldier in the long column was bearing one, which meant that, despite the mountainous terrain and cool temperature, they were all sweating heavily. The army had been on the move since before dawn, and its temporary camp near the town of Zela was now several miles to the rear.

Romulus peered up at the sun, which occupied the blue sky alone. Not a single cloud was present to shade the earth below. It was early, but there was a fierce intensity to the disc's rays that he had not seen since Parthia. The day was going to get hotter, and with it came the distinct possibility of battle, and death. *If only I'd had the strength to forgive Tarquinius before he disappeared*, he thought. *Now I might never get the chance to say it.* Again the grief welled up, and Romulus let it fill him. Constantly trying to batten the feeling down only made it worse.

Every single excruciating moment of that last day and night in Alexandria felt like yesterday. Most vivid of all was Tarquinius' unexpected thunderbolt, the revelation that he had murdered the belligerent noble who had confronted Romulus and Brennus eight years before outside a brothel in Rome. The pair had only fled because they both thought that Romulus was responsible for the killing. Unintentionally, of course.

Tarquinius' guilt still stung Romulus, but he'd have given anything to see the blond-haired haruspex reappear, his double-headed axe slung over his shoulder. Instead, only the gods knew where he was. He could easily have been among the hundreds of legionaries and sailors who had died that night. Yet the three of them had almost made it, Romulus reflected sourly. If it hadn't been for those bastard slingers, Tarquinius would be here by his side.

He and Petronius had dragged the unconscious haruspex out of the shallows and laid him safely on dry ground. Then, screamed at by frantic *optiones* and centurions, they had joined the battle to defend the island. The ensuing battle was short, vicious and decisive. No infantry in the world could better the Roman legionary in a confined space such as the Heptastadion. The enemy troops had been hurled back onto the mainland, with heavy casualties. It was bittersweet knowledge for Romulus, who, bloodied and battered, had come to find Tarquinius in its aftermath.

Bizarrely, there had been no sign of the haruspex; only a reddened imprint in the sand remained where he had lain. A quick search of the area had revealed nothing either. Even with the glow from the lighthouse and the fire on the docks, there were plenty of places to hide among the boulders on the shore.

In some ways, Romulus had not been surprised by Tarquinius' disappearance. He still wasn't. He had had no further chance to search for his friend at the time. His only option would have been to desert, but, angered by the disappearance of one of his new recruits, Romulus' *optio* had placed a watch on him night and day. To make matters worse, the following afternoon Caesar's triremes had evacuated the entire army and sailed along the coastline to the east of Alexandria. Full of despair, Romulus was among their number. He'd tried to rally his spirits by imagining that Fabiola had heard his shout and would soon send word to him. It worked— partially.

Having learned a lesson in the Egyptian capital, Caesar had moved to meet his allies, who were led by Mithridates of Pergamum. Although he bore the same name as the king who had once tried Rome to its limits, Mithridates was no relation and was a trusted supporter of Caesar's. Comprised of Syrian and Judaean soldiers, his relief force had already encountered the main Egyptian army, which was commanded by the teenage King Ptolemy and his aides. After an initial setback, Mithridates had sent for help from Caesar, who was delighted to leave Alexandria's claustrophobic streets behind. His le- gionaries had all felt the same, with the obvious exception of Romu- lus. Not even a stunning victory against the Egyptians, when thousands of enemy troops died and the young king had drowned, could lift his mood.

With control of Egypt in his hands, Caesar returned to Alexan- dria, and Cleopatra, the king's sister. She had become his lover, so naturally, Caesar installed her as queen. Not that Romulus cared. Frantic, still heartbroken, he had resumed his search for Tarquinius. But weeks had gone by since the battle in the harbor, and whatever trail there might have been had long gone cold. In a city of more than a million people, what chance was there of finding one man? Bor- rowing whatever money he could from his new comrades, Romulus had spent it in the temples and marketplaces, hoping against hope he would discover something.

Not as much as a snippet.

Two months later, when the legions were leaving the city, Rom- ulus had been in debt to the tune of a year's pay. *I did my best,* he thought wearily. *There was no more I could have done.*

Bucinae rang out, dragging Romulus back to the present. The call meant "Enemy in sight." At once the army ground to a halt. Thump, thump, thump went the fascines on the ground. Romulus looked to Petronius, who marched on the outside of the rank. After his heroism in saving the other's life, Romulus and Petronius had become firm friends. Petronius had even helped to look for Tarquinius, which Romulus was still grateful for. "Can you see anything?" he asked.

Everyone was trying to see why they had stopped. There was a palpable hunger in most men's eyes. A battle would make a change from the boredom of the previous few months. Keen to establish his authority over all Rome's vassal territories, Caesar had first visited Judaea and Syria. Intimidated by his troops' mere presence, the local rulers had fallen over themselves to pledge their allegiance. With plentiful tributes collected, the legions' peaceful travels had continued with a voyage to Cilicia on the coast of Asia Minor.

Caesar had then headed for Bithynia and Pontus, where King Pharnaces was stirring up all kinds of trouble. A son of Mithridates, the Lion of Pontus and scourge of Rome twenty years before, Pharnaces was as warlike as his father. While Caesar and his men were trapped in Alexandria, he had raised an army and begun a brutal war against Calvinus, the Roman commander in the area. Inflicting heavy losses on Calvinus, Pharnaces' men had subsequently castrated all Roman civilians who fell into their hands.

Which was why Romulus and his comrades found themselves in a steep-sided valley in northern Pontus just after daybreak. Caesar did not take such affronts lightly, and after months without even a skirmish, his legionaries were feeling bored and restless. They were glad that Pharnaces' increasingly humble overtures of peace had been ignored. Now they were hunting down his army, intent on a confrontation. Caesar's plentiful Republican opponents in Africa and Hispania and political matters in Rome could wait until this matter was dealt with.

Hearing that the enemy was camped near Zela, Caesar led his legions north from the coast at a fierce pace, covering nearly two hundred miles in less than two weeks. It reminded Romulus of the last part of his fateful journey with Crassus' host. The obvious difference was that Caesar was a military genius, a title that his former ally certainly did not deserve. How could a disaster like Carrhae befall the general who foiled defeat and death at every turn? It felt good to serve under Caesar.

To reach Pontus, they had also marched through the province of Galatia. Deiotarus, its ruler, was a fierce, longtime ally of Rome but had supported Pompey at Pharsalus. Recently, he had begged forgiveness of Caesar, which was duly given. Deiotarus' famed cavalry and ten cohorts of infantry were a welcome addition to the general's three battle-worn, understrength legions. Trained in the Roman manner, his troops were loyal and courageous.

Nearing Zela the day before, the combined forces camped to the west of the town. Deiotarus' Galatian horsemen had then reconnoitred the area, returning with news that Pharnaces' host was located a few miles to the north. Protecting the road to the Pontic capital, Amasia, it was positioned in the same place Mithridates had occupied when he defeated a large Roman army a generation earlier. Clearly this was deliberate, and while few legionaries regarded this as a good omen, they were not unduly worried either. Had Mithridates not succumbed to the Republic's might in the end?

"There!" cried Petronius triumphantly, pointing at the hill slightly off to one side. "That must be it."

Tying his chinstrap, Romulus stared at the flat-topped mount. It lay on the other side of an almost dry stream. Atop it, he could discern the outlines of hundreds of tents. The neighing of horses carried faintly through the thin air; mixed with the sound were the shouts of alert sentries. Soon figures began to emerge from the tents, and cries of alarm drowned out the previous noises. The legionaries began muttering excitedly. Their early arrival had caught Pharnaces' army by surprise.

Realizing Caesar's tactic, Romulus chuckled. As he'd learned in the arena, knowledge and preparation contributed significantly to success in war, along with an unerring eye for swiftly taken opportunities. Caesar was master of all three. His order for every man to carry a fascine might have raised a few grumbles, but no one was seriously unhappy. When piled with others, they would form the core of a defensive earthwork.

Romulus wondered what else was in Caesar's mind. From Zela, the legions had followed the road to Amasia, which alternated on both sides of a low-running stream. At the moment, they were on its eastern bank. The watercourse that he could see below the enemy-occupied hill was probably an offshoot of it too, but neither was deep enough to prevent them getting to grips with their opponents. A short distance in front of their position, the valley split, forming a rough T shape. The stream below Pharnaces' army emerged from the left arm, while the road continued due north, over the hills. No one could take this route without risking a flank attack from the enemy. Not that Caesar would try to avoid battle, he thought.

"Those bastards won't give up the high ground," declared Petronius. "They'll want us to slog up the slope instead."

"Caesar's far too canny for that," said a soldier in the rank behind. "Even if we did catch the fuckers napping."

Laughs and loud murmurs of agreement met this comment.

Romulus indicated the slope to their left. "A position on the top of that is as good as Pharnaces'."

Men looked to see who had spoken. The valleys that protected their enemies would also provide their own defense. Each army could then watch the other in a stalemate that might last for days. At Pharsalus, Caesar's legions had faced off against Pompey's for a week before the fighting began.

"That means carrying these damned fascines up there," growled a voice farther back.

"Fool! You'll be glad of them if the enemy attacks," growled Petronius.

Guffaws and jeers rained down on the anonymous legionary, who fell silent.

The *bucinae* sounded, silencing the soldiers' mirth. "About turn!" screamed the centurions. "Re-form your ranks, facing west."

†

Less than an hour later, the entire army had reached the hilltop. With half the infantry and the Galatian cavalry spread out in a protective screen, the remainder set about digging a ditch to enclose their camp. The earth from this was mixed with the fascines to erect a rampart that was taller than a man. While the Roman legionaries built the front and rear walls, Deiotarus' soldiers constructed the sides. The result of their efforts was not sufficient to withstand a sustained attack, but would do for now.

Some time later, the train of mules that carried the tents and their yokes arrived in the valley below. Leaving the baggage behind had meant the legionaries were ready to fight at a moment's notice. Romulus knew that it was a common ruse of Caesar's. "Arrive at an unexpected time, and victory is often there to be taken," he muttered as they marched downhill to escort the mules up. How could it be done here, though?

Their opponents watched them for the rest of the day. Riders galloped up and down the hill opposite, carrying messages and orders to Pharnaces' allies in the area. Deiotarus' cavalry made sallies right up to the Pontic fortifications, finding out as much as possible. Enemy riders did the same to the Roman position. By the time darkness fell, the legionaries were aware that they faced a host more than three times their size. Pharnaces possessed superior cavalry, greater numbers of infantry and other classes of troops not even in Caesar's possession. He had Thracian peltasts, *thureophoroi*, Judaean skirmishers and slingers from Rhodes. There was heavy horse similar to the Parthian cataphracts, and large numbers of scythed chariots. Confrontation on flat ground had to be avoided at all costs. Storming the enemy's heavily fortified position did not seem a good option either. A nagging sense of unease began tugging at the edges of Romulus' mind.

The sun went down in a blaze of red, illuminating the doubled Roman sentries on the earthen ramparts. There would be no surprise attack under the cover of darkness. Sitting outside their leather tents, the rest of Caesar's soldiers shared *acetum*, vinegary wine, and *bucellatum*, the hard biscuit eaten when on campaign. Petronius and the six other soldiers in Romulus' *contubernium* took their ease by a small fire, laughing and joking. The same scene was being played out all over the camp, yet Romulus did not feel comfortable. Although he had formed a friendship of sorts with his comrades, loneliness still gnawed away at his insides. More than ever, he wished that Brennus were still alive, and that Tarquinius had not disappeared.

Naturally, his thoughts made no difference. Romulus sighed. Even Petronius, whom he trusted with his life, could never know the real truth about his past. Tonight, though, it was not his origins as a slave that he wanted to share. It was his doubt. Romulus could not get over the casual arrogance of Caesar's soldiers, the certainty in their minds that Pharnaces and his huge army would be defeated. Had that not been the attitude of most of Crassus' legionaries before Carrhae?

Yet to mention his experience in that doomed army would attract attention of the most unwelcome kind. At best he would be branded a liar, at worst a deserter. All Romulus could do was keep his mouth shut and continue to trust in Caesar.

†

The following dawn was crisp and clear, presaging another sunny day. The trumpets sounded, waking the men as normal. Army routine did not change merely because an enemy was nearby. After a light breakfast, most soldiers were given the duty of reinforcing the rampart that surrounded their camp. While the fascines and dug earth had served well for one night, much still needed to be done. Sharpened wooden spikes were fitted to the outside of the fortification, just below the level of the sentries' walkway. Deep pits were excavated in irregular rows, their bottoms decorated with spiked iron caltrops. Slabs of rock were broken apart with hammers and chisels and embedded in the ground, pointing crazily upward like the teeth in a giant demon's mouth. Romulus was fascinated to discover that these defenses had also been deployed at Alesia, running for more than fifteen miles and facing in two directions.

Of course their preparations were necessary: The huge force that faced them was made up of fierce warriors who had already tasted success at the expense of a Roman army. They were on hallowed ground too, the site of a historic victory over Rome by Mithridates. In such situations, defeat was only ever a whisker away.

The *ballistae*, which had been taken apart for ease of transport, were reassembled. Facing north toward Pharnaces' army, they were positioned on the *intervallum*, the open ground that ran around the inside of the earthworks. Work parties with mules were sent out to collect stones of suitable size for the two-armed catapults. Artillery was probably Caesar's sole area of superiority, thought Romulus, remembering the withering fire laid down by the Forgotten Legion's *ballistae* during its last battle.

The memory brought twinges of sadness and guilt. As always, the emotions were followed by gratitude. *If Brennus hadn't sacrificed his own life, I would not be here,* thought Romulus. This bitter pill made it harder not to blame himself also for what had happened to Tarquinius. Remembering that the haruspex had been the one who wanted to enter the Egyptian capital, he managed to shove away the guilt. Each man was master of his own destiny, and Tarquinius was no different in that respect.

The bright sunshine eventually lifted Romulus' mood. Fortunately, the Twenty-Eighth had been chosen to form the defensive screen in front of the camp. While some of Deiotarus' Galatian cavalry was also given this duty, the majority had been sent out in squadrons to study the surrounding terrain. Delighted with their easy task, the men of the Twenty-Eighth watched their toiling comrades and laughed behind their hands so the officers would not see.

Some time later, Romulus glanced at the enemy position. "Jupiter's balls," he cried. "They're on the move."

Petronius swore loudly. Across the valley, thousands of men were emerging from behind the Pontic fortifications and forming up. Weapons flashed in the early-morning sunlight, and the creak of chariot wheels and shouted orders traveled through the air. Soon it was obvious that Mithridates' entire army was leaving its camp.

The Roman officers' response was instantaneous. "Close order! Raise shields!" they roared, pacing up and down the front of the ranks. Hefting their javelins, the legionaries obeyed at once. Although the slope before them was steep, an assault by the enemy would prove dangerous. There was no need to panic, though: Descending into the valley and then climbing to their position would take a while. If that happened, their comrades on the ramparts would have ample time to join them.

"It must be a parade," said Petronius scornfully. "Mithridates wants to tell his soldiers how brave they are."

"Maybe he wants Caesar to deploy more men out here," Romulus countered.

Petronius frowned. "To slow down the construction of the fortifications?"

Romulus inclined his head. If their entire force constantly had to defend their camp, it would never get built.

"He's probably just showing off his army. Boosting their confidence. It is much bigger than ours, after all," muttered Petronius.

This was quite plausible. Romulus grinned, glad of the Roman legionary's psychological advantage over other troops.

The pair glanced at their camp, wondering how their general would respond. It was not long before a red-cloaked figure had climbed onto the ramparts, followed by a group of senior officers and a single trumpeter. A loud cheer rose up at the sight of Caesar, who was deliberately making himself visible while getting a better view of the enemy. Lifting a hand to shield his eyes, Caesar peered into the distance. He studied Mithridates' host for a long time.

Romulus did likewise. At the very front he could make out groups of slingers and archers, the missile troops that led most attacks, their purpose to cause as many casualties as possible. Behind them, the war chariots formed up in the center, with thousands of peltasts and *thureophoroi* arrayed in a tight square close behind. On the left wing sat the Pontic heavy cavalry, while on the other an unruly mass of lightly armed Thracian horsemen assembled.

"That looks like battle order to me," Romulus muttered.

"It does," agreed the other with a suspicious growl. "Here comes Mithridates now."

Rapt, they watched a rider on a magnificent black stallion emerge from the camp gates to rousing cheers from the waiting host. He was followed by a number of mailed warriors on similar steeds. Crying out in a deep voice, Mithridates moved slowly across the front of the host. Loud, admiring shouts rang out in response, and the distinctive sound of swords being hammered on shields mixed with that of clashing cymbals and pounding drums. Like those in any army, the Pontic soldiers reveled in the attention of their master. Reaching the center, Mithridates spent a long time enjoining the charioteers, and Romulus' unease grew. By the time the king had addressed his entire force, the noise levels on the other side of the valley had grown to a threatening crescendo.

"Let them shout," said Petronius contemptuously. "It makes no odds to us."

Perturbed, Romulus took a look at Caesar, whose stance had not changed. *Nothing seems to panic this general,* he thought with relief.

Caesar turned to confer with his officers. After a few moments, he faced the Twenty-Eighth, every man of which was watching him intently. "They're just showing off, comrades," he declared confidently. "It's nothing to worry about. There'll be no battle today. Finishing our fortifications is far more important." At his words, an audible sigh of relief went up. Satisfied, Caesar clambered down to the *intervallum* and disappeared.

"As you were," shouted the officers. "Back to work."

Once again, pickaxes and shovels rose and fell. Carrying rocks for the *ballistae,* the braying mules were urged forward toward the walls. A surveyor emerged from the front gate, talking with a colleague. Behind him scuttled a slave clutching the *groma,* the device that helped his master to lay out a rectangular grid of the camp every day. A pair of straight, crossed sticks on a vertical pole, the *groma* had a lead weight dangling from the end of each of its four arms.

Relaxing, Petronius and the rest of Romulus' comrades began chatting among themselves. Once again, their job was the easiest on offer. The *optiones* and centurions did little to stop the idle banter. If Caesar was unconcerned, so were they.

Romulus' study of the enemy did not let up, however. Mithridates continued talking, and at last a long, rousing cheer went up from his assembled troops. Romulus cursed.

"Caesar got it wrong," he blurted. "The bastards are going to attack."

Petronius gave him an incredulous glance, but this changed as he too studied the Pontic host. Other men began to notice as well.

Mithridates had already moved to one side, allowing the slingers and archers to lope down the slope first. Next came the scythed chariots, their axles creaking loudly. Alongside those trotted the heavy cavalry and the Thracian horsemen, forming a second wave of men and steeds. Taking up the rear were the peltasts and other infantry. Romulus' main concern, though, was the Pontic chariots and the massive amount of mounted support they had on each wing. If Mithridates' army was making the crazy decision to attack uphill, he and his comrades would struggle to hold back an all-out attack. Most of Deiotarus' riders were absent still.

Soon the roiling mass of chariots and horsemen had reached the bottom of the opposite slope. There was a pregnant pause and, in the lines of the Twenty-Eighth, everyone held their breath. Would the enemy move off along the valley floor, or make the fateful decision to charge upward, toward their lines?

Romulus was glad to see that their *optio* was now observing too, but neither he nor any of the centurions seemed alarmed yet. It wasn't that surprising, he supposed. Attacking up a hill was most unwise. Romulus scowled, worried that this was more than just an enemy maneuver. There was no harm being prepared, in warning Caesar. Was the officers' belief in him so strong that they couldn't see what was happening right before their eyes?

The lead slingers and archers leaped into the water, quickly followed by their comrades. Holding their bows and slings high, they soon waded across, looking up at the Roman position. Horses whinnied as they were forced into the stream, yet the heavy cavalry maintained good order while crossing. Typical of irregular troops, the Thracians traversed in a disorganized mob, shouting and laughing. Loud rumbling noises and splashes ascended from the chariots, which were also being driven into the calf-high water without hesitation. On an area of flattish ground, the Pontic soldiers reassembled, quickly reassuming their original positions. All were now glancing upward, while their officers pointed and shouted commands.

"They couldn't be that stupid," breathed Petronius.

"I wouldn't be so sure," replied Romulus grimly.

There was a short delay as the last enemy warriors urged their mounts into line. Then, started by the lead charioteers, an angry shout left their throats and, as one, they began to move forward. Uphill.

"Jupiter!" Petronius exclaimed. "They're mad."

Their centurion finally acted. "We're under attack!" he shouted. "Sound the alarm!"

Raising his instrument to his lips, the nearest trumpeter blew a short, sharp series of notes over and over again. The response of the Twenty-Eighth was fast, the officers ushering the cohorts into close order while reducing the gap with its neighbor on each side. Deiotarus' horsemen—scarcely a hundred strong—moved together uneasily. Then the legionaries working on the ditches and ramparts took in the closely packed ranks climbing the slope. Led by their officers, they charged onto the *intervallum* and ran for their shields and *pila*.

It was slow, thought Romulus. Far too slow.

The protection they needed—the remainder of Deiotarus' cavalry—was nowhere to be seen. Furthermore, it would take the legions in the camp half an hour to find all their gear, assemble and march out to do battle. By that time the Twenty-Eighth would have been annihilated. Looking around, Romulus could see the same shocked realization appearing on men's faces. Yet they had to stay put: Without their protection, their ill-prepared comrades inside the walls would suffer the same fate.

The confident atmosphere that had prevailed all morning evaporated. What had seemed like a cushy job was going to be the death of them all. No one spoke as they watched the enemy moving uphill, taking their time to conserve their horses' energy. Having fought the Romans before, Mithridates' men would know that they were at no risk from javelins until they were within thirty paces, perhaps fifty down an incline like this. The *ballistae* were still within the walls, so there was no means of preventing the enemy from ascending the slope unchallenged. The Pontic horse would have ample time to regroup before charging. Romulus' mouth felt dry at the prospect.

An uneasy silence reigned over the Twenty-Eighth; angry shouts and cries rose from the camp as the rest of the army struggled to get ready. Six centuries of roughly eighty men had to join up to form a cohort; ten of these assembled units made a legion. While the process happened smoothly, it took time. A good general did not march his men out to battle unprepared, thought Romulus. He and his comrades would just have to manage.

It was not long before the enemy host had come to within two hundred paces of their position. Now Romulus could make out the slingers and the archers. Clad in simple wool tunics, they were similar to the mercenaries he had fought against in Egypt. Each man carried two slings, one for short range and another for longer distances. The spare was wrapped around their necks, while a leather pouch on a strap contained their ammunition. Many also carried knives. Dressed in white tunics, the archers were better armed. As well as their recurved bows, many wore swords on their red leather belts. With occasional hide or linen cuirasses and helmets, these were troops that could close with the enemy as well as fire arrows from a distance.

Yet neither type would pose a threat to the legionaries' shield wall, Romulus thought. It was the men in the chariots behind, and the heavily armed horsemen on either side, who would do that. Although he knew of the Persians' disastrous attempt to use scythed chariots against Alexander at Gaugamela, Romulus still felt uneasy. The men around him had not been shown how to fight such vehicles, as Alexander's had. Pulled by four armored horses and controlled by a single warrior, they had curved blades as long as a man's arm protruding from the end of the traces and from both wheels. They promised devastation.

Nor had the Persian chariots been backed up by heavy cavalry, as the Pontic ones were. These horsemen could sweep around to their rear and thus prevent any retreat. Dread surged through Romulus at the memory of the Parthian cataphracts. With conical iron helmets, scale mail that reached below the knee, and carrying long jave-lins, those opposite closely resembled the mailed warriors who had smashed apart Crassus' legions with such impunity. The sun's rays flashed off the chain mail covering their horses' chests and flanks, reflecting blinding light into the legionaries' faces.

The threat posed by Pharnaces' army was sinking in around Romulus. Men were looking very uneasy. *If they knew what I had seen at Carrhae,* he thought, *many would run now.* Thankfully they didn't, so their wavering lines held. Their *optio* looked to the centurion, who cleared his throat self-consciously. "Steady, lads," he ordered. "We won't have to hold the bastards for long. Caesar is on his way."

"Fucking well better be," commented Petronius.

Nervous laughter rippled through the ranks.

They had little opportunity for any further contemplation as the Pontic archers and slingers loosed their first volley. Hundreds of ar-rows and stones shot up, darkening the sky. This was the opening gambit of most battles, aimed at causing maximum casualties and softening up the enemy before a charge. Although his shield was made of layers of hardened wood and covered with leather, Romu-lus still felt his jaw clench.

"Front rank, on your knees!" shouted the officers. "The rest of you, shields up!"

Hundreds of *scuta* banged off each other as men rushed to protect themselves. Those at the very front, including Romulus and Petronius, did not do the same. Instead they dropped to the ground, allowing their shields to cover them completely, while the men in the second row angled theirs obliquely before them. Those farther to the rear held their *scuta* directly over their heads. This was a method used by the Forgotten Legion to withstand Parthian arrows, and Romulus was pleased to note that Caesar used it too. The normal deployment—with the front row remaining on their feet—allowed many soldiers to suffer injuries to their lower legs from well-aimed shafts.

There was a heartbeat's delay, and then the air filled with gentle whirring sounds as the arrows came down to earth. An instant later, loud crashes announced the stones' arrival too. His muscles tight with tension, Romulus waited, knowing what the next noise would be. He hated it as much as the first time he had heard it. Listening to men scream was much harder to do now than during the rage and immediacy of one-on-one combat, when it became part of the red hot blur of battle.

Sure enough, strangled cries of pain broke out everywhere. Soldiers collapsed, thrashing at the shafts that had found the gap between shields to pierce their flesh. Others had gained enough momentum to drive through the legionaries' *scuta* and into their arms and faces. Fortunately, most of the stones just clattered off the shields and bounced away, but a few did find targets, cracking bones and denting helmets. Given the number of missiles released, it was inevitable that there were fatalities. Not many, but the unlucky few slumped to the dirt, their weapons falling from slack hands.

Romulus' dream of getting to Rome was fading. He gazed uneasily at the massed enemy ranks, asking for Mithras' continued favor.

Everyone else was praying to their favorite gods too.

Their work done, the slingers and archers fell back. It was time for the chariots to attack. Romulus could make out at least fifty. Enough to hit most of the Twenty-Eighth head on, while the Thracians and Pontic heavy cavalry rode around to their undefended rear.

Their situation was grim now, even critical. Still there was no sign of Caesar or the other legions.

Flicking their reins, the charioteers signaled their horses to pick up the pace. At last it was possible to make them out clearly. They were clad in composite scale cuirasses and laminated armpieces, with crested Attic helmets were not dissimilar to those worn by junior Roman officers. Each carried a long-handled whip, which he used to encourage his beasts to the trot. A moment later, it was the canter. Having conserved their steeds' energy, they had room to ask everything of them. With jingling traces and the blades on their wheels spinning and flashing, the chariots surged forward. Although the slope was steep, the ground was not that uneven and they were able to pick up speed quite fast. With loud whoops and cheers, the cavalry forces split off to the sides, eager to complete the pincer movement. Last of all came thousands of peltasts and *thureophoroi*, their weapons raised in readiness. Theirs would be the final job, to charge into the Roman lines after the chariots and horsemen had smashed them apart, and prevent any attempt to regroup.

The fear among the legionaries grew palpable, and again the Twenty-Eighth began to waver, despite the officers' muttered reassurances and threats. More centurions moved to stand in the front rank, and the standard-bearers lifted their wooden poles for everyone to see. The tactic helped somewhat. No one ran—yet. Men looked nervously to their comrades, muttered anxious prayers and eyed the heavens. They were all about to die: chopped apart by the chariots or cut down where they stood by the horsemen. Where in the name of Hades was Caesar?

At last the centurions at the back ordered the soldiers there to turn about and face the enemy. *If only we had some of the long spears which the Forgotten Legion used*, thought Romulus. Those weapons had been able to stop any cavalry. Instead they had just their *scuta*, swords and a pair of javelins each. In less than twenty heartbeats, the chariots would hit their lines. Then they would be hit from the rear by hundreds of cavalry, before the enemy foot soldiers finished the job. Romulus spat on the ground. He hoped that their deaths bought enough time for Caesar and the other legions to emerge fully prepared.

Less than a hundred paces remained between the tightly packed chariots and the Roman front ranks. They left nowhere to go. It was a case of being run down by fast-moving armored horses, or cut apart by the blades they pulled. The grinning charioteers knew it too, and urged their teams to greater speeds.

"Ready *pila!*" bellowed the centurions. The fearful soldiers obeyed, cocking back their right arms and preparing to release.

Now the legionaries could see the steeds' nostrils flaring with effort, their heads bobbing up and down. Their hooves pounded on the hard ground, and their harness jingled. Romulus fancied he could almost hear the scythed blades whirr as they spun round on the wheels.

Fifty paces until they struck. Time began to move in a blur. A wheel on one chariot struck a rock, sending it up at a crazy angle and throwing its driver free. It overturned, dragging its horses into those of another team. Both chariots careered crazily to a halt and a hoarse cheer went up from the legionaries. But the rest were still closing in fast. Behind Romulus, a man cursed their bad luck, Caesar and all the gods. Another began to wail with fear. Anxious to release his javelin, Petronius shifted from foot to foot beside Romulus.

Twenty-five paces, thought Romulus. He could clearly see the stubble on the face of the charioteer heading for them. Good killing distance for their *pila,* and their only chance to make some dent in the enemy numbers. He looked to the centurion, whose mouth was opening to give the order. Before he could give it, a piece of lead took the officer in the center of the forehead. Released by a slinger as a parting shot, it was as clean a kill as Romulus had ever seen. The crack with which the small piece of metal struck left no doubt as to its lethality. The centurion dropped soundlessly, without giving the order to release.

Romulus' head spun frantically, searching for the *optio*, but he was at the rear with the *tesserarius*, ensuring that no one tried to flee.

All around them, the other centuries were throwing their javelins. Tall as a man, their long wooden shafts were topped by a pyramidal iron tip that could punch through shields and armor to kill. In graceful clouds, they climbed into the air, falling among the charioteers in a shower of lethal points. Many enemy warriors were struck down, losing control of their teams of horses, which panicked and collided with one another. The three that would reach Romulus and his comrades were unaffected, though, and the charioteers grinned with satisfaction.

Behind them ran thousands of peltasts and infantry.

Of Caesar there was no sign.

IV

THE TEMPLE OF ORCUS

Jovina did not hear what Scaevola said to Fabiola. Sensing an opportunity, though, the madam darted forward to her side. "This is the new owner," she declared with a flash of real malice. "We're to sign the deal later today."

Old bitch, thought Fabiola in alarm. She had already made up her mind to sell.

Scaevola's eyebrows rose sharply. "It's this whore I should be talking to then, eh?"

Confusion mixed with the triumph on Jovina's face. "You know Fabiola?"

"Let's say that we have a certain amount of . . . shared history." He sniggered. "Don't we, gorgeous?"

His men leered, all unshaven jaws, rotten teeth and broken noses.

Jovina took the opportunity to fade into the background.

Fabiola's cheeks flushed with impotent rage while Sextus and Vettius bristled in front of her. Laying restraining hands on their arms, she considered her options. It was six to two, or six to three if she threw herself into the fray as well. The odds were not insurmountable, but it didn't feel like the right time to have it out with

Scaevola. She had bigger fish to fry than this malevolent bastard, which was also the reason she wouldn't walk away.

Fabiola found the *fugitivarius* studying her face for signs of fear.

She would give him nothing. *Go on the offensive,* Fabiola thought. *Get him on the back foot.* "You piece of filth," she hissed. "Get off my property. Now."

Scaevola didn't move a step. "Don't have forty slaves backing you up now, eh?" he chuckled. "Jovina's not telling stories then. Good. Ruining your whorehouse instead of hers will be even more satisfying."

"We'll see about that," Fabiola replied boldly, ignoring her pounding heart. She remembered Scaevola's previous leanings, one of the reasons he had pursued her so hard. "Proven followers of Pompey are liable to be executed."

"Pompey?" The *fugitivarius* looked shocked. "I'm no supporter of his." Smiling at Fabiola's surprise, he winked. "In fact, me and my lads do some work for the Master of the Horse. Discreet stuff, you understand."

Fabiola's hopes sank. An expert at deception, of course Scaevola would have changed sides. She could imagine what type of jobs Marcus Antonius had him doing. Murdering innocent men in alleyways sprang to mind.

"I've thought about you plenty since we last met," said Scaevola, licking his lips. "Asking the gods that our paths might cross one day. Now my prayers have been answered! I'm going to enjoy hearing you scream." He rubbed at his crotch and his men laughed.

Fabiola felt sick, and her courage frayed. Nearly being raped by the *fugitivarius* was one of her most terrible memories.

The provocation got to Sextus at last, and he pulled out his sword. Vettius raised his club in support, but their actions were mimicked at once by Scaevola's five men. With a sudden burst of energy, Jovina darted to safety, peering around the corner of the hallway like a wizened, frightened child.

"Wait," Fabiola ordered her men. "Not yet." *Help me, Mithras,* she thought. *What can we do?*

The two sides glared at each other, the room seeming much smaller with so many drawn weapons. It was an impasse. Positioned by the doorway, Vettius and Sextus were preventing the *fugitivarius* and his thugs from leaving, but attacking them would result in fatalities on both sides.

Scaevola grinned. "We can wait here all day. Or would you rather fight now?"

"Vettius? I'm coming in."

Fabiola had never been so glad to hear Benignus' voice in her life.

Ducking his head to enter, Benignus eased his bulk through the arched entrance. His eyes narrowed, and he immediately moved to stand beside Sextus and Vettius. In one hand he gripped a metal-studded club like Vettius', in the other a broad-bladed dagger. Fabiola felt a surge of relief. The two doormen dwarfed their opponents, and despite his disability, Sextus was a skilled fighter.

"We can take them if we have to," Fabiola muttered. Scaevola and his heavies looked much less confident now. At least half of them would die if a fight started, an outcome only a fool would look forward to. "Give the dogs a chance to leave and they will. Make toward Jovina, but stay together."

Fabiola's men obeyed, keeping her safely to their rear as they moved around the side of the room. The others' instinctive response was to shuffle nearer the door. The maneuvers took place in silence, yet the atmosphere could be cut with a knife.

Scaevola muttered an order and his gang retreated outside. He waited until they were gone, showing Fabiola that he was not scared to face her followers alone. "We'll resume this matter later," he purred, making the mocking bow that she hated. Bellowing at his men to hurry, the *fugitivarius* was gone.

Fabiola let herself sag back against the wall.

"He's a nasty piece of work," said Jovina from the hallway. She pursed her lips. "Dangerous."

"Damn you! Sextus and I have better reason to know that than anyone else here," Fabiola shouted. "You were quick enough to tell him that I was the new owner too. We haven't even drawn up a bill of sale!"

Jovina made a show of innocence, which failed miserably.

"I should just walk out," Fabiola cried. "Leave you in the shit as you deserve!"

"No!" Tears sprang to Jovina's rheumy eyes, and she raised her joined hands in supplication. "Please," she whispered. "I am an old woman. He frightens me so much."

Fabiola bit down on her anger. The madam was completely untrustworthy, but there was no need to act prematurely. Jovina would be of use while she got to know her way around the Lupanar. After thirty years in charge, she was a mine of potential information. She just needed to be kept on a short leash. "I've been thinking," Fabiola said brightly. "Better to pay half the amount we agreed up front, and the rest in twelve months. Depending on how well business has picked up, of course."

Jovina looked unhappy, but she shrank before Fabiola's stony gaze. There would be few—if any—offers to better her former slave's one. "Very well," she simpered. "It doesn't matter to me."

"Good. Write down what we've agreed then."

Meekly, the madam shuffled to her desk and found a strip of clean parchment. Dipping a stylus into a glass inkpot, she scrawled a few lines on it before adding a signature at the bottom. She waited in silence as Fabiola countersigned it. "Satisfied?" she ventured.

Scanning the completed document again, Fabiola slipped it into her purse. There was little doubt in her mind that Jovina had written all that she needed to take ownership of the brothel, but she was no expert in legal terminology. Everything had to be correct with this purchase. "I'll have my lawyer check it over," she replied curtly. "If it meets with his approval, the money will be delivered by the following day."

Expecting nothing less, Jovina nodded.

"I'll take immediate possession," Fabiola announced. "Do you want to stay on?"

The madam began to answer, but another heavy bout of coughing prevented her.

"Will your health allow it?"

Wiping sputum from her lips, Jovina composed herself. "The gods will decide," she said. "With your permission, I'll stay. For a little while."

Fabiola could see that Jovina was trying to preserve her own dignity. She would allow her that. "Very well," she answered, all business now. Indicating that Sextus should check the situation outside, Fabiola stalked to the door. "I'll be back in two days, the gods willing."

Jovina bobbed her head gratefully.

"It's safe, Mistress," called Sextus.

With Vettius taking up the rear, Fabiola emerged onto the busy street. There was no sign of Scaevola or his men. She scanned the faces of all those in sight, but, to her relief, recognized none. Once more this was just another small thoroughfare in Rome. *Why bother having me followed?* Fabiola thought, weariness filling her. *The bastard knows that I'll be here every day in future.* Old fear swamped her anew. How was she going to defend the Lupanar against Scaevola's thugs, let alone turn the fortunes of the business around? That was before the *fugitivarius* tried to take his revenge on her. To Fabiola's shame, her next inclination was to walk away from the brothel and never return. Jovina would be powerless to stop her, and Scaevola would never dare attack her at Brutus' house. In a heartbeat, all her problems would disappear.

At that prospect, Fabiola's spirits plunged into the depths. This opportunity had seemed perfect—heaven sent, even. She glanced at the sky, willing a sign to appear. Nothing did. Maybe new dealings with the Lupanar were just not meant to be. Contemplating the climb-down made Fabiola feel like a complete coward, but she was terrified of Scaevola. What else could she do?

It was then that she stumbled on the uneven ground, and nearly fell.

Solicitous as ever, Sextus caught her with a strong grip. Fabiola muttered her thanks and they exchanged a look. The slave saw her fear. "Don't worry, Mistress," he muttered. "Think of all the dangers that we've survived since you first met that whoreson. The gods will not desert us now."

Fabiola managed a smile. Sextus was right, she thought. Their lives *had* been charmed. Taking strength from his words, she headed in the direction of her *domus*. The first thing to deal with would be Brutus' reaction to her recent purchase. Even if he approved, Fabiola did not think that he would want his legionaries standing guard outside a brothel. Her lover was in the business of winning back popularity for Caesar, not losing it. Yet she had to have protection against Scaevola. Secundus, the veteran who'd repeatedly saved her life, came to mind, but Fabiola discarded that idea at once. With their pensions and land grants honored, he and his men were now loyal to Caesar.

Apart from Sextus and the doormen, Fabiola was on her own again. She made a snap decision. It was time to call on every possible means of help, and not just the aid of Jupiter and Mithras, her favorite deities. There were darker gods than those in Rome. *I will make an offering to Orcus*, Fabiola decided. Fear clutched her at the very idea. Despite all her past troubles, she had steered away from worshipping the god of the underworld.

Now it was time.

†

Brutus had not returned when they reached the *domus*, which pleased Fabiola. She had still not composed herself totally and didn't want to have to try. Too much was going on in her mind. She could put up a blank façade for the servants and the legionaries on guard, but hadn't banked on Docilosa's ability to read her like a book. Since becoming friends in the Lupanar, they had been through much together. Short, plain and similar in age to Fabiola's mother, the former domestic slave was now her closest confidante. Fabiola wasn't that surprised, therefore, when Docilosa noticed her low mood.

"What's happened?" she cried. Rather than greeting Vettius warmly, she glared at him. "What's he doing here? Did that hag do something?" Docilosa was the only one who knew where Fabiola and Sextus had gone.

"I'm fine," Fabiola protested. "And Jovina's ill. Close to Hades, I'd say."

Vettius nodded in pleased agreement.

"Small loss she'll be," shrugged Docilosa. She had as much reason as Fabiola, and more, to hate her former owner.

"The old crone has no fight left in her," Fabiola went on, keen to relate her success. "I forced her to sell me the Lupanar—on my terms."

Docilosa's eyebrows shot up. "Is that the best way to move forward? When you escaped that world, you never wanted to return to it."

"This is different," replied Fabiola, trying to sound convincing. "I'm the owner now, not a whore. No one will be picking me out from the line."

"The fools will try," responded Docilosa tartly. "You'll be the best-looking woman there."

Fabiola smiled. "In that case, they'll have Vettius and Benignus to deal with. And Sextus." An image of the *fugitivarius* popped into her mind and her face fell. Over-amorous politicians and merchants were going to be the least of her worries.

"What's wrong, then?" Docilosa asked. "You look scared."

Fabiola's chin trembled. "Somebody came into the brothel while I was there."

"Who?" Docilosa demanded. "Memor?"

Vettius growled low in his throat.

Fabiola shuddered. "Not him." The cold, scarred *lanista* had enjoyed her company on frequent occasions near the end of her time in the Lupanar. Of course the feeling had not been mutual; Memor's only purpose in her life had been as a source of information, a function he had ultimately fulfilled by revealing some of Romulus' story since the twins' traumatic parting. While coupling with the *lanista* had been unpleasant, it paled into insignificance beside what Scaevola would do to her. "Someone far worse," she whispered.

Docilosa's brow furrowed. Who could instil such fear in her normally indomitable mistress? She took her time, studying Fabiola's miserable face. "Is it Scaevola?" she finally ventured.

Knowing nothing of what had gone on before, Vettius looked confused.

Unable to stop tears from welling in her eyes, Fabiola nodded. "He knows I'm the Lupanar's new owner too."

Scowling, Docilosa thought hard. "How many copies of the bill of sale are there?"

"I'm no fool," replied Fabiola. "One, and I have it here."

"Is it notarized yet?"

"Of course not."

"Tear it up," her servant crowed. "Burn the damn thing, or throw it in the sewer. Without proof, Jovina hasn't a leg to stand on. The purchase will never have existed! Then you can stay here." She waved at the legionaries lounging around the courtyard. "Scaevola can't harm you inside these walls."

Fabiola did not reply. She was stung by the abject misery in Vettius' eyes. If she didn't buy the brothel, his and Benignus' fate would again be uncertain. Leaving the doormen after her manumission had felt disloyal. Of course it had been because Jovina wouldn't sell them, but to do it a second time would feel like betrayal. It would also mean giving up her greatest desire—because of Scaevola. Fabiola's jaw set.

Docilosa read her emotions, and her face turned thunderous. "You want to press on regardless? Why?"

"You don't understand," answered Fabiola in a monotone. No one, not even Docilosa, could know of her plans to kill Caesar yet. "The Lupanar is part of my future."

Vettius was overjoyed, but Docilosa scowled. Fabiola's tears had gone, though, leaving only cold resolution on her face. Experience had taught her not to argue with her mistress at times like this. "If you're sure," she muttered.

"I am," said Fabiola, squaring her shoulders. "Tomorrow I will make a vow to Orcus. In return, I'll ask for Scaevola's death."

Docilosa went a pale shade of gray. Such oaths were not lightly taken. Placing her thumb between the forefinger and index finger of her right hand, she made the sign against evil.

"I do not ask you to follow me in this," said Fabiola, staring at her. "If you wish to leave my employ, I will release you without prejudice."

"No," Docilosa replied firmly. "If you're this determined, the gods must be watching. I'm in too."

"Get me three pieces of lead then." Prayers and curses to gods were often written on small square sheets of the gray metal and then folded up. Accompanied by coins and other offerings, thousands were thrown daily into temple fountains all over Rome by citizens in need of divine aid. "You know where to go."

Docilosa left without another word.

Fabiola dismissed Vettius a moment later, promising the delighted doorman that she would see him at the brothel soon. The moment she was alone, Fabiola fell into a deep reverie. Her curse on Scaevola would have to be carefully thought out. Malevolent deities such as Orcus were known for twisting vows and promises back on themselves. She had no wish to see the *fugitivarius* dead and then suffer some dreadful punishment as a result.

†

A heavy covering of low-lying cloud the next dawn promised rain in plenty. The gods did not fail to deliver. By the time Fabiola was ready to leave, water was falling from the skies in torrents, drenching anyone foolish enough to venture outdoors. The open-air courtyard in the center of the house soon resembled a swimming pool. Although it was early morning, the poor light made it feel like sunset. Thunder was grumbling overhead too, firing out occasional lightning bolts to illuminate the dull, gray streets. Summertime had vanished.

"You'll catch your death," Docilosa protested as she helped Fabiola into a hooded military cloak commandeered from one of Brutus' legionaries. "Or fall into the Tiber and drown."

"Stop fussing," said Fabiola, touched by her servant's concern.

Dressed similarly to Fabiola, Sextus was already set. Today he was armed to the teeth, wearing two daggers as well as his sword. Fabiola was not without protection herself. Under her cloak, a leather strap was slung over her left shoulder, and from it hung a plain but serviceable sheathed *pugio*. She was proficient in its use, having ordered Sextus to teach her long ago. *Anyone who attacks me needs to be prepared to die in the attempt,* thought Fabiola fiercely. *I will choose my own fate, and being mistress of the Lupanar is part of that path.* They were brave ideas, but her stomach still clenched with fear every time Scaevola came to mind. The *optio* in charge of Brutus' men had offered her an escort, but like the day before, she had refused it. Her visit to Orcus' temple was a private matter, and Fabiola wanted no gossip about why she was visiting such an ill-omened place. With Brutus absent on business, the *optio* had accepted her decision. Naturally enough, his soldiers looked relieved. Who went out in such weather unless ordered to do so?

"I'm coming too," Docilosa declared, taking her own cloak from an iron hook on the wall.

"No," said Fabiola firmly. "You'll stay in the *domus*. This is for me to deal with. No one else." She saw the pain in Docilosa's eyes, and her tone softened. "No harm will come to us out there. Neptune will protect us!"

"The ocean has certainly come to Rome today," Docilosa conceded with a reluctant smile. She gave Fabiola a fierce hug, before pushing her awkwardly away. "Go on," she muttered, her voice catching. "The sooner you leave, the sooner you'll be back."

"Yes." Swallowing the lump in her own throat, Fabiola followed Sextus to the entrance. The legionary on duty there peered out into the deluge before giving them the all-clear. The instant they had emerged, the postern gate slammed shut behind them. To Fabiola, it sounded like the doors of Hades closing. She clenched her fists, trying to shake her superstitious feelings.

Despite their heavy cloaks, Fabiola and Sextus were both drenched within a hundred paces of the *domus*. Underfoot, the unpaved surface had turned to a glutinous sludge, which made swift passage impossible. It squelched over the sides of their sandals, covering their feet in a smelly layer of brown mud. Trying not to inhale, Fabiola did not look closely at it. The dung heaps in the flooded alleyways on either side would be running out to mix with this morass, and it would be the same wherever they went. *Move on*, she thought grimly. *We can wash later.*

The dreadful weather meant that the streets were almost empty. The open-fronted shops that formed the ground floors of most buildings were still open, but there were few customers within.

The stallholders who normally occupied the spaces on each side of the narrow thoroughfares were nowhere to be seen. Soaking merchandise would not sell to anyone. The beggars, thieves and cripples were absent too, taking whatever shelter they could find under archways or in temple porticos. Like half-drowned rats, slaves on errands darted back and forth, ordered out by their masters despite the downpour. Patrolling sections of Antonius' legionaries were also evident. Marching close together, they held their *scuta* in against their bodies, their best protection from the driving rain.

Like Brutus' *domus*, their destination was situated on the Palatine Hill, which meant at least that their rain-soaked journey was short. Keeping their eyes peeled, Fabiola and Sextus soon reached a nondescript street not far from the Forum. Entering it, the air became cold and forbidding. Fabiola suspected it was because the empty lane was dominated by the temple. The buildings directly adjacent to it lay derelict, adding to the louring atmosphere. Their doors swung to and fro in the wind, and water poured down from roofs whose gutters were long rotted away.

It was usual for such venues to be thronged with salesmen, food vendors, acrobats, jugglers and soothsayers. Their customers—the worshippers—were absent today, though, so the traders had stayed at home. That suited Fabiola well. Sextus looked pleased too. It was far easier to assess a situation for danger when few people were about.

A plain altar carved from a large piece of granite occupied the central ground before the shrine itself, its surface covered in disquieting red-brown stains that no rain could wash away. Fabiola did not let her gaze linger on the stone slab, moving it to the carved columns that held up the triangular decorated portico. They were shorter and less grand than those of many other shrines, while the steps up to the entrance had not been cleaned in an age. Yet the depictions of demons and evil spirits sprang out from the faded paint above. There were sharp horns, probing tongues, mouths full of sharp teeth and outlandish weapons galore. Fabiola recognized Charon, the blue-skinned Etruscan demon of death, with his feathered wings and massive hammer. At gladiatorial games with Brutus, she had witnessed a living man play Charon's part, entering the arena to mock screams from the audience. There his role was real, and gruesome. The memory of his hammer smashing the skulls of the fallen to ensure that they were dead still revolted Fabiola.

The figure over their heads looked fully capable of the same, but Charon paled into insignificance beside the painted representation of Orcus himself. Occupying the central part of the triangular portico, the god's stern, bearded face was enormous, with a diameter at least twice the length of an ox cart. His dark eyes stared down fiercely, transfixing Fabiola. She could not bring herself to look at Orcus' hair, which was a writhing mass of snakes. Ever since another prostitute had placed a venomous serpent in her bed, she had been terrified of the creatures.

She jumped as Sextus touched her elbow. "Let's get inside, Mistress," he urged. "This rain will give us a fever."

There was no point holding back now. Praying that her plan would not backfire, Fabiola climbed up the steps to the entrance, followed closely by her slave. Past the rows of fluted columns were two tall doors, their surfaces covered with strengthening iron strips. They were shut, and Fabiola quailed. Was Cerberus waiting to devour her on the other side? *Come on*, she thought angrily. *I am alive, not dead.* Rallying her courage, Fabiola stepped up to the portals and thumped on the wood with a balled fist.

Apart from the rain drumming off the ground behind them, there was silence.

She banged harder this time. "Open up! I wish to make an offering."

A long pause followed, and Fabiola scowled. There were definitely people inside, she knew that. A temple complex such as this was no different to any other in Rome: It was where the priests and acolytes lived, ate, slept and worshipped. Apart from occasional sacred days—and today was not one—they were open to the public every day of the year. She raised her hand again, but as it fell, the door was pulled silently ajar. Startled, Fabiola lowered her arm and took a step backward.

A gray-robed priestess stood framed in the entrance. She was young, perhaps the same age as Fabiola. Short, with long brown hair pinned up behind her head, she had a wide face with a short nose. Piercing green eyes studied Fabiola, disconcerting her.

"Enter." She moved aside.

Fabiola was reminded of someone, but was so wound up that she gave it no further thought. Pushing back the hood of her cloak, she crossed the threshold with a mental prayer to Mithras for his protection. Fabiola felt no qualms about this; it was not unusual to ask things of many gods.

The corridor within ran from side to side away from the doors and was even dimmer than the street. Occasional small oil lamps hung from brackets, casting long, flickering shadows on a bare, stone-flagged floor. Grotesque paintings of gods and demons covered the walls, their limbs cleverly moving in the guttering light cast by the lamps. The threatening atmosphere was a deliberate construct, Fabiola realized, generating anxiety in visitors' hearts the instant they set foot inside. Yet this was the temple of Orcus, the god of the underworld. It was right to be scared here. Despite herself, Fabiola shivered. *Do not forget your purpose,* she thought, shoving down her rising dread. "I wish to make a request of the god. In private," she said, opening her clenched fingers. On her palm lay three neatly folded pieces of lead. She had spent hours composing the curses inscribed within them. With the threat from Scaevola more immediate, all referred to him, requesting his death in the most terrible of ways. For now, Caesar came second.

The priestess was unsurprised. People came here for every reason under the sun: twisted with hatred, seeking retribution for wrongs done to them, asking for revenge on enemies, lovers and superiors. Extreme weather did not remove such needs, nor did it affect the desire of certain devotees not to be seen by others. "Follow me." She walked off, her bare feet slapping off the floor.

Nervously, Fabiola and Sextus followed. In silence, they passed a succession of doors, all of which were closed. Fabiola wondered who might be in the chambers beyond. From one came the low sound of men chanting. She couldn't make out the words, but the tune was slow and mournful and did little to calm her jangling nerves.

The priestess came to a halt at last. Producing a key from within her robes, she unlocked the door before them, which opened noiselessly, adding to the air of pressure. Inside was a large windowless chamber, its plastered surfaces painted an ominous, dark red color. As in the hallway, the only light came from a few oil-burning lamps on the walls. There was barely any furniture, apart from a plain cement furnace on a square platform of bricks, situated at the back of the room. Staring in, Fabiola felt a warm current of air bathing her cheeks. A strong smell of incense also carried through the doorway. A deep red glow in the oven's opening revealed the source of the intense heat. To one side of it lay a pile of fuel, and on the other sat a small altar decorated with a statue of Orcus.

"You may make your offering here," said the young priestess. "Without interruption."

Fabiola's grip on the lead squares grew so tight that she felt them begin to bend at the edges. She stopped, worried that any damage might affect her requests of the god. Nothing must go wrong. Her very life depended on it. Nodding firmly, Fabiola walked in, tailed by Sextus.

The priestess also entered, shutting the door. Moving to the altar, she bent her head in prayer. Unsure what to do next, Fabiola did the same. Compared to the cool of the corridor and the rain-soaked streets, this room was like a *caldarium*, the hottest place in a bathing complex. Thanks to the incense that was burning, the atmosphere was heavy and intense. Despite her soaked clothing, Fabiola felt sweat break out all over her body. She was used to the fuggy warmth of a full Mithraeum, but this was different. Some temples had fires to throw small offerings on, but not this roaring furnace, which reminded Fabiola of what Hades might be like. Fresh fear gripped her, yet she forced herself to stay calm. Orcus was no ordinary god. Gifts to him were cast in their entirety into the flames, there to be consumed. Hence the need for the oven.

Orcus, Fabiola thought, raising her eyes to the statue. Implacable, it stared right back. *Mighty god of the underworld, hear me,* she entreated. *Once again, my life is in danger from Scaevola. He is an evil man and a murderer who will stop at nothing. I have no real means of stopping him without your help. Rid me of this whoreson, and I'll be in your debt forever. I will erect an altar to you, and there a goat will be sacrificed once a year for the rest of my days.* As an extra incentive, Fabiola leaned forward and placed a stack of silver coins before the figurine. A sharp intake of breath from the priestess proved that the amount was impressive.

There was a loud crackling sound and flames belched up inside the furnace. Startled, Fabiola craned her head to see. Neither Sextus nor the priestess had done anything, but the fire was now roaring as if a smith was working a pair of bellows on it. She looked around, expecting to spot a demon hard at work, but all she could see were the four crimson walls, pressing in on her like a tomb. Long yellow-orange flames licked at the oven's opening, making it seem like the glowing maw of a ravening mythical beast. Terror overcame Fabiola at last and she froze.

"This is a propitious moment," intoned the priestess. "Make your offering."

Her voice nearly made Fabiola jump out of her skin. She looked around at the gray-robed girl and nodded, jerkily. Did she seem vaguely familiar? There was no time to ponder. With the priestess urging her forward, Fabiola opened her hand. There, on her palm, the three lead squares lay, inert and innocuous-looking. Like the hatred in her heart, though, they were far from that.

"Throw them in as deep as you can," ordered the priestess.

Stepping as close as she could bear, Fabiola drew back her arm and flung the pieces of metal into the fire. They were lost to sight in the blink of an eye. She sighed. It was almost done, but what remained was critically important. Fabiola had no wish to bring down divine retribution upon herself for this act. As other Romans did, she made her offering on specified conditions. She was so wound up about this that she began whispering out loud instead of praying silently. "Keep me safe from harm, great Orcus," she muttered, staring into the bright blaze. "And those who are important to me. Romulus. Brutus. Sextus. Benignus and Vettius. Docilosa."

There was a sharp intake of breath from behind her, and Fabiola realized that her request had not been internal after all. She glanced around at the priestess, whose face had gone white and pinched-looking.

"Who is Docilosa?"

"My servant," replied Fabiola, startled. "Why?"

Visibly disappointed, the priestess answered with another question. "Not a slave?"

"She used to be," admitted Fabiola, avoiding any mention of her own origins. She felt a little discomfited now. "But she has been a freedwoman for nearly six years now."

Hope filled the other's face. "What age is she?"

A tremor of suspicion tickled Fabiola's memory. "I don't know, exactly. Probably about forty."

The priestess's composure cracked now, leaving the grief of a young girl in its place. "Who was her owner?"

"Jovina," said Fabiola. "The owner of the Lupanar."

"Orcus be praised," gasped the priestess. "Mother is still alive!"

It was Fabiola's turn to be shocked. "Sabina?"

The priestess stiffened. "You know my name?"

"Docilosa has mentioned you many times," explained Fabiola, smiling. "She has grieved every day since your parting, and searched for you in countless temples. She never gave up hope of seeing you again."

There was a flicker of a smile. "Where is she?"

"In my house," said Fabiola. "It's not far."

Sabina's expression softened for a heartbeat, and then grew hard once more. "Why are you her mistress? Is Jovina dead?"

Fabiola bit back her instinctive retort to the interrogation. Under normal circumstances, she would not tolerate this level of rudeness from anybody. This was not a typical situation, though, and Docilosa was very dear to her. Moreover, Sextus already knew of her past. "Jovina is still alive, although only the gods know for how much longer. She used to own us both."

"You weren't a domestic slave like my mother, I take it," Sabina snorted.

Fabiola's nostrils flared at her presumption. An ordinary household slave was worth far less than a good-looking virgin, so Gemellus had sold her as a whore. It wasn't as if she'd had any choice in the matter. "No," she said quietly. "I wasn't."

Sabina's top lip curled with disdain.

"If you'd been more of a looker, that might have been your fate," said Fabiola, riled by her arrogance. "Thank the gods it was not."

A retort sprang to Sabina's lips, but she bit it back. "Who bought you, then?"

Fabiola took a deep breath. "My lover saw fit to buy my manumission and, because I asked him, that of your mother also."

At this, Sabina grew a fraction less surly. "Why would you do such a thing?"

"Because Docilosa has been a good friend to me," Fabiola replied. "She'll want to come and see you at once. Is that permitted?"

"Visitors are not encouraged, but there are ways around it," Sabina said craftily. "We can use a room like this to meet. The best time is midmorning, when the temple is busy. None of the priests will notice then."

"Good," Fabiola declared briskly, concealing her dislike. "I'll tell her." She turned to go.

Sabina wasn't finished. "You must have an urgent need to visit in such weather," she said, probing

"My business for being here is my own," Fabiola retorted. "It's nothing to do with you."

"You forget yourself," snapped Sabina. "I am a senior priestess here and, as such, privy to the god's thoughts and wishes."

Furious, Fabiola nonetheless forced her expression to become humble. To have achieved such a position from slavery while so young, Sabina must be a woman of immense ability. In addition, by angering one of Orcus' important disciples, she herself risked losing any chance of her request being granted. "Forgive me," she muttered from between clenched teeth. "It's nothing much. Just some trouble from a business rival."

"You work in the Lupanar still?"

"No," replied Fabiola quickly. She grimaced at her instinctive denial. "Yes. I bought the place from Jovina yesterday."

Sabina's eyes narrowed. "I see. Why?"

Fabiola did not like this unhealthy interest in her affairs. What was behind it? Placed on the back foot by her fear of Orcus and Sabina's confidence, though, she had no easy answer. There was no harm in telling some of the truth, she supposed. "My lover is in Caesar's army, and I've been on campaign with him for over two years," she replied. "I've had enough. I want to stay here in Rome, and running the Lupanar is something that comes naturally to me."

"It would," said Sabina haughtily.

Fabiola wanted to claw her eyes out, but she dared do nothing. They exchanged a frosty glance. Sabina could see her anger, she thought, and was reveling in it. Unless Docilosa could bring some influence to bear, here was a potential enemy.

The next question came. "Who's your lover?"

"Decimus Brutus."

Sabina's eyebrows rose. "One of Caesar's right-hand men? You must be very . . . persuasive."

Fabiola fought the color that rose to her cheeks and lost. *Damn the girl,* she thought. *Where does the venom come from? Docilosa's not like this.* Then she glanced at the statue on the altar beside her, and was shocked back to where she was. Orcus was not the jovial Bacchus, nor the caring Aesculapius. Even the powerful triad of Jupiter, Minerva and Juno were less dread-inspiring than the god of the underworld. While they were all powerful, they did not take a person's soul for eternity. What could it have been like for Sabina, sold here as a six-year-old acolyte? Fabiola wondered. There was a hardness to the other's mien that perhaps she had not noticed before. Maybe being sold into a brothel was not the only way to Hades?

"As you say," she murmured, moving toward the exit. Sextus gave her a reassuring look, and she managed a small grin in reply. With luck, the grilling was over. More importantly, Fabiola hoped that Orcus had not been angered by her clash with one of his priestesses. Extra prayers would have to be offered up to Jupiter and Mithras, asking for their intervention with their brother deity.

They reached the door without hearing Sabina speak again. Turning the iron handle, Fabiola glanced around. With her back to them, the priestess was on her knees before the altar. It was as obvious a sign of dismissal as Fabiola had ever been given, and her heart sank. She could think of nothing else to say, so she just closed the door behind her.

Deep in her misery, Fabiola paid little attention as they walked back to the entrance. Who knew what malevolent influence Sabina could bring to bear? Afterward, she would blame herself for not concentrating, but in reality there was little she could have done to prevent what happened next.

As Fabiola drew alongside one of the many doors in the passageway, it opened. Still wishing to remain anonymous, she didn't turn her head. There was an angry gasp from Sextus, though, and Fabiola heard his *gladius* snickering from its scabbard. She came back to reality with a bang. What was he doing? Drawing a weapon inside a temple would draw down the wrath of any deity, let alone Orcus. Turning, Fabiola's mouth opened in rebuke. She was just in time to see a stocky man plunging a sword deep into Sextus' side.

It was Scaevola.

V

VISIONS

ALEXANDRIA, EGYPT

Soaking up the warm sunshine, Tarquinius walked slowly along the street's central section, among the tall palm trees and ornate fountains. At least thirty paces across, the boulevard had to be three times wider than the biggest avenue in Rome. On its own, it was impressive. Taken with the lofty buildings on each side, the luxuriance of the trees' shade and the whispering water all around, it was truly awe-inspiring. Despite its widespread reputation, the haruspex had never believed that the Egyptian capital could be quite so impressive. Yet it was. This, the stunning Canopic Way, was not even unique in Alexandria, the most grand of cities. Equally impressive was the Argeus, the main thoroughfare that ran from north to south, and which intersected with the Canopic Way at a magnificent crossroads.

While he took little pleasure from the sights, every one of the metropolis' five quarters lived up to the same standard. Countless royal palaces dotted the northern parts; near the center were the striking Paneium, a man-made hill topped by a temple to Pan, and the Sema, the marble-walled enclosure that contained the tombs of the

Ptolemy kings as well as that of Alexander of Macedon. In the western quarter, where Tarquinius was now heading, were the main part of the library, and the Gymnasium, the grand building where young men were taught Hellenistic values and sports including running, wrestling and javelin-throwing. Though he was not a man who was easily surprised, the haruspex' jaw had fallen open the first time he saw its immense porticos. Each was more than a *stade* in length—nearly an eighth of a mile—making the Gymnasium dwarf any structure he'd ever seen, apart from the Pharos, Alexandria's mighty lighthouse.

Always one to remain inconspicuous, Tarquinius kept the hood of his light wool cloak up. With his long blond hair and gold earring, people had always stared at him. Now, though, they had even more reason. The slingshot had left a deep depression in the left side of his face, which accentuated the scar left by Vahram's knife. Tarquinius did not care. All his emotions were muted by a heavy blanket of grief, his constant companion since that night in the harbor.

Falling back into the cold black water, the haruspex had been sure that his life was over. Yet again, he'd been wrong. A good part of him still wished that he had not been. Killing Caelius outside the brothel had been sweet revenge for the death of Olenus, his mentor, but the repercussions of his act had been profound. At the time, it had seemed the right thing to do. Now, he was not so sure. Time could not be turned back, though, and Romulus was gone with Caesar's legions, to whatever fate the gods laid out for him. With luck, that would include a return to Rome. Tarquinius scowled. If that vision wasn't wrong too.

Coming to a short time after Romulus and Petronius had carried him onto the sand, Tarquinius had been overwhelmed with shame. All he'd wanted to do was vanish. Somehow he had crawled up the rocky slope off the beach, finally falling into a shallow gully. Lapsing in and out of consciousness, he remained there until dawn the next day, waiting for the demon Charon. Death seemed the only apt punishment for the content and timing of his confession. Romulus had been rightfully incandescent, and Tarquinius doubted if the young soldier would ever forgive him. The pain he'd seen in the other's eyes hurt more than the crushing injury to his face and left the haruspex with little reason to live. Yet, injured and alone, he had not died. After many days of agony, existing on brackish rainwater from rock pools, and shellfish, he had recovered—physically. In turn that meant that the gods still had plans for him. Whether it was Tinia, the greatest Etruscan deity, or Mithras, his guide since Margiana, who was behind it all, Tarquinius had no idea. Nor did he have a clue to his purpose, but he knew better than to fight against a will greater than his.

By the time the haruspex had ventured back into the city, the fighting was long over. Caesar's legions had sailed east, joining with their allies from Pergamum and taking the fight to the Egyptians. At Pelusium, the boy king Ptolemy and thousands of his troops were killed. Caesar had returned to Alexandria in triumph. Cleopatra was installed as queen, and the legionaries who had been reviled by the population swaggered about the streets like conquering heroes. Tarquinius was forced to go to ground. Although he had been press-ganged into the Roman army against his will, he was technically a deserter. It was also possible that he might meet Romulus, and that prospect was too painful. With nowhere else to go, he had fled to the vast necropolis that lay southwest of the city walls. There, among the gardens, groves and myriad tombs, Tarquinius' companions were the criminal poor, lepers and the embalmers of the dead. In the shelter of a crumbling mausoleum to some long-dead merchant, he was content to live a solitary existence. Days blurred into weeks, and then months. Most of the graveyard's residents gave him a wide berth; those who did not received short shrift. Age and injury might have been starting to take their toll on the haruspex, but he was still lethal with a sword or his double-headed axe.

Caesar had finally departed Alexandria a week previously. Feeling relieved that he was free to move about and guilty that he had not encountered Romulus, Tarquinius began venturing into the city on a daily basis. Haruspicy, his favored method of discovering what the future might hold, had proved characteristically unhelpful. The winds off the sea, which lay to the north, and from Lake Mareotis, which was to the south, were a daily feature in the city. To Tarquinius, expert at reading air currents, they were refreshing but little else; the clouds he saw merely offered shade from the sun, and the birdlife, more varied and colorful than in Italy, was nothing other than that. After nearly twenty-five years of soothsaying, the haruspex was used to this episodic dearth of information. When his need was greatest, the world around him often revealed nothing, and when he did not care one way or another, it deluged him in detail. Although it was difficult to find enough privacy to sacrifice an animal, Tarquinius had managed it twice. Neither occasion had been fruitful, but he had not completely lost faith in his abilities—as had happened in Margiana. His gut feeling was that he would find out by another method, and it was time to locate that source.

To this end, Tarquinius had been visiting the great library daily. Thankfully, the warehouses that had burned down on the night of the pitched battle between the Roman legionaries and the Egyptians had not meant its total destruction. That was no thanks to Caesar, he thought darkly. All the general had been concerned with was a diversion to panic the enemy troops, who considerably outnumbered his men. No, the library's survival was due to the fact that it had two locations. The one on the dockside—which had been entirely consumed by the flames—was only a small part of the whole, with the majority of the documents being stored in a complex of spacious buildings near the Gymnasium.

It was here, therefore, that Tarquinius came to study each day. It was the fulfillment of a lifelong dream to do so, and his grief lifted a fraction each time he crossed the threshold. Inside were many tens of thousands of papyrus rolls on poetry, history, philosophy, medicine, rhetoric and every other subject one could think of. Collected for more than two hundred years, the library of Alexandria comprised the single greatest collection of information in the world. As well as his future path, Tarquinius also hoped to find a clue to the mysterious origins of his people. Despite decades of searching, the haruspex was no wiser about where the Etruscans had come from.

The complex was far more than a library or a storage place for scrolls. It was a combination of school, shrine and museum, also containing immaculate gardens, a richly stocked zoo and an observatory. Naturally, the temple was dedicated to the Muses, and was overseen by a priest of high rank. For generations, Greek scholars from all over the Mediterranean had come to the library as paid tutors, working together and sharing their knowledge with those who came to learn. Men who knew far more than Tarquinius did had spent years here: Archimedes, studying the rise and fall of the River Nile and inventing the screw that could lift water up great heights; Eratosthenes of Cyrene, who lectured on the route to India by sailing west from Hispania, who posited that the world was round and had calculated its circumference and diameter. Others had propounded theories about the sun's effect on the planets and stars, or had advanced medical science by their study of human anatomy.

Humility became a new emotion for Tarquinius as he paced the covered walkways of the library's various wings, discovering the existence of more information than he could absorb in a lifetime of study. To him, the shelves filled with linen- and leather-covered scrolls and parchments were like all the gold and jewels in the world. Even though the majority of the information had been catalogued, he found scant word of the Etruscans. A few fragments of crumbling papyrus referred to a people who had journeyed from the lands beyond Asia Minor. There was mention of a city called Resen on the River Tigris, and little else. Nothing to fill in around these skeletal details, which Tarquinius already knew from Olenus. In turn this made him wish that he'd had an opportunity to do some investigation after Carrhae. It was a futile thought, for he, like all the other Roman captives, had been kept under lock and key day and night when in Seleucia. Soon Tarquinius began dreaming about a return trip to Parthia.

Perhaps that was where his future lay? While part of Tarquinius' heart rejoiced at this thought, much of it ached at its utter finality. Would he ever see Romulus again? Although there was no guarantee of a reunion by remaining in Alexandria, the haruspex was reluctant to leave until he unearthed, or was given, some kind of meaningful sign of his purpose.

For weeks, Tarquinius concentrated his search in the library section that contained material on astronomy and history. It was no good. He found nothing. Keen to keep a low profile, he did not ask too much of the librarians, translators and scribes, who tolerated his presence with reluctance. It was Tarquinius' fluent Greek and medical knowledge that had allowed him entry in the first place, but that did not mean that they liked the silent, scarred stranger wandering up and down the covered walkways, or sitting alone, watching the debates between the resident scholars. He did not fit in.

There was, however, one scribbler, as the translators were known, who enjoyed Tarquinius' company. Aristophanes was a stout, balding Greek in late middle age, whose main interest was in astronomy. Like his colleagues, he wore a nondescript off-white short-sleeved tunic. His shoulders were stooped from a lifetime of leaning over documents; his fingers stained black from the ink in his reed stylus. Aristophanes' work area was one of the small courtyards which bordered the book-lined corridors. Perched on a mat surrounded by scrolls and parchments, he deftly copied ancient tracts onto clean pieces of papyrus each day. This part of the library was also where the haruspex spent a lot of time. Inevitably they had spoken; Tarquinius wanted to read a particular text about Nineveh, but could not locate it and had asked the Greek for help. As they searched, a prolonged debate about the merits of papyrus versus those of calf-skin parchment developed. Although they never found the relevant scroll, a friendship developed, one based on scholarly topics, and which avoided personal matters. Other than the fact that he was Etruscan, Tarquinius mentioned little about his past, and Aristophanes was content not to ask.

That morning was no different, and the two men resumed their discussion of the previous day, about whether it was possible to accurately measure the movement of the stars.

"They say that there's a boxlike device on Rhodes that shows how the sun, moon and planets travel through the sky," the scribbler confided. "Made of metal, with dozens of little hidden wheels and cogs that move in unison. Apparently it can even predict lunar and solar eclipses. Not sure I believe it myself."

Tarquinius laughed. He'd heard rumors of such a thing when visiting Rhodes himself.

Aristophanes frowned. "What?"

"Look around you. Think of the wealth of knowledge that has been gathered here," he replied. "Why wouldn't that appliance exist?"

"Of course, you're right." Aristophanes smiled ruefully. "I've spent too long here. Can't see what's in front of me anymore."

Tarquinius thought for a moment. While the data he studied in the library was fascinating, all too often it felt sterile, even dead. "Rhodes, you say?" he asked.

Aristophanes nodded. "In the Greek school there. One day I'll visit it," he said wistfully.

Perhaps I should also go, reflected Tarquinius. He'd stolen enough for the passage. Suddenly, the library's tranquility was broken from outside by the distinctive tramp of men marching in unison. The noise came to a halt by the main gate, and was followed by the hammering of a weapon butt on the timbers. Shouted commands rang out, demanding entry.

Aristophanes looked perturbed. Even the recent fighting had not affected the library's status as an island of calm in the city. "What in the name of Zeus do they want?"

Tarquinius was on his feet before he knew it, clutching for a sword that wasn't there. The orders had been given in Latin, not Greek or Egyptian. That indicated Roman soldiers were present, which meant trouble. Legionaries might ask awkward questions. He felt the air about him move. *Danger*, the haruspex thought. Was it to him, though, or to someone else?

"What's wrong?" Aristophanes had seen his response. "Are they after you?"

Calm down, thought Tarquinius. *Few, if any, Romans in the city would recognize me.* He took a deep breath. "Not exactly," he said slowly, knowing that the only exits apart from the main entrance were locked. He'd tried them already, seeking an escape route in advance in case it should ever be needed. "I don't like them, that's all."

The Greek gave him a skeptical look. He knew that Tarquinius was from Italy, and had gleaned that he'd served in the army. There was more occurring here than his friend was letting on. Yet, like most residents of the city, whether Egyptian or Greek, Aristophanes had little love for the new effective rulers with their arrogance, crude manners and martial tendencies. "Go back under the portico," he advised quietly. "Even if they come in here, the sunlight is so bright that they'll only see a shadow. Just another scholar studying some old tome."

Grateful, Tarquinius rolled up the tract on Assyria that he'd been perusing and did as Aristophanes said. Facing the rows of shelves, he could peer over his shoulder at anyone who came into this wing. What then, though? There was still no way out. With his heart thudding in his chest, he looked up at the patch of sky that was visible overhead. The air was calm, and the clouds made no sense. Tarquinius cursed under his breath.

To his surprise, the soldiers who clattered into the courtyard a few moments later were a mixture of Romans and Egyptians. First came two squads of ten well-presented legionaries, then the same number of royal guards, resplendent in green tunics, Greek helmets and bronze breastplates. Taking half of the area each, the two groups spread out in a protective screen, their spears and swords ready. Aristophanes and his accoutrements were simply stepped over and ignored. An officer whistled the all-clear and in walked a striking young woman; she was accompanied by several fawning courtiers and senior librarians. Tarquinius' mouth opened. Knocking his pots of ink flying, Aristophanes jerked up and prostrated himself face first upon his reed mat. He had no time to warn Tarquinius, but there was no need.

Here was Cleopatra, sister to the dead king Ptolemy. Lover to Caesar, she was now the sole ruler of Egypt. A goddess to her people. What was she doing here? the haruspex wondered.

"Abase yourselves," cried one of the officials.

Hastily Tarquinius went down on his knees, and then, responding to a sidelong glare from the prone Aristophanes, he leaned forward and placed his forehead on the tiled floor. He had only had a few heartbeats to study Cleopatra, but that was enough to take in her assured manner. The queen was clad in a flowing cream linen gown hemmed with silver thread, her hair was tied up in braids. Long ringlets fell on either side of her pale-skinned face, and ringing her head was a uraeus crown, symbol of the Egyptian pharaohs. Made of solid gold, it was encrusted with jewels and featured a rearing cobra at the front. A string of massive pearls hung around Cleopatra's neck; gold and silver jewelry winked from her wrists and fingers. Her big mouth and hooked nose were easily compensated for by a curvaceous and attractive figure. Full breasts moved enticingly under the see-through fabric of her dress, the well-cut folds of which clung to her belly and thighs. She was a riveting sight.

The official spoke again. "You may rise."

Carefully averting his gaze from the nearby soldiers, Tarquinius got to his feet. He recognized no one, but there was no point tempting fate. It would only take a single challenge for him to be skewered by a *pilum*, or tied up like a hen for the pot and tortured. Aristophanes was now just a few steps from Cleopatra, and dared only to rise to his knees. "Your Majesty," he said, his voice trembling. "You honor us with your presence."

Cleopatra inclined her head. "I come seeking knowledge. It is important that I find what I am looking for. Apparently this is where the relevant scrolls are to be found." Her voice was deep and attractive, but there was no mistaking the threat within her words.

A cold sweat broke out on Aristophanes' brow. "What type of information does Your Majesty require, exactly?" he asked.

There was a long pause, which Tarquinius used to study Cleopatra sidelong. A jolt of energy shot through him as his eyes passed across her flat belly. *She is pregnant,* he thought, shocked as much by this as by the sudden return of his divinatory skills. *Cleopatra is going to bear Caesar a child.* He glanced again. *A son. The man who is set on being the sole ruler of Rome is to have an heir. Cleopatra is here to find out what the future holds for her and her offspring.* Immediately he thought of Romulus. Was this the threat he'd sensed?

Cleopatra turned coy. "Not much," she purred. "Just the pattern of the stars over the next year or so. The outlook for each sign of the Zodiac as well."

Aristophanes looked aghast. "Your Majesty, I am no expert in these matters," he stuttered.

Cleopatra smiled. "You only have to find the correct scrolls.

These men will interpret the meanings for me." She indicated the robed figures behind her, every one of whom now looked terrified.

Aristophanes' swallow of relief was very loud. "Of course, Your Majesty. If you would follow me?" With a quavering arm, he pointed at the corridor behind Tarquinius.

The haruspex froze. He had anticipated none of this. All he could do was try to remain calm. Any sudden move would bring down the most unwelcome attention.

"Lead on," Cleopatra ordered Aristophanes.

The Egyptian guards parted at once, allowing the scribbler to scuttle away. Forming up in four files of five, with Cleopatra in the middle, they held their spears upright now. Half followed Aristophanes, then came the queen and the sweating scholars, followed by the remaining ten. The little column moved off the courtyard and onto the covered walkway where Tarquinius stood, rigid as a statue. The smell of sweat and oiled leather filled the air as they passed. Most barely gave him a second glance, just another badly dressed scholar.

Tarquinius bowed his head as Cleopatra went by, but his senses were on high alert. He felt a joyous air about her—a pride in her pregnancy. *What a catch she has made for herself,* he thought. No less a man than Julius Caesar. Of course her play was not that surprising. A shadow of their former selves, the Egyptian royal family had been reliant on Roman military power for some years. To first gain Caesar's affections and then become pregnant by him, Cleopatra had shown her desire to remain ruler of her country, and more. The recent battles had left her teenage brother Ptolemy dead; with her sister Arsinoe a prisoner, she now had no real rivals.

There was something else in the energy surrounding her. Tarquinius closed his eyes, using all his ability to discern what it was. The shock of it rocked him back on his heels. While Cleopatra would move to Rome for a number of years, she would not rule by Caesar's side. Their son would die young. Violently, too. Murdered by the order of . . . a thin young noble Tarquinius did not recognize. Why? The haruspex could see that this man loved Caesar, yet he was responsible for the killing of his son. Which meant that he would hold no love for Romulus either. *Rome is at the center of all this*, the haruspex thought. *Should I go back there?*

"You!" demanded one of the legionaries. A dark-skinned veteran with heavy stubble covering his jaw, he glowered at Tarquinius' ragged appearance. "What's your business here?"

Too late, the haruspex realized he'd been muttering to himself. "I'm studying the ancient Assyrian civilization, sir," he answered obsequiously, proffering his scroll in evidence.

The soldier's eyes narrowed.

Tarquinius' heart stopped. Worried about Romulus and startled by the command, he had answered in fluent Latin rather than the more common Greek. Which was not a crime, but with most scholars in the library being Greek, it was a trifle unusual.

The legionary thought so too. "Are you Italian?" he demanded, moving a few steps closer. He lowered his *pilum* until the pyramidal iron head pointed straight at Tarquinius' breastbone. "Answer me!"

The haruspex had no wish to start justifying who he was and why he wasn't in the army. "I'm from Greece," he lied. "But I spent some years in Italy as a tutor. Sometimes Latin seems like my native tongue."

"A tutor?" The other's expression turned sly, and he poked his *pilum* tip at Tarquinius' scarred, caved-in left cheek. "Explain those injuries then."

"The Cilician pirates raided the town where I lived," he replied, his mind racing. "They tortured me before selling me as a slave on Rhodes. Eventually I escaped and made my way here, where I've made a living as a scribe since."

The veteran considered his words for a moment. Until Pompey

had crushed them twenty years before, the bloodthirsty Cilicians had been the scourge of the entire Mediterranean. Once, they had even had the gall to sack Ostia, Rome's port, thereby threatening grain supplies to the capital. The legionary had heard the tale from his father and plainly this pathetic figure was old enough to have been around then.

They heard Cleopatra's raised voice coming back down the corridor. Aristophanes had found the texts she required. The soldier's attention turned away, and Tarquinius breathed a long sigh of relief.

Surrounded by her guards, the queen emerged, her cheeks aglow with excitement. Hurrying behind came Aristophanes, his arms full of tightly rolled scrolls, which were giving off a fine cloud of dust. Last came the learned men, now looking frankly petrified. With the correct texts found, the full weight of Cleopatra's expectation would soon be on them.

On the other hand, Aristophanes was jubilant. Catching sight of Tarquinius, his face lit up. "Guess what I also found, my Etruscan friend?" he called out in Latin. "That text from Nineveh which you gave up looking for weeks ago."

In slow motion, Tarquinius' gaze moved to the swarthy legionary. It only took a moment for the scribbler's words to sink in.

"Etruscan?" snarled the soldier, wheeling toward the haruspex. "You lying bastard. Probably a Republican agent then, aren't you?"

Too late, Aristophanes realized what he'd done. His mouth opened in an O of shock as Tarquinius dropped the scroll he was holding and ran for his life.

"Spy!" screamed the legionary at his comrades. "Spy!"

Tarquinius ran as if Cerberus and all the demons in Hades were after him, but the heavily armed men in pursuit were younger and fitter than he was. Despite his small head start, he had little chance of reaching the main entrance, let alone the streets outside. He cursed the lapse of concentration that had made him speak in Latin. Dread filled him as he pounded through the gardens, drawing startled looks from the slaves tending the plants. His claim of being a scribe would not bear up to any scrutiny, so the legionaries really would take him for a spy.

His real story was too fantastical; he also had to keep his divining abilities secret. Which meant there would be only one outcome. Death, by torture. The haruspex' lips twisted with bitterness. So the return of his abilities had been a cruel joke by the gods, devised to let him know that he could do nothing further to help Romulus, whose life he had ruined.

Then, perhaps fifteen paces away, Tarquinius saw the open door in the wall. Beside it stood a terrified-looking scribe, who was beckoning frantically. If he got through it, there was the smallest chance that the portal could be closed before the legionaries saw where he'd gone.

Pumping his arms and legs until he thought his heart would burst, Tarquinius sprinted toward it.

VI

"VENI, VIDI, VICI"

PONTUS, NORTHERN ASIA MINOR

I t was a severe offense for an ordinary soldier to shout orders, but Romulus knew that if someone didn't, he and the men all around him would die. The trio of chariots was going to smash their part of the line apart. Throwing back his head, he roared, "Aim short! Loose *pila!*"

The surrounding legionaries responded to the order instantly. Doing this was better than just staring death in the eyes. Lunging over their *scuta*, they hurled their javelins in unison. Dozens of the wooden shafts shot forward at the enemy chariots. At almost point-blank range, it was hard to miss. Barbed metal points punched through the horses' armor, running deep into their chests, necks and backs, while others transfixed two of the drivers, throwing them backward onto the hard ground. Staggering and bucking with pain, their injured steeds were now out of control. They had reached such a momentum, though, that they continued moving forward. Running slightly to the rear of the others, one charioteer and his team remained unhurt. Screaming at the top of his voice, he shook his traces to encourage his horses onward.

The first two chariots collided with the closely packed Roman lines. Romulus watched in horror as the wounded steeds smashed into the shield wall nearby, still pulling their chariots with their deadly spinning blades. Some of the men directly in their path were crushed against the soldiers behind, while others were knocked down and trampled. It was the legionaries a few steps farther out who suffered the worst fate, though. This was the moment when the scythed weapons played their part. Screams of terror rose as they struck, and blood sprayed everywhere as limbs were chopped off indiscriminately.

Romulus managed to drag his attention back to the last chariot. His eyes widened. It was no more than ten steps away. The horses were going to hit the soldiers two or three over from Petronius, who was on his right. Army steeds, they were trained to ride men down. Romulus' knuckles whitened on the shaft of his remaining *pilum*, which felt utterly useless. The scythes on this side were going to strike Petronius, and him.

Cries of terror rose from the legionaries. A few threw *pila*, but their shots were poorly aimed, and flew over the chariot bearing down on them. Complete panic threatened to paralyze Romulus, and he felt his gorge rise. His muscles were locked rigid. *This is what it feels like to see death approaching*, he thought.

"Lie down," shouted Petronius. "Now!"

Romulus obeyed. It was no time to worry about the men behind. Throwing his *scutum* forward, he flattened himself on the stone-covered ground. Alongside, he heard Petronius doing the same. Some men copied them, while others, panicking, turned to flee. It was too late for that. Romulus cringed; the cheek piece of his helmet bit into the side of his face. The pain helped him focus. *Mithras*, he prayed frantically. *Don't let me end my life like this: cut in two by a fucking scythed chariot.* Beneath his ear, the earth was reverberating with the thunder of pounding hooves. It scared him even more.

With a terrible whirring noise, Romulus heard one and then the other set of blades go over his body. Screams of agony rang out as the legionaries to their rear took the brunt of the chariot's impact. Beside him, Petronius lay motionless, and Romulus' mouth went dry. *He must be dead,* he thought, sorrow filling him. *Petronius has saved my life, like Brennus did—by giving his own in return.* An instant later, the chariot had gone. Incredulous, Romulus twitched his fingers and toes. They were all still there and his heart leaped first with joy, and then with guilt that he was alive while Petronius was not.

Someone gave him an almighty shove. "That should pay you back for saving my skin in Alexandria!" The horsehair crest on Petronius' helmet had been neatly cut off, but beneath it the veteran's face was grinning and unhurt.

Romulus shouted with joy. "I was sure you were dead."

"Fortuna might be a capricious old whore," laughed Petronius, "but she's in a good mood with me today."

They looked behind them. The chariot that had just cut men apart had come to a complete halt, the depth of the Roman formation finally using up its momentum. Like starving wolves, the nearest soldiers swarmed forward, desperate to kill man and beast. The horses were cut down, stabbed in their bellies or their hamstrings cut. Their unfortunate charioteer was no coward. Instead of trying to surrender, he reached for his sword. He didn't even get to pull it out of the scabbard. Instead, four or five screaming legionaries buried their *gladii* in his neck and arms. As the blades were withdrawn, the charioteer's body toppled to one side. They were not finished with him yet, though. Still filled with the terror of what the scythes might have done, one of the soldiers swept his sword down, decapitating his enemy. Blood sprayed all over his legs as he stooped over the head. Ripping off the helmet, he held aloft the dripping trophy and bellowed a primeval cry of rage, which was echoed by all those who saw.

The charioteer's face still bore a grimace of surprise.

Despite causing heavy casualties, the chariots had not broken apart the Roman formation. Large holes gaped where men had fallen: serious damage to the shield wall when the battle had only just commenced. Although the gaps could quickly be filled, the legionaries' relief did not last. A new sound filled their ears. It was more horses. Bitter curses rang out.

Through the back ranks, which were facing the opposite direction, Romulus and his comrades saw the Pontic cavalry. It had ridden around the Twenty-Eighth's flanks and was now about to fall on its ill-prepared rear. Even in the best of circumstances, it was almost unheard of for infantry to stop a charge by horses. At Pharsalus, specially trained legionaries had managed it, stabbing at the enemy riders' faces with their *pila* and panicking them into flight. The Forgotten Legion had also done it with specially forged long spears, which horses would not ride onto. Neither option was available here today, and, fully aware that they had only their javelins to throw before they were ground into the dust, the soldiers at the rear cried out in fear.

They were not the only men with death staring them in the face, thought Romulus, remembering the infantry running behind the chariots. The surviving centurions were of similar mind. "About turn. Re-form your ranks," the nearest one cried. "Quickly, you useless bastards!"

Romulus spun around at once. He wished he hadn't.

Waving their swords and spears, the peltasts and *thureophoroi* were closing in fast. Battle cries and screams rose as they came. The Roman shield wall was still in disarray and many legionaries flinched. Memories of these men's ferocious kinsmen in Alexandria were still strong. With the cavalry closing in from behind, and a horde of fierce infantry about to attack the gaps in their line, their doom seemed certain.

Romulus felt like a piece of metal lying on an anvil with the smith's hammer raised high above him. When it came down, he would be smashed into smithereens. Despairing, he raised his eyes to the clear blue sky. As usual, he saw nothing. Since having a terrible vision of Rome when in Margiana, Romulus rarely tried to use the soothsaying skills that Tarquinius had taught him. On the rare occasions that he had, the gods seemed to mock him by revealing nothing. *Damn them all,* Romulus thought. *Who needs to divine now anyhow? A fool can see that we're going to die.*

Whether they thought the same or not, the centurions did not panic. Veterans of numerous campaigns, they were the epitome of discipline, and the backbone of the legions at perilous times like this. Chivvying the men together, they closed the gaps left by the chariots. Romulus swore aloud with relief as he understood their purpose. The centurions had realized that one tiny crumb of advantage remained to the Twenty-Eighth: that of height. It gave them a little time. Because the enemy foot soldiers had to run uphill, their charge was a lot slower than the chariots had been.

Romulus' resolve stiffened, and he glanced at Petronius.

The veteran gave him a clout on the shoulder. "This is what it's about, lad," he growled. "Backs to the wall. About to die, but with our comrades around us. Can't ask for more than that, can we?"

There were fierce nods from the men who heard his comment.

Their acceptance brought tears of pride to Romulus' eyes. None knew his history as a slave, but they had seen his courage at first hand and now he was one of them. The rejection that he and Brennus had suffered at the hands of other legionaries in Margiana had left a deep scar on his soul. Here on a barren Pontic mountainside under the hot sun, the soldiers' recognition was a powerful and welcome balm. Romulus' chin rose with new determination. If he had to die, then he would do so among men who took him for one of their own.

"Elysium awaits us," shouted Petronius, lifting his *pilum* high. "And we die for Caesar!"

A loud, defiant cheer followed his cry. The word "Caesar" was repeated along the line like a mantra. It visibly strengthened the shield wall, which had been wavering before the crushing numbers of enemy troops rushing up the slope. Even the legionaries who were about to be struck by the Pontic cavalry joined in.

Romulus' spirits were deeply stirred. Since being press-ganged into the Twenty-Eighth, there had been no real chance for him to gain an understanding of the soldiers' unswerving devotion to their general. He knew that Caesar had earned his troops' loyalty the hard way—by leading from the front, by sharing their hardships and rewarding their fealty well, but he had not really seen it for himself. The night battle in Alexandria had been a shambles, and the decisive victory over Ptolemy's forces soon after had not been a hard-fought struggle. Romulus had heard over and over how amazing a leader Caesar was, but neither of these clashes had provided him with the evidence that he desired. If he was to serve in one of the general's legions for the next six years or more, then he wanted to believe in him. Now, that conviction was taking seed in his heart. To see that men retained faith in Caesar as their death approached was truly remarkable.

All chance of thinking disappeared as the peltasts and *thureophoroi* rushed in. Romulus had not really appreciated the variety of nationalities that made up Pharnaces' army until that point. Unlike the Roman legionaries and Deiotarus' men, who armed and dressed in much the same manner, no two of the warriors charging uphill looked alike. Attracted by mercenaries' high wages and the chance of plunder, they had come to Pontus from far and wide. There were Thracian peltasts like those Romulus had seen in Alexandria: unarmored and carrying long-bladed *rhomphaiai* and oval shields with spines. There were different varieties of peltast too—men armed with javelins and curved knives. Some individuals wore padded linen armor, while others carried round or crescent shields made of wicker and covered in sheepskin. A few, no doubt the wealthier men, had shields with polished bronze faces.

Plenty of the approaching infantry were *thureophoroi* from Asia Minor and farther west. Bearing heavy oval or rectangular shields faced with leather, they had Macedonian crested helmets with large cheek pieces and rounded peaks over the eyes. Like the peltasts, few wore any armor, just simple belted tunics in an array of colors—red-brown like the legionaries, but also white, blue or ocher. Most carried javelins and a sword, but some were armed with long thrusting spears.

The enemy's left flank was made up of thousands of Cappadocians, fierce bearded tribesmen in pointed fabric hats, long-sleeved tunics and trousers, and carrying hexagonal shields. They bore longswords similar to that which Brennus had owned, as well as javelins or spears.

On their own, none of this variety of troops would have caused a Roman legion much difficulty. The trouble was, thought Romulus, there were just too many of the whoresons. Even with the rest of the army, any victory would be hard won. The fate of the Twenty-Eighth was sealed, but afterward how could even Caesar prevail?

Petronius laughed, startling him. "We've got two things to be grateful for," he said.

Romulus strained to read his mind. "They're sweating their guts out to reach us, while we just stand here waiting?"

"And our *pila* will be far more effective thrown downhill."

The enemy officers were thinking the same thing. While they had to hit the Twenty-Eighth before the remainder of the legions emerged, there was little point throwing winded soldiers at a rested foe. They halted their men a hundred paces away, well outside *pilum* range. All the legionaries could do was mutter prayers and try to ignore the terrible sounds from the rear as their comrades battled to hold back the Pontic heavy cavalry. The more inventive officers there were ordering their men to stab their *pila* at the enemy riders as had been done at Pharsalus, but the ploy was only partially working. Holes were being punched in the Roman ranks, which threatened to split the Twenty-Eighth apart. If that happened, Romulus thought, they'd all be dead even sooner than he'd imagined.

Acid-tipped claws of tension were now gnawing away at his belly. Thankfully, he would have no time to brood. The approaching peltasts and *thureophoroi* would reach them soon. Despite the agonizing effort of climbing the hill, the enemy infantry regained their wind fast. Perhaps twenty heartbeats went by before they charged forward at the Romans like hunting dogs. There was no tight shield wall like the legions used, just a heaving mass of screaming men and weapons. The eager Cappadocians were a few steps ahead of the rest of the Pontic troops, but it would only be moments until battle was joined all along the front. A few fools threw their spears as they ran; they barely flew more than fifteen paces before skidding onto the rough ground, harming no one. Obviously following orders, most held back until they were much closer.

The centurions had no such compunction. With the steep slope affording their *pila* extra distance, they had to cause the maximum number of casualties before the Pontic infantry hit. "Ready javelins!" came the order when the enemy was about fifty paces away. "Aim long!"

Closing his left eye, Romulus focused on a bearded peltast who was slightly ahead of his companions. Carrying an oval shield that had been painted white, he bore a larger than normal *rhomphaia*, and looked well able to wield it. Remembering the man he had fought in Alexandria, Romulus could imagine the injuries the warrior might cause. Gripping his *pilum* hard, he drew back his right arm and waited for the command.

Every man was doing the same.

"RELEASE!" bellowed the centurions in a loud chorus.

Up went the javelins in a dark shower of metal and wood. With the steep drop of the slope offering only blue sky behind them, they looked quite beautiful flying through the air. The Pontic infantry did not look up, though. Determined to close with the legionaries, they broke into a sprint.

Romulus studied the peltast he had aimed at, wondering if his aim had been true. An instant later, the man went down with a *pilum* through the chest, and he cheered. There was no way of knowing, but Romulus had a strong feeling that it was his hit. Packed as dense as a shoal of fish, the enemy were running without their shields raised, which meant that every javelin struck down or injured a warrior. They were so numerous, though, that a couple of hundred fewer made little difference. Even when a second volley of *pila* had landed, there were few discernible gaps in their lines. This made Romulus feel incredulous, and fearful. Now it was down to the *gladii* that he and his comrades all carried. That, and their Roman courage.

He began to beat his sword on the side of his *scutum*.

Grinning, Petronius did the same. Others emulated them, drumming their iron blades faster and faster to create a terrifying din for the Pontic troops to approach.

"Come on, you bastards!" Romulus screamed, desperate to come to blows with their foes. There had been enough waiting. It was time to fight.

Every centurion who wasn't facing the enemy cavalry was in the front rank. Twenty steps from Romulus and Petronius, so too was the *aquilifer*. Atop the wooden staff he bore was the silver eagle, the legion's most important possession, and a symbol that encapsulated the unit's courage and pride. With both arms holding up his standard, the *aquilifer* could not defend himself, which meant that the legionaries on each side had to fight twice as hard. Yet their positions were highly sought after. To lose the eagle in battle was the greatest disgrace any legion could suffer, and men would perform heroic acts to prevent it. For the legate to place it in such a position showed how desperate the struggle would be. Although Romulus had been forced to join the Twenty-Eighth, he too would shed every last drop of his blood in its defense.

"Close order!" roared the officers. "Front ranks, shields together! Those behind, shields up!"

Shuffling together until their shoulders nearly brushed, the legionaries obeyed. They had done this so many times: on training grounds and in war. It was second nature. Clunk, clunk, clunk went their *scuta*, a metallic, comforting noise. Their bodies were now covered at the front from their heads to their lower calves. All that projected forward from the solid wall were the sharp points of their *gladii*. The soldiers behind were also protected from enemy missiles by the wall of raised shields.

The Pontic infantry were almost upon them. It was time for their javelins. Hurled indiscriminately, the enemy missiles filled the air over the two sides for an instant before landing among the legionaries with a familiar whistling noise. Thanks to the strength of their shields' construction, few men were hurt. Their *scuta* were peppered with spears, though, which rendered them impossible to use. Frantically, they ripped at the wooden shafts in an attempt to dislodge them. It was too late. With an almighty crash, the two sides met.

At once Romulus' vision narrowed to what was directly in front. Everything else was irrelevant. It was just him, Petronius and the legionaries nearby who mattered. A wiry gray-haired peltast carrying a *rhomphaia* with a notched blade aimed himself at Romulus. He was perhaps forty years old, and the muscles on his deeply tanned arms and legs were bunched like cords of wood. Baring his teeth, the veteran drove his oval shield forward at Romulus, trying to knock him over. With his left leg braced behind his *scutum*, Romulus took the impact without difficulty. *Stupid move*, he thought. *I'm heavier than the fool by half his weight at least.*

That wasn't the peltast's plan.

Even as they grappled, pushing their shields against one another, his *rhomphaia* came hooking overhead. Meeting the top of Romulus' bronze-bowl helmet, it easily split the metal in two, cutting a deep wound in his scalp. The force of the blow made Romulus see stars. He staggered, his legs buckling beneath him. With a snarl of fury, the peltast tugged on the handle of his *rhomphaia* to free it from the helmet. Fortunately, the blade stuck for a moment. Half-dazed and in absolute agony, Romulus knew that he had to act at once, or the peltast's next blow would spread his brains all over the hard ground. Instinct made him drop to his knees, pulling the *rhomphaia* over the edge of his *scutum* and away from his opponent, making it more difficult to retain a good grip. A loud curse told him that his tactic had been successful.

More importantly, though, he could see around the edges of their two shields to the peltast's unprotected calves. Reaching forward with his *gladius*, Romulus severed the large tendon on the outside of his enemy's left knee. It wasn't a mortal blow, but it didn't have to be. No man could receive an injury like that and stay standing. With a loud scream, the peltast let go of his *rhomphaia*, which had just come free of Romulus' helmet. He fell awkwardly, landing on his side, but managed to keep his shield in front of him. Pulling a dagger, he lunged at Romulus' sword arm.

In slow motion, Romulus leaned out of the way. This was no rookie, he thought dazedly. Blood was now running down his forehead and into his eyes, making it difficult to see. The crippled peltast swept his knife forward again, but did not have the reach to harm Romulus. That was no relief to him. It would only be a heartbeat before another Pontic warrior jumped over to fill the gap. He had to stand up. Dragging in a breath, Romulus got to his feet, lifting his sword and *scutum*. Desperate now, his enemy made a final attempt to stab him in the leg.

Summoning all his strength, Romulus stamped down on the peltast's outstretched arm with his hobnailed sandal. He crushed it to the ground, and there was a dull crack as the bones broke against a protruding rock. With a keening cry of pain, the man released his dagger and his shield, leaving himself defenseless. Romulus took a step forward and stabbed him through the neck, feeling the blade grate off the cartilage of his windpipe as it slid home. The peltast's screams stopped abruptly, and his body went into a spasm of twitching as he died. Blood sprayed all over the front of Romulus' *scutum* as he pulled out his sword.

He had enough sense remaining to look up at once. Romulus knew that his chances of staying alive in the next few moments were down to pure luck, and the gods' goodwill. Concussed, he was in no state to fight any skilled opponent. Luckily, the burly peltast who came leaping over his comrade's corpse was so eager that he tripped, sprawling in a tangle of limbs at Romulus' feet. It was a simple case of shoving his blade in on the right side of the man's back, between the lowest ribs. "It's a good way of killing," Brennus had told him once. "Puts the man out of action at once. It's a mortal blow too. Cuts the liver, you see. The blood loss from that will kill very fast." Romulus had never used the ruse until now. Gratitude filled him yet again for the skills he'd learned from the huge Gaul. Without them, he would never have survived his first months as a gladiator—and Brennus' advice was still useful.

Petronius' voice came through a thick fog. "Daydreaming will get you killed, lad."

Romulus looked around. "Huh?"

Suddenly seeing the split helmet and the blood covering Romulus' face, Petronius blanched. "Are you all right?" he demanded.

"Not sure," Romulus mumbled. "My head hurts like a bastard."

Petronius glanced at the enemy. As it sometimes did, the tide of battle had ripped apart the two sides in their part of the line. It was a heaven-sent moment. Both sets of combatants would use the brief opportunity to rest before throwing themselves at each other once more. "Quick," he muttered. "Let's get that helmet off. It's no fucking use to you in two pieces."

Gritting his teeth, Romulus let his friend undo the chinstrap and ease the battered metal off his head. He waited nervously as the other probed the gash with none-too-gentle fingers. It was hard not to scream with the pain, but somehow he managed.

"Just a flesh wound," Petronius pronounced. Untying a sweat-soaked strip of cloth on his right wrist, he bound it around Romulus' head twice, tying it in place. "That'll have to do until the surgeon can see to it."

Wiping the blood from his eyes, Romulus laughed at the absurdity of it. There were so many *thureophoroi* and peltasts charging toward them now that the idea of having his injury treated was ridiculous. They were outnumbered by more than ten to one, never mind what was going on behind them. The thunder of horses' hooves was so loud that the Pontic cavalry must be making another charge into their rear. The Cappadocians were making short shrift of the unfortunate legionaries on the right flank. It would not be long before that section of the line gave way entirely. The end was in sight.

Petronius caught the meaning of his grim humor. He grinned. "We're screwed."

"I'd say so," Romulus answered. "Look, though." He pointed.

Petronius didn't take it in for a moment. Then he saw. "The *aquila* is still in our hands," he roared proudly.

Men's heads turned, eager to take in any crumb of hope. Not far to their right, the symbol of the Twenty-Eighth was being jabbed aloft. Grabbing the standard from the dying *aquilifer*, an ordinary legionary was shouting encouragement to everyone not to give in. Waves of Pontic warriors were trying to reach him, keen to snatch the glory of winning a Roman eagle from their enemies. None succeeded. The soldier's comrades had sword arms bloody to the elbow from their stout defense of the standard. Thrusting and stabbing like men possessed, they cut down all who came near.

"Can't give up yet," Romulus enjoined. "Can we, lads?"

"Mars would never forgive us," announced a short legionary with a nasty gash to his right arm. "Elysium's gates only open for those who deserve it."

"He's right," shouted Petronius. "What would any comrades who've gone before us say? That we gave up while the *aquila* was still ours?"

Romulus watched the sunlight glinting off the eagle's outstretched wings and the golden thunderbolt gripped in its talons. Memories of Brennus dying on the banks of the River Hydaspes ripped at his heart. He and Tarquinius had fled the field once before when an eagle yet flew. Never again. "Charge!" Romulus bellowed, his skull pulsing with sharp needles of pain. "For Rome and for victory!" Raising his *scutum*, he ran madly at the enemy, who were advancing once more.

Petronius was one step behind. "*Roma Victrix!*" he screamed.

Their courage fanned white-hot by the pair's words, the nearby soldiers followed.

The Pontic warriors were not put off by a few crazy Romans committing suicide when defeat was imminent. As anxious to close as the legionaries, they roared hoarse battle cries and increased their own speed.

Romulus focused on the only man he could make out distinctly with his blurred vision: a giant peltast carrying a bronze-fronted shield with a demon's face painted on it. The creature's slanted eyes and grinning mouth seemed to beckon him, promising a swift path to Elysium. Certainly the man bearing it looked unassailable, a monster whom he was in no state to fight. *So be it*, Romulus thought defiantly. *There'll be no shame when I meet Brennus again. I'm going to die facing the enemy, and defending the eagle with all of my strength.*

Ten steps separated him from death. Then five.

The huge peltast raised his *rhomphaia* in expectation.

Romulus heard a sound that had never been more welcome. It was *bucinae*, sounding the charge. Over and over they played the notes that all legionaries recognized.

Caesar had arrived.

The noise provided enough distraction for the enemy warriors to hesitate, wondering what the Roman reinforcements would do. The giant facing Romulus stared over at their right flank, which had been crumbling before the ferocious Cappadocian assault. His face took on a surprised look, and Romulus risked a glance himself. To his amazement, he saw the Sixth Legion leading the charge to support the collapsing section. Depleted from years of war in Gaul, and most recently the campaign in Egypt, it mustered no more than nine hundred men. Yet here they were, running at the Pontic infantry as if they were ten times that number.

They were doing it because they believed in Caesar.

Steely determination filled Romulus once more. He stared at the big peltast, trying to gauge his best option. Injured, lacking a helmet and only two-thirds the size of the other, he needed some weakness to exploit. He could see none. Bile rose in Romulus' throat as he took the last few steps, *scutum* raised high and *gladius* ready. Despite the rest of the army's arrival, death was going to take him anyway.

To Romulus' utter amazement, a fist-sized stone whistled past his ear and struck the peltast between the eyes. Splitting his skull like a ripe piece of fruit, it punched him into the ranks behind as if he were a child's doll. Gray brain matter splattered out as he went down, covering the men on either side. Their faces registered shock and horror. The rock had struck so fast that it appeared that Romulus had miraculously slain their huge comrade.

Then the rest of the volley landed. While the Twenty-Eighth had been fighting for its life, the *ballistae* had been readied outside the camp ramparts. Taking a great risk that some of his own men would be slain, Caesar had ordered the artillerymen to aim at the front of the enemy's densely packed lines. It was a risky tactic—which paid off in the richest style. Firing from less than two hundred paces away, the twenty-four catapults' efforts were lethal. Every stone killed or maimed a man, and many had enough velocity to spin off or ricochet onward, wounding plenty more. Wails of dismay rose from the stunned Pontic troops.

Romulus could scarcely believe his luck. He had been convinced that his last moment was upon him, but Caesar's shock approach had swept that concern away. His energy renewed, Romulus leaped over the body of the peltast, smashing his shield boss into the face of a warrior with a hooked nose. Beneath his fingers there was an audible crunch as the cartilage broke, and the man went down, bawling. Romulus stamped on him for good measure as he stepped over to engage the next enemy.

On his left, Petronius had killed one of the big peltast's comrades and was trading blows with another. On Romulus' other side, a tall legionary with steely blue eyes was hacking with grim determination into a dazed-looking *thureophoros*.

His instincts urging him on, Romulus barged farther into the mass of confused warriors. A few heartbeats later, the next shower of stones from the *ballistae* landed. This time, though, they were directed at the middle of the Pontic host. Aware that Roman reinforcements had arrived but unable to do a thing about it, the enemy soldiers were also helpless beneath the rain of death. Panic took them, and they began to look over their shoulders.

Romulus saw the same emotion appear in the faces of the peltasts and *thureophoroi* facing him. An instant before, they had been about to annihilate the Twenty-Eighth. Now the tables had turned. It was a moment to seize.

"Come on," he shouted. "The whoresons are going to break and run!"

Hearing his cry, the legionaries close by redoubled their efforts. Behind them, although they could not see it, the Pontic cavalry had broken away to prevent their being enveloped from the rear. Free now to attack the main body of their foes, the centurions turned around their battered men and led them downhill into the fray.

Following closely came three more legions, led by Caesar himself.

The sight was too much for the Pontic infantry. They stopped dead in their tracks. Then, all along their lines, grim-faced legionaries slammed into them. Full of new confidence, the Romans used the full advantage of their higher position to hit the enemy like individual battering rams, knocking many warriors completely off their feet. Even the Cappadocians, who had been so close to winning the battle, were taken aback by the ferocity of the Sixth's attack.

All across the Pontic host, the soldiers' bravery evaporated, to be replaced by terror.

Romulus saw their change in mood. This was the moment in which defeat changes to victory. Exultation replaced all his fear and the pain in his head faded into the background. *A single heartbeat is all it takes,* he thought. Delighted, Romulus watched as the panicked peltasts and *thureophoroi* took to their heels and ran. Dropping their weapons and shields, they pushed and shoved past each other in the eagerness granted by pure fear. All they wanted was to avoid the avenging swords of Caesar's legionaries.

There was to be no mercy, though. Few things were easier in battle than chasing a fleeing opponent, downhill. It was a simple matter of keeping up the pursuit. Thousands of men were trying to get away at the same time, and any chance of rallying them was minute. Who would choose to stop and fight when none of his comrades were doing so? thought Romulus. Yet the Pontic soldiers' primeval attempt to survive was their own undoing. Killing them now was as easy as knocking lemons off a tree. Disciplined like no others, the legionaries followed their adversaries, slaying them in their hundreds.

They brought down the enemy warriors by slashing them across their unarmored backs, or by hamstringing them. Those following then dispatched the injured with simple thrusts of their *gladii*. Yet even this efficiency did not account for all the dead. Plenty of men fell on the steep slope, tripped by tufts of grass or a loose strap on a sandal. They had no chance to get up. The other peltasts and *thureophoroi* simply trampled them into the dust. Their terror had grown so great that sense and reason were lost. All the Pontic soldiers could do was run.

At the bottom, the killing continued. Romulus watched in horror as dozens of warriors were knocked from their feet in the press and then shoved under the water by comrades trying to cross the stream. Wading in up to their thighs, the legionaries slew the drowning men with casual blows from their swords, or even their *scuta*. Still there was no resistance on the enemy's part, just blind panic. Despite the slaughter, thousands managed to ford the watercourse, fleeing up the hill toward the safety of their fortifications.

Soon there were large numbers of Romans on the far bank. Under the calm instruction of their officers, they reassembled in good order and began marching up to the Pontic camp. The running warriors wailed with terror as they saw that their adversaries had not halted.

Romulus glanced back at the trumpeters, who were descending with everyone else. Would the recall be sounded? After all, the battle was won. Ominously, the *bucinae* remained silent. There was to be no letup. "On! On!" shouted the centurions. "Up the slope! Their position has to be taken!"

Still full of battle lust, Romulus and Petronius charged after the foe.

†

Little more than four hours after the battle had started, it was over. Pursued right up to their fortifications, the Pontic forces had been granted no chance to regroup at all. After a short but vicious clash, the ramparts were stormed and the gates opened. Thousands of legionaries poured in, intent on more slaughter. In the confusion, King Pharnaces had barely made off with his own life, riding away with just a few horsemen. His escape only occurred because the victorious Roman soldiers had paused to loot his camp.

It scarcely mattered that Pharnaces was gone, thought Romulus as he stood with Petronius, looking across the valley. Both hillsides were covered with the bodies of the dead and injured. Only a small fraction were Roman casualties, and any of the enemy host who had survived were now prisoners. He gazed up at the clear blue sky, and the blazing hot sun that filled it. It was barely midday. How swiftly the gods had changed whom they bestowed their favors upon! The whole pantheon was smiling on Caesar and his army today. Romulus bent his head in silent worship. *Thank you, Mithras Sol Invictus. Thank you Jupiter, and Mars.*

"What a morning," said Petronius. His face, arms and *gladius* were covered in spatters of dried blood. "Who'd have thought we'd live through that, eh?"

Romulus nodded, unable to speak. As his adrenaline rush subsided, the pain from his head wound redoubled; it was becoming unbearable. He was swaying from side to side like a drunk man.

Petronius saw at once. "Lean on me, comrade," he said kindly.

"Let's head to the stream and get you cleaned up. Then we'll find a first-aid station where a surgeon can check that wound for you."

Romulus didn't argue. He was just grateful for Petronius' steady arm. There was no one else to help. Like many others, the pair had become separated from their units in the frantic pursuit of the enemy. It did not matter for now: the battle was over, and the cohorts could reassemble back at the camp.

After a slow descent, they reached the brook, which was clogged with hundreds of corpses. Moving upstream to a point where the water still ran clear, the two friends stripped naked and climbed in. Plenty of other legionaries were doing the same, eager to wash away the sweat, dirt and encrusted blood that covered their bodies. Weak and wobbly, Romulus stayed in the shallows and let Petronius clean the wound on his head. Having cold water run over it dulled the pain somewhat, but Romulus was not well. His vision was blurred, and although Petronius was by his side, the veteran's voice came and went as if he were walking around him.

"Better get a surgeon now," Petronius muttered as he helped Romulus onto the bank. "You'll need a good sleep after that."

Romulus grinned weakly. "I want a few cups of wine first, though."

"We'll find you a skin somehow," Petronius replied, not quite able to hide the concern in his eyes. "Good lad."

"I'll be fine after a few days," protested Romulus, reaching for his tunic.

"That's the spirit, comrade," said a strange voice. "Caesar's legionaries don't ever give up!"

"Especially those from the Sixth!" cried another.

There was a rousing cheer.

The two friends turned. Another group of soldiers had arrived, also intent on washing off the grime of battle. Romulus recognized none of them. With rusty, battered chain mail and notched swords, the men showed an arrogant ease that spoke volumes. A number of them had flesh wounds, but none was badly hurt. These were some of the legionaries who, vastly outnumbered, had stopped the right flank from dissolving before the Cappadocian attack. The Sixth Legion.

Their leader was a strongly built brute with black hair. Several bronze and silver *phalerae* were strapped to his chest over his mail. Stepping closer, he eyed Romulus' long, gaping wound with a critical stare. "A *rhomphaia* did that. Caught you unawares, eh?"

Embarrassed, Romulus nodded.

The soldier clapped him on the shoulder. "But you survived! Killed the bastard who did it too, I expect."

"I did," Romulus declared proudly.

"It'll never happen to you again either," the other confided. "Good legionaries learn fast, and I can tell you're one of those. Like us."

The newcomers gave him approving looks, and Romulus' heart swelled with pride. Here were some of Caesar's finest, accepting him as one of their own.

"Been wounded before too, I see," said the burly legionary. He pointed a thick finger at the purple welt on Romulus' right thigh. "Who'd you get that from?"

His wits addled, Romulus wasn't thinking straight. "From a Goth," he answered truthfully.

He didn't see Petronius' surprised reaction.

The soldier stopped. "Which legion are you boys in again?"

"The Twenty-Eighth," replied Petronius warily, sensing danger. He began trying to usher Romulus away.

"Wait." It was an order, not a request.

Avoiding eye contact, Petronius stopped.

"The Twenty-Eighth never served in Gaul or Germania," the black-haired legionary growled.

"No." Romulus knew enough of his new unit's history to answer, although he had no idea where this was going. "It didn't."

"So where the fuck did you ever fight a Goth then?" the other demanded angrily.

Romulus stared at him as if he were an imbecile. "In the *ludus*."

The big legionary's face was a picture of shock and outrage. "What did you say?"

Romulus looked at Petronius, who looked similarly stunned. Finally realizing what he'd said, his hand reached down for his *gladius*. It wasn't there—he was still naked, and his weapon was lying on top of his clothing a few steps away.

"I don't believe this," snarled the soldier, raising his bloody sword. "A slave in the Twenty-Eighth? Can't let that go unanswered, can we?"

Shouts of indignation left the men's throats as they swarmed in, seizing Romulus by the arms. He was too weak to resist, and when Petronius tried to intervene, he was clubbed to the ground in a hail of blows and kicks.

The immense danger of the situation began to sink into Romulus' fog of pain.

The black-haired legionary's next words proved it.

"I reckon we should finish off today properly," he cried. "Nothing like watching a crucifixion with a skin of wine."

At this, there was a loud cheer.

VII

THE AFFAIR

THE TEMPLE OF ORCUS, ROME

Sextus roared in agony as Scaevola pulled free his blade. Still clutching his own weapon, he collapsed to the floor in a heap. Fabiola screamed. Sextus' cloak and tunic were already saturated in blood. More was pooling on the mosaic tiles around him, filling the tiny cracks between each colored piece. Even if his wound wasn't mortal, Sextus would soon die from this loss. Yet she had to defend herself first. Unsheathing her *pugio*, Fabiola pointed it toward the *fugitivarius*. It felt like a child's toy. "Don't come any closer," she said, hating her quavering voice.

"What's that, bitch?" Scaevola asked, stepping over the injured Sextus, who could only watch. "I came here to ask for your life, and look! Orcus has answered my prayer before I've even left the premises." He grinned, revealing sharp brown teeth. "A man can't ask for more than that."

Fabiola did not answer. She didn't have the skill to fight off a powerful man like Scaevola with only a knife. And how could she leave Sextus behind? Feeling terrible, she backed away. If she could reach the entrance hall, there were bound to be people about. Priests, priestesses, or other members of the public. Someone who could help them.

Sensing what she was up to, Scaevola lunged after her, slashing and cutting with his *gladius*. "Why don't you run?" he taunted. "I'll even give you a little head start."

His leering face made Fabiola shake with uncontrollable fear. No matter where she went, or what she did, the *fugitivarius* seemed to pop up. It was all she could do to keep moving backward. Frantic, she glanced over her shoulder. It was at least twenty paces to the large doors that led onto the hall. Too far. Despair overtook her. What had she been thinking? To ask Orcus for help and then immediately insult his priestess had been beyond foolish. This had to be the deity's answer. Right on cue, Scaevola thrust his sword at her midriff. Fabiola threw herself sideways; she escaped being gutted by a finger-breadth.

I have angered the gods, and now I'm going to die in this dark corridor, she thought dully. *Caesar will never pay for what he has done. I'll never see Romulus again.* The last thought pained Fabiola most, and her feet came to a standstill. The *pugio* fell from her nerveless fingers to clatter on the floor.

Scaevola crept closer. "I'm going to gut you first, and then carry you outside," he whispered. "How would you like to be fucked while you're dying, you little whore?"

Fabiola stared at him, her eyes dark pools of misery. She could imagine nothing worse.

The *fugitivarius* drew back his blade. "Let's get the first bit over with then."

"Hold!" shrieked a voice taut with fury. "What sacrilege is this?"

They both turned to see Sabina standing over Sextus' prone form. Her hands were red with his blood, and her wide face was outraged.

"He did it," Fabiola stuttered, pointing at Scaevola. "Attacked us as we walked along the corridor."

"I've sworn to kill this woman," snarled the *fugitivarius*. "Came here to pray for that. And look—Orcus himself delivered her to me." Self-righteousness oozed from every word.

"How dare you assume to know what the god does!" screamed Sabina, spittle flying from her lips. "Only his priests or priestesses may speak for him. For any other to do so is heresy."

Scaevola swallowed uneasily.

Sabina leveled an accusing finger at him. "You have already drawn blood inside the temple, which is forbidden. A huge offering will have to be made for Orcus to forgive that, and if this man dies," she said, indicating Sextus, "you will be cursed with the most terrible fate imaginable. For all eternity."

His eyes darted to Fabiola, promising rape and murder anew.

It was all she could do not to lose control of her bladder.

"The same would apply if you murder her," hissed Sabina, her voice threatening. "Think carefully."

Despite himself, Scaevola flinched. Even the murderous were ruled by superstition.

Drawn by Sabina's cries, several priests spilled into the corridor from the main hallway. They gasped in horror at the sight of Scaevola holding a bloody sword over Fabiola.

"Fetch the *lictores* to arrest this dirtbag," shouted Sabina. "He has grievously injured a slave and offered violence to this devotee."

Casting frightened looks over his shoulder, one darted off at once. The others shuffled about, unsure what to do. As priests, none was armed or trained to fight men like Scaevola.

Nonetheless, his *gladius* lowered to point at the floor. "You win once more," he spat at Fabiola, his face purple with fury. "But that's the last instance. From now on, best watch your back night and day. We'll have a fine time together before I slit your throat."

Realizing that she was not going to die there and then, Fabiola recovered some of her courage. "Get out," she answered in a flat tone. "You vermin."

Furious, the *fugitivarius* hawked and spat a gob of phlegm in her face. Then, with his sword raised threateningly, he shouldered his way past the watching priests and out of the door. Awed by his confidence, they did not try to stop him.

Wiping the spit off with her sleeve, Fabiola ran back to Sextus. Sabina was already ripping open his tunic to examine his injury. It was still bleeding profusely, but that was not the worst of it. Fabiola bit her lip to stop herself crying out. Scaevola's *gladius* had entered Sextus' abdomen from the right, just over his hipbone. Running deep into his belly, the razor-sharp iron would have cut his intestines to ribbons. It was a death wound, and looking at Sextus, Fabiola saw that he knew it too. Her throat closed with sorrow, preventing her from uttering a word. It was her fault that her slave lay here like this. *I should have brought some legionaries too,* she thought bitterly.

"I'm sorry, Mistress," Sextus muttered. "Didn't see him coming."

"Stop it," she cried, feeling even worse. "No one could have anticipated that Scaevola would be here. Rest now. I'll have the best surgeon in Rome sent for."

Despite his pain, Sextus smiled, breaking her heart. "Save your money, Mistress. Aesculapius himself would struggle to cure me." A bout of shivering struck him as shock began to set in. After a moment, he managed to rally himself. "I have a request to make of you."

Fabiola hung her head, unable to meet his open, accepting gaze. "What is it?" she whispered, knowing the answer. He had made it of her during Scaevola's first ambush, a lifetime ago.

"A simple grave will be enough," he replied. "Just don't leave my body out on the Esquiline Hill."

"I swear it," said Fabiola, leaning down to clasp his hand through her tears. "There will be a fine memorial over it too. The most faithful slave in Rome deserves no less."

"Thank you," Sextus murmured, closing his eyes.

Trying to compose her maelstrom of emotions, Fabiola covered him with her cloak. Her loyal servant was about to die, and Scaevola was still at large. While the threat of the *lictores* might make him lie low for a few days, the cruel *fugitivarius* was not going to give up now. She only had to look at Sextus to know that every word of Scaevola's threat was real. Fabiola's skin crawled as her imagination ran away with the thought. With great effort, she forced the horrifying images from her mind. It could have all happened here, in this corridor, yet Orcus had seen fit to send a priestess out to stop it all. She could take some consolation from that. "I owe you my life," she said to Sabina. "I am grateful."

She received a brittle smile in response. "What he did was an outrage. I would have done the same for anyone."

The way she said it made Fabiola feel very small and unwelcome. Why Sabina was like this, she still had no idea. Yet the ice-cool priestess was the least of her worries right now. "If you could send word to my *domus* for a litter," asked Fabiola briskly, "I can remove my slave from here."

Sabina gestured at one of the priests, who hurried to her side. "Tell him where to go," she said. "I have to prepare the cursing ceremony for the vile creature who attacked you. What is his name?"

"Scaevola," Fabiola answered. Goose bumps rose on her arms as she imagined what the young priestess might demand of Orcus. "Among other things, he's a *fugitivarius*."

"I see." Sabina did not seem surprised. She turned to go, then stopped. "And my mother? When will she visit?"

"Tomorrow," reassured Fabiola.

This produced a small, pleased smile.

†

In the event, it was not possible for Docilosa to visit the temple the next day.

Accompanied by twenty legionaries, Fabiola arrived at Brutus' house with the unconscious Sextus carried alongside in her litter. Once she had settled him in a bedroom beside her own and deputized a number of slaves to care for their comrade, she went in search of Docilosa. Fabiola found her in bed, her broad cheeks flushed with fever. Her servant barely recognized her, and Fabiola decided not to mention Sabina. The time would be right when Docilosa was recovered, when she could immediately go to visit her long-lost daughter.

Upon his return, Brutus was shocked and incensed to hear what had happened. Fearing his reaction, Fabiola did not mention that the *fugitivarius* was responsible for Sextus' injury. Fabiola wanted to unburden her worries about Scaevola, but she worried that Brutus would forbid her from taking over the brothel. Then there would be no chance of continuing with her plans. She'd have to mention the *fugitivarius* at some point, but also dilute the threat he posed. So she told Brutus that their assailant had been a dangerous lunatic, who had been overpowered by some acolytes. As ever, he believed her story.

Brutus was even more surprised when Fabiola sprang the Lupanar's purchase on him but, in the throes of her expert all-over massage, soon came around. Fabiola's explanation of how the prostitutes could wheedle information from clients, in order to discover those who still sympathized with the Republican cause, pleased him immensely. "Since Pharsalus, Caesar's taken too many of the bootlicking bastards to his bosom," Brutus growled. "I don't trust a single one of them." *Just the type of men I want*, thought Fabiola. Naturally, she did not admit a thing. She had planted the seeds of doubt in Brutus' mind already, and would win him over in time.

It was time to mention Scaevola's involvement with the other brothel. Brutus was horrified to hear that the *fugitivarius* was back on the scene. "I'll just have a few squads of soldiers take the bastard out and execute him," he roared. Unsurprisingly, he calmed down when Fabiola told him of Scaevola's involvement with Marcus Antonius. "Damn it," he said, rubbing his tired eyes. "That prick Antonius wouldn't be happy if one of his henchmen was killed by my legionaries. I'm sorry, my love. We'll have to think of another way."

Fabiola had been expecting that response. It galled her immensely, but a different method to rid herself of Scaevola and his menaces would present itself at some stage. If she could stay alive that long. Fabiola's hunch that Brutus would not want legionaries standing guard outside a whorehouse was correct, but he gave her permission to recruit as many guards as she pleased. "I don't want you spending too much time at the Lupanar, though. It's safest here," he said, his brow furrowed. "Street heavies aren't the same as my trained soldiers." Fabiola gave her lover a lingering kiss and, lying through her teeth, assured him that she'd do as he said. After a brief visit to Sextus' bedside, Brutus retired, leaving Fabiola to brood over the dying slave by the flickering glow of an oil lamp.

She had dosed him with plenty of *papaverum*, so he was unconscious most of the time now. His face had taken on the waxy gray color of those near death, and on the rare occasion that he opened his unfocused eyes, Fabiola did not think Sextus saw much. He was in no pain, so she could do no more. Holding his calloused hand as she had never done in life, Fabiola considered her situation. It felt more dangerous than ever.

To set out on the most perilous of paths without Brutus being fully on board felt downright foolish. He was right about paid guards not being of the same quality or reliability as legionaries. The only dependable men Fabiola had were Benignus and Vettius. With at least a dozen thugs of his own, Scaevola was a lethally dangerous enemy to have. Making the Lupanar impregnable was almost impossible, which meant that her life would be in constant danger there. Fabiola clenched her teeth. Her original refusal to walk away from the purchase of the brothel was not going to change now. Caesar had raped her mother, and tried to do the same to her. How else could she recruit nobles to murder him other than in the Lupanar?

Sextus died during the night, slipping away while Fabiola dozed alongside. When she opened her eyes in the cold light of dawn and saw his unmoving form, she felt enormous guilt at not being awake at the moment of his passing. Yet, she reflected wryly, it was Sextus' manner to die as he had lived: in the most unassuming of ways. Still, Fabiola's heart ached now that he was gone. Since the dark day they had fought side by side for their lives, the one-eyed slave had been a pillar of support to her. In the weeks ahead, Fabiola would sorely miss his skill with a sword. As she pictured Scaevola's malevolent face as he attacked them in the temple, fresh fear filled her. Had buying the Lupanar been a good idea?

Then Fabiola looked down at Sextus' body.

To walk away now might mean she was safe—but the victory would be Scaevola's. Furthermore, her loyal slave's death would mean nothing. "I will avenge you, Sextus," she whispered. "At any cost."

†

Once burial arrangements had been put in train for Sextus, Fabiola set about completing her purchase of the Lupanar. Accompanied by a squad of legionaries, she first made a quick journey to the *basilicae*, the covered markets in the Forum. Among the moneylenders, scribes and soothsayers there, she found a portly lawyer recommended by Brutus. Fabiola was delighted to hear from him that the bill of sale written by Jovina was legally binding. After a greasy-haired scribe had penned two notarized copies—one for each of them—Fabiola deposited the original in a nearby bank.

In these plush premises, replete with fountains, Greek statues and urns, she also presented the parchment with which Brutus had gifted her. It granted up to 175,000 *denarii* in credit. The teller's eyes nearly fell out of his head when he read the amount. This fortune, to a woman? Of course, he dared say nothing, instead checking with a superior that Brutus' seal was genuine before silently composing the document that the confident young beauty demanded.

When it was finished, Fabiola scanned the close-written text herself. It was made out to Jovina for seventy-five thousand *denarii*—half the money she'd agreed to pay the old hag. Even this was an absolute fortune, a sum that only a few years ago she would not have been able to comprehend. Yet it was only part of the money which Brutus had freely given her. He'd offered even more, but, keen to show him that she was not greedy, Fabiola had refused. There was plenty here for her to buy the services of gladiators, street toughs, members of the *collegia*—whoever Benignus and Vettius could round up to defend the Lupanar.

"I need cash as well," she said to the clerk.

"How much, madam?" he asked.

"Twenty thousand *denarii* should do it," Fabiola replied, thinking trips here were probably best left to a minimum. The sturdy legionaries outside wouldn't always be present, and it was a long journey back to the Lupanar. She might not be able to make it too often. "Give me half of it in *sestertii*."

The teller blinked. In this respectable establishment, it was more usual for customers to use credit notes like the one he'd just written. "If Madam doesn't mind waiting," he said. "It will take a few moments to count out such a large amount."

"I'll be back for it in an hour," Fabiola answered. Since she was so close to Jupiter's temple on the Capitoline Hill, a quick visit was called for. She needed help more than ever, and Rome's greatest god had helped her on many occasions before. So too had Mithras. After her bad fortune with Orcus, perhaps she could renew her loyalties to these two deities.

Fabiola had no idea whether the requests that she had made of the god of the underworld were void because of what had happened. She had little stomach to return to his shrine and find out either. It was hard not to believe that her visit there had been a big mistake. *Stop it,* Fabiola chided herself. *You met Sabina there. Docilosa will be so pleased when she finds out.* Her conscience bit back at once. *Sextus is dead, and it's your fault.*

To that, Fabiola had no answer.

†

The next two days passed in a blur of activity, and Docilosa's fever raged on, obviating the need to tell her about her daughter. Keen to avoid possible trouble from Sabina, Fabiola made sure to send an explanatory note to Orcus' temple. Hopefully that would suffice. Despite the expense, Sextus was buried in a small plot on the Via Appia, and a carved stone tablet placed at the head of his grave. It read simply: "Sextus: brave heart and faithful slave." Fabiola did not attend the burial; she had too much on her plate. Scaevola was still lying low to avoid the *lictores,* but who knew how long that would last? She had to maximize the breathing space this granted her. Fabiola tried to bury her intense guilt about missing Sextus' funeral under the myriad of things she had to do. It didn't work.

She'd quickly realized that it wasn't just the competition that had dragged down the brothel's business. The place was run-down and shabby, with cracks in the plaster and damp trickling down the walls in many rooms. The worn, dirty bedclothes were in need of replacing, the floors were covered in dust, and Fabiola's stomach turned when she saw the heated baths. Previously it had been her favorite room. Now mold was growing in the tiny cracks between the tiles, and the green-tinged water obviously hadn't been changed in months. Even the remaining girls didn't look attractive. Old, worn-out, diseased or simply uncaring of their appearance, they had barely registered Fabiola's arrival until Benignus had announced who she was. After a brief pep talk in which she told them exactly how things were going to change, Fabiola left them to absorb her orders. Half of them would be sold as kitchen slaves. The remaining prostitutes would improve their act or the same would happen to them. It was tough, but Fabiola could see no other way to do it. There was no point worrying about the parlous state of the brothel either. The best thing to do was close it down for a week and refurbish it from top to bottom. Then, after recruiting some heavies, she would need a coterie of the best-looking women available in the slave market.

When Fabiola finished her initial tour she understood why Jovina had been so delighted at her reappearance with half the money. "It just needs a lick of paint," the madam simpered as they went into her old office, which was just off the reception area. It was a large room with a desk, several battered chairs and an altar covered in candle stumps. In one corner sat the repository for the brothel's takings, a large iron-clad trunk with several padlocks.

"The place has gone to rack and ruin," Fabiola replied dryly.

"I haven't been well," Jovina muttered, clutching her copy of the bill of sale tightly. "Things got on top of me."

"I can see that. You can cope with getting it cleaned, I presume?"

"Of course." Jovina smiled, revealing her few remaining pegs.

"The girls won't have anything to do while the brothel is closed, so they can all pitch in. The domestic slaves too. I want it finished by tonight, because the builders will be arriving at dawn," announced Fabiola, her face lighting up as she pictured the Lupanar restored to its former glory. "Is that clear?"

Jovina didn't argue. Part of her was glad to see new blood in charge. "It is," she said, a grudging respect creeping into her voice.

I don't deserve that yet, thought Fabiola. *Maybe when the customers return—if Scaevola hasn't burned the building down around our ears by then.* But she wasn't going to let her worries ruin everything. She smiled at

Jovina, pleased that someone who had ruled her life for years was acknowledging her ability. "Good. Benignus!"

He came running from his position by the door. A broad grin had been permanently plastered on both the doormen's faces since Fabiola's arrival. She looked after them as Jovina never had. "Mistress?"

Lifting a small leather pouch from the desk, Fabiola tossed it to him.

Surprised by its weight, his eyebrows rose.

"Find me men who can fight. Try the *ludi*. Go to the slave market too. If you have no luck there, then round up some citizens," she ordered. "Tough-looking ones."

Benignus was delighted. "How many?"

"At least a dozen, but more if you can find them. Big, small, old, young—I don't care. Just make sure that they can handle themselves. They are to live here and defend the Lupanar from that vile piece of work Scaevola. Offer them fifteen *denarii* a month." Fabiola's jaw hardened. "For that kind of money, I expect them to fight. And die, if necessary."

Lifting his club in anticipation of bloodshed, Benignus nodded eagerly.

"You and Vettius will be in charge," she went on. "Feel free to knock heads together whenever you want. Make sure that they know not to touch any of the girls. Warn them that the first one who does will be killed."

Benignus was beaming from ear to ear now. This was what he and his comrade had been wishing for.

"Off you go," said Fabiola. "It might take a while."

Bobbing his head, the shaven-headed doorman hurried out of the door.

Fabiola followed him, tailed by Jovina, her new shadow. She was keen to decide how the reception area could be improved. Apart

from the bedrooms where the prostitutes entertained the customers, this was the most important room in the building, the one that
gave a good or bad first impression. Making it look elegant and
classy once more would be an important part of the Lupanar's
facelift.

Fabiola was still musing over the details when she became aware
of a conversation going on between Vettius and someone just outside the entrance.

"I'm sorry, sir, but the business is closed for refurbishment," said
Vettius politely. "We reopen in a week's time."

"Do you know who I am?" growled the man in a deep, cultured
voice.

Vettius coughed awkwardly. "The Master of the Horse, sir."

Fabiola's hand rose to her mouth. What was Marcus Antonius
doing here?

"Exactly," declared the other. "Now stand aside."

Pursing her lips, Fabiola stalked to the door, determined to see
off this unwelcome visitor. Antonius was Scaevola's employer, and
while he probably knew nothing of her feud with the *fugitivarius*,
she wanted nothing to do with him. He was Caesar's most loyal
follower.

Bumping into the cloaked figure that strode across the portal,
she nearly fell. Quickly Antonius stooped and grasped her arm, preventing her from doing so. Fabiola found herself face-to-face with
the second most powerful man in Rome and her breath caught in her
throat. This close, his animal magnetism was overpowering. "Marcus
Antonius," she stuttered, taken aback. "What are you doing here?"

He smiled, discomfiting her further. "I might ask the same thing
of you. No one told me that Venus herself had come to live in the
Lupanar."

Fabiola flushed, and her heart hammered in her chest.

"Do you work here?" Antonius asked.

"No. I'm the owner," she answered.

He eyed Jovina, who instantly affected not to notice. "Since when?"

"A few days ago," Fabiola replied, angry that he had her so utterly on the back foot. "It's a new business venture."

"And you have experience in the field?"

There was a titter from Jovina, hastily converted to a cough.

Fabiola stared daggers at the old madam. "Some." She wasn't going to go into more detail.

"I missed meeting you before then," murmured Antonius. "Shame."

Fabiola ignored his comment. What was less easy to disregard was his roving eyes, which were busily undressing her. In return, she couldn't help but admire his burly physique and bulging muscles. Jupiter, he had presence. "My apologies, but we're closed until next week, sir," she said, trying to keep her voice from quivering. "Perhaps you could come back then?"

"You don't understand." He gave her the full weight of his penetrating stare. "I haven't had a woman in two days."

"In that case, I'm sure something can be arranged," Fabiola whispered, not sure what she even meant. "Go and get the cleaning started," she barked at Jovina.

With a disappointed look, Jovina disappeared up the corridor. No longer the madam, she had to obey.

At once Fabiola led Antonius into her office. "Sit down and have some wine," she said. "I'll fetch my best lookers in a moment."

He shrugged off his cloak, revealing a plain military tunic. An ornate *pugio* hung from his leather belt. "Have we met before?"

"In Gaul. After Alesia," Fabiola replied, blushing like a girl. How could she not have noticed his easy grace then? She had been too relieved to see Brutus again.

"Ah yes. Decimus Brutus' lover." The corners of his lips tugged upward. "I remember your beauty now—and your naïveté in front of Caesar."

Fabiola's cheeks burned at the memory. "I'd had too much wine," she muttered.

They looked at each other for a long moment.

Fabiola was at a loss for words. After all the men she'd unwillingly had sex with, she had never really thought to desire one. Yet every fiber of her being wanted Antonius. Right now. "I'll fetch those girls," she faltered.

It was as if he knew. Standing, Antonius paced toward her on the balls of his feet. "No need," he murmured. "What I want is right here."

"I'm the owner," Fabiola protested weakly. "Not a whore."

Ignoring her, Antonius pulled her close, fondling her full breasts and kissing her neck.

Fabiola reveled in his touch, and shoved him away with great difficulty. *What is going on*, she thought, panicking. *I never lose control.*

"Come now," he murmured. "I can see you want me."

A sound outside the room saved Fabiola from herself. Had that been a stifled cough? Raising a finger to her lips, she pointed. Antonius watched, smirking, as Fabiola darted to the door and threw it open. To her immense relief, there was no one in the corridor or reception area, but fingers of unease still tickled her spine. She beckoned urgently to Antonius. If someone—particularly Jovina—had eavesdropped on their conversation, Brutus would find out. Fabiola quaked at the thought of his reaction.

"When can I see you?" asked Antonius.

"I don't know," she said, still confused. Then, despite herself, she kissed him on the lips. "We can't meet here."

"One of my properties will do. I'll send a messenger telling you where to go." Antonius gave her a deep bow. Checking the street was clear, he ducked outside.

As she watched him go, Fabiola's heart was filled with a mixture of emotions: elation at the desire she'd felt, and sheer terror that someone had overheard what had gone on in her office. Despite this, she couldn't halt the surge of anticipation at the thought of seeing Antonius again.

Fabiola smiled as another thought struck.

If she became Antonius' lover, Scaevola wouldn't dare to harm her.

VIII

RHODES

THE ISLAND OF RHODES, OFF ASIA MINOR

Tarquinius walked up the narrow street from the harbor, old memories flooding back. He had been here decades before, as a young man. Of the many places he'd visited after Olenus' death, Rhodes had been one of the most interesting. Before arriving here, he had been in the legions, fighting under both Lucullus and Pompey in Asia Minor. In marked contrast to Tarquinius' quiet upbringing on a *latifundium*, his army career had provided the haruspex with comradeship, military experience and a means of seeing the world. His lips twisted upward in a wry grin. For the most part, those four years had been a good time in his life. Although Tarquinius hated Rome for everything it had done to the Etruscans, his people, during that period he had come to feel a grudging admiration for its soldiers' efficiency, courage and sheer determination. Even after his lucky escape from Caesar's men in Alexandria, he felt it.

Tarquinius muttered an instinctive prayer of thanks to Mithras. While the god had not permitted him to discover much of worth in the library, he had to be responsible for guiding his tiring legs down a street where a riot against the Romans was about to break out. Forgetting Tarquinius, their quarry, the chasing legionaries had joined their beleaguered comrades, allowing the haruspex to reach the port, and a ship to Rhodes. His escape had seemed heaven sent. Or were the gods just playing with him? A glance at the cloudless sky revealed nothing. It had been the same for weeks. The only thing he ever saw was a brooding sense of menace over Rome. If Tarquinius tried to see who might be at risk, his vision vanished. So he had no idea if he had to worry about Romulus, his sister Fabiola or someone else he knew in the capital. He'd had a recurring and unsettling nightmare about a murder in the area of the Lupanar, a bloody scuffle that ended with a man lying blood-covered and motionless while other indistinct figures shouted over him. Tarquinius took it to be his killing of Caelius, which told him nothing. Resigned, he shrugged. For whatever reason, he had reached Rhodes, another place of great learning. Maybe here he would find some answers.

Reaching an open area dominated by a brightly painted Doric temple, Tarquinius stopped. A small sigh of satisfaction escaped his lips. He'd climbed up from the main settlement, with its grid of parallel streets and residential blocks, to reach this: the Agora, the beating heart of the town. A bustling marketplace full of stalls, it was also the historic meeting place for the local citizens. A grand shrine to Apollo overlooked it; there were plentiful altars to other gods; and his destination, the Stoic school, was only a block away.

Tarquinius could vividly remember the first time he had walked into the Agora. It hadn't been that long after he'd run from the legions, when fear of discovery had been his constant companion. He'd deserted after facing up to the fact that joining the Roman army had been no more than a futile attempt to forget Olenus and his teaching. He'd realized that was no way to live his life. Thus, after a search of Lydia in Asia Minor had revealed little evidence of the Etruscans' origins, he had come here, to Rhodes. The Stoic school in the city had been a center of learning for centuries, the home of scholars such as Apollonius, and Posidonius, whom the haruspex had heard speak on a number of occasions. This was where rich young Romans came to learn rhetoric and philosophy and to hone their oratorical skills for the cut and thrust of the Senate. Sulla had been a pupil here; so too had Pompey and Caesar.

Tarquinius' first visit had gleaned him little insight into the Etruscans' past, or his own future. He frowned, hoping that this occasion would be different. That his persistent dream would be explained. To have reached Rhodes for the second time, especially when he hadn't expected it, felt most promising. Winded and desperate when he'd reached the merchants' harbor in Alexandria, the haruspex had leaped on the first ship that would take a paying passenger. Fortunately he'd had enough money to pay the captain, a hard-nosed Phoenician. Yet once on board, despairing that he would never discover what to do next, Tarquinius had sunk into a depression that had lasted for days as the merchant vessel hugged the coast of Judaea and Asia Minor. However, then it had sailed into Rhodes. Was it just a coincidence? Tarquinius wasn't sure. As so often before, his attempts at divining had revealed little or nothing of use. Perhaps his coming here was a big joke on the part of the gods, to show him the futility of his life? He hoped it was not so. Surely his visions of Rome and of the Lupanar meant something?

Since the trauma of his parting from Romulus had been added to by his flight from Alexandria, Tarquinius had been ravaged by self-doubt. This was unsurprising. Despite making a journey as remarkable as that of the Lion of Macedon, the haruspex hadn't managed to discover where his mysterious people had come from. While his companions, two of the bravest men possible, had fallen by the wayside or disappeared, he had come full circle, unscathed except for his scars. He railed against the injustice of it. Brennus had chosen a hero's death, fighting a berserk elephant so that his friends could escape. Romulus was alive, but he was a conscript in one of Caesar's legions: Facing death on a daily basis in the civil war, he would be lucky to survive. To Tarquinius, there increasingly seemed little point in living.

Realizing that his dark thoughts were dragging him into an abyss, the haruspex took control. It was not his fault that Brennus wasn't here. The Gaul's last stand had been fated to happen, predicted not just by Tarquinius, but by an Allobroge druid. In addition, the vision he'd had of Romulus entering Ostia, Rome's port, had been one of the most powerful of his life. His protégé *would* return to the city of his birth one day. Tarquinius just hoped that Romulus' homecoming turned out to be all that he wished.

The haruspex had little desire to return to Italy. After all, he thought, what did it matter if, as his vision kept revealing, there was danger in Rome? It mattered if it affected someone dear to him, bit back his conscience. Despite himself, Tarquinius was beginning to wonder if the Republic's capital wasn't the best place for him to be. A visit to the brothel outside which he'd killed Caelius, and changed Romulus' life forever, might trigger the release of more information.

The bark of shouted orders rang out behind him, and Tarquinius turned. Led by a centurion and a *signifer*, two files of legionaries came trotting up the street. They were at least a century strong, and dressed in full battle dress. Many of the locals looked unhappy at the sight. More than a hundred years after their country's acquisition by Rome, the Greeks still resented their masters. Tarquinius didn't like seeing them in a place like this either.

No doubt the soldiers were from the half-dozen triremes he'd seen tied up in the harbor. What they were doing here, Tarquinius had no idea. A peaceful place, Rhodes had long been under the Republic's influence. There were no pirates left hiding in the coves along its coast—Pompey had seen to that. Nor were any of his supporters to be seen; the island's population was far too small to provide the numbers of recruits they needed to fight Caesar.

Eager to remain inconspicuous, Tarquinius stepped into a small open-fronted shop. Amphorae lay everywhere inside: on piles of straw, and stacked three and four high on top of each other. An old desk covered in rolls of parchment, inkpots and a marble abacus sat in the middle of the floor and a crude wooden bar ran partway along one wall. He could hear the proprietor moving around in the back.

The legionaries clattered past without as much as a sideways glance. A line of slaves and mules followed behind them. Tarquinius noted that all the beasts' saddlebags were empty. Suspicion flared in his mind, but his thoughts were interrupted by the arrival of the shopkeeper, who emerged from his storeroom carrying a small, dusty amphora with a heavy wax seal.

The last of the passing soldiers got an angry glare. "Dirty whoresons," he muttered in Greek.

"They are," agreed Tarquinius fluently. "For the most part anyway."

Startled by the scarred stranger's sharp hearing, the shopkeeper paled. "I meant no offense," he stammered. "I'm a loyal subject."

Tarquinius raised his hands peaceably. "You have nothing to fear from me," he said. "Can I buy a cup of wine?"

"Of course, of course. Nikolaos refuses no man a drink." Visibly relieved, the shopkeeper set down his load. Producing a red earthenware jug and a pair of beakers, he placed them on the bar. Filling both, he offered one to Tarquinius. "Are you here to study?"

Tarquinius took a long swallow and gave an approving nod. The wine was good. "Something like that," he replied.

"Better hope that what you're looking for isn't gone by tomorrow then." Nikolaos pointed. "Those bastards were heading to the Stoic school."

Tarquinius almost choked on his second mouthful. "What are they doing?"

"Taking everything of value that isn't nailed down," lamented the other. "If the remnants of the Colossus itself weren't too big to transport, they'd probably take those too."

Tarquinius grimaced. Like all visitors to Rhodes, he had walked the site where the largest statue in the world had once stood. Although it had been knocked off its marble pedestal by an earthquake nearly two centuries before, giant pieces of the god Helios were still strewn on the ground to one side of the harbor. Even these were an impressive sight. Great bronze plates shaped into body parts lay surrounded by iron bars, filler stones and thousands of rivets. All gave testament to the Herculean toil that must have gone into the figure's construction. Now, though, they were good for nothing except scrap. Unlike the treasures in the school, which might hold the key to revealing his future.

Tarquinius couldn't believe it. Even this was to be denied him.

"You're sure?" he demanded in a thin, strained voice.

A little scared of his new customer, the shopkeeper nodded. "It started yesterday. They say that Caesar wants plenty of riches to display in his triumphs. Statues, paintings, books—they're taking it all."

"What right has the arrogant dog? He was fighting damn Romans at Pharsalus, not Greeks," shouted Tarquinius. "This is an already conquered land!"

Hearing the noise, a number of passersby glanced in curiously.

Nikolaos looked most unhappy. Such talk was dangerous.

Tarquinius threw back the last of his wine and slapped down four silver coins. "More," he snapped.

The other's attitude changed at once. The money would pay for an amphora of good wine. With a greasy smile, he filled Tarquinius' cup to the brim.

Tarquinius studied the ruby liquid in his beaker for long moments before drinking the lot. As if the alcohol could help, he thought morosely. Why was he being thwarted like this at every turn? The gods' motives were infuriating—outrageous even—but he was helpless before them.

"Another?" asked Nikolaos solicitously.

He got a terse nod. "And one for yourself."

"My thanks." Nikolaos bobbed his head, deciding that perhaps this customer wasn't so bad after all. "Last year's vintage was a good one."

There was no more chat, however. Ignoring the shopkeeper, Tarquinius stood at the counter, downing more and more wine. Its effects darkened his mood even further. He'd only just arrived, and already his journey to Rhodes had been a complete waste of time. With the school plundered of its valuables, what chance was there of finding information to help him decide what to do? He felt like a blind man feeling his way around a room, looking for a door that he would never find. *Rome*, his inner voice said. *Return to Rome.* He ignored it.

More than an hour passed. On the next occasion Tarquinius lifted the jug, it was empty.

Nikolaos rushed over. "Let me refill that."

"No. I've had enough," replied Tarquinius brusquely. He wasn't so miserable that he wanted to end up unconscious, or worse. Bacchus was no god to see him into Hades.

"Will you go to the school now?"

Tarquinius barked a short, angry laugh. "Not much point, is there?"

"I might be wrong about the soldiers," the shopkeeper offered lamely. "It was only rumor, after all."

"Those whoresons wouldn't march all the way up here with mules for nothing," snarled Tarquinius. "Would they?"

"I suppose not." He dared not argue further. The stranger was too confident, and the double-headed axe poking out from under his cloak looked well used.

Tarquinius took a step toward the door, and then turned to stare at Nikolaos. "This conversation never happened." His dark eyes were mere pits in his battered face. "Did it?"

"N-no," replied the shopkeeper, swallowing. "Of course not."

"Good." Without looking back, Tarquinius wove out onto the street. *Which way?* he wondered. *Might as well visit what I came here for,* he decided abruptly. *See what's left, if there's anything of worth remaining in the place.* Feeling more weary than he had in his entire life, the haruspex walked slowly across the Agora. In the busy crowd of shoppers, businessmen, and sailors from the port, he was just another anonymous figure. Not that he cared.

As he reached the corner of the street that led to the Stoic school, Tarquinius' sandal caught on a discarded piece of clay tile. He pitched forward, badly grazing both of his knees on the rough ground. Cursing, he struggled to get up.

"Bit early to be legless, isn't it?"

Tarquinius looked up, bleary-eyed. Standing over him was a figure wearing a bronze helmet with a transverse crest of red and white feathers. Bright sunlight shining from above obscured the centurion's face. From his position, all Tarquinius could really make out were the ornate greaves protecting the officer's lower legs and his well-made *caligae*. "It's a free world," he muttered. "And I'm not in the legions."

"Look like you might have been one day, though." A muscled arm reached down, offering him help. "That's a handy-looking axe you have there."

Tarquinius paused for a heartbeat and then accepted the grip. He wasn't going to fight what happened anymore.

With a heave, the centurion pulled him to his feet. A solidly built man in middle age, he wore a long mail shirt, crossed decorative belts with a *gladius* and *pugio*, and a leather-bordered skirt. The webbing strapped to the front of his chest was covered with gold and silver *phalerae*.

The haruspex saw with alarm that the highly decorated officer wasn't alone. Behind him, in neat ranks, stood the soldiers he had seen earlier. At the very rear were the mules, now laden down. Contempt filled the watching faces, and Tarquinius looked down in shame. He was a proud man, unaccustomed to being laughed at by ordinary rank-and-filers.

The centurion was interested by this odd-looking fool with his scarred face, blond hair and single gold earring. He wasn't a run-of-the-mill Greek. "What's your name?" he demanded.

The haruspex saw no point in lying anymore. "Tarquinius," he muttered, anger swelling within him at what the Romans had just done.

"Where are you from?"

"Etruria."

The centurion's eyebrows rose. The drunk was Italian. "What brings you to Rhodes?"

Tarquinius pointed past the waiting soldiers. "I wanted to study in the school, all right? You, and your friends've screwed that up, though."

Shocked growls rose from the legionaries at his nerve, but the centurion raised a hand for silence. "You question Caesar's orders?" he asked icily.

The Romans do what they will. They always have, thought Tarquinius wearily. *I cannot change that.* Looking into the other's eyes, he saw death. There were worse ways to die, he reflected. A *gladius* thrust couldn't hurt that much.

"Answer me, by Mithras!"

The words struck Tarquinius like a lightning bolt, stripping away the drink-induced fog from his brain. For some reason, he remembered the raven that had attacked the lead Indian elephant by the Hydaspes. If that hadn't been a sign from the warrior god, then he was no haruspex. This *had* to be another. He was not to die now. "Of course not, sir," Tarquinius said in a loud voice. "Caesar can do as he pleases." He stuck out his right hand in the gesture only a Mithraic devotee would use.

The centurion looked down in disbelief. "You follow the warrior god?" he whispered.

"Yes," Tarquinius replied, touching the blade-shaped scar on his left cheek. "I received this in his service." It wasn't so far from the truth. Again he shoved forward his hand.

With an oath, the officer grabbed it with his own and shook it hard. "Caldus Fabricius, First Centurion, Second Cohort, Sixth Legion," he said. "I had you for a troublemaker."

"Not at all," Tarquinius smiled. "Mithras must have guided me to you."

"Or Bacchus!" Fabricius grinned. "Well met, comrade. I'd love to talk, but I'm in a real hurry this morning. Will you walk with me?"

With a grateful nod, Tarquinius fell in beside the centurion. He was strangely relieved now that the threat of immediate death had gone. Of course the wine had fueled his foolhardy bravado, he thought. Yet he'd only drunk it because of the Romans looting the school. Always expect the unexpected, he thought. Meeting the centurion was tangible evidence of Mithras' favor.

"They had the most incredible artifacts in the school," revealed his new friend. "Instruments and metal contraptions such as I've never seen. There's a strange-looking one in a box with dials on the front and back. You wouldn't believe it, but it has little arms that move around, showing the position of the sun, moon and the five planets. Incredible! On the other side is a face that can predict every eclipse. The old man in charge of it wept when I took it from him. Said it had been made in Syracuse, by a follower of Archimedes." He laughed.

Tarquinius shoved down his throbbing resentment. There was little point being angry at the plundering, he thought. Fabricius was just following orders. Excitement bubbled up in him that the device

Aristophanes had described was so near. Its origins were revolution-
ary too. Everyone knew of the amazing machines Archimedes, the
Greek mathematician, had built to defend his city against the Romans
during the second Punic war. To discover that he might have influenced, or even designed, an even more incredible device was astonishing. "Is it here?"

Fabricius jerked a thumb over his shoulder. "It's on one of the
mules. Well wrapped up, of course, so the damn thing doesn't break."

"You're taking it all to Rome?"

"For Caesar's triumphs," answered the other proudly. "To show
the people yet again what a leader he is."

The last of Tarquinius' drunkenness fell away. On their own, the
images of the city under a louring sky and his nightmare about the
Lupanar weren't enough to make him journey back to the capital.
This was very different, though. Out of nowhere, a possible solution
had appeared. He couldn't ignore it. "Is there room on the ships for
another passenger?"

"Want to get back to Italy? I would too." Fabricius gave him a
nudge. "Be proud to have you on board."

"Thank you." With renewed energy, Tarquinius strode down
to the harbor alongside the centurion. Mithras was guiding him to
Rome, on the same ships that would carry off the contents of the
Stoic school.

Who was he to argue with a god?

IX

CAPTIVITY

PONTUS, NORTHERN ASIA MINOR

Petronius could only limp after Romulus as the gloating legionaries dragged him up to their camp, over the bodies of the Pontic dead. At the fortifications, the big soldier and his companions were prevented from immediately crucifying Romulus by the lack of wood. What few trees grew on the mountain had been cut down during the camp's construction. Yet their anger was such that four of them found axes and went off in search of some. The others lolled about in the afternoon sunshine, drinking extra rations of *acetum* that they had wheedled from the quartermaster.

Trussed up with ropes, Romulus was left to lie in the center of the group. The sun's rays beat down on his wound, turning his head into a throbbing mass of agony. His throat was parched, but of course no one gave him any water. He was barely aware of Petronius' presence, and only reminded of the others by the occasional kick that they gave him. The irony of the situation was not totally lost on him, however. To have endured so much just to end up a candidate for crucifixion in a remote location like Zela seemed farcical. But that was the nature of fate, Romulus thought numbly. The gods could do whatever they liked.

Tarquinius had been wrong. There would be no return to Rome. Soon afterward, Romulus lapsed into unconsciousness.

He was woken by angry shouting, and, confused by his concussion, took a few moments to work out what was going on. Standing on one side of him were the black-haired brute and his companions, their arms full of freshly chopped timber. On the other were Petronius, their *optio* from the Twenty-Eighth and an unfamiliar centurion. Threats and counter-threats filled the air between the veterans and Petronius, who still appeared to be on his own. Romulus' heart filled to see his friend defend him against such odds.

The *optio* did not seem inclined to intervene, but at length the centurion raised his hands for silence. At once the veterans obeyed. Senior officers could, and did, call down the harshest of punishment for any infraction of discipline.

The centurion looked briefly satisfied. "I want to hear, from one man at a time, what in the name of Hades is going on here." He aimed his vine cane at Petronius. "You came crying to your *optio* about this, so you can start."

Quickly Petronius recounted how they had gone to wash in the river after the battle, and how the veterans had struck up a conversation over Romulus' wound. "It's all a mistake, sir. Look at him— he's half-stunned. Probably wouldn't know who he just fought, never mind where he got an old scar on his leg from. Silly bastard never fought a Goth."

Studying Romulus' bloody, dazed appearance, the centurion smiled. "That sounds plausible, but the accusation of slavery is a serious one all the same." He looked at the black-haired legionary. "What have you got to say?"

"The dog's not that badly hurt," he said furiously. "And he admitted that the wound had been made by a Goth, sir. In a *ludus*! How much evidence does a man need?"

Angry mutters of agreement rose from his companions, but none dared to challenge their superior officer directly.

With a frown, the centurion turned to the *optio*, a squint-eyed Campanian whom Romulus had never taken to. "Is he any kind of soldier?"

"He is, sir. A good one," replied the *optio*, raising Romulus' spirits for a moment. "But he did join the legion in strange circumstances."

Interested, the centurion indicated he should continue.

"It was during the night battle in Alexandria, sir. Me and my section were guarding the Heptastadion when he and another dodgy-looking type appeared from nowhere. They were Italian and well armed, so I press-ganged the pair of them on the spot."

He got an approving nod for that. "Where had they come from?"

"Said they'd been working for a *bestiarius*, in the south of Egypt, sir."

"And is this the other one?" demanded the centurion, pointing at Petronius.

The *optio* scowled. "No, sir. He disappeared the same night. Unfortunately, I didn't notice the whoreson was gone until the battle was over. Couldn't find a trace of him anywhere."

"Suspicious," muttered the centurion. "Very suspicious." He nudged Romulus with his foot. "Are you an escaped slave?"

Romulus focused on his accuser with difficulty. After a moment, his gaze flickered around the other watching faces. All but Petronius' were filled with hatred or indifference. Utter weariness filled him. What was the point of carrying on? "Yes, sir," he said slowly. "But Petronius, my comrade, had no idea."

Despite Romulus' get-out clause for him, Petronius looked devastated.

"See, sir?" cried the black-haired soldier, his outrage resurgent. "I was right. Can we crucify the bastard now?"

"No. I've a better idea," snapped the centurion. "Caesar intends to hold massive celebratory games when he returns to Rome. There'll be a need for more bodies than the schools or the prisons hold. This scum might have escaped the arena once, but he won't manage it twice. Clap them in chains. Both can be used as *noxii*."

Mollified by this, the veterans grinned.

Scarcely believing his ears, Petronius bunched his fists. Being condemned to die fighting wild beasts or criminals and murderers was a degrading fate. Then he saw their captors' gloating faces. If he tried to fight, he'd be dead in a heartbeat. Life was still precious. Petronius unclenched his hands, and he did not resist when two legionaries tied him up with a length of rope.

"No, sir," croaked Romulus, struggling against his own bonds. "Petronius has done nothing wrong!"

"What?" sneered the centurion. "The fool made a comrade of a slave. He deserves the same miserable death as you."

"How was he supposed to know?" shouted Romulus. "Leave him be!"

The centurion's response was to stamp down on his head with the studded sole of one of his *caligae*.

Darkness took Romulus.

†

Probing fingers in his wound woke him. Romulus opened his eyes, finding himself in the camp's *valetudinarium*, a series of large tents near the headquarters. It was near sunset, he was still tied up, and a sallow-skinned surgeon in a bloody apron was examining him. There was no sign of Petronius, just a bored-looking legionary standing guard nearby. Despairing, Romulus closed his eyes again.

Soon the Greek pronounced the absence of a fracture. He cleaned the wound with *acetum* and placed a neat line of metal clamps in the skin to close it. Each one delivered a stabbing pain as it was inserted. After this, a rough linen bandage was wrapped around Romulus' head. Dressed in an old tunic, he was discharged from the *valetudinarium*. There were countless other casualties who needed the surgeon's care more than he did. Pulling Romulus to his feet, the legionary frogmarched him to the camp jail, a wooden stockade by the main entrance. There he was flung inside. As he sprawled to the floor, the door slammed shut. Romulus lay motionless for a moment, letting the misery of what had happened wash over him.

"Romulus?" Petronius' voice was very close.

Romulus managed to roll onto his chest and look around. There were seven soldiers in the prison, but his friend was the only one who'd come over. Petronius ushered him to a corner away from the rest. They sat down on the hard-packed dirt together.

"I'm sorry," said Romulus in a low voice. "You shouldn't be here. It's all my fault."

Petronius sighed heavily. "I can't say that I wasn't angry when it happened."

Romulus began to speak, but the other raised his hand.

"The way those bastards turned on me like a pack of dogs disgusted me. Made me think, because I was like that once," said Petronius ruefully. "Yet I'm a citizen just like them. How was I supposed to know that you were a slave? Didn't seem to matter a damn, though. Not one cared that you've proved your courage to me and the whole Twenty-Eighth. Slaves have fought for Rome before too, against Hannibal." He sighed again. "No longer, obviously."

Romulus waited.

Petronius locked eyes with him. "I owe you—my comrade—more than I owe either those bastards from the Sixth or that centurion."

This acceptance negated all the rejection Romulus had received earlier. He and Petronius were blood brothers; they had the same bond as he and Brennus. Overcome with emotion, he could do no more than extend his right arm. Petronius reached out and they gripped forearms in the military manner.

"Do you know what happens next?" Romulus asked.

"Caesar and the Sixth will be shipping out to the coast as soon as the mopping up is over, and taking us with them," replied Petronius with a scowl. "Apparently there's unrest in Italy. Veterans unhappy with their lot, according to our new comrades." He jerked his head at the other men.

"What did they do?" asked Romulus.

"Broke and ran during the battle," said Petronius disgustedly.

"Surprising they haven't been crucified."

"I guess Caesar needs plenty of fodder for his games," Petronius answered.

They exchanged a look of dread.

†

A month or so later, Romulus, Petronius and the other prisoners traveled to the southwest of Asia Minor, where Caesar's fleet was waiting. Forced to march in chains behind the wagon train, they were treated brutally on the way. As well as eating the dirt left in the air by the Sixth's passage, they were given hardly any rations or water. If any of them so much as looked at one of the guards, a merciless beating followed. It paid to lay low and say nothing, which is what the two friends did. They shunned their companions, preferring their own company to that of cowards who had fled the battlefield. Impossible to ignore, however, were the visits of the black-haired veteran and his comrades. Every day without fail, insults and derogatory comments filled the air. The ordeals lasted until their tormentors grew bored and left, or the officer on duty sent them on their way.

Fortunately for Romulus, his concussion had improved quickly. His wound had healed well too. After ten days, the surgeon visited the stockade to remove the metal clips, leaving only a long red scar that was visible through Romulus' close-cut hair. It would serve as a permanent reminder of a *rhomphaia*. Not that his life would be long, he thought bitterly, staring at the fleet of triremes that would carry them to Italy. Thus far, the routine of marching and pitching camp had maintained a weird air of normality to their existence. The ships brought reality hammering home. So too did the lack of any communication from Fabiola. Even if she had heard his shout and sent word to him, he knew that no one would bother to search the *noxii* for one man called Romulus. Their sighting of each other in Alexandria now seemed cruel.

He and Petronius had not been denying their fate, though. In addition to the twenty miles they'd had to travel each day, both had done as much exercise as they could, running on the spot, push-ups, and wrestling with each other. As soldiers, their fitness, or lack of it, could mean life or death. Yet their hard work was a futile gesture, because in their new vocation, that of the *noxius*, everyone died. It was the whole premise of their presence in the arena. Despite this, the friends were determined to prepare themselves as well as possible.

Embarking on the triremes in balmy summer weather, they had an uneventful voyage to Brundisium. During it, Romulus thought often of Brennus and Tarquinius. He and the Gaul had first met the haruspex on the reverse of this very passage, when they had been sailing to war with Crassus' army. How full of hope he'd been then, and what incredible things he'd seen since. Now here he was, returning by the same route, in chains. It felt lonely and unreal—and hopeless. There would be no lingering revenge on Gemellus. No joyful reunion with Fabiola when he reached Rome, just a terrible death before a baying mob. Tarquinius had been right. His road would take him to Rome—but to a miserable end.

Only the presence of Petronius, sturdy and somehow cheerful, had made it possible for Romulus not to withdraw completely into himself. Reaching Italy also helped to lift his spirits a fraction. Hearing Latin spoken all around for the first time in eight years was a joy, as were the familiar sights of Roman towns. Romulus even took pleasure from the sight of the autumn countryside filled with its *latifundia*. What was less welcome was people's reaction to the pair and their companions. While the veterans of the Sixth received rapturous applause and garlands of flowers wherever they went, the prisoners were reviled and spat upon.

After several weeks of this, Romulus was glad to see the walls of Rome at last. Instead of being instantly disposed of, the prisoners were thrown into a stockade for the night while the Sixth prepared itself for trouble. Caesar had a welcoming party to deal with. Rebellious veterans from, among others, the Ninth and Tenth legions were camped outside the city walls in their thousands. Gossip about the troublemakers had swept the column as it marched north from Brundisium, even reaching the captives. After Pharsalus, a number of legions had been sent back to Italy, where their promised pensions failed to materialize. Disgruntled, they had soon begun to demonstrate, and threatened worse. Caesar would need them to carry the campaign against the Republicans to Africa and they knew it, so the officers sent by Marcus Antonius to quell the mutiny had been stoned from their camps. Even Sallust, a charismatic ally of Caesar's, could not bring the rebels to heel. He had been lucky to escape from them with his life.

Uncaring that Caesar had returned, the veterans marched on Rome to demand their rights. Armed to the teeth, they were a brooding threat to the Republic's stability. Nonetheless, Caesar had taken the Sixth to within a mile of their position and set up his own encampment. Knowing that they were greatly outnumbered had filled the Sixth with unease, but nothing happened on the first night. Although his own death was near, Romulus couldn't help wondering what the general would do. Incredibly, by midmorning the next day it was all over. The delighted guards told Romulus and the others all about it.

Accompanied only by a few men, Caesar had entered the rebels' tent lines in the cold of an autumn dawn. Inside, he had climbed the podium outside the headquarters. As news of his presence spread, a great crowd of mutineers gathered to hear what he had to say. According to the stunned men who'd been with him, Caesar had simply asked them what they wanted. A long list of grievances followed, culminating with the demand that all the veterans be discharged. In a neat maneuver that totally disarmed them, Caesar promised to release every man from service at once, and to honor their rewards in time. Crucially, he addressed the rebels as "citizens" rather than "comrades," showing them that they were no longer part of his army.

At once the shocked legionaries had begged their general to have them back, to help win the struggle in Africa. Caesar repeatedly demurred, even starting to leave, but their pleas grew more frantic. Promises were made that he would need no other troops to achieve victory. With masterful reluctance, he had accepted the service of all except the men of the Tenth. It, Caesar's most favored and rewarded legion, had disappointed him most, so its soldiers had to be let go. With their huge pride in their unit called into question, the Tenth's veterans had demanded that Caesar decimate them, as long as they were taken back into his army. In a final gesture of magnanimity, he had given in, welcoming the Tenth to his bosom like wayward children, and ending the rebellion at a stroke.

When he heard the story, Romulus' admiration for Caesar soared. For months, Petronius had filled his ears with talk of Alesia, Pharsalus and other victories. In Pontus, he'd seen with his own eyes what Caesar could do, but this quality made him unique. Not only could Caesar lead armies into battle against terrible odds and win, he could lead men like no other. Crassus had been the polar opposite of this, commanding in an impersonal and uncharismatic manner. Even though he had only served under Caesar for a short time, Romulus was glad he had had that experience before he died.

Once the mutineers had been dealt with, there was no further delay. Caesar headed into the capital to meet with the Master of the Horse and the Senate. The Sixth was demobbed for the moment, its soldiers beating an instant path to the local taverns and brothels. After a few days, they would go home to their families. The prisoners were disposed of the same day too. With a dozen soldiers as escort, the centurion who had pronounced sentence on the two friends led the group into the city.

Petronius had never seen Rome before, and was amazed by the thick Servian walls, the sheer size of buildings and numbers of people. Romulus, on the other hand, felt a sense of dread as they walked the streets through which he had run errands as a boy. This was not how he wanted to return home. Even the sight of Jupiter's massive temple atop the Capitoline Hill produced only a flicker of joy in his heart, and this small pleasure was drained away by passing the crossroads near Gemellus' house. Despite the financial difficulties Hiero had told him of, the merchant might still be living there. A dull resentment filled Romulus' belly. He was only a hundred paces from the door of the man whom he'd dreamed for years of killing, and he was unable to do a thing about it.

Finally they neared the Ludus Magnus, the main gladiator school, and old fear made Romulus' heart skip a beat. It was from this place that he and Brennus had fled, unnecessarily as it turned out. It had been Tarquinius who killed the fiery nobleman, not Romulus. By now, his initial fury at the haruspex' revelation had crumbled to a lingering bitterness at what might have been. It was hard to feel otherwise. Brennus could still have been alive if they hadn't run, and they might both have earned the *rudis*. Yet Romulus was not naive: underneath lay the knowledge that Tarquinius would have acted as he thought best—and according to the wind, or the stars. Had his accurate divinations not been a comfort through the ordeals of Carrhae and Margiana? After so long together, Romulus knew the haruspex well; he did not think Tarquinius was a man to act maliciously.

The realization helped him to square his shoulders as he read what was inscribed on the stone over the main gate: "Ludus Magnus." The first time Romulus had seen them, as an illiterate thirteen-year-old, he'd only guessed the two words' meaning. Thanks to Tarquinius, though, he could now read them. It was odd that they were here, thought Romulus. There were four *ludi* in Rome, yet here he was, outside his old training ground. An ironic smile flickered across his lips as the centurion demanded entry.

A moment later, their hobnailed *caligae* echoed in the short corridor that led to the open square within the thick walls. It was midafternoon, and dozens of gladiators were engaged in physical training with each other and against the *pali*, the thick timber posts as tall as a man. Trainers armed with whips walked among them, pointing and shouting commands. With wicker shields and wooden weapons that were twice the weight of the real thing, the fighters danced around each other, thrusting and stabbing. Romulus recognized none of them, and his heart bled. Sextus, the little Spaniard, and Otho and Antonius, two other friendly gladiators, were probably all long dead. It was also likely to be true of Cotta, his trainer. He scanned the balconies for Astoria, Brennus' Nubian lover, but there was no sign of her either, only the menacing shapes of the *lanista's* archers, watching for any signs of trouble. It was not that surprising that Astoria wasn't around, Romulus thought gloomily. Memor would have sold her to a brothel.

Romulus' attention was drawn back to the present by other familiar classes of fighter—Thracians with their square shields and curved swords, and *murmillones* in their distinctive fish-crested helmets. There were even two pairs of *retiarii* sparring against the same number of *secutores*, his own former category of hunter. He stopped for a moment to watch. Instantly, there was a sharp prod in his back. "Get a move on," snarled one of the legionaries, poking him again with his *pilum*. "Follow the centurion."

Romulus swallowed his anger and obeyed. Soon he and the

others were lined up in front of a familiar figure, one whom he'd never thought to see again. Memor, the *lanista*. The years hadn't changed him that much. Maybe his skin was a darker shade of brown, thought Romulus, and his shoulders slightly stooped, but the *lanista*'s mannerisms and the way he ordered the gladiators about were exactly the same as before. So was his sarcastic manner. Romulus' stomach clenched. Would Memor recognize him?

"What have we here?" the *lanista* drawled. "Deserters?"

"Cowards mostly," the centurion replied. "They ran away in the middle of a battle."

Disapproving, Memor flicked his whip along the ground. "They'd be no damn good as gladiators then. Why weren't the dogs crucified?"

"The games celebrating Caesar's recent victories are short of recruits," growled the centurion. "They are to be classed as *noxii*."

Memor's lip curled. "Not my usual line of business, that."

Only because there's no money in it for you, thought Romulus sourly.

"Taking them on would be seen as a favor to Caesar himself," responded the other.

At once Memor was all beams and smiles. "Why didn't you say? It would be my honor to prepare the sons of whores for death. I might even be able to make them perform well." He gave the prisoners an unpleasant stare. Oddly, it stayed longest on Romulus and Petronius. "Why are those two here?"

The centurion snorted. "One is a damn slave who had the cheek to join the legions."

Memor's bushy eyebrows rose. "And the other?"

"His fool of a friend. Tried to defend the slave when he was exposed."

"Interesting," said Memor, pacing before the chained men in an appraising manner. His whip trailed after him, its weighted tip drawing a line in the sand. He came alongside Petronius, staring at him like a leopard looking at its prey.

The veteran met his gaze with contempt.

"Still proud, eh?" Memor grinned. "I can soon change that."

Petronius had the wisdom not to answer.

Memor moved to stand before Romulus, who, keen not to be recognized, looked away. But the grizzled *lanista* grabbed his jaw and twisted his head around, making Romulus feel thirteen years old again. His deep blue eyes met the black pits that were Memor's, and they stared at each other for a long moment. "Which is the slave?" Memor asked abruptly.

"The one you're looking at," replied the centurion.

A frown creased Memor's lined forehead. "Big nose, blue eyes. You're strong too." He let go of Romulus' chin and pulled up the right sleeve of his russet military tunic. Where a slave brand might have been, there was a linear scar, partially obscured by a tattoo of Mithras sacrificing the bull. To expert eyes, however, it was obvious that Romulus had been a slave once. Brennus' excision had been that of a battlefield surgeon, quite unlike the skilled art of those who specialized in removing brands from wealthy freed slaves, and the tattoo Romulus had paid for in Barbaricum only sufficed to divert passing glances. Memor knew at once what he was seeing. Stepping back, he sized Romulus up. "By all the gods," he said, his face coloring with old anger. "Romulus? Isn't that your name?"

Resigned, he nodded.

The centurion looked surprised. "You know him?"

Memor spat a violent oath. "The scumbag belongs to me! Eight years ago, he and my best gladiator got out one night and murdered a noble. Of course the bastards ran away. Disappeared completely, although I heard a rumor they'd joined Crassus' expeditionary force."

The centurion chuckled. "I don't know about that, but he was certainly in one of Caesar's legions."

"I *was* in Crassus' army," muttered Romulus. "Thousands of us were taken captive after Carrhae. I managed to escape with a friend some months later."

Petronius' and the centurion's faces were the picture of shock. Apart from Cassius Longinus and the remnants of his command, no further survivors from the disaster in Parthia had returned to Rome.

Memor spun back. "You and the big Gaul? Where is he?"

"Not him," said Romulus heavily. "He's dead."

Disappointment filled the *lanista*'s features.

With his grief over Brennus' death scraped raw once more, Romulus could still see Memor's mind working. After all, he too had been an excellent gladiator—at only fourteen years old. Now he was a grown man, who had served in the army. An even better prospect. "Surely this one could return to me rather than being killed off?" Memor asked. He paused, then couldn't help himself. "He's my property, after all."

"Don't try your luck. The whoreson joined the army as a slave, which means he's under my jurisdiction until he dies," snapped the centurion. "I don't care if he's fucking Spartacus himself. He and his friend go into the arena and they don't come out."

There was to be no way of making back the money he'd lost from Brennus' and Romulus' disappearance. Furious, Memor lifted his whip. "I'll teach you," he hissed at Romulus.

"Don't damage them either," warned the centurion. "Caesar will be expecting a top-class spectacle, not just some cripples being mauled to death in double-quick time."

Cheated of even this, Memor stepped back. "Shouldn't be ungrateful, I suppose. It'll be a pleasure to see you die," he said with a cruel smile. "I believe that the *bestiarii* have a fine selection available at the moment. Tigers, lions, bears and the like. Apparently there are even more exotic creatures too."

The other prisoners gave one another fearful looks. Even Petronius shuffled his *caligae* to and fro. Romulus managed to keep his face blank. He was also scared, but he was damned if Memor would get to see it.

"I'll leave that decision up to you," offered the centurion, tossing the keys for the padlocks to Memor. "They're on in two days." With a curt nod, he led the legionaries out of the yard.

"Unchain them." Memor handed the keys to one of his men, a skinny Judaean with buck teeth and a scraggly beard. "Then find the worst cell you can. Tell the cook they are to get no food." Still in a bad mood, he stalked off.

Rubbing their skin where the neck rings had chafed, the prisoners followed the Judaean to a dank, windowless chamber with mold growing on the walls. It was barely big enough for two or three of them to sleep side by side, let alone eight. There were no bunks or blankets either. Smirking, Memor's man walked off.

The two friends moved away from the doorway. There was no point spending any more time in the cell than they had to. Leaning back against the wall, they watched the gladiators, who, with the excitement over, had gone back to their training.

"Two days until we go to Hades," muttered Petronius. "Not long."

Fighting despair once more, Romulus nodded grimly.

Petronius thumped one fist into the other. "Why did that black-haired bastard have to interfere? If it hadn't been for him . . ." He sighed.

"We cannot understand the gods' purpose," said Romulus. Even to his ears, the words sounded hollow.

"Spare me your piety." Clearing his throat, Petronius spat on the sand. "We don't deserve a fate like this."

Romulus' spirits hit a new low.

They were damned.

X

CAESAR'S GAMES

TWO DAYS LATER . . .

S cowling, Fabiola totted up the figures on her parchment again. It made no difference: They were as depressing as the first time she'd calculated them. Time had passed since her takeover of the Lupanar, and business was still not improving. It wasn't as if she hadn't been busy, she thought angrily. The brothel had been redecorated from top to bottom and the baths refilled. Fifteen heavies recruited by Vettius lounged around the entrance and the street, ready to fight at a moment's notice. Unless one had a very large force, attacking the premises now would be tantamount to suicide. Thanks to some well-placed bribes at the slave market, Fabiola was the owner of a bevy of new prostitutes: dark-eyed, brown-skinned Judaeans, Illyrians with raven tresses and pitch-black Nubians. There was even a girl from Britannia with red hair and a cream complexion that Fabiola could have wished for herself.

Posters advertising the Lupanar's revamp had been put up all over Rome too, aimed at attracting both new custom and old. A common method of raising public awareness, this should have resulted in a flood of men through the door. Instead, it had been a mere trickle. Fabiola sighed. She had underestimated Scaevola's ability to affect her business. There could be no doubt that the brothel's failure to take off was thanks to the *fugitivarius*, whose blockade of the Lupanar had begun the day after Antonius' visit. Her hopes that Scaevola would find out about her affair with the Master of the Horse and just disappear had proved fruitless. While Fabiola didn't think Antonius knew of her feud, she hadn't dared mention it to him yet either. Any time she ever thought about it, her new lover seemed to mention the *fugitivarius*—in glowing terms.

Scaevola's initial tactics had been blatant: open intimidation of potential customers by his thugs right outside the brothel. Incensed, Fabiola had sent Vettius and his men out to deal with them. After a pitched battle and a handful of casualties, the *fugitivarius* had withdrawn his forces to the surrounding streets. The situation had then settled into an uneasy peace, broken by the occasional bloody skirmish. While the fighting was bad for business, the damage done by Scaevola's ever-present heavies was even worse. It was impossible to stop them too. Fabiola's guards could not protect the Lupanar and also stand on every street corner day and night.

It was all rather depressing, thought Fabiola morosely. Brutus' funds weren't limitless, and the place wasn't making any money. While she didn't mind spending most of her time in the brothel, the poor trade meant that she was having little luck in discovering anyone of senior rank who was prepared to join a conspiracy against Caesar. Every one of her prostitutes had been drilled to repeat the smallest detail let slip by a client about the political situation. Thus armed, Fabiola planned to focus her attention on those who spoke badly of Caesar in any way. Information, though, like customers, was proving to be thin on the ground. She could only suppose that, eager to avoid trouble, most people were keeping their lips sealed.

For weeks Fabiola sat in the Lupanar, brooding. Even Brutus, who was working from dawn till dusk on official matters, had noticed her ill humor. "Buying the damn fleapit was a bad idea from the start," he cried during one of their now regular arguments. Alarmed by the volatility of Brutus' reaction, she had turned on a charm offensive to allay his concerns. It had worked—for the moment. Now Fabiola was careful to be at home before he was, ready to pay him the attention he was used to. She could not afford to upset Brutus too much, especially now that Marcus Antonius had become a regular lover.

That impulsive move had made her life far more complicated, and dangerous. By this stage, however, Fabiola could not help herself. It had all begun with a simple plan: that in the Master of the Horse she would have a safety net in case Brutus ever abandoned her, or that Antonius would prove to be another possible ally against Caesar. Of course it was all an exercise in self-deception. Antonius was known throughout Rome for philandering with senators' wives, so he wasn't about to lose his heart to Fabiola, or to favor her above all others. He was also Caesar's most ardent supporter, threatening bloody murder to anyone he thought harbored the smallest disloyal thought about the Republic's dictator. If he learned of Fabiola's plans for Caesar, she might as well write her own death warrant. The best thing she could have done was to end the affair after the first occasion.

Fabiola had known all this within a few days of encountering Antonius, and yet here she was, still meeting him whenever he demanded it. Guilt about her infidelity to Brutus ravaged her, but it wasn't enough to stop her. The fact that Brutus did not deserve it wasn't adequate either. Fabiola hated her weakness, but did nothing about it. Deep down, she knew why. The reason she was involved with Antonius was that she was enthralled by his animal magnetism, his brooding presence, and his confident manner. The Master of the Horse was an alpha male from his head to his toes, while Brutus, a decent man through and through, was not. In Antonius' presence,

Fabiola wasn't always the one in charge. It was a most unusual situation for her and, after so many years of controlling men, she liked it. She relished too how Antonius undressed her with his eyes, the way he ran his hands over her naked body and the feeling when he was deep inside her.

Fabiola dreaded Brutus' reaction if he discovered her illicit relationship. He didn't like the Master of the Horse at the best of times, and, when aroused, his temper was ferocious. So Fabiola took the most elaborate precautions when meeting Antonius. Smuggling herself out of the brothel with only Vettius or Benignus as protection, she would meet him in discreet inns just outside Rome, or at one of his private residences in the city. Jovina suspected something was going on, but knew better than to ask. Now that she was no longer in charge, none of the slaves or whores would tell her a thing, which cut off her eyes and ears at a stroke. Fabiola was aware how easy it would be for one slave to gossip with another, or a customer. Scandal like her affair would spread faster than the plague, hence the meetings off the brothel's premises. Docilosa and the two doormen were the only ones who knew the truth. Benignus and Vettius adored Fabiola so much that they did not care what she did, and while Docilosa disapproved, her mind was wholly taken up by Sabina, with whom she had been reunited after her fever abated.

Although Antonius did not talk much about official business during their trysts, inevitably he let the occasional snippet fall. Fabiola pounced on these gems like a magpie and now knew of more than half a dozen men who were suspected of plotting against Caesar. Many, like Marcus Brutus and Cassius Longinus, were former Republicans who had been pardoned by Caesar after Pharsalus. Their names filled Fabiola's mind day and night, frustrating her hugely. How could she meet them in private and win them over? By virtue of her sex and former status, Fabiola did not socialize with the nobility that much. Of course Brutus took her to plays, and to feasts, but these were hardly the places for her to foment high treason. What she needed was for those who hated Caesar to walk through the brothel's door. She scowled. There was little chance of that happening with Scaevola's blockade in place. It was endlessly frustrating— a vicious circle that had gone on for months. To break it, she would have to broach the subject of the *fugitivarius* with Antonius.

Sudden shouts from the street made Fabiola's face brighten. Rather than Scaevola or his thugs, it was the sound of excited, drunk citizens. Drawn by the prospect of Caesar's games, thousands of people were already flooding the capital's streets. To celebrate his recent victory over Pharnaces in Asia Minor, several weeks of entertainment had been laid on, beginning a couple of days prior. Brutus had been raving about the quality of gladiators who would be fighting. The resulting influx of visitors into the city had seemingly diluted the *fugitivarius'* ability to affect Fabiola's business, and in turn that was bringing in more customers. She glanced at the little altar in the corner. Perhaps Mithras or Fortuna might send her some of the nobles Antonius had mentioned.

What about Romulus? she thought guiltily. *How could I forget him?* Her resolute refusal to believe that her twin was dead had carried her through for years, culminating miraculously with a sight of him in Alexandria. Yet there had been no news of Romulus since. With a civil war in full flow, Caesar's legions were constantly on the move, and it was proving hard to get any meaningful information from them. The quartermasters and senior officers whom Fabiola's messengers had contacted were less than cooperative. Busy obtaining supplies and equipment, recruiting new men to replace their losses, and preparing for Caesar's new campaigns, they had more on their plates than finding one ordinary soldier among thousands. It was not as if Romulus was an unusual name, one centurion had apparently scoffed.

Stuck in Rome, Fabiola had resigned herself to not seeing her brother again until the war was over and Caesar's troops returned home. If he survived, of course. There was no guarantee that he would. A fresh wave of guilt washed over her. To Fabiola's shame, resentment followed in its wake. Wasn't she doing all she could? She still prayed daily for Romulus. Couriers armed with information had been dispatched to every legion in the army. She couldn't help it if they found nothing. Was it so wrong for her to have some pleasure in the meantime? After all, she wasn't a Vestal Virgin.

"Mistress?"

The sound of Docilosa's voice cut through Fabiola's reverie. "You know not to call me that," she said for the thousandth time.

"Sorry," Docilosa replied. "Old habits." Wearing a hooded cloak, she looked ready to go out.

"Off to see Sabina?" Fabiola inquired.

There was a shy grin. "Is that all right?"

"Of course," Fabiola replied warmly. "Whenever you like." Docilosa's joy over her reunion with Sabina warmed her heart. Pangs of sadness always gripped her at the same time, though. What might it have been like to see her own mother once more after so many years? She would never know. "Be careful. Keep your eyes peeled for Scaevola."

Docilosa lifted her hood. "Don't worry. Vettius won't let me out until the street's clear." Like all the brothel's residents, she had grown used to blending into the crowd at once.

Fabiola nodded, her guilt about Romulus and desire to see Antonius returning with a vengeance. She was unaware of her grim expression.

Docilosa didn't move from her position. "What's wrong?" she asked. "You've not been yourself in recent days."

Fabiola forced an unconvincing smile. What was sparking Docilosa's sudden interest? "It's nothing," she muttered.

Her servant raised one eyebrow. "Expect me to believe that?"

"There's a lot on my mind," Fabiola offered. "Scaevola's still about. Business isn't increasing like it should. My coffers aren't bottomless."

"We're doing everything that can be done in those departments," Docilosa answered stolidly. She studied Fabiola's face. "There's more than that going on—I can see it in your eyes."

Fabiola looked down, wishing that her servant would just leave. She was poor at concealing her emotions from Docilosa, and still wasn't ready to reveal her plan to kill Caesar. Now she had two more dirty secrets—her pleasure in having an affair with Antonius, and her shameful resentment of Romulus. Suddenly these private thoughts seemed too much to bear on her own. Fabiola glanced at Docilosa. "I . . ." she faltered.

"Tell me," Docilosa urged. "I'm listening."

I should explain, thought Fabiola. *Every little detail. She'll understand. She did when I couldn't cope with the idea of Carrhae any longer.* Fabiola's memory of her meltdown on the very day Brutus had appeared with her *manumissio* was strong. It was Docilosa who had listened and calmed her, before sending Fabiola out to face her lover in what had proved to be the most important meeting of her life. "It's about Caesar," she began. "And Romulus. And . . ." Her voice dried up.

Docilosa finished Fabiola's sentence for her. "Marcus Antonius?"

She nodded, unable to miss the stern disapproval in Docilosa's tone.

There was no time to continue the conversation. A customer had arrived. Speaking a few words to Vettius over his shoulder, he entered. A big, burly man in a plain cloak and tunic, he had a sheathed *gladius* hanging from a belt. It was the mark of a soldier, thought Fabiola. Then he turned toward her, and her stomach turned over. There was no mistaking the determined blue eyes, the long straight nose and the mop of curly brown hair. It was Marcus Antonius.

"Surprise!" He half bowed, sending a strong whiff of wine in her direction.

"Antonius. What are you doing here?" Fabiola hissed. Her nerves were unraveling fast. Jovina was in the kitchen, but could venture up the corridor at any moment. If the old madam saw him, she would put two and two together in the blink of an eye. "You're drunk," she chided, taking his arm and trying to usher him toward the door.

Antonius wouldn't budge. "Might have had a little wine," he admitted with a grin. "Nothing wrong with that."

Fabiola hid her impatience. By now, she knew all about his excessive drinking. Antonius was a wild-living soldier who cared nothing for what others thought. He commonly attended political meetings while under the influence, and had even vomited in front of the entire Senate once. Now his bravado had brought him here, in broad daylight. "Are you alone?" she demanded.

"Of course." He sounded hurt. "No *lictores*, no guards. I even left my chariot at home." He tugged at his workingman's tunic. "Look. Just for you."

Impressed, she touched his cheek. Antonius' British war chariot was his pride and joy. So was his fondness for wearing military dress. "No one saw you coming in?"

"I hid my face all the way here," he declared, lifting a fold of his cloak dramatically. "Only the doorman knows."

"Good," replied Fabiola, but her worries remained. Even without his coterie of followers, Antonius was recognizable to all. Despite his protestations, he would have been noticed. On the other hand, it was excellent that Scaevola and his men would have seen him enter the Lupanar. They might think twice before attacking it again. But Antonius' visit was still a double-edged sword. Fabiola couldn't afford for him to stay longer than the time it would take to be entertained by a prostitute. He'd also have to leave discreetly, or Brutus would hear that the Master of the Horse, his enemy, was frequenting the Lupanar.

Antonius eyed her cleavage, and Fabiola felt a surge of desire. "I have to have you," he muttered. "Now."

Fabiola wanted him too. Badly. She glanced at Docilosa, who took the hint.

"I'll go and find Jovina," she declared. "There's something I need to ask her."

Bless her, thought Fabiola, knowing that the madam would be kept out of the way. *Despite what I do, Docilosa remains loyal. There'll be no problem when I tell her about Caesar. Romulus will return one day too. My actions won't interfere with that.* She lost track of any further coherent thought as Antonius dragged her into a lingering kiss. At length, Fabiola managed to pull away from his roaming hands. "Not here," she scolded. "We're practically in public view."

"All the better," Antonius growled. "I'd fuck you in front of all Rome."

Pouting, Fabiola led him to the first bedroom, which she knew was empty. Quickly they stripped off their clothes, squeezing and caressing each other's flesh in a tide of lust. Goose bumps rose on Fabiola's skin as Antonius kissed her neck and ran his fingertips slowly down her back and on to her buttocks. His hand paused for a moment before moving around to the front, and cupping Fabiola's moist sex. She moved her thighs apart to allow him to insert a finger. He moved it in and out, bending to suck on her nipples at the same time. It wasn't enough. Moaning, Fabiola pulled away and climbed onto the bed. On all fours, she looked back at him.

"Well?"

Growling, Antonius leaped up to join her. With a great shove, he thrust his erect member deep inside her. "Gods above, you feel good," he cried, moving his hips. Fabiola encouraged him, reaching back with one hand to pull him farther in. Driven by their lust, they moved faster and faster, losing all awareness of anything else. All that mattered was their overwhelming pleasure. Fabiola surrendered herself to her feelings. Sex had never felt like this before. As a prostitute, she had enjoyed it on a rare handful of occasions with young, attentive clients. With Brutus, it was nice; familiar even. Not once, though, had it been the same as this earth-moving sensation, which threatened to overcome her. Unconsciously, Fabiola's right hand slipped between her legs, searching. Her fingers slipped onto the nub of flesh she used to tease herself and began to rub. She pushed back against Antonius even harder.

A moment later, there was a quiet knock on the door. Fabiola barely heard it.

Antonius certainly didn't. Holding on to Fabiola's waist, he was driving into her, oblivious.

The second rap was louder. A low voice joined it. "Mistress?"

Fabiola stopped moving. "Vettius?" she said, astonished at the doorman's gall.

"Yes, Mistress."

Even from the other side of the door, Fabiola could sense his embarrassment. Her annoyance subsided. It had to be serious for the doorman to interrupt her at a time like this. "Is something wrong?"

Vettius coughed awkwardly. "Brutus is coming down the street. He's no more than a hundred paces away."

"You're sure?" cried Fabiola, her lustful thoughts vanishing into the ether. Brutus almost never visited the brothel. What did he want?

"Yes, Mistress," came the reply. "I can delay him at the door, but not for long."

"Do it," she hissed, already turning to Antonius. "Stop!"

He was too far gone. With his face flushed a deep red, he came inside her.

Fabiola pulled away and rounded on him. "Didn't you hear? Brutus will be here in a few moments."

Antonius' lip curled. "What do I care? You're mine, not his. Let the dog in and I'll soon put him right."

"No," Fabiola cried, seeing all her plans turning to dust. "He won't stand for it."

Antonius laughed and pointed at his *gladius*. "Will he not?"

Panic constricted Fabiola's throat. Even when he was naked, Antonius' arrogance knew no bounds. Pulling on her dress, she racked her brains for a way to budge him. "What would Caesar say to all this?" she finally demanded. "This is hardly fitting behavior for his deputy."

At once Antonius' expression became surly.

Fabiola knew she had him. He looked like a boy about to be disciplined by his father. "Do you want to bring disgrace down on Caesar? He's barely returned from Asia Minor, and you're bringing his name into disrepute." She shoved Antonius' tunic at him, and was relieved when he shrugged it over his shoulders. His *licium* followed, and then his belt. A few heartbeats later, Fabiola was pushing Antonius out into the reception area. "Go on," she said urgently. "Send a messenger next time."

He pulled her in for a last kiss. "What'll I say if Brutus sees me?" he asked, all innocence now.

"Tell him you'd been out drinking and heard about the new whores here. You wanted to try one out."

He liked that. "I'll say they're well worth the money!"

Fabiola smiled. "Leave," she pleaded. "Or my life won't be worth living."

"Can't have that now, can we?" Pinching her backside, Antonius bowed and was gone.

Fabiola took a couple of deep breaths. *Calm down*, she thought. On the narrow street Brutus could not miss Antonius; naturally, he would engage him in conversation. She had a little time. Darting into her office, Fabiola looked into the small bronze mirror on her desk. Her face was red and sweaty, and her normally immaculate hair had come undone. She looked disheveled—like someone who had just been having sex. That had to change—fast. Fabiola reached for one of the little clay vessels on the desktop, dabbing some white lead on her cheeks. An expert at applying makeup, she soon changed her appearance to a more sickly one. Leaving her hair down, she wiped away some of the sweat, but not all. She wanted to appear feverish.

It wasn't long before she heard Vettius talking to Brutus at the front door. True to his word, the huge doorman delayed him as long as possible. Fabiola panicked, suddenly unsure of her ability to deceive her lover yet again. Somehow, though, she had to.

"Fabiola?"

Her reflexes took over. "Brutus?" she said in a weak voice. "Is that you?"

"What are you doing in here?" He stood framed in the office doorway. "Gods, you look terrible. Are you ill?"

With relief flooding through her, Fabiola nodded. "I think I've got Docilosa's fever," she said.

Moving to Fabiola's side, Brutus lifted her chin. Studying her pale complexion and the bags she had carefully painted under her eyes, he swore. "Why are you even up?" he demanded in a worried voice. "You need a surgeon."

"I'm all right," Fabiola protested. "A day in bed and I'll be back to normal."

"Jovina should be looking after the front of the shop," he muttered.

"I know," said Fabiola. "I'm sorry."

His face softened. "No need to apologize, my love. But you're in no shape to be working."

Fabiola sat down on the edge of the desk with a sigh. "That's better," she sighed. There would be no rest until she discovered his purpose. "What brings you to the Lupanar so early in the morning?"

"I could say the same of Antonius," Brutus answered with a flash of anger. "What in the name of Hades did he want here?"

Careful, thought Fabiola. *Remember what you told Antonius to say.* "You know what he's like. He'd been on an all-night drinking session, and came in on impulse. Our advertisements about the new whores must be working." She smiled broadly.

Brutus scowled. "The prick should go somewhere else."

"He will," murmured Fabiola. "A man like him rarely plows the same furrow twice." The truth of her own words shocked her. Why was she risking everything with such a rake?

Brutus grimaced. "True enough." Then he grinned, becoming the person Fabiola was so fond of. "I came to see if you would accompany me to Caesar's games this morning, but with you being ill, it's out of the question, obviously."

Fabiola's ears pricked up. Even though Romulus was no longer a gladiator, she thought of him every time the arena was mentioned. "Is there something special on?"

"This morning, you mean?" Brutus looked pleased with himself. "Yes. There's a beast appearing that they call the Ethiopian bull. It's half the size of an elephant, but with two horns and an armored hide. Impossible to kill, apparently. I thought you'd like to see it."

Fabiola knew the animal wouldn't just be walking around to be admired. "Who's fighting it?"

Brutus shrugged. "A pair of *noxii*. Deserters from one of Caesar's legions, I think. No loss, in other words."

His casual manner made Fabiola feel nauseous. Who deserved to die like that? "Thank you," she whispered. "But I couldn't."

XI

THE ETHIOPIAN BULL

ONE HOUR LATER...

I t was only midmorning, but the amphitheater was already full. Above Romulus' head, the crowd was shouting with anticipation. All the prisoners knew why too, and fear stalked among them, increasing their unease. As a consequence of the street gossip that had swept into the *ludus* the previous afternoon, few had slept well. Memor had relished delivering the news himself, watching each man closely for signs of terror. Petronius had stared at the wall, refusing to meet the *lanista*'s gaze, but Romulus had been forced to. Two strapping gladiators had pinioned his arms while another pulled his head around to hear Memor reel off the host of fanged and toothed creatures they might be pitted against. In the face of such cruelty, he had managed to keep his composure—just.

Apparently Caesar had paid astronomical sums for the most exotic animals available. Some had never been seen in Rome before. Consequently, wildly inaccurate descriptions were rife. Waxing lyrical, Memor mentioned them all. Even the most common beasts to be used were enough to send men witless. Lions, tigers, leopards and bears were all lethal predators. Just as dangerous were elephants and wild bulls. Old memories had been triggered in Romulus' mind at the *lanista's* gruesome descriptions. He had witnessed a contest between *venatores* and big cats once before. Not one man had survived the brutal display, and the injuries they sustained before dying had been horrendous. Thankfully he'd concealed his distress from Memor, but his mind was filled all night with the images of the young *venator* who had endured only to be executed for his anger at the crowd's cruelty toward him. It was crushing to know that even if, by some miracle, he survived, there was virtually no chance of mercy. By dawn, Romulus' eyes were red-rimmed with exhaustion and fear. What he would have given to have had Brennus or Tarquinius by his side. But they were gone, long gone, and now he faced his own journey to Hades. Petronius' presence helped, but only a little.

During the march from the *ludus*, the guards had done nothing to stop their charges from being abused by the crowd. The degradation reminded Romulus of the walk he'd made through the streets of Seleucia before Crassus' execution. This felt even worse, though. Rather than being Parthian, his attackers were of his own nationality, and today he understood all the insults. Covered in spit, rotten fruit and vegetables, he and his companions had finally arrived at Pompey's magnificent complex on the Campus Martius, the plain of Mars. It was a place that Romulus had fought in before, but, hurried to the cells below the audience's seats, he did not get to appreciate its grandeur. With its people's theater, temple to Venus and chamber for the Senate, it was a monument to extravagance that had cost Pompey an absolute fortune to construct. Despite this, it had won him little popularity with the masses. His opulent house nearby stood empty now, its pattering fountains and graceful statues mocking Pompey's fall from grace.

At least the general's end in Egypt had been quick, thought Romulus. Infinitely better than what awaited him and the other men in the barred chamber. He tried not to think about what a lion's claws might feel like as they ripped apart his flesh. The pain as a bull gored him to death. Or having his head ripped off by an elephant—that was how he had seen Vahram, the cruel *primus pilus* of the Forgotten Legion, die. It was impossible now not to imagine these terrible fates. Romulus paced up and down, swallowing the bitter-tasting bile that kept rising from his stomach. His urge to vomit was overwhelming, but he would not let himself. Some prisoners were praying to their gods, while others just sat, staring into space. Petronius was furiously doing push-ups. *As if that would help,* thought Romulus. He said nothing, though. Each man faced death in his own manner, and it was not for him to laugh at it.

He and his companions were in an iron-barred cell beneath where the spectators sat. Theirs was just one of a line of similar cages, designed to hold gladiators, *venatores* and lowly *noxii*. Along the back of the pens ran a long passageway, with regular corridors down to the arena. Apart from the guards, there was no one else around. The gladiators who would fight later hadn't arrived yet, and the animals were kept in a separate area, which was even more secure. They could tell where it was from the cacophony of roars, snarls and bugling. Promising death in multiple ways, the noises chilled the blood.

It wasn't long before Memor reappeared, looking smug. Half a dozen guards with spears and bows were with him. Romulus knew where the *lanista* had been: settling the running order with the master of ceremonies. Deciding all of their fates. Nausea washed over him anew, and his knees wobbled. Locking them was the only way he could stay upright.

"Steady," whispered Petronius in his ear. "Don't give the fucker any satisfaction."

Quickly Romulus regained control. He glanced at his friend, nodding his thanks.

Memor came to a halt outside the cage and beamed in at them. "Who wants to go first?" he asked. "Any volunteers?"

Behind Romulus a man was sick, puking up the paltry breakfast of porridge they'd finally been given at the *ludus*. The acrid smell filled all of their nostrils, adding to the tension. No one spoke.

Ignoring Petronius' hisses, Romulus raised his hand. What did it matter which particular animal killed them? He just wanted to get it over with.

"Not you," growled the *lanista*. "Or your friend."

The pair exchanged a glance. He had something else planned for them. It wouldn't be a better way to die either.

No one else would look at Memor. Growing bored, he stabbed a finger at the three nearest men. "You, you and you can be the first act of the day. And your adversaries?" He paused, smiling cruelly. "A pack of starving wolves."

Romulus looked at the trio, and wished he hadn't. There was more fear in their faces than he'd ever seen on a battlefield. Perhaps Crassus' terror before he died had matched it, but he wasn't sure.

The exit into the arena was formed by the end of the corridor between the cages. Two of the guards were already busy lifting a giant locking bar that allowed them to open it. Once this was done, one pulled wide the cage door while his comrades stood by with ready spears.

"Outside," Memor ordered. "Now."

One of the prisoners ran to the bars and ripped open his tunic, exposing his chest. "Kill me now," he begged. "For the love of the gods, please!"

Indifferent, Memor studied his bitten fingernails. "Get them into the arena," he snapped. "Quickly."

The bowmen among his guards moved right up to the cage. Notching arrows to their strings, they leveled them at the unfortunate soldiers.

"They will loose on the count of three. First into your legs, and then your arms. After that, your groin," said the *lanista* calmly. "One."

The men looked at each other. A pair of them began to weep like children.

"Two."

With dragging feet, the condemned trio walked out into bright autumn sunlight.

Memor smiled as his guards closed off the exit.

Despite themselves, Romulus and Petronius rushed to the front of the cage. So did the three others. Through gaps in the brickwork, it was possible to see the circle of golden sand upon which so much blood was spilled. With a clean layer raked into place, it was empty except for their erstwhile comrades. Who, with their limbs paralyzed with fear, stayed close together.

A loud announcement was made that these were legionaries who had left their comrades to die at Zela. This was met with a chorus of insults from the audience. Pieces of bread and fruit rained down on the deserters' heads, and those in the front rows spat or threw coins. Cowering, the trio moved away from the hurled objects and into the center of the arena. Gradually the torrent of abuse died down. The master of ceremonies was waiting for this exact moment.

"Cowards like these deserve no mercy," he cried in a deep, booming voice. "What animal could deliver an apt punishment?"

Speculation from the curious crowd filled the air.

"The merciless creature which, if given the chance, will slaughter the shepherd's entire flock. Or attack the unwary traveler on a winter's night," the announcer shouted. "The mighty wolf!"

Cheers of excitement greeted this revelation.

Falling to his knees, one of the men raised his hands to the heavens, which prompted more whistles and catcalls of delight. Nobody was going to help this wretch. His companions shuffled from foot to foot, their gaze fixed on the other side of the arena. Romulus saw at once what was attracting their attention. There were three metal grilles set close together in the enclosure's wall. Already they were opening, pulled upward by ropes attached to a ring at the top of each. No doubt urged by spiked prods wielded by their out-of-sight handlers, eight lithe animals emerged into the light. Their thick fur was a combination of colors from gray to brown or black, and they stood larger than most dogs. With intelligent faces and pricked upright ears, they were magnificent examples of the wolf, which lived all over Italy.

Romulus held his breath. He had only rarely glimpsed these creatures before, in the mountains of the countries he'd marched through. Wary of humans under normal circumstances, they lived as far from them as possible. Of course it didn't stop hunters trapping them for events like this, and despite the artificial environment, the wolves would not hold back from killing the three soldiers. Although their heavy coats hid the evidence, they were starving. To make sure of a good spectacle, the beast handlers would have given them no food for many days.

Sure enough, the predators had only advanced a few steps before their gaze fixed on the arena's occupants. Growling and snarling, they immediately split up, some moving straight at the soldiers, while others went to either side. Then they began to close in, slinking along with their bellies almost touching the sand.

"I've seen them chasing a deer in the hills near my home," Petronius muttered. "It's incredible to watch. They hunt together, like a team."

Although filled with horror, Romulus could not drag his eyes away. The man who had fallen to his knees was now praying loudly to Mars, and begging for forgiveness. The other two had moved back to back and were shouting threats and waving their arms to keep the wolves at bay. It made little difference, and the audience howled with amusement and bloodlust at their helplessness. More food and coins were thrown in an attempt to anger the wolves, but few struck their targets.

It didn't matter, thought Romulus. The crowd was going to get its wish soon enough.

Sensing his weakness, the predators moved in on the kneeling figure first. Two leaped at the same time, grabbing him by the arm and neck and knocking him to the ground with ease. Savaging the howling soldier's flesh with their powerful jaws, they held him down as their companions swarmed in for a feed. The man struggled and thrashed about, his screams piteous to hear. Thankfully the din did not last for long, but it was enough for the two other legionaries to lose all self-control. Hopeful of a last-chance redemption, one ran to the edge of the enclosure where a prominent noble was sitting. There he begged for his life. It made no difference: His potential savior completely ignored him, drinking wine from a silver goblet rather than look down. When the soldier tried to climb out of the arena, guards thrust at him menacingly with their long spears. This didn't stop his now crazed efforts to escape, and at length he was stabbed in the chest. Dying, he was thrown back onto the hot sand. Three wolves began feeding on him at once, ripping open his belly to get at his intestines first.

Meanwhile, the last deserter made for the exit from which he'd been expelled, and began ripping at the bricks with his bare hands. "Help me," he shouted, reaching his bloodied fingers through a tiny gap in the wall. "For pity's sake!" From only an arm's length away, Romulus and Petronius watched in total revulsion as a wolf jumped onto the man's back. Placing its large paws on his shoulders, it sank its teeth into the back of his head. Stumbling backward with his arms flailing, the soldier was a perfect target for another wolf. It darted in and grabbed hold of his groin, eliciting a cry of agony that made Romulus wince and turn aside.

He could not block out the terrible sounds of distress as the deserter was torn apart half a dozen paces away. Or the delirious shouts from the people sitting overhead. While Romulus had no sympathy for men who would run and leave their comrades in the midst of a battle, he didn't think that they deserved to die like sheep, or deer. Crucifixion was brutal beyond belief, but this was worse. To the rabid citizens above, however, this was justice being done.

It was a long while before all the shrieking stopped, but the men's deaths did not bring silence to the arena. Instead the screams were replaced by the growls of wolves arguing over their prey, and the noise of bones being cracked by powerful jaws. The spectators began to lose interest and soon, the predators were forced out of the arena by dozens of slaves. While some banged drums and cymbals to cause confusion, others carried shields and flat pieces of wood. Walking close together in a long line, they herded the wolves back through the open grilles and into their cages.

During this interlude, Memor reappeared in the corridor. With a cruel wink at Romulus, he picked the second trio of soldiers and sent them out to face two bears and a pair of wild bulls. Still giving the friends no clue as to what they'd face, he disappeared again. Romulus' stomach clenched into a tight knot, and he sat down. He was damned if he'd watch another spectacle like the previous one. Besides, his fear was threatening to overcome him. Although death had been omnipresent in his life since Gemellus had sold him into the Ludus Magnus, some tiny chance of survival had always appeared. He'd beaten an older, more experienced gladiator; he'd survived the slaughter at Carrhae to be taken prisoner; he'd escaped the almost-certain annihilation of the Forgotten Legion by a vast Indian army. Now, with his ears ringing with the dying howls of his fellow captives, his life seemed to have come to a complete dead end.

He glanced at Petronius, who was sitting beside him. The veteran's eyes were closed, and he was muttering a prayer to Jupiter. *He's more composed than I am*, thought Romulus with surprise, *and the poor bastard shouldn't even be here. He could have walked away and left me to it. A true friend, he didn't.* Shame filled Romulus. How could Petronius face death like a man when he was acting like a scared child? His comrade deserved more respect.

"Time's up," Memor's voice broke in.

Romulus looked up. Hands on hips, the smirking *lanista* was standing a few paces away. Only the metal of the cage separated them. "What I'd give for a chance to rip your throat out," he said from between gritted teeth.

Memor grinned. "Sorry," he said. "If that happened, my guards would kill you. Then the good people of Rome wouldn't get to see the final spectacle of the morning. Can't have that, can we?"

Romulus got to his feet.

Deep in his own world, Petronius stayed where he was.

Dusting his hands off, Romulus moved right up to the bars. All he was going to show from this moment on was steely determination. "What have you got in store for us, you old shitbag?" he demanded fiercely.

Surprised, Memor took a step back. He was quick to recover his poise, though. "An Ethiopian bull," he replied. "Some call it a rhinoceros."

Studiously ignoring the *lanista*, Petronius stood up and watched the guards opening the exit. The only sign of his inner tension was his jaw clenching and unclenching. The wilder rumors in the *ludus* had included an armored beast with the colloquial name of "Ethiopian bull." They had been terrifying.

Trying to protect his friend, Romulus had denied all knowledge of it. A pointless gesture, he now saw. He gripped the bars tightly, remembering the capture of a rhino he'd witnessed when working for Hiero. It had taken nearly a score of slaves with ropes and nets to subdue the giant two-horned creature enough to get it in a cage. More than one slave had died in the process. Plenty of others had been hurt in the weeks and months that followed. Irritable and aggressive, the rhino had been Hiero's prize capture. It could even be the same beast, Romulus reflected. How ironic. He closed his eyes and sent up a prayer to Mithras. *Grant us a swift death.*

Memor chuckled. "You should never have run away," he said, almost regretfully. "Might have even won a *rudis* by this stage. Made me a fortune in the process. Now look at you."

There was a clunking sound as the heavy planks of the exit were lifted and then placed on the ground. Blinding sunlight poured into the cage, making it difficult to see out into the arena. As usual in breaks between bouts, the audience was largely silent. All that could be heard were the voices of mobile food vendors hawking their wares of sausages, bread and watered-down wine, and bookmakers offering odds on the gladiator fights that would take place later in the day.

"Burn in Hades, Memor," Romulus spat. Without waiting for a response, he trotted out onto the sand. It was the only gesture of defiance he could make. That, and dying like a man.

Casting dreadful aspersions on the *lanista*'s parentage, Petronius followed.

Memor did not reply. Instead the planks were replaced, leaving the friends stranded in the arena. People noticed the activity on the sand, and turned from their conversations. "Deserter scum," shouted a portly figure in a ragged tunic. "Cowards," cried another. Their accusations were infectious and soon insults were pouring down on the pair.

The fact that desertion was not their crime was irrelevant, thought Romulus. Place anyone in this circle of death and the citizens would assume that they were guilty. And he was, technically. Although he'd been press-ganged into the Twenty-Eighth, Romulus had joined Crassus' army as a slave. Yet, even facing this most brutal of ends, he was glad that he had. What momentous things he had seen in only eight years—and what friends he'd made in Brennus, Tarquinius and Petronius. His only regret now was not being able to speak with Fabiola for just a few moments. That, and not being reconciled with the haruspex.

"This Ethiopian bull," said Petronius. "Does it really have a horn as long as a man's arm?"

"Yes." Romulus could still picture the slave he'd seen being gored by Hiero's rhinoceros. His had been a lingering death. "At least that length."

"It's twice as big as any bull?"

"Or more," Romulus admitted. "Aggressive too. One small help is that it's half-blind."

"So what? We can't hide anywhere." Fear surfaced on Petronius' face at last, but he did not panic. "What do you think we should do?" he asked, his deferential tone giving Romulus the leader's role.

Romulus scanned the perimeter of the enclosure. There were no spikes to prevent animals jumping out, but at regular intervals stood spearmen and archers. Any attempt to escape would win them the same fate as the deserter a short time previously. He looked up at the sky, hoping against hope to be given a sign. A clue. Anything at all. He wasn't. It was just another glorious autumn morning. "Don't know," he said heavily. "I can't think."

Petronius barked a derisory laugh. "Me neither," he said. "Still, it was good knowing you."

"Aye, comrade," answered Romulus. "It was."

Ignoring the shouts of the crowd, they gripped forearms.

A short delay followed. Initially, Romulus thought it was a cynical ploy by Memor or the master of ceremonies to increase their fear and terror. He caught sight of the *lanista* making his way to the seating area just to one side of the dignitaries' box, which was protected from the hot sun by the *velarium*, a large cloth awning. As the man responsible for providing the deserters, Memor had to be on hand if the *editor*, or sponsor, wanted to quiz him. Today, of course, this was none other than Caesar himself. The great general's seat was empty, though. The box was occupied only by the announcer, a short figure with oiled hair and a self-important manner, and a couple of bored-looking senior officers. Caesar probably wouldn't turn up until much later in the day, thought Romulus. What interest would he have in watching men being torn apart by beasts? There was no martial skill in that.

"Why haven't they sent the damn thing in?" asked Petronius uneasily. "I just want it to be over."

Without answering, Romulus studied the crowd.

Even it had fallen silent.

Romulus cocked his head and listened.

A moment later, *bucinae* blared from outside the amphitheater. An expectant air fell over the waiting citizens, and the master of ceremonies jumped to his feet, self-consciously patting his pomaded hair. Memor looked over his shoulder, and Romulus gasped. "It's Caesar," he whispered. "He's come to watch us."

Petronius managed a laugh. "Us losers? He'd want to see the Ethiopian bull far more."

Romulus smiled lopsidedly. "True enough."

A party of legionaries led by a distinguished-looking centurion emerged into the box, giving it a quick once-over. When the officer was happy, the announcer was given a nod.

Raising his hands to attract attention, he stepped forward. "Citizens of Rome. Earlier than expected, we are to be graced by the presence of the *editor* of today's games!" He paused.

Excitement rippled through the spectators, and suddenly all eyes were on the dignitaries' box. A few of the more enthusiastic in the crowd began to clap and cheer.

"He is the conqueror of Gaul, Britannia and Germania," cried the master of ceremonies. "Savior of the Republic. The victor at Pharsalus, in Egypt and in Asia Minor!"

Always happy to hear of Roman military successes won in their name or otherwise, the audience yelled approval. Thanks to Caesar's well-oiled propaganda machine, they were fully up to score with his awesome credentials, and loved him for it. Caesar had been immensely popular for years, and his recent victories over Pompey and the diehard Republicans were regarded by most in the same light as his previous triumphs. A man who lived by the same creed as his soldiers, who always won when it seemed impossible, Caesar embodied the stubborn nature of Rome.

"Descended from Venus herself, and the most important scion of the Julii clan," bellowed the announcer. He waved his arms, stirring up the crowd even more. "I give you the recent victor at Zela: Julius Caesar!"

This was met with the loudest roar of all.

A trio of slaves appeared in the arena. Each bore a placard upon which had been inscribed a single short word. The first read "Veni," the second "Vidi," and the last "Vici." Yet again, Romulus was impressed by Caesar's self-confidence. I came, I saw, I conquered. This succinct appraisal of the battle had swept through Caesar's celebrating army, and now it was being used to win over the Roman mob. Judging from their uproarious response, the move was a shrewd one.

Then the man himself appeared in the box. Clad in a white toga with a purple stripe running around its edge, Caesar acknowledged the people's cries with languid waves of his right hand. A good number of staff officers, senators and hangers-on crammed in behind him, eager to share in the glory. Of course the watching citizens did not give a jot for anyone except Caesar. The applause went on long after he'd taken a seat.

Meanwhile Romulus and Petronius stood on the hot sand, waiting to die.

After several circuits, the slaves bearing the placards disappeared from sight, and the self-important announcer waved for calm. There was a gradual reduction in the noise levels as the excited audience sat down, eager for the next part of the show to begin.

"In his generosity, Caesar has today arranged for an animal

never seen before in Rome. Captured in the wilds of eastern Africa, it has been transported here for your pleasure. Many men have died to bring it to this arena. Now it will kill two more: the *noxii* before you."

There was a deliberate pause, and the crowd shuddered with anticipation.

"Bigger than the largest of oxen, fiercer than a lion, and with an armored skin tougher than the legionaries' *testudo*, Caesar presents—the Ethiopian bull!"

Romulus and Petronius exchanged a glance full of fear—and determination.

Moving silently on oiled pulleys and chains, a large iron portcullis opposite Caesar's position rose up. Soon a gaping black square was visible: the opening into a cage. Nothing emerged, and Romulus had a momentary fantasy that the creature within had already managed to escape. Loud shouts and the sound of weapons being dashed off bars deep inside the bowels of the amphitheater soon dispelled this hope.

There was a series of annoyed grunts and then an immense brown-skinned animal trotted onto the sand. Hairless except for the tips of its wide ears and the end of its tail, it had a long, sloping head. From its nose projected two sharp, fearsome-looking horns. Its feet were large and three-toed, and there was a prominent hump of bone at the base of the skull, between the ears.

The rhino paused, its small, piggy eyes squinting as they adjusted to the bright light.

As one, the audience gasped with shock at the creature's outlandish appearance. This was stranger than the giraffe and zebras imported by Pompey, and more exotic than the elephants they were now used to seeing on a regular basis.

Romulus' heart stopped. It was bigger and more dangerous-looking than he remembered. "If we stay still, it won't see us," he whispered to Petronius.

"What damn good is that?" the other retorted.

Knowing that the two soldiers might try this ruse, Memor nodded at the archers, who loosed half a dozen arrows into the air. Aimed carefully, they smacked into the sand a few paces short of the pair's position. Their message was clear: Move, or the next ones won't miss.

Romulus took a step forward, his mouth dry with tension.

Smirking, the bowmen relaxed.

The rhino's head turned at the movement. It snorted with suspicion.

Romulus froze. So did Petronius, who was picking up an arrow.

The armored beast squealed a few times, and then pawed the ground. It had seen them.

Closing his eyes, Romulus prayed with all the fervor he could muster. *Let me die fighting at least, great Mithras. Not like this.*

Lowering its head, the rhino charged.

XII

ROMULUS AND CAESAR

Within a few heartbeats, the rhino was thundering toward them at full gallop. Although the arena was large, it would be upon them in a few moments. Despite this, Romulus' feet felt anchored to the spot. His life was over. In slow motion, he scanned the watching crowds. The wealthy toga-clad nobles and the grimy poor in their threadbare tunics. Caesar, on his velvet cushion, with his followers and soldiers arrayed around him. The greasy master of ceremonies. Memor, who looked delighted now that Romulus' fate was sealed. The guards on the edge of the enclosure with their bows and spears.

A daring plan took root in his mind.

"Quick! Grab an arrow," hissed Petronius. "It'll be some kind of defense."

"I've got a better idea," muttered Romulus. "You go left, and I'll go right."

"Why?"

"The beast can only follow one of us. When it does, the second can try to grab a spear from a guard." Romulus jerked his head at the nearest. "Look. It's pointing downward, in case he needs to use it quickly. A lot of them are standing like that. Jump up, give the shaft a hard yank and there's a chance of gaining a weapon that would actually be useful. Then the one who's armed can protect the other."

"The archers will be ordered to shoot us down if we do that," breathed Petronius. A fierce spark lit in his eyes nonetheless. "Won't they?"

"Probably. It'll be dangerous for both of us."

There was a heartbeat's pause as both considered the obvious: Whoever the rhino pursued would die.

"It's worth a try," said Petronius after a moment's consideration.

"Better than just dying like cowards."

"It is." Petronius took a deep breath. "Ready?"

The ground was already shaking from the rhino's approach. Its head was down, presenting the most terrifying of sights: its long front horn, which could gore deep into flesh. If it missed, the creature's wide skull, backed up by the weight of fifteen men, would smash bones, crush ribs, or both. Helpless from any of these injuries, its victim would then be trampled to death.

"Go!" shouted Romulus. Arms and legs pumping, he sprinted off to one side. His fear gave him an extra turn of speed, but he dared not look around until he'd counted fifteen or twenty paces. Then, not having been run down, he glanced back. His heart rose to his mouth as he saw the rhino charging after Petronius. With a daring jink to one side, the veteran avoided its first attempt to gore him in the back. He was now running in the opposite direction to it. Not for long. The enormous beast turned remarkably fast and pounded after Petronius again. With nowhere to hide, it would only be moments before it caught up.

Romulus turned away. Every single instant was vital. If both of them weren't soon to be bloody corpses on the sand, he had to forget Petronius. The guard he'd seen slouching over the low side of the enclosure was about two dozen steps away. Gripped by the action, the man hadn't moved, and his dangling spear was just within arm's reach. Acting as if he was searching for an exit, Romulus ran along the brickwork, silently counting his strides. He was careful to keep his gaze averted from the spearman.

The air filled with insults as the nearby spectators showed their contempt for his perceived cowardice. "Miserable dog!" "Trying to save your own skin? Fool!" "Spineless whoreson!" Romulus ran on regardless. In the distance, he could still hear the angry snorts of the rhino. There had been no screams, however, which gave him heart that it had not yet killed Petronius. Ten steps. Fifteen.

Romulus gritted his teeth as he drew closer. The guard had to be watching whatever was happening to poor Petronius, or he was lost. Twenty paces and he risked a look up. The broad-leafed blade was pointing downward, its dull-witted owner oblivious to his approach. *Mithras, help me*, he thought. One more step, and Romulus bent his knees, leaping high into the air. With both hands, he grabbed hold of the shaft just below the head and pulled downward. There was a strangled cry of surprise as the guard followed his weapon into the arena. Landing awkwardly, he found himself staring up at his own spear, which Romulus had reversed to point at his heart. The man had enough sense not to reach for his sword.

"Stay there, you bastard," growled Romulus before tearing off to help Petronius. As he ran, he could hear the angry shouts of the other guards and the shocked cries of the spectators. Arrows and spears would be loosed at him any instant, but he couldn't think about that. What was happening before his eyes was far worse than that. Romulus cursed himself that he had not run faster. The rhino had already struck Petronius a glancing blow. Although his friend was still running, he was listing to one side and clutching his ribs. His free hand clutched his only weapon, the useless arrow. The damn beast was right behind him too.

Romulus gauged the distance between them. Thirty paces at least.

If he threw the spear now, it had little chance of even hurting the rhino.

If he didn't, Petronius was a dead man.

Romulus slowed down, and closed his left eye. Taking aim at the armored beast's shoulder, he hurled the spear forward in a powerful curving trajectory. As he did, his gaze locked with that of Petronius. The veteran gave him the tiniest of smiles. It spoke a thousand emotions. Pride that Romulus' attempt had been successful. Respect for his courage and ability. And the love that comrades bear each other.

The spear came down at speed, striking the rhino squarely between the shoulder blades. It glanced off its thick hide.

"No!" Romulus screamed.

The creature's front horn hit Petronius in the middle of his back, lifting him high in the air. Punching through his abdomen with ease, it emerged red-tipped from just under his sternum. A great cry of agony left Petronius' lips. Spitted like a wild boar on a spear, he struggled to free himself as the rhino shook him effortlessly from side to side.

Cheers of excitement rose from the crowd. Mingled with these were shouted commands.

Overcome by grief, Romulus paused. He was dimly aware that no one had shot him down yet, but he did not know why.

Blood dribbled from Petronius' lips as the rhino dropped its head and let him fall. It moved back a step, preparing to smash him into a pulp. Then it saw Romulus. Pawing the ground with a huge foot, it bellowed with anger. Here was another troublesome human to kill. Ignoring Petronius, it began to move toward Romulus.

That's it, he thought, looking at the spear, which was lying on the sand behind the rhino. *My effort was wasted, and I'm a goner.*

Somehow Petronius dragged himself partially upright. Along with the blood that was streaming from the gaping hole in his belly, there were loops of torn intestine and feces visible. "You ugly brute," he shouted, ashen-faced. "Come back."

As Petronius had intended, the rhino's attention was drawn from Romulus. Grunting, it turned around.

Romulus came alive again. Even as he died, Petronius was trying to buy him time. He could not waste that. As the rhino smashed its head down on his friend's already broken body, he darted around the bloody sight to the spear. The long wooden shaft felt hot in his hand as he swept it up. It was a heavy hunting weapon with a leaf-shaped iron blade, suitable for killing boar or lion. Romulus had no idea whether it could do the same to the mighty creature that had killed Petronius. For that was surely what had happened. The rhino had now struck his comrade several times with immense force. He'd heard a muffled cry after the first impact, but nothing since.

Something made Romulus look up at the nearest spectators. Without realizing, he had moved to stand just below the dignitaries' box. Not twenty steps away was Julius Caesar, his face alive with interest. Romulus glanced at the closest guards, who had their weapons raised and ready. Remarkably, they were not aiming at him. *I am being allowed to fight on,* he realized with a thrill. Turning his gaze back to the rhino, Romulus winced. It had finished with Petronius' corpse, which was now nothing more than a misshapen bundle of bloody rags. It hadn't seen him. Not moving a muscle, he waited to see what it would do.

Snorting through its broad nostrils, the beast walked away from Romulus. *Its eyesight really is poor,* he thought with a flush of excitement. It gave him the tiniest window of hope. *Now I might have a chance of striking a lucky blow. But where?* Before he'd moved a step, Romulus despaired. The rhino's hide was thicker than the chain mail worn by legionaries. Stabbing it in the hindquarters or even its belly would not kill, or even wound it badly enough to stop it goring or trampling him. Its massive bony head was invulnerable, and the great muscles of its neck afforded no weakness either. *Its heart,* he thought. *Somehow I have to reach that.*

The rhino was now about twenty paces away, and impatient members of the crowd were throwing things at it to make it turn around. All this did was to anger the creature even more, and it trotted toward the far side of the enclosure.

Romulus took a step toward it, and another. Each one he took made it easier to continue, but then he had to pass by Petronius' mangled remains. Romulus couldn't help himself. He looked down, and revulsion filled him. His friend's features were barely recogniz-able amid the blood and broken bones of his skull. Fury bubbled up in Romulus that a trusted comrade had died like this. It was so un-just. The least he could do was to make a good attempt at killing the rhino. With renewed determination, he gripped the spear with both hands. Instead of advancing, he retreated toward the timber planking of the enclosure's edge. A truly desperate idea was germi-nating in his mind.

Catcalls and jeers erupted from the watching citizens.

They died away when Romulus shouted at the rhino. "Come on," he yelled. "Here I am."

Despite the clamor, the creature heard his cry. Spinning more gracefully than he could have imagined, it raised its head and bugled a challenge. Its front horn was red and sticky all the way down to its base. *That's Petronius' blood,* thought Romulus with a tremor of fear. Warm wood touched his back and he stopped. *Mine will soon join it— but maybe not, if the gods are willing. Either way, this is the end of the line.* He was glad that it would be over quickly. This level of dread was hard to live with. Planting his feet wide, Romulus watched as the rhino gave more indications that it was about to charge. Pawing the sand, it flattened its wide ears and snorted. Its head went up and down a few times, and then it came for him. Picking up pace, it quickly reached the speed of a galloping horse.

Shouts and cheers rose from the spectators, who were at last getting what they wanted. Their jaded palates had been tickled by the bizarre-looking rhino, but all the running about was boring. Soon this idiot would be crushed against the wall, and then the gladiator fights—the real entertainment—could begin.

Although it was utterly terrifying, Romulus stood his ground. Where could he run to, anyway? At least now he was armed, and could give a good account of himself before he was sent to Elysium. His pulse was going like a trip-hammer, and all he could think of was the people he had loved. His mother. Fabiola. Juba. Brennus. Tarquinius. And brave Petronius. His sister was the only one who was definitely alive, but he would still never see her again. *Gods grant that Fabiola is well, and happy,* thought Romulus. *I will see her one day, in paradise.* With that, he readied himself for the only move he could think of. He tossed the spear off to his right, making sure it landed straight, with its point toward him.

The audience responded with incredulous laughs. "Too scared to use it now?" shouted one man.

The sand beneath Romulus' feet began to shake. The rhino loomed larger and larger in his vision. Every instinct he possessed was screaming at him to run, to hide, to jump out of the way. He thought his heart was going to leap out of his chest, but somehow Romulus managed to keep his feet right where they were. If he moved prematurely, the rhino would turn and catch him. If he left it a heartbeat too late, it would smash every bone in his body against the wall behind.

His entire world had shrunk to a tunnel directly in front of him. It was filled with the angry rhino.

Romulus thought his muscles would remain frozen when the time came to move. *Great Mithras, give me courage,* he pleaded. An image of Brennus standing alone against the elephant flashed before his eyes. Then one of Petronius, buying him time. Romulus grimaced.

That was enough. There was time for a last deep breath before the armored beast hit him and ended this charade forever.

He took it.

With the rhino no more than three steps away, he hurled himself to one side.

There was an almighty crash as the creature collided with the heavy timber planks, breaking some and cracking others. Its momentum was such that its horns and the front half of its head drove through to the other side, trapping it. Flying splinters covered Romulus' back as he landed face first in the sand. Fortunately he'd closed his eyes, so the yellow grains only filled his mouth. Above and behind him, he heard the furious rhino thrashing to free itself from the wooden prison around its massive neck. Angry bellows echoed through the planking as it pushed and pulled. Ominous creaking sounds told Romulus that he didn't have long.

Desperate, he got to his knees and faced his foe. He was so close that he could have reached out and touched its armored brown hide. A kicking hind leg nearly brained Romulus as his right hand reached out, searching in the sand for the spear. Where was the damn thing? He began to panic. The rhino's struggling was so dangerous that he couldn't afford to look down. When his fingers closed on the wooden shaft, he gasped out loud with relief. Lifting the spear, Romulus studied the great expanse of leathery skin before him. It was just possible to make out the ribs. From his hunting experiences, he knew the heart's position behind the left elbow. Yet the foreleg on this side was pawing about so much he couldn't get a clear thrust in.

A number of timbers broke at once and the rhino lurched backward a step.

Romulus cursed. If he didn't act now, all his efforts would have been in vain. Trusting his skill, he shoved the spear into the rhino's side with all his might. He felt the blade grate off a rib, slow down momentarily and then slide deep inside the chest cavity.

Romulus ran the shaft in to the length of his forearm and more, twisting it to make sure. The sharp blade had to do many things: slice apart lung tissue, cut large blood vessels and penetrate the heart. It had to do all of those to bring down this leviathan.

A deafening bellow left the rhino's throat, and it broke free of the planking. Staggering backward, it coughed up a fist-sized ball of bloody froth. To Romulus' horror, its beady eyes fixed on him. They were still just a few paces apart. Good killing distance. *I had my chance,* thought Romulus, his hope turning to despair. *I wasn't good enough.*

The rhino took a step toward him, and then its front legs buckled and gave way. Its hindquarters followed suit, and it sank down with a groan. Torrents of pinkish fluid began to pour from its mouth, staining the sand. More was issuing from around the spear shaft, which was jutting from its chest. From the blood's bright red color, Romulus knew that he'd hit a major artery. He didn't know how, but he'd delivered the rhino a mortal blow. Gratitude filled every pore of his being. Petronius had been honored, and avenged. No doubt the archers would loose any moment, and end his life. But when he entered Elysium, Romulus knew that he could hold his head up high, even among heroes like Brennus and Petronius.

He came back to the present as the rhino kicked a few more times. A moment later, the great horned head slumped forward and lay still.

Silence covered the huge amphitheater like a blanket.

Romulus glanced up at the stunned and shocked faces of the audience. No one could believe what he'd done. It was unthinkable that an unarmed man could survive a bout against a creature as fearsome as the rhinoceros.

A pair of hands began to clap. Slowly at first, but then the speed increased.

When the crowd saw who was applauding, they hastily joined in.

Cheers and shouts of congratulation replaced the vitriol that had fallen on Romulus' ears only moments before. The hypocrisy of it was stupendous.

Romulus looked up, and saw that it was Julius Caesar himself who was leading the ovation. A great lump of pride filled his throat, and tears pricked his eyes. At least one person present could see his bravery. Somehow this recognition eased the pain of Petronius' death.

"Who is this man?" cried Caesar. "Bring him to me at once!"

The master of ceremonies scurried over to a furious-looking Memor and whispered in his ear. The impotent rage twisting the *lanista*'s face quickly disappeared and he set off down the nearest set of stairs. The thunderous applause continued, and Romulus took the opportunity to honor Petronius' body. He hadn't been afforded this luxury with Brennus, which made it all the more important. Turning his back on Caesar, Romulus crouched down and clasped the veteran's bloodied right hand in his. "Thank you, comrade. I will ask that the proper rites are performed. That you have a decent grave," he whispered. Unlike Brennus, whose body was probably picked over by birds of carrion. Tears ran down Romulus' cheeks as he gently closed Petronius' staring eyes. "Go well."

When he stood, there were four of Memor's men pointing spears at his chest. The *lanista* was just behind them. There was a grudging respect in all of their gazes, except for Memor, who looked like a snake deprived of its prey. Romulus didn't care. Greater people were now involved, and the *lanista* would no longer decide his fate. In a tight phalanx, the five forced him back under the seating, past the cages and outside again. They entered the spectators' part of the arena, a novel experience for Romulus. It was too much to take in. He was still reeling from the shock of Petronius' death and the enormity of what he'd done.

Emerging from the dark into bright sunlight again, Romulus

squinted. He was now in the dignitaries' box, surrounded by legionaries, high-ranking officers and senators. In their eyes he saw a mixture of emotions: respect, amazement and fear; and, in a few, revulsion and jealousy. Awe filled his own heart as he was shoved forward to stand before Caesar. Although Romulus had seen the general numerous times when in the Twenty-Eighth, he'd never been this close. In late middle age, with thinning gray hair, prominent nose and high cheekbones, Caesar was nothing special to look at. Despite this, his self-confidence was obvious and there was a palpable aura of command about him. Instinctively Romulus bowed from the waist.

"Leave us," Caesar ordered Memor's men. He jabbed a finger at the *lanista*'s chest. "You stay."

Bowing and scraping, the guards vanished.

"I understand that this slave was to die as a *noxius* for illegally joining the legions?"

"Yes, sir."

Caesar frowned. "And the other?"

"His comrade, sir. Apparently the idiot tried to defend him when he was exposed."

"Someone also tells me that you used to own this slave. Is that true?"

"Indeed, sir. I bought him as a boy. He was trained to be a *secutor*," replied Memor in an unctuous tone. "But he ran away more than eight years ago. Murdered a noble, you see."

Caesar's gaze fell on Romulus. "Two capital offenses," he said softly.

What have I to lose, thought Romulus. "I didn't kill the nobleman, sir," he protested.

"He would say that, sir," Memor interjected.

"Keep quiet," snapped Caesar, his dislike of the *lanista* obvious. "If you didn't, who did?" he asked Romulus.

"My friend, sir."

"Him down there?"

"No, sir. Another man—an Etruscan."

"Where is he?"

"I don't know, sir," Romulus answered truthfully. "He disappeared in Alexandria after being wounded by an Egyptian sling stone." Responding to Caesar's surprised look, he explained. "We were both forced to join the Twenty-Eighth."

Caesar seemed amused. "You had no choice in the matter?"

"No, sir."

"Innocent of all crimes, eh?" Caesar tapped a fingernail against his teeth. "That's what everyone says."

His legionaries tittered.

"I am guilty of one charge, sir," Romulus butted in. He would pretend no longer.

"Which is?"

"When my friend and I ran from the *ludus*, we joined a mercenary cohort in Crassus' army. Told them we were Gaulish tribesmen."

"This story gets taller and taller," scoffed Caesar. He glanced at Memor and saw him trying to conceal his reaction. His expression grew fierce. "Speak!"

"I heard that rumor, sir," the *lanista* admitted reluctantly. "After the news of Carrhae, I never thought to see the whoreson again."

"There are few whoresons who can kill a rhinoceros single-handed," mused Caesar. "So you and the other prisoners were taken to Margiana?"

"Yes, sir. Fifteen hundred miles from Seleucia, to the ends of the earth," said Romulus, staring into the general's eyes. "The Forgotten Legion, we called ourselves."

There was a small smile of acknowledgment. "Yet you escaped. That was well done. Did you have companions?"

"One, sir. The same man who killed the nobleman," answered Romulus, starting to prune his story. There was no point stretching

Caesar's tolerance too far. "We reached Barbaricum and found passage to Egypt, but our ship was wrecked on the Ethiopian coast. Luckily we survived, and the gods continued to show us favor. A *bestiarius* took us on, and we traveled with him to Alexandria."

"Where you joined the Twenty-Eighth."

Romulus nodded.

"I've heard many tall stories, but this is the best yet," Caesar cried.

More hoots of amusement rang out from his followers, and Romulus realized that his fate was still most uncertain. Caesar's next move was therefore most unexpected.

"Longinus!" the general called. "Where are you?"

A grizzled officer in an ill-fitting toga stood up. "Sir?"

"Ask this slave about Carrhae. Questions that no one else but a veteran of the battle could answer."

Longinus glared, his whole stance showing that *he* didn't believe Romulus' story. "How did Crassus' son die?" he demanded.

"Publius led a combined charge of cavalry and mercenaries against the Parthians, sir," replied Romulus at once. "The enemy pretended to flee, but then they swept around his forces and slaughtered nearly every man. Only twenty mercenaries were allowed to return. Then the bastards cut off his head, and paraded it in front of the whole army."

Longinus was too plain a man to conceal his surprise. "He's right, sir."

"Keep asking."

Obediently, the officer interrogated Romulus about Crassus' whole campaign. All his answers were correct, and at last Longinus gave in. "He must have been there, sir," he admitted. "Or else he's been talking to every survivor who made it home."

"I see." There was a long silence as Caesar considered his options.

Romulus looked out at the battered shape that was Petronius' body. He'd probably be joining him very soon. *So be it,* he thought. *I don't care any longer. I have done my best.*

"I have seen many things as a general and a leader of men." Caesar's voice was pitched to carry around the whole amphitheater. "Never have I seen such bravery as these two *noxii* showed today, though. Unarmed and condemned to die, one was resourceful enough to steal a spear from a half-asleep guard. Disregarding his own safety, he tried to wound the rhinoceros in order to save his friend." Caesar looked around at the audience, which was hanging on his every word.

Romulus was stunned. *Maybe I'm dreaming, or already dead,* he thought.

"The *noxius* failed, but then his comrade bought him some time with his own life. Even though the survivor was then armed with a spear, I thought that the beast would kill him. But it didn't! Against all the odds, he slew a creature that had walked out of legend. Furthermore, he turned his back on me—the *editor*. Why? To honor his friend," Caesar shouted. "I say to you that this man is a true son of Rome. He may have been born a slave, and committed crimes. Today, however, I name him a citizen of the Republic."

Romulus' mouth fell open. Instead of death, he was being offered life. Freedom.

Memor looked appalled, outraged even, but he kept his mouth shut.

To tumultuous applause, Caesar turned to Romulus and offered him his right hand. "What is your name?"

"Romulus, sir," he replied, firmly taking the grip.

"If all my soldiers were as brave as you, I'd only ever need one legion," joked Caesar.

Romulus was overcome by gratitude. "I offer you my service, Caesar," he said, dropping to one knee.

It was Caesar's turn to look surprised. "You wish to be part of my army? Soon we will be shipping out for Africa, where much bloodshed awaits us."

"I can think of no greater honor, sir."

"A soldier like you will be welcome," replied Caesar in a pleased tone. "Which legion would you join?"

Romulus grinned. "The Twenty-Eighth!"

"A good choice," smiled Caesar. "Very well. You shall have your wish." He beckoned to one of his officers. "Have this man—Romulus—taken to your camp and fitted out with an ordinary legionary's gear. He can bunk in with your soldiers until next week, when I send new orders to the Twenty-Eighth. Then he is to accompany them to his old unit. Clear?"

"Sir!"

Caesar turned away.

The officer jerked his head at Romulus. It was clear that the interview was over. Romulus struggled to overcome his intimidation and awe. *I made a promise,* he thought. "Sir?"

Caesar looked around. "What is it?"

"Petronius—my comrade—served in the Twenty-Eighth," began Romulus.

"So?"

"He was a good soldier, sir. I promised him that he would receive a decent funeral, with all the proper rites."

Caesar was taken aback. "Determined, aren't you?"

"He was my friend, sir," replied Romulus stolidly.

The surrounding officers and senators looked outraged by his audacity.

Caesar stared at Romulus long and hard. "Good enough," he said at length. "I'd do the same myself." He glanced at the centurion in charge of his guards. "See that it's done."

Romulus saluted. "Thank you, sir."

"Until we meet again," answered Caesar.

This time, Romulus felt his elbow being taken. His audience was over.

"*Lanista!*" Caesar's voice was frosty. "A word, if you please."

Romulus didn't get to hear what the general had to say to Memor. Alternately sad and ecstatic at what had happened, he was led off by a lean soldier with a bad limp. "Caesar likes you," this man whispered as they left the amphitheater. "But don't go thinking you're something special now. You're not—you're just a plain legionary, like me. Never again speak to an officer unless he addresses you first. Unless you want a good flogging, of course."

Romulus nodded. No longer having to conceal his identity was worth any harsh discipline.

"Don't expect any special treatment from your comrades either. They won't give a shit about what you did here today," the soldier went on. "All they'll care about is how you fight against the fucking Republicans in Africa."

Romulus caught the nervousness in the other's voice. "How bad is it over there?"

There was a resigned shrug. "The usual when fighting for Caesar. By all accounts, we'll be outnumbered two or three to one. The bastards also have vast numbers of Numidian cavalry, while we have next to none."

Resigned, Romulus eyed the temple of Jupiter that loomed over the city. He couldn't visit it just yet. Nor would he get to see Fabiola. Instead, more danger beckoned.

In Africa.

XIII

STRANDS OF FATE

Fussing like an old woman, Brutus put Fabiola to bed. Aided by Docilosa, he fetched warm blankets, watered-down wine and an assortment of herbal remedies. Guilt filled Fabiola. Unlike her "fever," his solicitousness was natural and unfeigned. She had to continue with her charade, though, at least until that evening. Lying back, Fabiola closed her eyes and tried to put the image of unarmed men being killed by a horned, armored beast from her mind. It was difficult, but the alternative—staring at Brutus' worried features—was little better.

Jovina had stepped in to run things from the reception area while Docilosa hovered in the background, her face a neutral mask. Fabiola knew well that this was only for Brutus' benefit. There were telltale signs that she could read: her servant's flaring nostrils, and the way she slapped down the glass of wine on the bedside table. As soon as he'd left, Docilosa would vent her spleen. It was unsurprising, thought Fabiola. Her coupling with Antonius had been an uncharacteristic moment of madness, which could have left her out on the street. Despite the calamitous outcome that had been so narrowly avoided, Fabiola still felt a surreptitious pleasure at what she'd done. They hadn't been caught, and that's all there was to it. She was her own mistress, and would carry on her own affairs as she chose. Docilosa wasn't going to tell her what to do. Who did her servant think she was, anyway?

Part of Fabiola knew that she was overreacting, but Docilosa's self-righteousness wound her up so much that she felt it impossible to let go. There would be no unburdening of her worries and guilt today, she realized. Best to get a good rest—she could always do with more sleep—and settle things with Docilosa tomorrow. Slowing her breathing down, she pretended to doze off. Satisfied by this, Brutus issued a string of orders to Docilosa and left. He was still keen to see the Ethiopian bull.

With a disapproving sigh, Docilosa sat down on a stool by the bed. She made a few attempts to talk, whispering questions at Fabiola. Still annoyed and set on her decision, Fabiola studiously ignored her. Eventually Docilosa gave up. It wasn't long before Fabiola actually surrendered to sleep. Running the Lupanar was draining work.

Despite the sleeping drafts which Brutus had made her drink, Fabiola's nap was far from restful. Instead, she was plunged into a dark nightmare in which Antonius knew all about her secret plan. Dragging her before Caesar, he laughed as his master raped Fabiola. Brutus was nowhere to be seen. Tossing and turning, Fabiola could not stop the horrifying dream. When Caesar was finished, she was turned over to Scaevola. That was too much. Fabiola woke up in a cold sweat, both of her fists clenched in the blanket. The room was silent. Was she alone? Her eyes darted wildly to the stool where Docilosa had been sitting. In her place perched an unhappy-looking Vettius.

Seeing her distress, he jumped up. "Should I fetch a surgeon, Mistress?"

"What?" she cried, startled. "No, I'm feeling better." Physically she might be, but Fabiola's mind was full of horrors. Damping them down as best she could, she sat up. "Where's Docilosa?"

His gaze flickered away. "Gone to see her daughter."

"When?"

"About three hours ago."

"She left me?" cried Fabiola in disbelief. "When I was ill?"

"She said that your fever had broken," Vettius muttered as if it were his fault. "Was she wrong?"

Fabiola considered what to say for a moment. There was no point making this bigger than it was already. "No," she sighed, throwing off the bedclothes. "It has gone. Go back to your post."

Vettius beamed happily. Looking after his sick mistress made him most uneasy. Now that she was recovered, all was well with the world once more. Picking up his club, he bowed and left her.

Watching his massive back disappear down the corridor, Fabiola wished that her outlook on life was so simple.

†

A few dozen steps from the Lupanar, Tarquinius was squatting in much the same position he'd occupied for a time eight years before. The spot brought back mixed memories. Back then, he had been waiting for Rufus Caelius, the malevolent noble who had killed Olenus. Unsurprisingly, every moment of the melee outside the brothel was crystal clear. He tried to block out the recollection of his single knife thrust, which at the time had felt so right. Although the haruspex felt it was destiny that had guided his blade, he was still being tortured by the consequences of his action, and the look in Romulus' eyes when he'd told him. Which was partly why Tarquinius found himself here once more, pretending to be a beggar.

It was strange how life worked in circles, he thought.

Fabricius had been as good as his word, taking Tarquinius down to the little fleet in Rhodes harbor. He'd insisted that his fellow devotee should travel on his own ship, the lead trireme. Tarquinius had accepted with alacrity. It seemed perfect: after Mithras' intervention, a passage back to Italy in relative comfort, with possible access to the ancient documents and artifacts he needed. Soon after their departure, though, the haruspex had discovered that most of the items that he wished to look at were on the other vessels. In a stroke, half his plan came undone. He had hoped on the journey to spend as much time studying as possible. In the event, however, the cargo arrangements were a blessing in disguise. When an autumn storm struck the fleet off the island of Antikythera, it was the ships laden with precious goods that sank, not the one with Fabricius and Tarquinius on board. Not that their trireme escaped unscathed. Braving waves taller than an apartment building, and hours of terrifying thunder and lightning, it finally limped into Brundisium with only the stump of its main mast remaining. At least a dozen members of the crew had been washed overboard.

Unharmed against all the odds, the haruspex chose to interpret his good fortune as most would. A deity—Mithras—was guiding his way. Although Tarquinius no longer knew what his purpose was, here was clear evidence that he had one still. He was grateful for this. Rome *was* where he needed to be.

Fabricius was also thankful to the warrior god. Nonetheless, he made an offering at the temple to Neptune before they left Brundisium. "Got to keep them all happy, haven't you?" he muttered. Like the Etruscans, Romans commonly worshipped a number of divine beings, depending on their need. Tarquinius was no different.

Reaching Rome, the centurion had taken him to a large house on the Palatine Hill. "I can do no less," he had insisted. "It's a place to rest your head." The building turned out to be the headquarters of a group of veterans, all followers of Mithras. There, in the underground Mithraeum, Fabricius introduced Tarquinius to Secundus, the *Pater* of the temple. Stunned by the presence of a Mithraic shrine in the heart of Rome, the haruspex had been even more astonished to recognize in Secundus the one-armed veteran he'd met outside the Lupanar years before. In contrast, the *Pater* had seemed unsurprised.

Meeting Fabricius and surviving the storm had substantially restored Tarquinius' faith in the gods. Just when it seemed that the obstacles in his way were too immense to overcome, they were removed. During the journey, he'd continued to see occasional images of Rome under a stormy sky. Clouds the color of blood told the haruspex that someone's life was in danger, but he had no idea who. The vivid dream about the murder at the Lupanar did not go away either, and so the brothel was Tarquinius' first destination once he'd had a night's rest.

Recognizing Fabiola soon after arriving, Tarquinius was surprised to discover that she was the Lupanar's new owner. Why she had bought the brothel, no one knew, but the knowledge gave him somewhere to start. Had she something to do with his nightmare? He'd also discovered that Fabiola was the lover of Decimus Brutus, one of Caesar's right-hand men.

The haruspex didn't go barging in to introduce himself as a friend of her brother, though. That wasn't his style. Instead Tarquinius sat outside, watching who came and went, gaining an understanding of what was going on. Within a few hours, he knew that all was not well in the Lupanar. The brothel was renowned throughout the city for its prostitutes' abilities, yet scarcely ten customers crossed its freshly painted threshold each day. It also seemed to have a disproportionately large number of armed guards, bullet-headed thugs armed with staves, knives and swords. These patrolled the almost empty street, eyeballing anyone bold enough to glance their way. To avoid their attention, Tarquinius had adopted the mien of a drooling, twitching simpleton. It worked nicely; the heavies gave him a wide berth.

This afforded him the time to consider what he was seeing. In Tarquinius' mind, the guards' strong-arm tactics weren't enough to explain the Lupanar's parlous state. They were there as a response to a threat, and those who wanted sex wouldn't be put off so easily. Important men were still visiting the brothel too—he'd heard passersby mentioning Marcus Antonius' name as a burly figure had gone in that morning. Antonius' must have been a brief encounter, Tarquinius concluded. Less than a quarter of an hour had elapsed before the grinning Master of the Horse emerged. No one had troubled him either, other than another noble. A pleasant-faced man of average build, he appeared most displeased to see Antonius. Could the danger he saw refer to either of them? Tarquinius wondered. What did it matter, unless it impacted on Fabiola? He felt frustrated and fascinated at the same time. If Romulus' sister was in peril, though, he felt a duty to help.

More was revealed at midday as he hobbled away in search of some food. In the surrounding streets, the haruspex noticed different groups of armed ruffians standing around. Directed by a stocky, brown-haired man in a mail shirt, they formed checkpoints reducing, or preventing, access to the Lupanar. Only the most insistent pedestrians—such as a plain-faced woman in middle age he'd just seen—managed to get past. It wasn't difficult to come to the conclusion that some kind of turf war was going on.

Tarquinius still wasn't sure if he should get involved.

Best to wait and watch instead.

†

Morose, Fabiola was sitting at her desk in the reception area when Docilosa returned. It was near sunset, which meant that her servant had been gone for several hours. By the happy look on her face, the visit had gone well. Seeing Fabiola, her features stiffened.

"You've recovered, then?" she asked with a show of concern.

The expert needling made Fabiola's hackles rise. "Yes," she snapped. "No thanks to you."

Docilosa made a small contemptuous sound and brushed past, into the corridor. "I'll be out the back, washing clothes," she said.

Furious, Fabiola bit her tongue rather than respond further. The anteroom a few steps away was full of prostitutes who would be listening to every word. Jovina was lurking about somewhere too. The less said in public, the better. Yet the situation could not continue in this manner. It would have to be resolved one way or another, and soon. Fabiola's nostrils flared. Docilosa's friendship was valuable to her, but not under conditions like these.

Before she could do any more, a trio of wealthy merchants from Hispania rolled in the door. Fabiola stood up to welcome them. Well-oiled, they insisted on recounting their story. After a hard week of selling their goods, they'd celebrated by going to Caesar's games that day. A drinking session followed that, and now, the Spaniards declared to Fabiola, they wanted the fuck of their lives. No street gangs were going to stop them visiting the Lupanar, which they'd heard of in their home country. "You've come to the right place, gentlemen," Fabiola purred, instantly spotting the heavy purses on their belts. Quite the madam now, she called the girls out to be inspected.

The inebriated merchants made their selection quickly and were led off to various bedrooms. Again Fabiola moved toward the corridor, but a pair of wide-eyed figures in workingmen's tunics were next through the entrance. She wondered why Benignus had let them in until she saw the money clutched in their fists. Ordinary citizens, they had won a small fortune at the day's games by making an outside bet on an aging *retiarius*, the underdog in a gladiator duel. As they told Fabiola, it was a gamble that had paid off richly when the favorite, a *murmillo* from Apulia, slipped on a patch of bloody sand, allowing the fisherman to stab him in the belly with his trident and end the fight at a stroke. Unhappy at the unexpected result, the bookmaker tried to renege on the wager, but the angry crowd had swarmed in around the two friends and forced him to pay up. Now they were here in the Lupanar to spend their winnings.

Caesar's games were certainly helping business, thought Fabiola as she watched the goggle-eyed pair disappear with their choice of girls. Maybe she should have gone to see them for herself?

No. Fabiola's reaction was instant. Her pretense to Brutus that morning had not been entirely selfish. Her gorge rose at the thought of seeing men die for little more than the crowd's pleasure. She would never be able to watch such spectacles without seeing Romulus on the circle of sand. Just imagining her brother made her heart ache. Where was he? How she wished to see him again! Although they'd both grown into adults since their last meeting, Fabiola had no doubt that they would get on famously. Twins, they'd been inseparable as children. What could be different now? Their bond was unbreakable. Feeling happier, Fabiola thought of Docilosa. Shame filled her. Her servant was almost as close as family. It was time to kiss and make up.

Ordering Jovina to cover the reception, Fabiola went in search of Docilosa.

†

Outside, Tarquinius was considering how much longer he would wait before calling it a day. Little of interest had happened since Antonius' hurried departure and brief conversation with his fellow noble. He noted the middle-aged woman from the checkpoint enter the brothel, and marked her down for a servant or slave. She was too old and plain to be a prostitute in a place like the Lupanar, that was for sure. Tarquinius was surprised to feel a surge of energy as the woman disappeared through the arched doorway. The insight he got was so brief that he almost missed it. An old sadness had recently been washed away, to be replaced by a deep joy. Anger was also present, a resentment at someone who had ideas above her station. Irritated, Tarquinius did not try to see more. The emotions of a servant were not what he wanted to know about.

Still, it was a start.

He scanned the patch of sky that was visible in the narrow gap between the buildings for a clue. It had a typical autumn appearance: heavy cloud cover, with the promise of rain before nightfall. Little else. The haruspex looked away, and a gust of chill wind swept down, carrying with it the threat of bloodshed. Tarquinius stiffened; fingers of fear clutched at him. He focused his thoughts, trying to understand. A moment later, he felt certain. Danger was in the air. Here. Was this the threat he'd seen so many times?

At once the haruspex' fingers fumbled under his cloak to the hilt of his *gladius*. He'd left the great two-headed axe in the veterans' house. It was guaranteed to attract unwanted attention. Thankfully, the solid feel of the sword calmed his racing heart. Tarquinius glanced up and down the darkening street, seeing nothing of concern. Somewhat reassured, he sat back, wondering if anything was about to happen. Did he need to worry about Fabiola's safety? It was a shock to realize how important it already felt to watch over her.

Half an hour passed, and darkness fell. The brothel's doormen retreated to the arcs of light cast by the torches on either side of the front door. Tarquinius began to wonder if he'd been imagining the threat. He was growing stiff and cold, and his belly was grumbling. Yet experience had taught him not to rush things, so he gritted his teeth and stayed put.

Some time later, the tramp of feet on the rutted ground drew Tarquinius' attention. Waking himself from a half-doze, he sat up. Illuminated by their torches, a large party was approaching the brothel from the other end of the street. The time of day made the number of guards unremarkable. Unless they were mad, anyone who ventured out after dark traveled like this. What did surprise Tarquinius as the group drew nearer was the fact that they were gladiators. He saw Thracians, *murmillones* and *secutores*, as well as a number of archers. Usually only a *lanista* used men like that as protection.

Was this more than a visit in search of carnal pleasure?

Tarquinius leaned forward, all his senses on high alert.

The heavily armed party came to a halt by the entrance. Looking uneasily at each other, the Lupanar's doormen gripped their weapons. Snickers of contempt rose from the gladiators, and a short, grizzled figure in a wool cloak pushed his way to the front. "Is this the way you greet all your customers?" he demanded.

An enormous slave with a wooden club shuffled forward. "My apologies, sir. We're having some trouble at the moment. Got to be prepared at all times."

The *lanista* sniffed. "Something to do with that rabble at the crossroads, no doubt. The bastards didn't want to let us through until I had my archers draw a bead on them. Then they opened up quicker than a whore's legs!"

His men laughed dutifully.

So he's not allied to that lot, thought Tarquinius with relief.

"No one stops the *lanista* of the Ludus Magnus from going where he pleases," Memor declared. "Tonight, I want the best-looking whore in the Lupanar."

With a respectful bow, the big slave indicated that Memor should enter.

"This visit is well overdue," declared the *lanista*, swaggering inside. "My balls are bursting."

More forced laughter from his gladiators.

An afterthought struck Memor, and he looked around. "Piss off back to the *ludus*," he ordered. "Come back tomorrow morning. I might have finished by then."

With relieved looks, his fighters did as they were told.

On the other side of the street, excitement and dread filled Tarquinius. Romulus had fought for the Ludus Magnus, which made Memor his former owner. Had the *lanista* any idea who Fabiola was? Was that the real purpose of his visit? *Of course not,* he told himself. *Memor will have forgotten Romulus long ago. He probably doesn't even know that Fabiola's running the place.*

Still gripped by uncertainty, Tarquinius prayed. *Guide me, great Mithras. Should I go inside?* In the night sky above, the stars were almost completely obscured. The glimpses he was granted through momentary breaks in the clouds were far too short to ascertain anything. The presence of danger that had been so strong was gone. Tarquinius felt the gods were mocking him, and forced himself to relax. Yet he also felt compelled to stay where he was.

†

Docilosa wasn't in the baths or the kitchen. Fabiola found her in the courtyard at the back of the brothel, washing bedclothes. Hardly a task to fulfill by torchlight; her servant was obviously avoiding her. They had time to exchange frosty looks before Catus, the main cook, distracted Fabiola with a query about the amount of food and drink that the extra doormen were going through. Leading her to the storerooms off the kitchen, he pointed in outrage at the empty shelves. "I'm using over a *modius* of grain a day making bread, Mistress," he whined. "Then there's the cheese and vegetables. And the wine! Even watered down, the dogs are finishing an amphora every few days."

Catus' list of complaints was long, but Fabiola had been putting off talking to him about it for some time. The balding slave was a hard worker, so she stood and listened, deciding what was to be done about each and directing him accordingly. While this was happening, she was aware of Docilosa creeping past her into the corridor that led to the front of the brothel. *Damn it, she's acting like a child,* thought Fabiola. *As I was earlier. That's not like her. I wonder if Sabina's planting ideas in her mind?* It was hard to concentrate. Warming to his theme now, Catus was droning on about the price of vegetables in the Forum Olitorium compared to what local farmers charged if bought from directly. "I tell you, it's a complete rip-off," he moaned. "The price in the Forum is three or even four times what the stuff costs wholesale."

Fabiola could take no more. "Fine," she snapped. "Find an honest farmer and offer him a contract to supply all our food."

Catus quailed before her anger.

Fabiola gentled. He'd never been given this degree of responsibility before. "The doormen will be here for the foreseeable future," she explained. "We have to feed them. Getting our supplies direct is an excellent idea, and one you're well capable of sorting out."

His chin lifted. "Thank you," he muttered.

"Come to me when you've found the right man," said Fabiola. "I'll have the lawyers draw up the correct paperwork." Leaving Catus grinning like a fool, she hurried off in search of Docilosa. It was good to sort out minor problems like this, but the sense of real urgency that had been tugging away at her would now not be denied.

Fabiola would always wonder how the situation might have unfolded if the cook had not accosted her when he did. As she entered the long corridor, she heard a woman screaming. The noise was not like the ecstatic cries that some of the prostitutes used to encourage their clients. No, thought Fabiola in alarm, it was the sound of someone who was absolutely terrified, and in fear of her life. She broke into a trot. "Vettius! Benignus!"

Ahead of her, Fabiola could see Docilosa, only a few steps from the reception area. Nearer to the source of the screams. Her servant's head was turning from side to side, searching for the right room. Finding it, she moved to its door.

Fabiola cursed. It was the one commonly used by Vicana, the

new British slave with red hair and fair complexion. To her horror, Docilosa's hand reached out to lift the iron latch. "No," screamed Fabiola. This was not what should happen. "Wait for the doormen!"

Ignoring her, Docilosa pushed wide the door. "Stop it," she cried at once. "Let her go."

The volume of the screams grew deafening. Above them, Fabiola could hear a man cursing. "Bitch," he cried. "Just do what I tell you." There was a loud slap, and the woman's cries stopped abruptly.

Docilosa took a step inside. "Leave the poor girl alone," she muttered, her voice shaking. "Don't hurt her."

"Mind your own damn business, you ugly old cow," snarled the man.

Docilosa entered the room completely. "Stop it!"

There was a chilling laugh. "Want a piece of this, do you?"

Terrified herself now, Fabiola sprinted toward the doorway. As she did, the doormen appeared round the corner from the reception.

Too late. They were all too late.

There was a choked cry, such as someone makes when tripping unexpectedly. It was followed by the sound of a body falling to the floor, and then the air filled with screams once more. "Shut up, you little slut," cried the man. "Or you'll get the same."

Fabiola slid to a halt in the doorway, and her stomach turned over at the sight inside. "No," she whispered. "Please, no." Docilosa was lying quite still on the floor, her back to Fabiola. Blood was already pooling around her—damning evidence. Over her stood a naked man holding a reddened dagger, his grizzled features contorted in rage. Cowering on the other side of the bed was a sobbing Vicana, her tear-stained face white with fear.

At first, the man didn't even notice Fabiola. He seemed crazed, or drugged. "That'll teach you," he muttered, poking a foot at Docilosa. "Interrupting my fun like that."

A towering fury took hold of Fabiola. She knew this creature, had slept with him on many occasions in the past. It was Memor, the *lanista* of the Ludus Magnus, from whom she'd wheedled information about Romulus. "You whoreson," she hissed, her nostrils flaring. "What have you done?"

Memor looked up, and his eyes cleared. "By all the gods," he said appraisingly. "You're a real beauty. Why weren't you out there to be picked from? I'd have chosen you first anytime."

Fabiola didn't answer. Although all her instincts screamed at her to run, she moved toward Docilosa. She couldn't stop herself, nor could she help her temper. "A shame my brother didn't kill you when he had the chance, you piece of filth," she cried.

His eyes narrowed. "What are you talking about?"

"Romulus," she threw at the *lanista*. "The one who ran away. You told me about him." Confusion twisted Memor's face, but then Fabiola saw the realization hit. "By Mercury," he breathed. "I've fucked you before."

Fabiola hawked and spat in his face. "I hated every moment."

His lips peeled back with anger. "You told me that Romulus was your cousin!"

"I lied. The same as when I told you that you were a stallion," she sneered. "Limp-pricked old goat." Fabiola's heart lurched as the words left her mouth. She was only a few paces from Memor and his knife, and the doormen hadn't yet arrived. *Should have kept my mouth shut,* Fabiola thought.

She was right.

"You whore," screamed the *lanista*, lunging forward with his blade.

XIV

SABINA

Panicking, Fabiola dodged backward. Memor's dagger whistled past, coming within a fraction of gutting her. She glanced back at the door. It was too far for her to reach. Where were Benignus and Vettius?

"Prepare yourself for Hades, because that's where you're going," muttered Memor, his eyes staring madly. "Like this ugly bitch." He kicked Docilosa in the belly. She gave a faint groan.

Fabiola could not take her eyes off his blade, which was covered in her servant's blood.

The *lanista* edged forward, leering. He wasn't watching the floor, wasn't prepared for Docilosa's hand to reach out and grab weakly at his ankle. Memor stumbled. Then his other foot landed in the pool of blood, and he skidded. Losing his balance, he fell awkwardly to one knee. Furious, he stabbed Docilosa a number of times in the back and belly.

Vicana screamed at the top of her voice.

Hating herself, Fabiola retreated to the doorway. An instant later, she was manhandled into the corridor by the two doormen.

Bundling into the room like a pair of raging bulls, Benignus and Vettius laid into the *lanista* with their metal-studded clubs. One of the blows alone would have crushed his skull, and the enraged pair landed more than half a dozen each before Fabiola managed to stop them. "That's enough," she screamed. "Stop it!"

Breathing heavily, and spattered in blood and gray brain matter, they stood back.

"He's dead," Fabiola shouted, looking down at the smeared mess of hair, flesh and bone fragments that was Memor's head. Tears sprang to her eyes.

Vettius was surprised by her reaction. "Of course he is."

"I wanted to grill the bastard about Romulus," Fabiola sobbed. "He used to be his owner."

A rattling breath from Docilosa attracted everyone's attention.

Overcome with remorse, Fabiola dropped to her knees by her servant's side. Docilosa was alive—barely. Fabiola ripped open her dress, cringing at the first bloody, open-lipped entry point she saw. It was small, yet had caused so much damage. Memor's knife thrust had been expert, entering her chest on the left side, just below the breast. Puncturing one lung, it had probably pierced the heart as well. A mortal wound. His other blows would have killed too, albeit more slowly. For now, they just increased the blood loss. Fabiola didn't think that one person could have so much in her. Docilosa's dress was drenched in it, and so was the floor around her. Her eyes were stretched wide, and staring into nothing. Her mouth gasped open and shut like a fish out of water, trying—and failing—to get enough air in.

"I'm sorry." Fabiola grasped one of Docilosa's reddened hands in both of her own. "You were right. I should know better." She looked beseechingly at her servant. "This is my fault too. If we hadn't argued, you wouldn't have been in the corridor when Vicana screamed."

A stream of fine bloody bubbles dribbled from Docilosa's lips onto the tile floor.

Fabiola squeezed her hand, praying for a response. Some proof of forgiveness, to give her hope.

There was none.

Docilosa's entire body gave a heaving shudder, and then relaxed.

Fabiola threw herself down to catch her servant's last breath. Then she gave in to her grief entirely. Tears ran unchecked down her face, mixing with Docilosa's blood. Fabiola didn't care. The only person who had shown her real friendship and kindness through the worst years of her life was dead. Their unresolved quarrel doubled her feelings of guilt. She would never be able to change that now. Time could not be turned back. Yet Docilosa had tripped Memor; had saved her, even as she died.

Paralyzed by her grief, Fabiola lay there, ignoring the doormen's pleas for her to get up. Jovina tried to help too, but to no avail. The old madam soon hurried back to the reception. "Customers could come in at any time," she muttered. Fabiola was oblivious to all of this. She wanted to die, longed for the floor to open up and carry them both off to oblivion. Even that thought was tainted by bitterness. Docilosa wouldn't be going where she was headed: Hades. Where else did she deserve? First Sextus had died, and now her blameless servant. No matter how hard Fabiola wished it, though, nothing happened. She thought vaguely of picking up Memor's dagger and using it to open the veins in her wrists. Death wouldn't take long that way. Then there would be no more pain, no more suffering. But she didn't. A short while later, when her nightmare of earlier returned to haunt her, Fabiola knew why.

She had a purpose in life that was greater than her own misery.

Her mother, Velvinna, had always been vague about her rape, but she'd been insistent that a noble was responsible. While Caesar had never actually raped Fabiola, he had tried to. His words then had, in her mind and heart, proved that he was the man who'd violated her mother. Deep down, however, Fabiola had to admit that this was no more than her strongly held suspicion, building on his strange re-semblance to Romulus. Caesar was only one of a thousand possible suspects. Yet he was also similar to the countless noblemen who had paid to use Fabiola's body, plenty of whom had seen the fear and reluctance in her thirteen-year-old eyes and carried on regardless. Fabiola needed someone to blame for that degradation, which had been repeated innumerable times. Her hatred of such men fes-tered within her; punishing a guilty party would give her some ease, and thanks to his assault on her, Caesar fitted the bill perfectly. Telling herself that he was her father helped to focus Fabiola's rage. If she committed suicide, he would escape her vengeance.

Fabiola pushed herself upright.

The doormen gasped.

She looked down at herself. Their reaction wasn't surprising: her dress was saturated in blood. Her hands and arms were also covered in it. "I look as if I've been stabbed," said Fabiola.

Benignus made the sign against evil. "Don't say that," he mut-tered.

Vettius helped her to get up. "No point bringing more bad luck on yourself," he agreed.

Fabiola grimaced. "Hard to see how I could do that."

Neither man answered.

"Best prepare a table in the kitchen," she said, forcing herself to remain calm. "We must lay out Docilosa, and clean her up. Put on her best dress. Vicana can get the hot water ready."

Taking the shivering British girl by one hand, Vettius disap-peared.

Benignus pointed at Memor's body. "What'll we do with this piece of shit?"

"Wrap him up in an old blanket. Then wait until all the custom-ers have gone," said Fabiola. "Carry him to the nearest sewer and drop the son of a whore in it. Let the rats feed on him. It's no more than he did for plenty of others. Tomorrow you can visit his second in command. I've heard that he's eager for promotion. Now his chance has come. A fat purse should help him forget all about Memor."

Benignus nodded. He'd done things like this before.

†

A short time after the *lanista* had entered, Tarquinius heard muffled screaming coming from inside the brothel. Unease filled him, but he could discern nothing of what might be going on. The response of the huge doorman outside was instant, though. Leaving his companions to hold the fort, he dived through the front door, his club at the ready. He was gone for a long time, which aroused Tarquinius' suspicions even more. He watched and listened intently, but the thick walls opposite muffled virtually all sound. He wondered if the screams had been anything to do with the *lanista*. His senses were telling him nothing, but the haruspex did not panic. Fabiola was unlikely to be in any danger. If a customer turned violent, it was far more likely that one of the prostitutes would get hurt. A quarter of an hour passed, and Tarquinius began to relax. No one had been ejected, which probably meant that the matter had been sorted out amicably. Of course there was another, darker possibility, but Tarquinius could detect no hint of bloodshed overhead. That didn't mean that it wasn't happening, of course. *Mithras,* he prayed. *Help me. Keep Fabiola safe.*

The silent figure that emerged from the gloom of the alleyway a moment later made him jump. It was a woman. On her own. The haruspex' eyebrows rose in surprise before he took in the newcomer's gray robe. Confusion reigned in his mind. What was a priestess of Orcus doing here, and at this time of night? Although few lowlifes would hinder the passage of someone who served the god of the underworld, the priestess had risked her life to venture out alone.

He watched as she walked straight up to the front door. The

four guards there looked quite taken aback by her sudden appearance. Scared too. The young woman said nothing, which discon-
certed them further. "Yes?" one ventured at last.

"I wish to visit my mother," said the priestess.

Tarquinius pricked his ears. To his knowledge, there were only
two women in the brothel old enough to have a child in her mid-
twenties. Jovina, and the servant he'd seen previously.

The guard coughed uneasily. "Who would that be then?"

"Docilosa," came the reply. "Fabiola's servant."

"It's very late for a visit," he said, glancing at his companions for
confirmation.

She wasn't to be put off. "It's urgent. She may be in danger."

"Docilosa?" The guard unsuccessfully tried to hide his smirk.

"The god has sent me."

The priestess's words wiped the smile off his face. Silently he
opened the door.

Tarquinius' stomach knotted with worry as he watched her hurry
within. Something was going on, but his senses were not picking it
up. Fabiola could be in mortal danger for all he knew. What chance
had he of gaining entry, though? Clenching his teeth with frustration, the haruspex cast his eyes to the strip of night sky framed
by the buildings above. After a few moments, he relaxed a fraction.
Blood *had* been shed inside, but it wasn't Fabiola's.

✝

"What's that?" Fabiola craned her neck and listened.

There was a loud, insistent voice arguing with Jovina. It belonged to a woman.

"One of the prostitutes?" queried the doorman.

"No. None would dare disagree with her."

"True," Benignus replied. "Who then?"

Fabiola moved to the door, which was ajar. "No, you can't go back there," she heard Jovina say. "Come back!" A chill of premonition struck her, and she stepped outside.

Sabina was coming down the corridor. When she saw Fabiola's appearance, her hand rose to her mouth in shock. "Sweet Jupiter, what's happened?" she asked. "Where's Mother?"

Fabiola didn't know what to say. This nightmare was going on and on.

"I knew something was wrong!" Sabina ran the last few steps. "Whose blood is it?"

Fabiola couldn't answer.

"One of your . . . girls?"

She shook her head in denial.

Sabina's head turned, and she peered in through the open door. For a moment, the young priestess didn't take in what she was seeing. Finally, though, it sank in. "Mother? Mother?" she screamed in disbelief. She darted in to kneel by Docilosa. Sobs racked her thin frame.

Following, Fabiola laid a hand on her shoulder.

Sabina jerked away as if a snake had bitten her. "You did this!"

"No," Fabiola protested. "It was him." She indicated Memor's body.

Sabina jumped to her feet. "You're lying!"

"Why would I harm your mother?" Fabiola cried, aghast. "I loved her."

From nowhere, a knife appeared in Sabina's right hand. "How did such a lowlife get his hands on her then? Mother was a free-woman! She had no right being in a filthy place like this." Her eyes glittered with malice.

"After Brutus bought her freedom, Docilosa chose to stay with me, and to come here," Fabiola explained, desperate that Sabina should believe her. "She just happened to be passing this room when Vicana cried out for help. Her bad luck."

With a terrible scream of pain, Sabina launched herself at

Fabiola. "Why did I stop the *fugitivarius?*" she hissed. "Better to have let him kill you too."

Sabina was quickly stopped by Benignus, who grabbed her arms from behind. Fabiola stepped forward to snatch the blade, letting it clatter to the floor. "I'm sorry," she said.

"Heartless bitch," spat Sabina. "It should be you lying there, not my mother."

"Perhaps," agreed Fabiola somberly. "But it isn't. My time is not today."

"Maybe not," snarled the other. "Your life will not be long, though."

Fabiola was struck dumb. Sabina sounded like an oracle.

"I curse you to deep unhappiness," the priestess snarled.

Fabiola's jaw hardened. She could take that. She deserved that.

"Brutus will not stay by you either." Sabina laughed at Fabiola's surprise. "Nor will the other you open your legs for so easily."

Docilosa must have told her about Antonius, thought Fabiola, reeling from shock. How else could she know?

"As for your brother—" Sabina began.

"No," shouted Fabiola in panic. "Shut her up," she ordered Vettius.

At once the doorman placed a meaty hand across Sabina's mouth. She did not try to prevent him, but her eyes still glinted with venom.

Fabiola bent to pick up Sabina's dagger.

The priestess's eyes opened wide.

"I'm not going to kill you, even though that's what you would have done to me," snapped Fabiola. She didn't want to anger Orcus again. "I'll even send a messenger to the temple so that you know where Docilosa's grave is."

Sabina's eyes filled with tears.

"Never come back here. On pain of death," Fabiola commanded. Then, to Benignus, "Throw her out."

He obediently manhandled the priestess out of the room. She didn't fight him.

Still shaken, Fabiola headed straight for the baths. All she wanted to do now was wash off Docilosa's blood, which had formed a thick crust on her skin. She tried to put Sabina's words from her mind, but it was impossible. They hung before her mind's eye, haunting her as she undressed. Not only was poor Docilosa dead, but her own destiny had been revealed—and it was unpleasant. Fabiola cleaned herself mechanically, going through the motions while her mind spun ever faster. By reasoning things through, she eventually managed to calm herself. Who knew if Sabina's prophecy was accurate? Even if it was, the priestess had said nothing about Fabiola failing to kill Caesar. Which meant that her plan *could* still come to pass. *So be it*, Fabiola thought, stiffening her resolve. *I can succeed.* The possibility of always being unhappy and losing Brutus was as nothing compared to achieving her heart's desire. Dying young didn't matter either. Only one thing did.

What would Sabina have said about Romulus if she'd been allowed?

Half of Fabiola wished she'd just let the priestess say her piece and have done.

The other half couldn't bear to think of it.

Fabiola occupied herself by going to the kitchen. One of the tables had been draped with a sheet so that Docilosa's blood-soaked corpse wouldn't lie on bare wood. With Vicana's help, Fabiola arranged it with the feet pointing toward the front door. Sending all the domestic slaves away apart from Vicana, she stripped Docilosa naked and began to wash the blood from her body. She used the opportunity to grill the British girl about what had gone on: It helped to take her mind off what she was doing.

"He was angry even when deciding which of us he'd have," revealed Vicana. "Said he liked my fair skin. Yet he still seemed preoccupied."

"Go on," Fabiola murmured, rinsing her sponge clean.

"Once the *lanista* was undressed, I offered him a massage. He didn't want that." Vicana sighed. "So I began stroking his prick to get him hard. Nothing happened."

Fabiola shrugged. It was common for customers to suffer from stage fright, especially if they'd been drinking.

"I took him in my mouth, but it was no good," Vicana revealed. "He seemed completely uninterested. Started muttering to himself."

That engaged Fabiola's interest. Any crumb of information was worth knowing. Memor had owned Romulus for several years. "Did you hear what he said? Think carefully."

"I didn't understand," said Vicana. "Something about Caesar and the fortune that an Ethiopian bull would cost to replace. How it wasn't his fault that it was dead."

Had the horned beast died before it could appear in the arena? It wasn't impossible. Fabiola had heard of many wild creatures that died of fright in the cages below the amphitheater. Why would Memor have cared, though? He had been a *lanista*, not a *bestiarius*, she thought, puzzled. It made no sense.

"I asked him if he was all right." Vicana touched her bottom lip, which was swollen and bloody. "He shouted that it was my fault and backhanded me across the face."

"And you cried out."

"I couldn't help myself," sobbed Vicana. "Then suddenly he produced a knife. He wanted to cut me while I pleasured him. That's when I really started screaming."

Twisted old bastard, thought Fabiola, feeling glad that Memor had never acted in that manner with her. Noticing Vicana's distress, she patted her on the shoulder. "He's gone now, and you're unharmed."

Vicana nodded bravely.

"Go on," said Fabiola. "Try to get some sleep. I'll finish preparing Docilosa myself."

The redheaded girl did not protest.

When she was alone, Fabiola sat thinking for some time. What had made Memor so angry? Was it really the death of the Ethiopian bull? She could come up with no reasonable explanation. She would have to ask Brutus later. Now, though, she had to make sure that Docilosa looked her best for her journey to the other side.

It was one of the saddest things Fabiola had ever had to do; it brought up old, painful memories. She did not shy away from the task, however. The tears that welled up in her eyes had been too long held back.

Tenderly Fabiola anointed her servant's body with oil, weeping as she imagined doing the same for her mother. Like so much in a slave's life, that had been denied to her. Velvinna's corpse would have been discarded like so much waste, tossed down a disused mine shaft or left out for the vultures. The thought made Fabiola want to hunt down Gemellus in whatever dark hole he currently resided and kill him—slowly. She made a resolution to have the doormen search him out whenever the opportunity arose. Finding him would be difficult, of course. The bankrupt merchant had been forced to sell his house in the Aventine, which meant that he could be anywhere. *I must stay focused*, thought Fabiola. *Caesar is my main quarry now.*

Docilosa's body was still warm. Once the stab wounds had been covered by her best dress, she could have been just sleeping. It was a fanciful pretense, but Fabiola wallowed in it for as long as she could. The proper rituals could not be delayed, however, and eventually she closed Docilosa's eyes and placed a *sestertius* in her mouth. Without this coin, Docilosa would have nothing to pay Charon, the ferryman.

Her funeral would take place the following night. No eight days of lying in state for Docilosa, the lowly ex-slave, thought Fabiola. There was no point. Who would come to pay their respects, apart from her and Sabina? Yet she was determined that her servant's passage to the other side would be conducted in the proper manner.

Professional mourners and musicians would be hired, and a decent tomb purchased. It was the least Fabiola could do for the humble woman who had become her only family. The anger she'd felt toward Docilosa earlier was gone now. In its place was a throbbing grief that physically hurt every fiber of her being.

There was a knock on the door. "Fabiola?"

She could see by the low level of oil in the nearest lamp that hours must have passed. Business should be done for the night. Would she get no peace? "Come."

Vettius shuffled in, looking nervous.

Fabiola tensed. "What is it?"

"Antonius is here."

She felt incredibly weary. "What time is it?"

"The water clock makes it sometime during the *Gallicinium* watch."

"Gods, the man is insatiable," muttered Fabiola. Sex was the very last thing on her mind right now.

"Jovina offered him his choice of girl, but he refused. Says he has to see you. To spend the night."

Claws of terror ripped at Fabiola again. Jovina was still at reception! She would interpret Antonius' behavior in only one way.

Vettius saw her mood. "Will I send him away? He's definitely the worse for wear."

She was touched by his loyalty. "Antonius is the Master of the Horse, Vettius. Drunk or not, he can come in here if he wants to."

"Of course, Mistress," he muttered. "Which room should I take him to?"

"My office," Fabiola replied, pulling herself together. At least there was no bed there. She could make a pretense of talking to him about business. Jovina might buy it before she ordered her to retire. "Bring some wine, and then stay outside the door in case I need you."

He did not inquire further.

A fresh pang of grief struck Fabiola. Laying his hands on Antonius would earn the huge slave a flogging, or even worse, yet both he and Benignus would do it if she asked. Fabiola almost wished that the doormen would argue with her sometimes. Their unquestioning devotion provided her with no feedback on her choices of action, whereas Docilosa had never been shy of making her opinions known. Even if Fabiola chose to disregard her servant's advice, as she had done up till now with Antonius, she had done so with an understanding of the other side of the argument.

Now, though, she was on her own again.

The walk up the corridor felt like several miles. Fabiola paused by the door where Vicana had been entertaining Memor. Benignus was inside, scrubbing the floor clean of blood and tissue. Beside him, the *lanista*'s body was nothing more than a lumpen shape under a blanket. Sensing her presence, Benignus looked up. "Can we get rid of him yet?"

Fabiola hesitated. She wanted no one to see Memor's corpse being carried out, but who knew how long Antonius would stay? He was stubborn, and persistent. It might be all night, as he'd demanded. If dawn arrived and he was still here, they'd have to keep the body hidden until the next evening. That made up her mind. "Antonius has called in. Wait around to see what happens. If more than half an hour goes by and you've heard nothing, he'll be with me for a while. It should be safe enough then."

Benignus nodded.

Flicking her hands through her hair, Fabiola made for the reception. After all that had gone on, she didn't look her best. Right now, however, she didn't care. The sooner she could get rid of Antonius, the better. Then she could get to bed. Even alone, Fabiola doubted that she would get any sleep, but lying down would still be preferable to the charade she was about to perform.

Pausing to ensure that her cleavage wasn't too prominent, she entered.

Antonius was leaning against one of the walls, tracing his fingers over the depiction of a woman sitting astride a man. Jovina sat at her desk, arms folded in clear disapproval. Her gaze met Fabiola's, and immediately slipped away.

Fabiola's heart banged off her ribs. Jovina's body might be frail and weak, but her mind was as sharp as ever. The bitch already suspected something was up. What would she think of Antonius' presence at this time of night, except that she and he were lovers? Worse still, who would the old madam tell? Keeping her face neutral, Fabiola raised an inquiring eyebrow.

"He won't even speak to anyone else," Jovina muttered. "Insisted I send all the girls away."

Antonius suddenly noticed her. "Fabiola!" he cried, moving away from the support of the wall. His wavering stance showed that his drinking session had continued since he'd left that morning. "Just been looking at a good position," he leered. "Fancy trying it?"

Jovina could scarcely conceal her interest now.

Fabiola bowed, trying to keep things formal. "Marcus Antonius. It's an honor to have you visit the Lupanar."

"I should damn well think so," Antonius slurred. Turning around to pick out his favored sex act, he nearly fell over. "Where is it?" He cursed, and then pointed in triumph. "That's the one I want."

Fabiola was struggling not to panic. "I'm sure one of the girls would love to satisfy you in whatever way you please," she purred, taking his arm.

Antonius looked annoyed. "What?" He leaned in closer, covering her in a haze of wine fumes. "I want you on top of me, not one of your whores," he muttered.

Fabiola shot a look at Jovina, whose face was registering both shock and glee. The emotions vanished at once, but Fabiola had seen them. Her heart sank. Jovina knew, and she couldn't be trusted to keep the information to herself. Giving in to fate, Fabiola led

Antonius to her office. "Tell the doormen to get inside, then lock up and go to bed," she ordered Jovina. "I'll see Antonius out later."

"He's got no guards with him," Jovina muttered, suspicion twisting her face.

"Do as I say," Fabiola shot back, not listening.

The old madam obediently scuttled out from behind her desk. It was then that Vettius arrived bearing a bronze tray with a jug of wine and two glasses. Fabiola cursed silently. As if Jovina needed any more proof that she was involved with the Master of the Horse. This time, the madam had enough presence of mind not to react, but Fabiola's mind had just been made up.

Jovina had to die. Tonight.

She balked for an instant at the ruthlessness of it, but then her fear took over. What choice had she? Brutus could not find out about Antonius, under any circumstances. None of the prostitutes would say a word—they were too scared of her—but Jovina was a different kettle of fish. Despite her sale of the brothel, and her illness, not all of her fight was gone. She would try to use the information as leverage. Fabiola knew it. That couldn't happen.

The doormen wouldn't turn down another dirty job.

A hand grabbed one of Fabiola's breasts, dragging her thoughts back to the present.

First Antonius had to leave.

†

As it turned out, Antonius was incapable of much. Once Fabiola had put a glass of wine in his hand and placed the table between them, he collapsed into a chair and began an incoherent ramble about the latest goings-on in the Senate. Fabiola carefully encouraged him, all the while watching his body language. It wasn't long before Antonius' voice died away, and his head fell on his chest. Fabiola didn't move a muscle. Even when he started to snore, she didn't stir.

Finally, she judged it safe to move. Opening the door, she found

Vettius just outside. Benignus was waiting with him. There was no sign of Jovina or any of the guards. Still she didn't register that Brutus had arrived without any protection of his own, something no one in his right mind would do at this hour.

"Safe to move Memor now?" Vettius asked.

"Yes. The fool's asleep." She took a deep breath. "There's something else I need you to do."

They looked at her questioningly.

"Jovina."

Vettius' brow wrinkled. "What about her?"

"She's got to go."

At first, neither man understood. Then they saw how serious Fabiola was, and their jaws dropped in unison. "Kill her?" Benignus breathed.

Fabiola nodded.

"But she's so old," he faltered.

"Jovina's a snake in the grass," Fabiola hissed. "You both know that. She'll tell Brutus about Antonius."

They didn't argue any further. Their mistress knew best, and it wasn't as if either cared for Jovina in any way. "When?" queried Vettius.

"Tonight," instructed Fabiola. "Get rid of Memor first, though. Now."

They hurried off to do her bidding. Fabiola remained by the door to her office, listening for any signs of Antonius wakening. She was pleased to hear only snores.

Soon the doormen reappeared, carrying the bundled-up blanket between them. Fabiola had already slipped the bolts on the front door and pulled it open. "Be quick," she urged.

They hurried toward her.

From Fabiola's office came the distinctive sound of a glass breaking on the floor.

Like murderers caught in the act, Vettius and Benignus froze.

"Outside," whispered Fabiola frantically.

"Fabiola?" Antonius' voice was sleepy but truculent. "Where in Hades have you gone?"

The pair of slaves had half made it out of the doorway when Antonius emerged, rubbing his reddened eyes. Pushing Vettius outside, Fabiola flashed her most brilliant smile. "You've woken up," she trilled. "I was just going to get a blanket for you."

Perhaps it was Antonius' military training, or her guilty manner, but all signs of drunkenness dropped away from him. "Vulcan's prick! Was that a body?"

For once, Fabiola was at a loss for words.

In a heartbeat, Antonius was by her side. Pulling wide the door, he stared at the two doormen, who were spotlit by the torches on either side of the entrance. As most slaves' would have been in such a situation, their feet were rooted to the spot. "What have you got there?" Antonius barked.

There was a pregnant pause.

"Answer me!"

"Nothing, sir," ventured Benignus. "An old blanket."

Antonius whirled around to Fabiola. "Was someone killed here tonight?" Fabiola struggled not to break down in front of him. Today was proving to be the worst day of her life. Could things get any worse? "Yes," she muttered.

"Who?"

"Nobody. A lowlife who started roughing up one of the girls. He killed my servant as well." Fabiola's grief over Docilosa surged up, out of control. "He deserved to die," she snarled. "Like anyone who crosses me," she added in a whisper.

"What did you say?"

Panicking, Fabiola looked away. "Nothing."

If Antonius had heard her final words, he chose to ignore them for the moment. "Whose body is it? Tell me!"

Fabiola quailed at his fierce expression. "Memor, the *lanista*."

Antonius' eyes widened. "An important man. I see your need for secrecy. So you waited until there was no one about, and then ordered your goons to get rid of the evidence. Clever. Except I saw it."

Fabiola didn't answer.

Antonius turned back to the doormen. "Go on, fuck off."

They goggled at him.

He raised a fist. "Beat it!"

Unable to believe their good luck, the pair hoisted their burden and disappeared into the darkness.

Fabiola exhaled slowly, knowing that the danger wasn't over yet.

Pushing her before him, Antonius shut the door. The bolts slid home with an ominous sound. Straightening, he looked at Fabiola with new respect. "Quite the siren, aren't you? Who'd have thought it?" he said softly. "Come too close, and you'll end up shipwrecked. Or dumped in a sewer." He laughed at his own joke. "Should I be worried? After all, it's not as if I've never knocked a woman about."

Fabiola began to feel afraid. Antonius was a big, powerful man. He could kill her with ease, and there was no one about to stop him. She backed away, but he followed and grabbed her by both arms.

"A word in your ear."

Terrified now, Fabiola bent toward him.

"Before getting any ideas, you should know something. Your little quarrel with Scaevola is no secret to me." He smiled at her surprise. "Been wondering why things have quietened down on that front? It's because I told him to back off."

Fabiola looked at Antonius, dumbstruck. That was why he'd had no guards with him.

"The *fugitivarius* knows that I'd kill him if he touched a woman I was fucking," Antonius confided amiably. His expression hardened. "But if I was tired of her *and* thought she had ideas far above her station? He'd bite my hand off to be slipped from the leash!"

He did hear what I'd said, thought Fabiola. She could hardly breathe. *Mithras,* she prayed. *Help me.* There was no response, and her hopes fell away into a dark abyss from which there was no return. She was unsurprised. This was her punishment for all that she had done. In that instant, Fabiola knew also that she didn't want to die. Not like this.

Antonius took her by the throat and squeezed. His blue eyes glittered cruelly, mocking Fabiola for her weakness. "Or I could just strangle you myself."

Choking, she began to lose consciousness.

Abruptly Antonius relaxed his grip, and Fabiola staggered away. Feeling like a mouse injured by a cat, she waited to see what he'd do next.

"I'd rather fuck you," he ordered. "Find a bed."

Numbly, Fabiola led him away.

Docilosa had been right all along. Why hadn't she listened? If she had, her servant would still be alive instead of lying cold on a table in the kitchen.

Antonius groped at Fabiola's crotch, revolting her. Yet she made no effort to stop him.

This was her lot.

†

Seeing the priestess being thrown out of the Lupanar thoroughly confused Tarquinius. The guards looked most unhappy as their huge companion roughly pushed her away from the entrance. They quailed when she cursed the building and all its inhabitants to Hades. The haruspex was perturbed and intrigued by this. Few people would dare to treat one of Orcus' followers in such a manner. For it to happen meant that someone—probably Fabiola, as she was in charge—was extremely confident of herself. Long after the priestess's outline had vanished into the darkness, he sat pondering the significance of what had transpired.

Tarquinius' conclusion came more from his powers of deduction than any sign from the wind or stars. All kinds of scenarios went through his head, but few made any sense. Docilosa wouldn't throw her own daughter out in the middle of the night, especially when she had come with a warning. Neither would Jovina, for fear of her new mistress's reaction. Why would Fabiola do it then? The haruspex dwelled on the question for an age, and eventually reasoned that Docilosa had been the woman screaming earlier. Had she been hurt, or even killed? A portent of this might have brought her daughter hurrying over, arriving too late. The priestess's reaction would have been extreme, prompting Fabiola to have her thrown out.

Had Memor been the violent customer? What had happened to him?

Before there was any chance of finding answers to these questions, Tarquinius' attention was drawn by the noise of footsteps. It sounded as if at least a dozen men were approaching the brothel, but only one man emerged into the arcs of light by the entrance. Weaving from side to side, he drew amused smiles from the guards, who didn't appear to have noticed anything untoward. The newcomer's companions stayed in the darkness, making Tarquinius very uneasy. Who were they? He was careful not to move from his position. Hopefully, they wouldn't notice him.

"Let me in!" demanded the powerfully built man. "I want to see Fabiola."

"Marcus Antonius?"

"Who else?" he sneered.

At once the guards opened the portal, allowing the noble to enter.

Tarquinius' interest in what was going on deepened. Fabiola had *two* lovers then: Decimus Brutus and the Master of the Horse. Given that he hadn't seen Antonius visit the brothel before, the men probably didn't know about each other. That meant Fabiola was playing a very dangerous game. Why? Again he scanned the sky, hoping for some information. Could he have been mistaken in his presumption that his disturbing dream involved his murder of Caelius? Perhaps it had happened tonight?

Tarquinius' hunch became certainty a short time later. The two enormous doormen emerged, carrying a lumpen shape wrapped in a blanket. Fabiola stood by the open door, hurrying them on. Their burden was clearly a human body, and was in all likelihood the man who'd caused someone to scream earlier. *Clever,* thought the haruspex. *Wait until everyone is in bed, and then get rid of the evidence.* He was pleased. Fabiola was a woman of some ability.

Tarquinius' opinion of her was strengthened when a bleary-eyed Antonius appeared in the doorway. After challenging the doormen, he had a muffled conversation with Fabiola. Then, to Tarquinius' surprise, he let them go. The door immediately closed, preventing any further insights. Drawing the conclusion that he *had* been guided to the Lupanar by his dream, the haruspex grinned. The gods wanted to show him that although there was danger in Rome, Fabiola for one was well able to look after herself.

There was no need for him to watch over her so closely.

Tarquinius had no idea how wrong he was.

XV

RUSPINA

Several weeks go by . . .

THE NORTH AFRICAN COAST, WINTER 47/46 BC

The sea was calm now, a different creature to the monster that had battered Caesar's ships on the three day crossing from Lilybaeum in Sicily. Under a clear blue sky, gentle waves rolled in, rocking the two dozen or so anchored triremes and flat-bottomed transports that lined the shore. Soldiers disembarked, gratefully jumping down into the shallow water before being handed their gear by their comrades. Using special timber frames, horses were lifted from the holds and then lowered into the sea. Their riders then led them ashore. Sacks of foodstuffs, spare equipment and dismantled *ballistae* were passed hand over hand by chains of legionaries to the ground above the waterline. Under the close supervision of a quartermaster with a tally sheet, they were piled in neat stacks.

Farther inland, the playing-card shape of a camp had been marked out; Caesar's tent and the pavilion for the headquarters had been pitched first, their positions in the center marked by a red *vexillum*. Hundreds of men were digging the first *fossa*, using the earth from their efforts to form the beginning of the defensive rampart. Centurions and *optiones* strode up and down, encouraging the toiling soldiers with alternating promises and threats. In a giant arc around them stood fully half the legionaries present, guarding against sudden attack by the enemy. In the midst of these was Romulus.

The scene was the picture of order, he thought proudly. The Roman army at its efficient best. He was only a small part of it, but he *belonged* now, which counted for so much. For the first time in his life, Romulus was somewhere that he wanted to be. He would be eternally grateful to Caesar for that. As a result, his dreams of seeing Fabiola and of killing Gemellus had been placed firmly on hold. He owed his freedom to Caesar and, in Romulus' mind, that debt had to be paid back before he could contemplate pursuing his own path again. He would repay Caesar by being a loyal and brave soldier for however long was necessary. Romulus adopted a practical approach to the effect this had on his plans. Thus far, the gods had seen fit to protect Fabiola, and with their help, she would continue to be safe. Just as they were saving Gemellus' miserable hide for him, he thought, gripping his *pilum* tightly. Every night, after his prayers for his sister's well-being, Romulus asked for the fat merchant to be alive if he ever returned to Rome.

Of course there was no guarantee that he or his comrades would survive. The campaign had got off to a bad start, with Caesar already proving fallible. Setting sail against the advice of his soothsayers and without instructing his captains where to land, Caesar and his men had run into severe weather, which had broken up the fleet. In another seemingly bad omen, the dictator had stumbled and fallen that morning as he jumped from his ship into the surf. In a master stroke, Caesar turned the ominous moment on its head by grabbing two big handfuls of shingle and shouting, "Africa, I have hold of you!" Everyone present had been able to laugh off their superstitious reaction.

Yet their situation remained critical.

Although few men had been lost, only a fraction of the force that had set out from Lilybaeum was in this anchorage. Instead of six legions, Caesar had only 3,500 legionaries, mostly cohorts from different units. More worryingly, thought Romulus, the dictator had fewer than two hundred horsemen, while the Pompeian troops in the area were dominated by Numidian cavalry. Romulus knew all too well how dangerous that could be: Crassus had also retained insufficient horse. He trusted that Longinus, the grizzled officer who'd interrogated him on Caesar's behalf, had passed on this critical detail. Unlike Crassus, Caesar trusted and relied on his subordinates, many of whom had served him for years.

However, there was little Caesar, or anyone, could do about this glaring weakness for the moment. The rest of the army had been carried off by the strong winds and heavy seas, and only the gods knew where they were now. Ships had been dispatched to scour the coast, but their quest could take days. Days in which the enemy could well discover their position.

Romulus grimaced. That eventuality did not bear thinking about. Caesar would cope. They all would—somehow. In the meantime, it was time to dig in and pray that their reinforcements arrived soon.

†

A week passed by without event. Most of the scattered fleet was rounded up and brought to join the small force that had disembarked with Caesar. While still severely outnumbered, his army had also been blessed with good fortune. The local Pompeian forces— more than ten legions strong—proved to be widely dispersed along the coastline. Led by Metellus Scipio, they had been caught napping by Caesar's arrival in the middle of winter. It was only a few days into the new year—hardly the time to start a campaign. Typically, that was just what Caesar had done. Now his enemies needed time to gather their strength, which afforded the dictator crucial breathing space.

The realization that Caesar had probably expected this lag phase helped increase Romulus' admiration for his leader. The man knew that most soldiers thought in a regimented fashion, only ever fighting in daylight and waging war when it was *supposed* to happen—in the summer. So he did the opposite. Yet Caesar's lightning-fast tactic had brought a major problem of its own: that of providing the legions with supplies. The empty transport ships were already on their way to Sicily and Sardinia, their mission being to bring back the grain for which there had been no space on the voyage over. In the meantime, though, Caesar's main business was not seeking battle with the enemy, but rather finding food for his men. For a number of reasons, this task was proving more difficult than anticipated.

Romulus had been pondering the problem himself. Stuck on sentry duty much of the time, there was little else to do. Caesar's army could not forage far inland for fear of being cut off from the coast and the reinforcements, which were landing daily. Several veteran legions had yet to arrive, and their presence in a set-piece battle would be crucial. Like the Twenty-Eighth—Romulus' unit—most of Caesar's legions had been formed during the civil war, and were relatively inexperienced.

They still needed food, though. Lots of it.

Unfortunately, local agriculture had been disrupted in a major way. As well as gathering all the food they could find, the Pompeians had conscripted large numbers of peasants into their army. The farms in the fertile landscape were thus largely empty, forcing Caesar's men to harvest any remaining crops for themselves. Inevitably, these did not last for long, and so the dictator had led his legions to the nearby town of Hadrumentum. The Pompeian garrison there barred the gates and refused to surrender. Caesar had neither the time nor the equipment to put a siege in place, so marched on to Ruspina, where he established his main base. Leptis, another local settlement, soon opened its gates to the Caesarean forces, but neither Leptis nor its neighbor was capable of supplying thousands of soldiers for more than one or two days.

The cavalry's horses were in even worse straits, until some veterans had the brainwave of harvesting seaweed from the shore. Washed in fresh water and dried in the sun, it supplied enough nutrients to keep the mounts alive if not well fed. Such ideas were thin on the ground, though, and the soldiers needed more than seaweed to be able to march—and fight. They had been on two-thirds of their normal rations since arriving, and that could not continue.

Hence the major foraging party, thought Romulus, looking over his shoulder at the long column behind him and the dust cloud hanging over it. He was grateful that the Twenty-Eighth had been given the honor of taking the lead, thus avoiding the choking powder thrown up by the passage of so many men. Led by Caesar himself, the patrol was thirty cohorts strong, and mostly made up of soldiers from his less experienced legions. They had set out less than an hour before, marching without their equipment and prepared for battle. Their main purpose was to spot fields of unharvested crops. Traveling south, they kept to the dirt road that led to Uzitta. Wheat was the preferred foodstuff, but Romulus and his comrades were no longer picky. Barley, oats and whatever other foods could be scavenged would fill their bellies. Yet they had come across precious little so far.

As the soldiers passed through tiny villages full of mud-brick houses, they were watched by the terrified locals, mainly women, children and the old. Under strict orders from Caesar, no looting took place. It was bad enough that they were taking the peasants' food, he said, without stealing what few valuables they had too. For once, it wasn't difficult for his hungry men to obey the order. They only had eyes for the fields around each settlement that contained the crops. Naturally, everything edible this near to Ruspina had already been harvested and hidden by the locals, or previously commandeered by Caesarean troops.

At least they had plenty to drink, thought Romulus. Thanks to the deep wells in Ruspina, every man's leather water bag was full. Marching was much easier when every drop of fluid didn't have to be treated as if it were gold. The fact that it was winter meant that the temperatures were nothing like the cauldron of the Parthian desert either. Romulus had terrible memories of the raging thirst he'd suffered while traveling through that alien landscape with Brennus and Tarquinius.

The thought of the haruspex now made Romulus feel sad, nostalgic even. The passage of time had diluted his anger over what Tarquinius had done. He'd admitted to himself that Caesar's grant of manumission might never have occurred if events hadn't happened the way they did. Yet it was hard not to wonder what would have happened if he hadn't had to flee Rome with Brennus. His life could still have been a success. *I might have won my freedom in the arena by earning the coveted* rudis. *Or died instead,* he reflected. *Who knows?* Romulus had not quite reached the point of forgiving Tarquinius, but he no longer felt the burning fury toward his mentor that he had in Alexandria. It had become a matter that they could discuss and sort out, man to man. If they ever met, that was.

Romulus sighed. What chance was there of that? Precious little. Best not to think about Tarquinius too much. No point worrying about things he couldn't change. Better to concentrate on the matters to hand, such as finding some food. With all the fields empty, that tactic didn't work for long. Thinking about winning the war worked no better—the Pompeians were so numerous that, despite Caesar's unparalleled leadership, success was by no means certain.

Only time would tell. Romulus tried another method, tuning in to the song being bawled out by someone in the rank ahead. As was often the case, it was about Caesar himself. Each lurid verse featured one of the many noblewomen he had conducted affairs with, while the chorus advised the men of Rome to lock up their wives when the "baldheaded lecher" returned to the city for good. Romulus joined in with gusto. The first time he'd heard the mocking chant, he had been shocked by Caesar's tolerance of it. Later, he'd come to see that it showed the huge affection in which the general was held by his men, and Caesar knew that.

"Halt!" bellowed Atilius, their senior centurion. "Halt!"

The order was repeated at once by the unit's trumpeter, who marched beside Atilius.

Wondering what was going on, Romulus peered into the distance. His comrades did likewise. Their German and Gaulish cavalry still only numbered four hundred or so, and a quarter of these were scouting the terrain before them. The eagle-eyed Atilius must have spotted some of the tribesmen returning. An instant later, Romulus' suspicion was confirmed by the sight of a small dust cloud, which preceded the arrival of a troop of horsemen. The Gauls had soon galloped in, passing the Twenty-Eighth. Riding with only small shields for protection, the pigtailed, lightly armed warriors ignored the questions thrown their way by the curious legionaries. Caesar, who had led them through the conquest of Gaul, was the only man they would speak to. As the commander, he was in the usual position halfway along the column.

Still nothing could be seen. The countryside was relatively flat with few trees, which meant that it was possible to see for up to a mile in front of the patrol's position. The legionaries began to relax, grounding their shields and taking sips of water from their carriers. Their officers didn't interfere. With no enemy in sight, there was no harm in this behavior.

A short while later, most of the Gauls came trotting back past the Twenty-Eighth.

"Look," said Romulus, spotting a familiar red cloak. "Caesar is with them!"

Even Atilius turned his head and stared. "They must want to show him something," he growled. Like many officers in the Twenty-Eighth, Atilius was a veteran of the Tenth, Caesar's favorite legion. He and his comrades had ostensibly been drafted in to form a nucleus from which the less experienced soldiers could learn backbone and discipline. In some circles, though, it was whispered that they were the mutineers who had marched on Rome just a few months before, posted out of their original unit to prevent more trouble. Either way, Atilius was a fine soldier and reminded Romulus of Bassius, the old centurion who had led him in Parthia.

Wondering where the other Gauls had gone, Romulus glanced over his shoulder. Half a dozen warriors were riding back to the rear. Adrenaline surged through him. "He's sent for the rest of the cavalry and the archers, sir," he cried. "Must be expecting trouble."

Atilius gave Romulus an appraising stare. The story of the slave who had been condemned to die in the arena yet instead won his freedom by killing a rhinoceros had traveled through the ranks of the Twenty-Eighth long before Romulus had arrived in Lilybaeum. Because of his previous history, he had been assigned to a different cohort from that in which he'd served before. To give him his due, the young soldier was physically fit, responded to orders well and performed his duties to Atilius' satisfaction. That made him no different to many of the legionaries under his command, and so the senior centurion was reserving judgment until an opportunity for Romulus to prove his real worth presented itself. "So he has. We might have to forget about our grumbling bellies until later."

"Yes, sir." Romulus could sense Atilius' coolness and suspected the reason behind it. It was the same, or worse, with a few of his new comrades, who disliked him for receiving what they saw as special treatment from Caesar. There was no outright hostility, just begrudging looks and a lack of camaraderie. Although it was hard, Romulus could cope with that. From the majority, though, he received a kind of reluctant admiration, as well as a good deal of ribbing about being the best man to fight the Pompeians' elephants, of which there were reputed to be 120. Romulus bore these comments with good humor, knowing that it was an eventual route to gaining their acceptance. With luck, fighting together would accelerate that.

He looked forward to more comradeship. Petronius' death had hit Romulus hard, accentuating the pain of his split with Tarquinius and reopening the wound of Brennus' last stand. Although he hadn't been able to save Petronius, at least he'd tried to. *Why didn't I stay with Brennus?* Romulus asked himself repeatedly. Beside that, even his manumission seemed trivial. *I could have died with my blood brother, instead of running like a coward.* Telling himself that Mithras had meant for him and Tarquinius to escape felt like an excuse—an easy way out.

A few moments after Caesar had ridden off, the *bucinae* blared from the general's position. He had issued his orders before leaving.

"Hear that?" Atilius grinned wolfishly. "Prepare to move out," he bawled.

Excitement and a little fear rippled through the ranks. The enemy had to be near.

Readying his *pila*, Romulus advanced alongside his comrades. His eyes scanned the terrain constantly, especially around the point where Caesar and the Gauls were heading. Soon the horsemen had become nothing more than a dust cloud. For an age, Romulus saw nothing. The tension continued to build. Only so much time could pass on African soil before they met the Pompeians, and now combat was imminent. Every man could sense it.

This feeling was heightened by the sight of the Gaulish cavalry halting at the top of a gradual incline. The legionaries followed Caesar's tracks up a long, sloping ascent. Nearing the crest, they saw that he had stopped in order to survey the area. Their general was talking animatedly to the Gauls' commander. His arm stabbed here and there, pointing out important details. Then Caesar turned to see how close his cohorts were. A smile crossed his face.

Instinctively, the soldiers' pace quickened.

Atilius was a dozen paces in front, so it was he who reached the crest and spotted the Pompeians first. "Jupiter above," Romulus heard him say.

Soon he was able to see the enemy for himself.

A plain stretched away from where Caesar was sitting on his horse. On the far side of it, about half a mile away, was an immensely wide formation of soldiers. The sheer length of the Pompeian line spoke volumes. There were thousands more men in it than in Caesar's foraging party. Many legionaries' faces paled.

Atilius sensed the mood. "Caesar is no fool," he bellowed. "He won't offer battle against that rabble unless he has to."

Romulus felt a tickle of unease. It wasn't certain that any fighting would take place, yet already the men around him were wavering. Not a good start, he thought. He was pleased when Atilius continued talking to his soldiers while raining abuse on the Pompeians. Reassured, the legionaries settled.

While he might not have desired battle, Caesar could not fail to respond to the enemy's presence so close to his own. Sharp blasts from the trumpeters soon had the cohorts assembling in a long line similar to that of the Pompeians. To match the enemy's width, however, his soldiers had to form up only one cohort deep. This was a major departure from normal tactics, which saw a minimum of two lines to face any enemy, and caused more uneasiness in the ranks.

"He must be worried about being flanked," Romulus confided to Sabinus, the legionary on his right. They'd become friends over the previous few weeks.

"I suppose," Sabinus grunted. "Never mind that we've got fuck-all cavalry to defend us there."

A short, black-haired man with a strong chin, Sabinus had been in Pompey's army at Pharsalus. Like thousands of his compatriots, he had surrendered and sworn loyalty to Caesar. They'd fought well since, in Egypt and at Zela. That had been against foreigners, though, Romulus worried, enemies who'd had nothing to do with the Pompeians. Today it was time to confront troops whom many of these soldiers would have previously fought beside.

Like any officer worth his salt, Atilius realized that his legionaries were still uneasy. First the *signiferi* and then the *aquilifer* were brought into the front rank. There were proud reactions when the silver eagle arrived, with loud vows being made that no enemy would ever lay his hands on the legion's most important possession. Atilius also had a word with his subordinates, who began walking along the ranks, addressing individual soldiers by name. The senior centurion did likewise, pinching men's cheeks and slapping their arms, telling them how brave they were.

Caesar himself rode along the front of the Fifth Legion, the tribesmen he'd recruited in Gaul and made into Roman citizens because of their loyal service. His exact words didn't carry through the air, but the rousing cheers that followed did.

Thus prepared, Caesar's cohorts waited to see what Metellus Scipio would do.

It wasn't long before the answer came.

To Romulus' amazement, large parts of what had appeared to be closely bunched infantry in the lines opposite were actually cavalry. Numidians. In a stunning exercise of subterfuge, Scipio had concealed the true nature of his forces until the last moment. Now they began to move, the large squadrons of horsemen galloping out to either side on the flat ground between the two armies. From the middle of the enemy's position ran thousands of foot soldiers: lightly armed Numidian infantry.

Scipio wanted a battle and, thanks to his clever tactics, he would get it. Despite Caesar's thinning of the line, his men now had every chance of being outflanked. There was little point in refusing to fight, Romulus realized, because the Pompeians would then harry them all the way back to Ruspina. By standing and fighting, though, they faced the distinct possibility of annihilation. As Crassus had at Carrhae. Bitterness filled him at the thought of serving under two generals who lost through lack of cavalry.

Caesar's few archers finally came trotting from the rear, their faces lathered with sweat. The 150 men had made the journey from Ruspina at the double in order to catch up with the foraging party. Without a rest, they were sent off in front of the main force. The remaining cavalry also arrived, joining up with the men around Caesar. The patrol was immediately split up, with two hundred Gauls being placed on each flank. It was a trifling number, and Romulus cringed when he looked out at the Numidian cavalry pounding across the plain toward them. There had to be seven or eight thousand in total. Twenty horsemen for each of Caesar's, and Numidians at that. The world's best cavalry, which, under Hannibal, had repeatedly helped to butcher Roman armies.

Thankfully, he had no time to dwell on the disparity between the two sides.

The *bucinae* sounded the advance.

Caesar's response to Scipio's offer of battle was to accept. It was typically brave of the general, but neither he nor his men could have prepared themselves for the onslaught that began moments later.

The cohorts marched forward, each keeping close to its neighbors. Pacing them on the flanks were the Gaulish cavalry. The air was filled with the characteristic sounds of thousands of marching men: the tramp of studded sandals in unison on the ground, the jingle of chain mail, the clash of metal off shields and the shouts of officers. Romulus could hear men coughing nervously and muttering prayers to their favorite gods. Few spoke. He cast his own eyes up to the heavens, wondering if anything would be revealed. All he saw was blue sky. Romulus clenched his teeth, taking comfort from the soldiers on each side of him and ignoring the tang of fear in the smell of their sweat.

This was the worst part: the anticipation before the actual battle started.

"Keep moving," roared Atilius from his position in the very center of the third rank. "Stay in line with the other cohorts!"

Soon they could make out the individual shapes of the Numidian infantry running toward them. Thin, wiry figures with dark hair and light brown skin, they wore short, sleeveless tunics belted at the waist with rope. Like their mounted comrades, they wore no armor, carrying only a small round shield for protection. Their arms consisted of light throwing spears and javelins, and a knife. Barefoot, they danced along the hot ground singly and in groups, closing in on the Roman lines like packs of hunting dogs.

"Don't look up to much, do they?" sneered Sabinus.

His comment was greeted with contemptuous grunts of agreement.

Romulus' spirits lifted. It *was* hard to see how the lightly armed skirmishers could have any meaningful impact on their lines. Although the Gaulish cavalry would come off worst, perhaps they, the infantry, could turn the tide in Caesar's favor?

They were now within a hundred paces of the enemy. Close enough to pick out individual men's faces. To see their lips twisted back in fury. To hear their ululating war cries.

Romulus licked his lips. It was nearly time.

An instant later, the *bucinae* sounded the charge.

"Up and at them, men," roared Atilius. "Wait for my call to release your *pila*."

The Twenty-Eighth surged forward.

Romulus' *caligae* pounded off the short grass. He glanced left and right, taking in the bunched jaws, the nervous faces and the downright terrified expressions of a few soldiers. As always, his own stomach was knotted with nerves. The sooner they closed with the enemy, the better. He scanned the figures running toward them, and felt slightly reassured. The Numidians looked puny compared to the heavily armed men all around him. Sabinus had to be right. What chance had these skirmishers of resisting a charge by legionaries?

†

Half an hour later, Romulus was of a different mind altogether. Rather than meet the legionaries in a clash of shield against shield, and engage in brutal hand-to-hand combat, the Numidians acted almost like horsemen. Fleet of foot, and unencumbered by equipment, they ran in toward the Romans, discharged a volley of javelins, and fled. If they were pursued, they kept running. When the exhausted legionaries stopped to take a breather, the Numidians swarmed back, flinging spears and throwing taunts in their guttural tongue. Nothing the Romans did made any difference. While few men had been killed, there were dozens of injured. It was the same story all along the line.

Here and there, frustrated groups of Caesar's soldiers had ignored their officers and broken ranks to charge the groups of the enemy that ventured close to their positions. Romulus had developed a healthy respect for the Numidians, whose tactics changed when attacked in this manner. They turned in unison like a flock of birds, but their purpose was altogether more deadly. The pursuing clusters of legionaries were quickly enveloped and overwhelmed by sheer weight of numbers. Then, before the watching cohorts could respond, the enemy skirmishers were gone again, running back toward their own lines.

Romulus was quite worried. Atilius and his officers had kept most of the Twenty-Eighth in position, but the Numidians' assaults were whittling away at the men's confidence. Without the officers' constant reassuring shouts, and the waving of the eagle, he thought they might have broken and run by now. Romulus could see by the wavering of the other cohorts' positions that the situation was the same everywhere.

The Gaulish cavalry was faring no better. Driven backward by the Numidians, they were struggling to remain anywhere near Caesar's flanks. Already the cohorts on the edges were having to defend themselves against harrying attacks from the javelin-throwing horsemen. Before long, the enemy riders would have enveloped the entire patrol, blocking off its only avenue of escape. Romulus had vivid memories from Carrhae of what befell infantry when that happened. He didn't mention a word of this to Sabinus or the men around him, but there was no need. They'd heard the story of Curio, Caesar's former tribune in Africa, who had come unstuck in this manner the previous year. Moreover, they could see what was happening for themselves.

Panic was creeping into the faces of many.

Romulus could feel the first flutters of it in his belly too.

XVI

LABIENUS AND PETREIUS

Caesar had seen what was going on. Soon orders were carried by messengers along his entire front that no one, on pain of death, was to move more than four paces from the main line occupied by his cohort. Romulus took great heart from this. Caesar was even roving between units, talking to the legionaries and bolstering their courage. In the cohort next to Romulus, he had seen a wavering *signifer* turn around and try to flee. Grabbing the man, Caesar had turned him bodily to face back toward the Numidians, telling him, "Look, the enemy's that way!" It had raised a shamefaced laugh from the surrounding soldiers, and bolstered the other units' courage.

Caesar's men held their lines still, but his fighting words could not stop the relentless harrying by the enemy skirmishers and horsemen. By the time an hour had passed, scores of soldiers had been injured in each cohort, and their cries did little to decrease the general unease in the ranks. Something drastic needed to be done if the situation wasn't going to spiral out of control. Romulus could feel his own determination being drained. Cursing the wraithlike Numidians, he shoved his black thoughts away.

To add to their distress, the Pompeian leader was revealed to be Labienus, not Metellus Scipio. Formerly one of Caesar's most trusted legates during the prolonged campaign in Gaul, Labienus had changed sides after Caesar's crossing of the Rubicon. Infuriated, Caesar had sent his baggage after him. Like many of the Pompeian leaders, Labienus had taken part in the battle of Pharsalus, but after Caesar's victory, he had traveled to Africa rather than surrender. An accomplished general in his own right, he now took the opportunity to urge on his own men and to harangue Caesar's battered cohorts.

Riding bareheaded into the no-man's-land between the two armies, Labienus taunted the legionaries with astute barbs that showed his awareness of their inexperience. "Greetings, raw soldiers! What are you doing?" he cried. "You're terrifying me!"

No one replied.

Urging his mount nearer Caesar's lines, Labienus continued in the same vein. "Has Caesar taken you all in with his honeyed words? Look at you now!" With a sneer, he pointed at their ragged appearance and the number of wounded. "What a place your general has guided you all to. I pity the lot of you."

The exhausted legionaries glanced at each other. Few received any reassurance. Here was one of Caesar's former leaders, whose men were winning the battle, insulting them with impunity.

Romulus felt differently. *Come closer, you bastard,* he thought, his fingers itching on the shaft of his javelin. The Pompeian leader was still out of range, though.

Emboldened by the lack of response from Caesar's men, Labienus moved his horse forward a dozen steps. Then a dozen more. "You're pathetic," he shouted. "Call yourselves Romans? The peasants from the little farms around here make better recruits than you!"

Before Romulus could react, Atilius pushed his way forward. "I'm no raw recruit, Labienus," he shouted, "but a veteran of the Tenth Legion."

Taken aback for a moment, Labienus quickly recovered his poise. "Really? Where's your standard then?" he demanded. "I can see none for the Tenth."

Atilius pulled off his centurion's crested helmet and tossed it to the ground. Staring proudly at Labienus so that he could be recognized, he stuck out a hand behind him. "A *pilum*," he ordered. "Now."

Romulus broke ranks to give Atilius his remaining one.

"I'll show you what kind of soldier I am, you whoreson," the senior centurion roared. "One of Caesar's best." Lunging forward, he threw the javelin with all his might at Labienus.

Romulus held his breath.

His *pilum* hummed through the air to strike the legate's mount squarely in the chest. Severely wounded, the horse collapsed, kicking, to the ground. Labienus was thrown free, but landed badly. There was a dramatic silence as he lay sprawled on the ground. Eventually, he picked himself up with a groan.

"Remember, Labienus, that it was a veteran of the Tenth who attacked you," shouted Atilius.

Romulus and his comrades cheered at the tops of their voices.

Labienus did not reply. Holding his left side, he hobbled away with the jeers of the Twenty-Eighth ringing in his ears. His horse was left kicking and bleeding in the dirt.

"Fine shot, sir," Romulus said to Atilius, remembering how he'd once brought down a Parthian archer at a similar range. "You taught him a lesson."

"It's a sad day nonetheless," replied Atilius quietly. "I served under Labienus a number of times. He's a good leader."

"But he's not with Caesar," said Romulus stoutly, feeling a flush of loyalty to the man who'd pardoned him. "He has to take the consequences of that."

Atilius squinted at him, and then a smile creased his lined face. "Aye, lad. He does."

†

Unfortunately, the senior centurion's effort at rallying the legionaries' spirits did not last for long. While the Twenty-Eighth steadied itself, the surrounding cohorts did not. The Numidian attacks grew ever bolder, with squadrons of horsemen riding in with the skirmishers to launch huge volleys of javelins at the Romans. Nervous of being struck down, the inexperienced soldiers clustered together, reducing their ability to fight back as well as making themselves more of a target. On and on it went. There were so many Pompeian troops that they could keep up a constant attack on the beleaguered Caesarean cohorts.

The only things that differed from Carrhae, thought Romulus, were the facts that the enemy javelins didn't have the penetrative force of the arrows from the Parthian recurved bows, and that the temperature wasn't quite as hot as the Mesopotamian desert. All the same, thirst and dehydration were beginning to rear their ugly heads. The battle had been going on all day now, and most men's water carriers were long since empty. They'd had no food since dawn either.

Caesar did not disappoint Romulus. Ordering the cohorts to spread out, he had alternate units turn about so that they faced the Numidian cavalry that was attacking their rear, while the others continued to confront the waves of skirmishers to the front. Atilius and the other senior centurions were entrusted once more with the task of rallying the men's morale. Then, in a simultaneous action, both parts charged at the enemy, hurling their remaining *pila*. To the legionaries' surprise and delight, the Numidians retreated before the ferocity of their attack.

At once the recall sounded.

"This is the first time we've got the fuckers on the run!" Sabinus cried.

"Our energy won't last," Romulus explained. "When we stop, they'll turn on us again. This is our chance to get away."

The *bucinae* repeated their command, and men's faces lit up at the chance of escaping the hellhole in which they'd been trapped all day. Forming up, the cohorts began retreating toward Ruspina with the remaining Gaulish cavalry formed up on the flanks as protection. They didn't get far before enemy reinforcements could be seen approaching from the south. Comprised of cavalry and infantry, the newly arrived Pompeians immediately set out in pursuit of the battered foraging party. Reinvigorated, their exhausted comrades followed close behind.

Seeing the new danger, Caesar had his men halt and turn about once more. Soon afterward one of his messengers came in search of Atilius. "Caesar wants six cohorts to lead a counterattack, sir," he panted. "Three from the Fifth, and three from the Twenty-Eighth. Says you've earned it."

Atilius' chest blew out with pride. "Did you hear that, boys?" he shouted. "Caesar has noticed your bravery."

Despite their cracked, dry throats, the legionaries managed a rousing cheer.

"What are Caesar's orders?" demanded Atilius.

"He wants an attack three cohorts wide, two deep, sir," came the answer. "Push the fresh enemy troops back. Give them a bloody nose that they won't forget. We just need enough time to get back to Ruspina." With a quick salute, the messenger was off to the next cohort.

Atilius turned to his men. "I know you're all tired, but give me one last effort. Then we can go home." He eyed the Pompeian reinforcements, which were descending from some high ground to the southeast. "We'll need to send them packing back over that. Can you do it?"

"Yes, sir," they mumbled.

"I can't hear you," Atilius bellowed.

"YES, SIR!" the men cried, fired by his enthusiasm and the honor granted them by Caesar. Romulus was particularly stirred by their mission. With no backup from their cavalry, it was perilous in the extreme. If anything went wrong, they'd be completely on their own. No less a man than Caesar had asked for it, though, and it was a chance to help every one of the tired soldiers in the patrol. Something Romulus had wanted to do, but could not, on the retreat from Carrhae.

The senior centurion smiled. "Good." Leading the cohort out of rank, he waited as two more picked from the Twenty-Eighth joined them. The Fifth's position was farther to the rear, and its three chosen cohorts were already waiting to one side of the retreating patrol. The senior centurions from the units conferred with each other before Atilius' cohort took the right flank, while the center and left flank were formed by two from the Fifth. The three remaining units assembled to their rear, and they set off.

When Atilius returned, Romulus couldn't help himself. "How come we have this position, sir?" They were in the place normally awarded to the most experienced part of an army; he had expected one of the Fifth's cohorts to take it.

Atilius looked pleased. "The others said that my javelin throw had earned me the honor. Now we all have the chance to win some glory."

Romulus grinned. Atilius seemed more and more like Bassius as the day went on. It was easy to follow such an officer into battle. Fearless, tough and prepared to take all of the risks that his soldiers had to, Atilius was the epitome of a leader. Romulus had to give Caesar the same credit too. Their general had played a huge part in maintaining his legionaries' morale, and could still be seen urging on those who were falling behind. Although he was in his midfifties, Caesar acted like a man half his age.

What more could a soldier ask for?

Determination filled Romulus that he would help drive back the advancing Pompeian troops, or die in the attempt. His leaders and comrades deserved no less.

Atilius glanced to either side, and raised an arm. "Close order," he ordered. "Shields high. Draw swords."

The distinctive sound of *gladii* sliding from their scabbards filled the air. Almost no legionaries had any *pila* left; after an entire day of combat fought back and forth over a large area, most had been damaged or were irretrievable. Their charge would hopefully lead them into close-quarters fighting for the first time. There they could use their deadly swords and the metal bosses of their *scuta* to exact revenge for the torture they'd been put through by the Pompeians. It was a pleasing prospect for the bitterly frustrated soldiers.

"Forward!" bellowed Atilius. He took off at a gentle trot, and six cohorts followed.

Soon they could tell that the enemy reinforcements were predominantly infantry, but were supported by a strong force of cavalry on each wing. Foot soldiers never liked facing horsemen at the best of times, yet all the men present knew of Caesar's tactic at Pharsalus sixteen months before. This stunning success had been at the root of their general's victory, and had been drilled into every one of his soldiers since. While they no longer had *pila* to jab at the riders' faces, the legionaries had the confidence of knowing that a charge on the enemy riders gave them a chance of breaking the attack. Horsemen were not invincible. That was the theory, anyway.

By the time they had covered a quarter of a mile, the Pompeians were closing fast. The cavalry were keeping their mounts reined in so that they didn't overtake the foot soldiers, but a swelling roar of anger could be heard from their ranks. These were men who had missed the whole day's fighting; no doubt their leaders had promised them the glory of winning the battle.

"Double time!" Atilius shouted. With an energy that scarcely seemed possible given their ordeal, he broke into a full run. In a clever move, the *signifer* was right beside him.

Battle madness, which had been lacking in the Twenty-Eighth all day, began to seize control of the men. Keeping silent as they'd been trained, they used the frenzy to push their tired bodies to the same speed as Atilius. It was at times like this when their mail shirts, helmets and *scuta* became as heavy as lead. Although the soldiers' muscles screamed for a rest, the cohort's standard meant nearly as much as the silver eagle. It could not under any circumstances fall into enemy hands. For it to do so would bring disgrace down on every man's head, a dishonor that could only be wiped away by its recovery.

Naturally, the other cohorts kept up with Atilius' men. With the safety of their comrades entrusted to their care, no one was prepared to be left behind. Caesar was watching.

The advancing Numidians were taken aback by the speed and ferocity of the Roman counterattack. They had been told that after a long day of fighting, their enemies were exhausted and ready to break. Instead, they were confronted by the sight of six cohorts bearing down on them like packs of vengeful wolves. Foot soldiers against cavalry? Surely only madmen would take part in such an assault?

The cavalry slowed noticeably, and the light infantry did likewise.

Atilius saw the Pompeians' hesitation at once, and acted on it. "Stay in close order! Keep your shields high," he shouted, increasing his speed and raising his *gladius*. "Remember, aim for their faces!"

Narrowing the gap between Sabinus and the man on his other side, Romulus gripped the hilt of his sword until his knuckles went white. His comrades were doing likewise, but their pace did not slacken. The Numidian cavalry was only about thirty paces away now, close enough for them to see the mounts' nostrils flare with nervousness at the line of approaching *scuta*. To pick out the features of individual riders, and the painted designs on the fronts of their shields. Charging a line of advancing horses was terrifying and Romulus gritted his teeth. If they failed, the remaining cohorts would be routed back to Ruspina. In that case, few men would survive. Everything depended on them.

The Pompeian officers did not react quickly enough to their men's indecision and their advance had slowed right down by the time the Caesarean troops hit. Screaming like maniacs to scare the horses, Atilius and his men barged into the Numidian cavalry. The faster-moving enemy riders broke open the front of the Roman lines, knocking soldiers to the ground, but most had lost their momentum. Shields slammed into the mounts' chests and *gladii* stabbed upward at their riders. Like all light cavalry, the Numidians wore no armor and carried only a small round shield for protection. They were not the type of troops to meet a charge by heavy infantry head on, and their javelins were unable to punch through heavy *scuta*. In contrast, the legionaries' iron blades bit deep into men's thighs, bellies and chests, injuring and killing Numidians aplenty. Horses were slashed across the neck or stabbed in the ribs, causing them to rear up in terror, spraying blood over everyone within arm's reach. Ignoring their dashing hooves, Caesar's men darted into the gaps, disemboweling the steeds or hamstringing them. The next rank of cavalrymen looked panic-stricken at the sight of frenzied legionaries emerging from the slaughter with bloodied *gladii* and snarling faces. Instinctively, they reined in, and some tried to turn their horses' heads around. Of course their fear was obvious, and the baying legionaries redoubled their efforts.

Within the space of a hundred heartbeats, the enemy attack on the Twenty-Eighth had come to a standstill. Romulus could see that the Caesarean standards were all still roughly in a line, which meant that the Fifth's cohorts were achieving the same results.

Pushing in behind came the other three units, which kept up their momentum. Exhilaration filled Romulus. After all the fear and setbacks of the day, it seemed that courage and determination were being rewarded at last. Already many of the horsemen were looking to the rear. All they had to do was keep up the pressure, and the Numidians would break and run.

Of course there were always leaders who could pull the fat from the fire. Screaming orders at his riders, an officer clad in Roman army uniform on a fine white stallion managed to drag the Numidians' rear sections away before the Twenty-Eighth had reached them. Galloping back three hundred paces, he rallied the panicked tribesmen before leading a stinging attack on the side of Atilius' cohort. Riding in at speed, the whooping cavalry threw their javelins in a thick shower and retreated, as they had all day.

The volley caused heavy casualties among the unprepared legionaries, whose shields were raised against attack from the front, not the side. At once the tactic was repeated, with similar results. Dozens of men were down now, and fear was mushrooming in the rest. It was a shining example of how the course of a battle could be turned around. Romulus watched the scarlet-cloaked Roman officer directing operations and cursed. If this went on, all their efforts would have been in vain.

"I know him," shouted Sabinus. "It's Marcus Petreius, one of Pompey's best generals."

Romulus watched Petreius gallop off to the far flank, no doubt to emulate his success here. "The bastard's got to be stopped, or they'll turn us over."

"What can we do?" Sabinus retorted. "He's out on the open battlefield on a damn horse and we're on foot."

Romulus didn't answer, but a daring idea was coming to mind. Breaking rank, he trotted over to Atilius, who was directing sections of legionaries forward into the Numidian lines. "A word, sir," he shouted.

The senior centurion looked around, surprised. "Make it quick."

"Did you see the attack on the cohort's right flank a moment ago, sir?"

"Of course I did," scowled Atilius. "Now the prick has gone off to repeat the same with the rest of his cavalry."

"I'll kill him, sir. Just give me two men," Romulus pleaded.

He had all of Atilius' attention now. "What will you do?"

"Make our way through the melee," Romulus explained. "Pick up some enemy javelins on the way. Somehow get close enough, and bring him down."

"Causing panic in his men," muttered the senior centurion. "With luck, they'd flee."

Romulus grinned. "Yes, sir."

Atilius scanned the open ground to their right. Apart from a few scrubby bushes, there was hardly any shelter. Waves of Numidian cavalry were sweeping back and forth across it to attack the Twenty-Eighth. "It's a suicide mission," he said.

"Maybe it is, sir. But if someone doesn't stop the whoreson, they'll soon break our attack."

"True." Atilius thought for a moment. "Three men less in the cohort won't save our skins either. Do it."

Romulus could hardly believe his ears. "Sir!" He snapped off a crisp salute and pushed his way back through the press to Sabinus' side. Quickly he filled the dark-haired soldier in on his plan.

"Been praying to Fortuna?" Sabinus asked sarcastically. "We'll need her guiding every step of the way to stay alive."

"Are you with me or not?" Romulus demanded. "We're defending the rest of the column, remember?"

Sabinus spat a curse and then nodded. "Very well."

"I heard what you said, comrade. Count me in too," said a thick-set legionary wearing a bronze helmet with its horsehair crest missing. He stuck out his right arm. "Gaius Paullus."

Romulus grinned and accepted the grip. "Let's go." Shoving through the ebbing and flowing ranks of legionaries, they soon reached the edge of the cohort. Injured men were everywhere here, screaming at the iron-tipped javelins that had struck them in their arms or legs. Those who had been hit in the neck or face sprawled uncaring on the ground, forcing Romulus and his two comrades to step over them. Mentally, he asked their forgiveness. It helped—a little.

Once in the outermost rank, Romulus took in the situation at a glance. There was no sign of an *optio* or centurion here, which meant that they'd been killed. The Numidian attacks had already left huge gaps in the side of the cohort. It would not be long before the beleaguered legionaries were either overwhelmed or ran away. Time was of the essence, but they also had to wait until Petreius returned from the left flank.

Ducking down behind their *scuta*, the trio weathered a number of Numidian attacks. There was no chance of defending themselves, just the ignominy of hiding away from the enemy javelins. Eventually, though, Romulus saw the distinctive white stallion reappear behind the regrouping cavalry. "There he is," he muttered, pointing.

"It's about three hundred paces," muttered Sabinus.

"A long way," added Paullus.

A strange calm fell over Romulus. "Leave your shields. Helmets too," he ordered. Wiping his bloody blade on the bottom of his tunic, he sheathed it. "Take off your mail shirts."

The other two stared at him as though he were raving mad.

"We stand out a mile in our gear," Romulus hissed. "It's also damn heavy. Without it, the Numidians might think we're riders whose mounts have been killed."

Understanding blossomed on their faces and they began to obey. The dazed soldiers nearby looked on uncomprehendingly as the three stripped themselves of all their equipment. Underneath their thigh-length chain mail, their padded russet jerkins were saturated in sweat.

"Gods, that feels good," said Paullus with a grin.

A shower of enemy javelins came scudding overhead and the smile disappeared from his face.

Swiftly they lifted their shields again until the attack had ended. Reaching out carefully, each man picked some Numidian light throwing spears from the dozens that lay scattered amid the bodies.

Romulus waited until the enemy horsemen had turned around. "Now!" he hissed. "After them!"

The trio shot forward like Greek sprinters at a games. The retreating tribesmen did not look back and, as Romulus had hoped, their mounts concealed the trio from the Numidians who were waiting to move forward. The crucial moment would be when the two lines met, and the new wave of attackers rode out.

They had covered about half the distance when Romulus saw horses' heads appearing in the gaps between the retreating cavalry. "Down on your bellies!" he shouted.

Sabinus and Paullus understood now.

All three threw themselves headlong to the hard ground. Pressing their faces into the dirt, they lay like dead men. Soon they could feel the earth shaking from the cavalry's approach. Romulus' heart was hammering in his chest, and he had to stop himself from trying to see what was going on.

An instant later, dozens of Numidians rode past at the canter. Shouting to each other in their own tongue, they didn't even look at the soldiers: just three more bodies on a littered battlefield.

Sabinus made to get up, but Romulus grabbed his arm. "Stay put," he whispered. "The others will see us. We wait until the first lot pull back, and then do the same again."

Fear mixed with determination in Sabinus' face. "What then?"

"Get in between their horses," said Romulus with as much confidence as he could muster. "Make a beeline for Petreius."

"And pray," muttered Paullus from his other side.

"If we're successful?" asked Sabinus.

"Head for our lines," Romulus replied. *What chance will we have?* he wondered. *Little to none.* The reality of their plight sank in. They'd committed themselves, though, and their comrades were depending on them.

The end of the Numidian attack was marked by a chorus of screams from the legionaries who'd been injured. Soon after that, the pounding of hooves shook the ground again as the light cavalry pulled back. Romulus waited until the last of the riders had gone past. "Now," he cried. "Run as if your life depended on it."

Jumping up, they tore after the Numidian horsemen. This time, they were closer behind the enemy, and once again none of the stationary riders saw them. Romulus counted his steps as he ran. Thirty paces, then forty. Fifty. Sixty. Still no one cried out or threw a javelin. Craning his head this way and that, he looked frantically for Petreius' scarlet cloak amid the press.

"There," shouted Paullus, pointing to their right.

Romulus stared into the confusion of horses and riders, seeing nothing. Then his vision cleared, and he recognized the Roman general about a hundred paces away. Petreius was surrounded by a group of officers and, like Caesar on the opposite side, he was pointing and gesticulating at his enemy's lines. A dozen guards on horseback ringed him, their spears at the ready.

Mithras, help me now, Romulus prayed. *I do this for all my comrades.* He glanced at the other two. "Ready?"

They each gave him a grim nod.

"Don't say a word if you're challenged. Just keep moving." Angling himself straight at Petreius, Romulus increased his speed. Within twenty steps, they had reached the ranks of the Numidian cavalry.

It was a perfect example of chaos, thought Romulus, so unlike a Roman cohort. Fresh riders were making their way through to the front, cheering and laughing with the tribesmen who had just returned. Men were dismounting to check their horses' hooves or to urinate on the dry ground. There were shouts and cheers and water bags were being handed around. No one even gave them a second glance.

"Stop running," Romulus hissed. "Act like one of them."

At once his companions slowed to walking pace. Covered in sweat and blood, and wearing tunics not dissimilar to the Numidians', the three deeply tanned legionaries could pass an idle glance. A sudden jolt of fear hit Romulus as he looked down. The *gladii* on their belts were a dead giveaway. His pace faltered for a moment. *Keep moving*, he told himself. *They're not looking. We have not been seen.*

He was right. No one confronted them as they worked their way through the mass of men and horses. One Numidian even nodded at Romulus, who grunted in reply and moved on before the warrior could ask him something. Soon they were nearing the back of the formation, and Petreius' group of officers and sentries. This party was a different prospect.

"We'll never make it to his side," Romulus muttered from the side of his mouth. "Those bastards are too alert. Are either of you good at long spear throws?"

Sabinus shook his head.

"Not me," Paullus answered ruefully.

Romulus sucked in a nervous breath.

"It's down to you then," said Paullus. "We can bring down a few of his guards. Protect you while you take aim."

Romulus counted their light throwing spears. He and Paullus had two each, while Sabinus had three. Seven in total. It wasn't enough, but would have to do. Then Romulus looked at the collection of enemy riders they were about to take on and his courage began to falter. "Come on," he hissed, moving into the open before fear made him freeze on the spot.

To their credit, Sabinus and Paullus were only a step behind. Fanning out on either side of Romulus, they readied their spears.

Romulus was so near Petreius that he could hear what the general was saying. Cocking back his right arm, he drew a bead on his target's chest. At this short distance, his iron-tipped shaft should penetrate the gilded breastplate that Petreius was wearing.

Ten steps away, one of the guards glanced uninterestedly at the trio. Then he frowned. Something wasn't right here. His gaze turned back and at once his mouth opened to shout an alarm. Before he could, Paullus' first spear took him in the chest. Without a word, the Numidian toppled backward off his horse. Another looked around in surprise. In a heartbeat, he'd noticed the wooden shaft sticking from his comrade's chest and the trio of ragged-looking men just in front of him. A loud cry left his lips and he prepared to throw his javelin.

"Quickly!" cried Sabinus.

Things started to happen very fast.

Romulus threw his first spear just as one of Petreius' officers unintentionally moved his horse forward a step. The weapon flew through the air, punching into the Numidian's belly with a gentle soughing sound. With a loud scream of pain, the man fell sideways to the ground. Petreius looked around, and realized what was going on. His face twisted with fear and rage, and he pulled his horse's head around to ride away. Romulus spat a curse. The Pompeian general knew that his life was worth more than staying to fight these assassins.

As he prepared to throw his second shaft, Paullus gave a surprised cough. Romulus looked around in horror to see a javelin protruding from the right side of the thickset legionary's chest. With no mail to stop it, the shaft had slid past his ribs to puncture the lung. It was a death wound. As if to confirm this, a stream of bloody bubbles was already leaking from Paullus' lips.

Yet he still had the strength to point urgently at Petreius before he collapsed.

Romulus spun back. Petreius was riding away, taking two guards with him. A moving target, with men milling around between Romulus and it. He had to take a shot, though, or the whole mission would be a failure. Paullus would have died for nothing. Romulus took a deep breath and lobbed the spear up in a curving arc, over the officers and guards. Swift as an arrow, it turned and came back down, striking Petreius in the left shoulder. The impact threw him sideways in the saddle, but he did not fall. Immediately one of his men rode in alongside to lend him support and together they cantered off.

Romulus' spirits plunged. He'd failed. Petreius wouldn't die from an injury like that.

A sword swept through the air, held by a Numidian officer. "Roman scum!"

Romulus ducked, narrowly missing losing his head. Moving back a step, he pulled his *gladius* from its scabbard. He parried the next blow, and the next, but his opponent was on horseback, which made defending himself much harder. The next time the Numidian slashed at him, Romulus took a different tack, darting around the other side of his mount to plunge his sword into the man's thigh. There was a muffled cry as the officer went down.

Romulus looked around. All he could see was snarling faces pressing in from all sides.

Where was Sabinus?

XVII

HOMECOMING

At the junction, Tarquinius stopped. The northern Italian countryside had been growing more familiar since before dawn, but he knew this spot better than anywhere in the world. It was where, twenty-four years before, he had looked back one last time toward the *latifundium* he'd called home. It felt very strange to be standing here once more. How much had he seen and done since then? Suddenly Tarquinius felt old, and tired.

He was relieved a moment later to feel an unusual surge of happiness. He had had many good times in the area. His parents had farmed not ten miles away. High on the cloud-covered mountain above, he'd learned the skills of haruspicy from Olenus. The ruins of Falerii, an ancient Etruscan city, also lay nearby. Tarquinius had been drawn back by vivid memories of it, and a desire to visit the peak—the same that dominated the landscape for miles around—one more time. Perhaps in the sacred cave where he had completed his training the gods would reveal their purpose to him at last. Fabiola seemed to be safe with Antonius, and certainly wasn't scared of the priestess of Orcus. There was no sign of Romulus either.

Given that he was still seeing storm clouds over the capital, the haruspex had decided to act on his impulse.

After a week's journey, here he was.

Lake Vadimon sat on one side of the road, and the low walls of an estate ran along the other. Through the empty fields and olive groves Tarquinius could make out the shape of a large villa. Behind it were the wretched slave quarters and the marginally better buildings that housed indentured workers. Although he had long reconciled himself to the inevitability of time, the haruspex couldn't help wondering if his father and mother might still live there. It was a comforting thought, but he knew it for a wishful fantasy. At the rate Sergius, his father, had been drinking, Tarquinius doubted he would have survived long after he'd left. Thanks to a lifetime of heavy labor, Fulvia, his mother, had been a virtual cripple. Almost certainly the pair lay in the unmarked graveyard situated on some rocky ground not far from the estate buildings. As purebred Etruscans, they would have preferred to have been interred in the streets of tombs outside the ruins of Falerii, but Tarquinius doubted anyone would have shown them that honor. Besides, few locals were prepared to climb the mountain and risk the evil spirits that were reputed to live there.

The haruspex had decided to disinter their bones and carry them up to the city of the dead himself—if he could find their graves. That necessitated approaching the villa and making some inquiries. Tarquinius knew that Rufus Caelius was dead—he could remember the exact moment that his knife slipped into the noble's chest—but a spasm of old anxiety still struck him as he took the road that led to the estate's entrance. As a young man, he'd been wary of the brutal redhead. Rightfully so, as it turned out. There was some justice in the world, though, the haruspex reflected. While Caelius might have been responsible for Olenus' death, the money he'd earned from his treachery had not saved him from losing his *latifundium*. Or his life. As ever, Tarquinius' guilt over Romulus being blamed for the killing was his first feeling, but he still felt a dark satisfaction over the deed. Because of it, he, Romulus and Brennus had all become comrades. Acknowledging his sentiment as selfish, the haruspex could console himself with the fact that his visions at that time had been accurate, which meant that the gods had laid out their paths. Therefore, and despite what Romulus might think, murdering Caelius had been the right thing to do.

That didn't stop Tarquinius' heart aching at the memory of the shock on Romulus' face as he'd told him.

According to neighboring farmers and the fat proprietor of a hostelry five miles back down the road, Caelius' estate was now owned by a retired soldier, a centurion who'd served with Caesar in Gaul. "A pleasant enough type," the ruddy-cheeked innkeeper had muttered over a cup of wine bought by Tarquinius. "All he wants to do is reminisce about the army. If you can listen to him drone on about that, he'll probably offer you a meal and a bed for the night."

Tarquinius' lips twitched at the idea of enjoying the luxury of Caelius' former home while the man himself rotted in Hades.

†

Fabiola shifted irritably under her bedcovers. Several goblets of wine and a dose of valerian had made little difference to her agitated mental state. She'd pulled the heavy curtains on the windows fully closed and doused all the oil lamps, but sleep still evaded her. The reason for her restlessness was simple. Weeks before, Antonius had begun visiting the Lupanar whenever he pleased. He was no longer prepared to be discreet. Naturally, all Fabiola's pleasure in their coupling had vanished since the night of Docilosa's murder, yet she was too scared to do anything. The unspoken threat of Scaevola always hung in the air when Antonius was around. Regrettably, that wasn't the worst of it. Although Fabiola's slaves were under pain of death to speak to no one, news of her involvement with the arrogant Master of the Horse was commonplace in the city. Brutus must have heard the rumors by this stage. Why hadn't he confronted her? Fabiola's anxiety had been growing by the day. Now it was virtually all she could think about—a permanent knot of tension in her belly.

She was grateful, therefore, not to have seen much of Brutus recently; her days at the Lupanar and his long hours at the Senate didn't afford them much free time. On the rare occasions they were together, Brutus had given away nothing. His manner had changed imperceptibly, though, becoming more neutral than Fabiola had ever known. He'd made no physical advances for a while either, and had pleaded exhaustion if she dared to try. This made Fabiola even more nervous. Brutus wasn't one for playing games, yet she had the distinct impression that he was withholding something from her. Why else would he be acting so strangely? Terrified, she had said nothing for days, watching for any sign that he knew but too frightened to bring it up herself. She scuttled to bed first at night and pretended to be asleep when he joined her. On the rare occasions Brutus was home before Fabiola, she waited until the sound of his snoring filled the air before creeping under the sheets.

Tonight was not one of those last instances. Brutus had been gone for the whole day, with no sign of his returning thus far. Her mind awash with sad memories of Docilosa, Fabiola had retired early, hoping to find some relief in sleep. Even this was to be denied her, she thought bitterly. Her favorite methods of lying still, deep breathing and trying to keep her mind blank made no difference. Hours had passed and she was still wide awake.

The familiar thump of the postern gate shutting was therefore most unwelcome. This late, it could only be Brutus returning. Quickly Fabiola rolled onto her side and faced the wall, decreasing her respirations to a convincingly slow rate. Some time went by before Brutus appeared, leading her to suppose that he might have work to finish. It wasn't uncommon for him to spend several hours poring over documents in his office. *Good*, she thought. *He'll be too tired to talk.*

The instant she heard him fumble with the door latch, Fabiola knew that her presumption was incorrect. A loud curse was followed by a belch, confirming her suspicions. Brutus had been drinking. That in itself was unusual, for he was a temperate man. Panic flooded Fabiola's every pore, forcing a cold sweat onto her forehead. She barely had time to wipe it away and resume her position before Brutus entered the room. *Jupiter and Mithras above,* she prayed silently. *Just let him fall on the bed and pass out. Please.*

She had no such luck. There was a prolonged pause during which Fabiola heard Brutus breathing heavily and muttering to himself. Then he came around to her side to see if she was awake. Fabiola kept her eyes firmly shut, and after a few heart-stopping moments, he weaved away again. Next he sat down on the bed with a groan. Making no attempt to remove his *caligae* and his clothes, he remained in the same position for an age. Fabiola dared do nothing other than continue her pretense of being dead to the world. Soon she judged that nearly a quarter of an hour had passed. He must have fallen asleep, she thought.

"Fabiola?"

Somehow Fabiola managed not to react. *What's he been doing?* she wondered in alarm. *Sitting there watching me?*

"Fabiola." His voice was louder this time.

Let him want sex, Jupiter, Fabiola pleaded. *I beg you.*

He leaned over and grabbed her shoulder. "Wake up."

"Huh?" she mumbled. "Brutus?" She rolled over and looked up at him in the sleepy kittenish manner she knew he loved. He didn't return her smile, and Fabiola's heart sank. She didn't give up, though. "Come here," she murmured, reaching out both her arms.

He pulled away. "Why did you do it?"

It was possible that Brutus was talking of something else, Fabiola told herself. "What, my love?" she asked, putting all her effort into sounding confused.

He scowled with fury. "Don't play it coy with me."

Shame filled Fabiola and she looked down, afraid to say a word.

"I could live with the infidelity," he spat. "You're only human, after all, and I haven't been around much. But with that fucking creature? I can't abide Antonius. You know that."

Although Fabiola's eyes had filled with tears, she dragged her gaze up to his. "I'm sorry," she whispered.

"So it's true?"

She nodded miserably. "I didn't mean to hurt you, though."

"Really?" His lip curled. "Imagine how I felt when he boasted of your exploits together to my face then. In front of a dozen others!" His wine-flushed face twisted with embarrassment and pain. "I've ignored the street gossip as malicious rumor until now, but there's not much to say when the Master of the Horse reveals in public that he's cuckolding you."

Finally a sob escaped Fabiola's lips. "I'm so sorry, Brutus," she cried. "Please forgive me."

He gave her a contemptuous look. "So you can do it again the instant my back is turned?"

"Of course not," she protested. "I wouldn't do that."

His response was instant. "Once a whore, always a whore."

Fabiola flushed and hung her head. Inside, she cursed her reckless behavior with Antonius. All her plans for the future were about to be washed away. Without Brutus' backing, she was a complete nobody. If he wanted, he could easily wrest the ownership of the Lupanar from her, and reclaim what was left of his money.

Brutus read her fear and scorn filled his eyes. "You can keep the damn brothel. The cash too. I don't want it."

Fabiola gave him a grateful look. "I'll gather my things. Leave at dawn," she said.

"Fine. Do not return. I don't ever want to see you again." Climbing unsteadily to his feet, Brutus lurched from the room. He didn't look back.

In the depths of despair, Fabiola sank down onto the bed. What had she done?

†

Thankfully the information given Tarquinius about Caecilius, the owner of the *latifundium*, was correct. Posing as a merchant who'd grown up in the area, he was welcomed into the villa's warm kitchen by the friendly majordomo, also a veteran. Over a plate of food and a cup of *acetum*, the haruspex was able to confirm that his father and mother were both dead—Sergius before Caecilius had even bought the place, and Fulvia two years later.

"Relations of yours?" asked the majordomo.

Tarquinius made an indifferent gesture. "An aunt and uncle."

Draining his beaker, the other wiped his mouth with the back of his hand. "Fulvia wasn't up to much by the end. Poor old creature. Some would throw such a person out on their ear, but Caecilius isn't like that. 'She's worked here for long enough,' he said. 'It's not as if she eats much either.'"

"He has my thanks," said Tarquinius, genuinely touched. "I would like to pay my respects."

"He should be back by this evening," said the majordomo. "You can tell him over dinner."

"Excellent." Tarquinius smiled. "Does anyone know where my relations are buried?" he asked casually. "It would be good to visit their graves."

The majordomo thought for a moment. "The *vilicus* would be the best one to ask," he said. "He's been here the best part of thirty years."

Tarquinius hid his surprise.

"Dexter's his name," said the other. "Another ex-soldier. Half the man he was, according to most, but still able to keep the slaves in line. You'll find him in the yard or the fields around the house."

Murmuring his thanks, the haruspex went in search of Dexter: the man who'd warned him about Caelius' plans for Olenus. He found the *vilicus* hobbling up and down the edge of a large field, shouting orders at the slaves who were picking weeds from the hand-high winter wheat. He was still an imposing figure. The injuries that he'd picked up in the legions were slowing him down, but his back was straight and his eyes were bright.

Tarquinius could tell that he was being sized up from the instant he came into view. He didn't care. His only crime in vanishing had been to break the terms of his indentured labor. Scarcely something to be concerned about half a lifetime later. "Greetings," he said. "The majordomo said I'd find you out here."

Dexter grunted irritably. "You a friend of his?"

"No," the haruspex replied. "I grew up in the area."

The *vilicus* stared at him, frowning.

Tarquinius waited, interested to see if Dexter would recognize him.

"I can't place you," he admitted. "You're about the same age as me though."

"Younger," the haruspex corrected. His graying hair and scars always made people think he was older than he was. "Tarquinius is my name."

Finally a look of recognition crossed Dexter's face. "Mars above," he breathed. "I never thought to see you again. Owe me some fresh meat, don't you?"

Tarquinius had to smile at that. "You have a good memory."

"Some things are still working," the *vilicus* answered with a scowl. He eyed the slaves for a moment, checking their work was satisfactory. "Why did you run and leave the old man after I warned you?"

Tarquinius sighed. "He wouldn't have it any other way."

Dexter looked unsurprised. "I didn't have you down as a coward." His expression turned crafty. "What did you do with his valuables?"

Tarquinius had prepared himself for this exact question and kept his face blank. As Caelius' strongman, the *vilicus* had often been party to his plans. The whole point of selling Olenus out had been to steal the sword of Tarquin, the last Etruscan king of Rome, and the bronze liver, a model for soothsayers to learn their art. "Was Crassus unhappy?" he asked by way of answer. "Turns out he could have done with their help."

"Damn your eyes," Dexter snarled. "What happened to them?"

"They were already missing when I got up there," Tarquinius said regretfully. "Olenus wouldn't tell me where."

They stared at each other without speaking.

It was the *vilicus* who looked away first, perturbed by the dark, bottomless pits that were Tarquinius' eyes. "It's of no matter now," he muttered uneasily. "Both Caelius and Crassus are long gone."

"They are," the haruspex replied. "To whatever place they deserve."

They exchanged another long look.

Dexter broke the silence. "What brings you back?"

"I'd like to visit my parents' graves. The majordomo told me to ask you where they were."

Dexter gave an awkward cough. "Workers only get a wooden marker. This long after, there's usually nothing left."

"Nonetheless, I thought you might remember where they were buried," said Tarquinius, his voice turning silky.

"Perhaps."

Tarquinius stood aside, leaving the track back to the villa and the graveyard beyond open.

Unsettled, Dexter barked an order at the slaves and then led the way up the hill. Reaching the rough quadrangle that served as the burial ground for slaves and indentured workers, Tarquinius was pleasantly surprised when the *vilicus* led him straight to a spot that looked up toward Falerii. It wouldn't have been a deliberate choice on the part of those charged with digging the graves, but it pleased him all the same.

"Here." Dexter pointed with the toe of one of his worn-out *caligae*. "They were buried in the same hole."

It would have been done to save space, but Tarquinius was still gratified by what felt like a small gesture on the part of the gods. Looking down at the unmarked sod, he remembered his mother and father as they had been in his youth on the family farm. Smiling, vital and proud. It was how they would want to live on in his memory. Sadness filled him as he thought of the manner of their parting, and that he had never seen them living again. Closing his eyes, he let their images fill his mind for long moments.

Dexter shifted from foot to foot, unhappy but no longer sure what to say.

Doubtless he would feel the same grief when he climbed up to the cave and visited Olenus' burial place, thought Tarquinius. What had it all been for? he wondered wearily. After all his wanderings, he was still the last haruspex. He'd discovered little about the Etruscans. Some of the knowledge Olenus had drummed into him had been passed on to Romulus, but if the gods didn't clear the way for them to meet again and be reconciled, it would all have been for nothing.

No, not for nothing, Tarquinius thought, dragging together the shreds of his belief. *Tinia and Mithras know best, and their will is divine. It is not for me to question them, and they have not forgotten me. I am needed in Rome. Why else would I have been drawn back to the Lupanar? Fabiola appears to be safe, but the unspecified danger and the storm over the city must signify something. With luck, I will be granted a sign at the cave.*

Keeping this to the front of his mind, the haruspex looked up the mountain slope. If he hurried, there was time to visit it and return safely before dark. Then, after dinner with Caecilius, he could creep out to check that the sword and liver were still undisturbed in the olive grove where he'd buried them.

It was as if Dexter had read his mind. "You know damn well where the artifacts are," he suddenly growled.

Tarquinius' fingers caressed the hilt of his *gladius*. "Even if I did, who would you tell?"

They eyed each other in silence. Dexter had been the scourge of every slave on the estate for decades, and had beaten men to death on many occasions. The last time he'd seen Tarquinius, he would easily have done the same. Now, there was an air of deadly confidence about the long-haired Etruscan. It was more than that, though, thought the *vilicus*. There was something in the other's eyes that put the fear of Hades into him. It was as if Tarquinius was looking into his soul, and passing judgment on it.

Suddenly Dexter felt old and beaten. "Nobody at all," he whispered.

With a brief smile of satisfaction, the haruspex brushed past.

It was time to honor Olenus and, for the thousandth time, to ask for guidance.

XVIII

FATHER AND SON

R omulus!"

He turned his head, searching for Sabinus' voice. Incredibly, his comrade was on the back of a horse beyond
the nearest Numidians. How Sabinus had got there, Romulus had
no idea, but he'd never been more pleased. Slashing at another rider,
he managed to barge around one mount and then another. Sabinus' last spear took down a further warrior, creating terror in the
enemy ranks. There were so many angry Numidians trying to get at
Romulus that all was chaos, but within four or five heartbeats, he
was by Sabinus' side. Spurred on by pure adrenaline, he took the
legionary's outstretched arm and leaped up behind him.

Urging the horse on with his knees, Sabinus directed it around
the side of the milling Numidians. They headed straight for the
Twenty-Eighth. Most of the enemy cavalrymen had yet to realize
what had gone on. However, four of Petreius' party gave chase, and
Romulus' hopes, which had soared, fell again. A horse carrying two
could never outrun those with single riders. The dun-colored beast
laboring beneath them was worthy enough, but it wasn't Pegasus.
Sabinus cursed and drummed his heels against its ribs—to no avail.

The chasing Numidians drew closer and closer, shouting insults as they came. A spear flew lazily through the air, landing just behind them. It was followed by another, which shot past to impale itself in the sand ten steps in front. Romulus glanced back, and his mouth opened in horror as a third javelin scudded in, striking their mount in the rump. Its head went up in shock, and its gait altered, slowing almost to a walk.

Sabinus knew instantly what had happened. Throwing his right leg over, he dismounted. "Come on!" he shouted.

Romulus didn't need any prompting. Half climbing, half falling, he got down. The horse stumbled off, the javelin still protruding from its hip. Romulus had no time to pity it. The Numidians were closing in fast, throwing spears at the ready. Perhaps fifty paces separated them.

The pair looked at each other. "Run for it, or fight?" Romulus asked.

"They'd ride us down like dogs," snarled Sabinus. "We fight!"

Pleased by his comrade's reaction, Romulus nodded.

They moved to stand side by side, and prepared to die.

Two spears whistled by, but missed. That left four Numidians, each of whom had one or two shafts left. The enemy riders were expert shots from close range, and Romulus knew that, without shields, the chances of not being injured or killed in the next few moments were slim to none.

That was until he heard the strident clamor of *bucinae* ring out behind him.

The Numidians saw what was happening before Romulus did. Their faces creased with anger, and they pulled up. One threw a spear in a last futile gesture, and then the four horsemen turned and fled.

Romulus looked around and saw a wedge of legionaries charging toward them, their shields raised high. In their midst was Atilius. He gasped with delight. The senior centurion must have been watching to see how they got on. There could be no other explanation for their rescue. Followed by Sabinus, Romulus trotted over.

"Didn't know you could ride," he muttered.

"I grew up on a farm," explained Sabinus. "We always had a few nags about the place."

Romulus clapped him on the shoulder. "I owe you one."

"My pleasure." Sabinus grinned, and Romulus knew he'd made a comrade for life.

Atilius halted his men as the two pounded in. "Get inside," he ordered, shoving legionaries aside. "There's no time to waste."

Gratefully they obeyed, and the wedge did a swift about-turn. Romulus glanced at the Numidian lines. To his surprise, the enemy cavalrymen were not trying to attack. Instead, they were milling around, shouting at each other. A few had even galloped off to the south. It didn't take much for fear to spread, thought Romulus. It was like watching the ripples in a pool after a stone went in. Riders looked at the ones who'd gone, and then followed. Then a few more did the same. Before the wedge had rejoined their comrades, the entire mounted force had disappeared in a great cloud of dust.

"You killed Petreius, then?" asked Atilius.

Romulus flushed. "No, sir, just wounded him."

"It was a good enough effort. He must have fled the field," the senior centurion said with a satisfied grin. "Look! The whoresons have lost their taste for a fight."

Romulus stared at the Numidian infantry, who were fleeing en masse from the center. The cavalry on the far flank wouldn't stay and fight now, when all their companions were running away. With daylight fading, it meant that they had won the vital respite Caesar's cohorts needed to retreat safely. Romulus let out a gusty sigh, realizing that he was exhausted. Yet his satisfaction over what he and his comrades had managed was far stronger than his aching muscles.

"It was well done."

Romulus looked up to find Atilius' gaze upon him. "A joint effort, sir. I couldn't have done it without Sabinus here, and Paullus too."

"Is Paullus dead?"

"Yes, sir."

"Many good legionaries have fallen today," said Atilius sadly. After a moment, though, his face cleared. "Thanks to you both, many will live to fight again. Caesar will hear of this."

Romulus thought his heart would burst with pride.

†

The Pompeian forces soon called it a day and pulled back to their camp. With night fast approaching, the battle could no longer be conducted effectively. Labienus had failed to annihilate the foraging party, and missed a golden chance to capture or kill the Pompeians' greatest enemy: Caesar.

As a result, the journey back to Ruspina was uneventful. In good order, Caesar's men marched and sang, aware that they'd had a lucky escape. Romulus couldn't get over Caesar's tactics, which had been both stubborn and courageous. Few leaders would have had the self-belief to continue fighting in such a desperate situation with fearful, inexperienced troops. Making his cohorts face different ways had been improvisation of the finest quality, as had the decision to launch a last-ditch counterattack. Crassus, the only other Roman whom Romulus had served under, had possessed little of the ability that shone from practically every action of Caesar's.

The next day, he and Sabinus were ordered to Caesar's headquarters and Romulus' excitement reached fever pitch. Atilius had been as good as his word, commending them both for bravery, and Romulus a second time for his initiative and effort in wounding Petreius. The senior centurion told them both about it just before they turned in, which meant that neither man slept well. They rose long before dawn, cleaning and polishing the gear they'd stripped from dead legionaries the previous evening. The battlefield had been littered with corpses, so it hadn't been hard to find mail shirts and helmets that fitted.

"What do you think he'll say to us?" asked Sabinus, combing out the horsehair crest on his helmet.

"How should I know?" Romulus retorted with a grin.

"You've met him before."

Romulus didn't talk about receiving his manumission, but, like everyone else, Sabinus would have heard the story. All the same, his comrade's awe came as a slight shock to him. It wasn't that surprising, though, he supposed. Very few ordinary soldiers ever met Caesar directly. It wasn't as if the general went about the camp every night, swapping stories over a few cups of *acetum*. Caesar held a status not far short of divine among the ordinary rank and file, so to have held a conversation with him was unusual. Romulus felt a surge of pride at this. "Caesar's a soldier," he said. "So he appreciates courage. I imagine he'll say that and give us each a *phalera*."

Sabinus looked pleased. "Some extra cash would come in handy too. My wife's always bitching about how little I send her."

"You're married?"

Sabinus grinned. "Chained to, more like. Have been for ten years or more. Three kids living, last time I was home. She keeps the farm going with the help of a few slaves. It's only a little place, about halfway between Rome and Capua." He caught Romulus' wistful look. "You'll have to come and stay when we're demobbed. Help me take in the crops, roll a slave girl or two in the hay." He winked. "If we survive that long, of course."

"I'd like that," said Romulus. The idea of having a wife, a family, a place to go back to was immensely appealing. As a former slave, he'd never really thought about such things, but it was easy to see how much it meant to Sabinus, despite the deprecating remarks.

What have I to look forward to? Romulus wondered. *Other than finding Fabiola and killing Gemellus, precious little. Where would I live? What could I do?* Greatly disquieted by these thoughts, he was grateful for the arrival of Atilius. They both scrambled up and stood to attention.

The senior centurion studied them with a practiced eye. "Not bad," he said. "You almost look like soldiers now."

This was the nearest Atilius got to praise, and they both grinned self-consciously.

"Come on then," he ordered. "Can't keep the general waiting, can we?"

"No, sir."

The other members of their *contubernium* muttered their good wishes as the pair scurried after Atilius like eager puppies.

It wasn't a long walk to the *principia*, the headquarters, which was situated at the intersection of the Via Praetoria with the Via Principia. These, the two main roads in the massive camp, ran north–south and east–west respectively. The area in front of the huge pavilion that operated as Caesar's office and command center was already filled with hundreds of legionaries, come to witness the awards ceremony. There was no sign of the general yet, but his senior staff officers were grouped by the tent's entrance. Resplendent in their polished cuirasses, gilded greaves and feathered helmets, they looked magnificent. Twenty handpicked soldiers from Caesar's party of Spanish bodyguards stood along the pavilion's wall, their irregular dress and weapons at odds with the rest of those present. Every legion's eagle was present, held proudly upright by its *aquilifer*. The general's own standard, the red *vexillum*, was also on prominent display. A quartet of trumpeters watched keenly to see when Caesar would emerge.

A short distance from the entrance stood a number of legionaries and officers. Their awkward stance told Romulus that these must be the others up for a decoration. Sure enough, it was to the end of this line that Atilius urged them. "Good luck," he whispered.

"What shall we do, sir?" asked Sabinus desperately.

"Salute, accept your award and thank Caesar," Atilius muttered. "Then wait to be dismissed."

They shuffled into place, nodding at the other candidates.

The trumpeters lifted their *bucinae* and sounded a sharp burst of notes.

"Attention!" cried one of the senior officers.

Every man present snapped upright.

Romulus and his companions were well placed to see Caesar stroll out into the morning air. Dressed in his scarlet cloak, gilded breastplate and leather-bordered skirt, he wore a *gladius* with an ornate gold and ivory hilt and a scabbard inlaid with silver. A highly polished crested helmet and calf-length leather boots completed his attire. His thin face and long nose gave him a regal air. Caesar looked every part the general.

"At ease," he said calmly.

Everyone relaxed except Romulus and the other men in the line.

Caesar walked forward and raised his hands. At once an expectant hush fell over the whole gathering. "Comrades," he began. "Yesterday was a long day."

"That's putting it mildly, Caesar," shouted a wag from the depths of the assembled men.

A loud gust of laughter rose into the clear air, and Caesar smiled. He liked this badinage with his men: It increased the bond between them. "It was a hard fight, against terrible odds," he admitted. "The enemy did his best to annihilate us. But he did not succeed. Why?" Again Caesar paused, and Romulus saw his art, how the man was a master of oratory as well as a great military leader. He glanced at the men around him, and saw how they were hanging on the general's every word.

"Why?" Caesar repeated his question. "Because of you." He pointed dramatically at a legionary near him. The man grinned delightedly. "And you. You and you." His forefinger stabbed at a second soldier, and then a third and fourth. "All of you fought like heroes!"

He let the cry swelling in every man's throat burst forth and, smiling, strode forward to the line where Romulus and Sabinus stood. The cheer went on and on, with the watching legionaries now drumming their swords on the metal rims of their shields to create a deafening wall of noise. Eventually, a single word rose above the crescendo, and Romulus struggled not to shout it himself. "CAE-SAR! CAE-SAR! CAE-SAR!" the soldiers cried.

The man is a genius, thought Romulus, his own pride brimming over. *There's no mention of Caesar's own ability, of the hours of fear and the terror, of the order to stay within four steps of the standards. Just stirring words to make every soldier here think he's as brave as Hercules. It works, too.* Romulus had never felt so glad to be a Roman legionary. Shoving back his shoulders, he looked down at his mail shirt and polished *scutum* boss, hoping that he looked respectable enough to meet his leader.

Eventually the din died away.

Caesar stepped up to the first man in the line, who saluted with alacrity. "Who is this?" he demanded.

"Centurion Asinius Macro, sir," boomed one of the senior officers. "First Century, First Cohort, Fifth Legion. Risked his own life on multiple occasions yesterday, most notably to rescue a section of his men who had been cut off by the enemy."

Caesar half turned, and a slave stepped forward bearing a bronze tray covered with decorations and leather purses. Picking a gold *phalera*, Caesar fastened it among the others on Macro's chest harness. He muttered a few words of congratulation, and handed over a purse before moving on, leaving the centurion beaming in his wake.

The process was repeated with each man: an announcement of his name and rank, and what he'd done to deserve his award. All the while, the watching legionaries shouted Caesar's name over and over. The atmosphere was electric, helping to dispel any lingering fears about the previous day from their minds. When Caesar reached Sabinus, Romulus had difficulty in not looking sideways. His pulse began to race. As with the others, their general clapped Sabinus on the shoulder and awarded him a silver *phalera* and purse. Finally he moved to stand before Romulus.

He snapped rigidly to attention.

"Legionary Romulus, First Century, Second Cohort, Twenty-Eighth Legion," cried the officer.

"And his reason for standing here?" asked Caesar.

"It was his idea to try and kill Petreius, sir," Atilius answered. "In just their tunics, he and two others crossed the battlefield to infiltrate the Numidians. They didn't succeed completely, but legionary Romulus injured the whoreson. The enemy broke and ran, when just a few moments earlier, Petreius had been successfully rallying them. If it hadn't been for Romulus' action, our counterattack would have been a complete failure."

Caesar raised his eyebrows. Of course he'd already heard the story. "You vouch for this man?"

"Yes, sir," replied Atilius confidently.

"Used to be in the Tenth, didn't you?"

"I did, sir."

Caesar nodded. "I heard about your little javelin throw yesterday. Well done."

Atilius beamed. "Thank you, sir."

Caesar turned back to Romulus. "A worthy deed, it seems." He frowned suddenly. "Have we met before?"

"Yes, sir," replied Romulus, his cheeks flushing.

"Where?"

"In Rome, sir. You granted me my manumission at the arena."

Recognition flared in Caesar's eyes, and he smiled. "Oh yes! The slave who killed the Ethiopian bull."

"Yes, sir," answered Romulus, his face burning now.

"Killing wild beasts is not your only skill, it seems."

"It was an honor to take part in the attempt, sir. Sorry that I didn't kill Petreius."

Caesar laughed. "Never mind, man! He ran away, and his men followed. That's all we needed, and it's thanks to you. There'll be another day to settle the matter."

"Sir."

Taking a gold *phalera* from the tray, Caesar attached it to Romulus' mail. "Continue like this and you'll end up an officer," he said, handing over two heavy purses. "Caesar does not forget good legionaries like you."

"Thank you, sir!" Grinning from ear to ear, Romulus thumped a fist on his chest in salute.

The general gave him a friendly nod and returned to his senior officers. "I give you—Caesar's bravest soldiers," cried one of the trumpeters. He lifted his instrument and blew a short fanfare.

A rousing cheer went up, with Romulus' voice straining itself hoarse among them.

Then, followed by his subordinates, Caesar entered his headquarters.

†

It was where he stayed for the following few weeks. Although enemy activity in and around his camp at Ruspina was vigorous, Caesar calmly ignored it all. With the defenses of the camp being increased daily—every craftsman available was making slingshot balls and javelins, catapults were mounted on every guard tower and the walls were fully manned day and night—Caesar had the confidence to remain out of sight, receiving reports and issuing his commands in response. His assurance was proved correct by the Pompeians' failure to attack. Even when Labienus' forces were reinforced by the arrival of Metellus Scipio and his army, Caesar's enemies did not act.

More legions and cavalry arrived from Italy, bringing with them much-needed supplies. There were regular skirmishes with the Pompeians, but none were decisive. Caesar's attempt to take the town of Uzitta, which was the main source for his enemy's water, failed, but the Pompeians lost many soldiers in their unsuccessful attempts to dislodge Caesar's forces from their positions. Eventually, realizing that there was little gain to be had from continuing the siege, Caesar led his ten legions off toward a settlement by the name of Aggar. They were harassed all the way by the Numidian cavalry, and struggled at one stage to move a hundred paces in more than four hours. What helped the beleaguered soldiers then was the knowledge that if they stuck together and did not break ranks, the enemy horse was able to do little more than injure a few men with their throwing spears.

Romulus was pleased when new training began for all the legionaries, teaching them how to fight alongside their cavalry. Three hundred men from each legion were then picked to remain in battle order each day, their purpose to act as close support for their horsemen whenever a skirmish began. In this way, the probing Pompeian attacks were resisted more easily. On a number of occasions the frustrated Scipio offered battle, but each time Caesar refused it. Although he knew that his general was waiting for the best moment to fight, Romulus began to grow impatient as time dragged by. He lost count of the times both armies faced each other, ready to fight, only to march away a few hours later.

Romulus was pleased that his comrades shared his sentiments. Fully part of his *contubernium* and century now, he sat around each night gossiping, wondering when the campaign would end. It seemed that everyone wanted the conflict to cease now. For some of the veterans who'd crossed the Rubicon with Caesar, the war had gone on for more than three years, and while he didn't say so, Romulus had been on campaign since he'd left Italy nearly a decade before. A sense of weariness that he'd never acknowledged before was awoken by the conversations about home, family and planting crops. Romulus' loyalty to Caesar was unswerving, but he too began to wish for a quick victory in Africa. Only Hispania would then remain as a potential campaign before they could all be demobilized. Yet Romulus' desire to leave the legions was always underpinned by his doubts as to what he'd do with his life. In some ways, dying in battle would be a simple way out.

It wasn't until Caesar's legions abandoned their attack on Aggar and made a night march to begin the siege of the coastal town of Thapsus that things started to look as if they might change. The fortifications had barely been finished on the first evening when news came of the Pompeian army's arrival. Scipio had come in hot pursuit. The ground around Thapsus was flat, facilitating a hard face-to-face encounter. At first glance, the situation didn't look good. The enemy outnumbered them in all parts of the army: infantry, skirmishers and cavalry; they also retained more than a hundred elephants, while Caesar had none. However, more than half of Caesar's men had fought under him for a decade or more, while the majority of the Pompeians were new recruits. Enemy deserters had also revealed that the elephants had only recently been captured and were thus not hardened in combat.

As well as sitting on the coast, Thapsus was protected by a large saltwater lagoon and an inward-pointing tongue of sea, which meant that it could be attacked in only two places. Shrewd to the last, Caesar had ordered a fort constructed on the route that afforded the best options to attack the town. This left a spit of land a mile and a half wide that ran between the sea and the lagoon as the only way to approach his forces.

As Romulus and his comrades had discovered at dawn, it was an avenue that Scipio had taken. Word had come from the outlying positions that a large army was advancing toward Thapsus in *triplex acies* formation. The classic three lines of soldiers used by most Roman generals, it had been strengthened by the presence of Numidian cavalry and the feared elephants on both flanks. In a surprise move, though, half the Pompeian army—including most of the Numidians—had been left to cover the second route by the fort. Consequently, Caesar's veterans now almost equaled their opponents. To the understandable delight of his entire army, the wily general did not attempt to avoid battle this time.

Instead his legions had marched out to meet the enemy.

The opportunity was too good to miss.

†

By midmorning that day, the two forces filled the spit of land entirely. Facing each other from a distance of no more than a quarter of a mile, they eyed each other closely, wondering what would transpire. The Twenty-Eighth, with Romulus in its midst, formed part of Caesar's center along with two other less experienced legions. His veterans from the campaign in Gaul, including the Fifth and the famous Tenth, were stationed on each wing, supported by hundreds of slingers and archers. Outside these were the horsemen, although the presence of water on both sides meant that any cavalry action would be limited. There simply wasn't enough space for them to maneuver.

Another reason to fight today, thought Romulus. Leaving the brunt of the fighting to the legionaries took away the advantage of the enemy's Numidians. Caesar's men were facing a greater number of Pompeian troops, but they were known to be inexperienced. There were about sixty elephants on each flank, and a large number of cavalry. None of this was causing much concern in Caesar's lines either. Five cohorts had been trained how to fight the massive beasts using their *pila*, and both they and the missile troops were aware of their vulnerable spots. Romulus eyed the eager-faced men around him. In a marked difference from Ruspina, confidence oozed from them. It was even more exaggerated among the veterans on the wings. Already their ranks were swaying backward and forward like reeds in the wind. Only the blows and curses of their officers were keeping them in line.

The day was to continue in this bloodthirsty vein. As Caesar prepared to address his men, his officers began beseeching him to allow the attack to start. Atilius and other cohort commanders were no different, breaking ranks to walk by the side of the general's horse and pleading for the honor of charging first. Smiling, Caesar told the senior centurions that the time would be right very soon. He had not anticipated the eagerness of the Ninth and Tenth legions on the right flank. Bullying their trumpeters to sound the advance, they ignored their centurions and pelted forward toward the enemy.

Romulus watched, first in amazement and then with growing impatience. Surely they had to join in? Otherwise the veterans' impetuous action could cost them dearly. His emotions were mirrored by the nearby legionaries. Despite the centurions' liberal use of their vine canes, the entire legion moved forward a good fifty paces toward Caesar.

With Atilius and his companions still by his side, their general took this in.

Pausing, the men of the Twenty-Eighth held their breath.

To Romulus' delight, Caesar shrugged, and then grinned. "It's as good a time as any. Felicitas!" he shouted, turning his horse's head. Drumming his heels into its sides, he headed straight for the enemy.

Atilius and the other senior centurions looked to their men. "You heard the general!" bellowed one. "What are you waiting for?"

Romulus, Sabinus and thousands of others answered with a deafening, incoherent shout. The cry was echoed by the entire army, which broke into a run toward the Pompeians. Soon it was possible to see the still-stationary enemy already quailing at the ferocity of their attack. This of course increased the Caesareans' determination, and they crashed into their opponents' lines like Vulcan smiting a piece of metal. First to hit the Pompeians were the Ninth and Tenth, who used their javelins to great effect. Thrown in dense volleys, they caused instant panic among the war elephants, which turned and stampeded back through their own lines. Without pausing, the veterans crashed into the bewildered ranks behind, breaking them apart like so much firewood.

The enemy troops did not know how to react, and the same story was shortly repeated all along the battle front. Spurred on by the success of the Ninth and Tenth legions, every soldier in Caesar's army flung himself at the Pompeians like a man possessed. Unprepared for this fervent zeal, their adversaries simply broke and ran. Dropping their weapons, they turned and fled along the spit. The narrow bridge of land, which had seemed so perfect for an attack, soon became a perfect killing ground. There was no escape to either side, and the Pompeians could not run fast enough to outstrip the enraged Caesarean legionaries. No quarter was spared, and thousands of the enemy died pleading for their lives.

It was almost as if every man was trying to end the civil war himself, thought Romulus as he watched his comrades cut down every soldier they encountered. It didn't matter whether they tried to fight, to run or to surrender. Wounded, whole or unarmed, they were slaughtered anyway. More than one Caesarean officer who tried to intervene was killed, and Atilius wisely let his legionaries do what they would. Although Romulus knew his comrades' reasons—they were sick of defeated Pompeians who had been pardoned by Caesar reneging on their words and rejoining the struggle—he could not bring himself to kill defenseless men. After their initial charge, when he'd downed a number of Pompeian soldiers, Romulus just ran alongside Sabinus and the rest, doing little other than watch the battle turn into a rout. His companions were so consumed by battle rage that they didn't even notice.

It was perhaps for this reason that Romulus saw the elephant before anyone else.

Terrified by the number of javelins and arrows launched by Caesar's legionaries and missile troops, almost every one of the great beasts had turned and run away. From what Romulus could see, they hadn't stopped yet. Except for this one. With numerous *pila* sticking from its thick, leathery skin like so many pins in a cushion, the elephant had done an about-turn and was now charging through its own retreating soldiers toward Caesar's lines.

Toward the Twenty-Eighth.

Bugling with pain and anger, it was smashing men out of its path like twigs. Its mahout was long gone, probably brought down by a spear or arrow, so the elephant was rampaging wherever it wished. Maddened now beyond reason, it killed everything in its path. The reactions of the Pompeians as they saw it coming varied, Romulus saw. Some panicked and ran toward the Caesareans, desperately pushing their comrades out of the way. Others managed to remain calm, throwing their *pila* at its eyes or trunk in an attempt to head it off. Another group froze on the spot, unsure what to do when faced with such a leviathan. All of these strategies were limited in their success, and Romulus' heart raced as he wondered what he would do.

The elephant surged through the last of the Pompeians' ranks, and directly into the middle of the Twenty-Eighth, which was close behind. Men flew screaming into the air as they were struck by its swinging trunk. Others were trampled into the sand, and an unlucky few were simply gored to death. In vain legionaries hacked at the beast with their *gladii*, wishing for the axes of the specially trained cohorts. Tarquinius and his deadly double-headed weapon popped into Romulus' mind. In the same heartbeat, he remembered Brennus. Old guilt burst forth like the rotten fluid in the center of an abscess, dragging Romulus' spirits to the depths. No matter what hope there was of returning to Rome, how could he have left his blood brother to die?

It was as if the elephant sensed his mental anguish. Lifting a screaming soldier on one of its tusks, it threw him high into the air before its piggy eyes settled on Romulus and his comrades. Swinging its trunk to and fro like a flail, it made straight for them. By this stage, the legionaries were so scared of the great beast that a path opened in front of it. Pushing and shoving, men scrambled out of the way. The sooner it could escape through their lines, the better.

Romulus didn't move. Instead he turned to face the elephant.

"Come on," Sabinus shouted. "Let's go."

In reply, Romulus threw his *scutum* to one side. He looked at his *gladius*, wishing it had the length of Brennus' longsword. It would have to do, though. Who was he to run from the gods' punishment? That was why the elephant was charging straight for him: It had to be. "Very well," Romulus muttered and took a step forward. He had no idea what to do when the creature reached him, but he was going to die facing it like a man. *No more running,* he thought, the agonizing memory of Brennus' last battle cry tearing at his soul.

His ears filled with the elephant's bugling, which was deafening at this range. Dimly, Romulus realized that he was not alone. He shot a glance to his right and was dismayed to see Sabinus there, his sword and shield ready. "Get out of here," he shouted. "This is my fate."

"Fool! I'm not leaving now," Sabinus retorted. "Imagine the abuse I'd get for deserting you."

Romulus had no time to reply. The elephant was only a few steps away. Raising his *gladius*, he lunged forward at it. To his surprise, it ignored him completely. Sidestepping neatly, it barged past, knocking him down in the process. Winded, Romulus was thrown backward. He looked on in horror as the elephant grabbed Sabinus with its trunk and bore him aloft. Sabinus screamed in fear. With both arms held by his sides, he was as helpless as a swaddled baby.

"You were supposed to take me!" Romulus shrieked.

Oblivious, the elephant swung Sabinus high and low, all the while trumpeting with anger.

Romulus jumped to his feet. Thankfully, he hadn't let go of his sword. Without thinking, he ran at the enormous creature. A slash at the nearest foreleg drew a furious squeal, but the animal didn't release Sabinus. Instead it swung its head at Romulus, forcing him to dodge out of the way or be smashed asunder by the sheer weight of its bony skull. A fierce lunge with its tusks followed, and Romulus shuffled farther away, trying not to lose his footing on the carpet of dead men and weapons. It was hopeless. The elephant was invulnerable to ordinary weapons. Soon it would kill him. Then he caught a glimpse of Sabinus' face, distorted with sheer terror, as it shot past. New energy filled Romulus at his comrade's plight. He couldn't just give in.

Raising his *gladius*, he ran in as the trunk went by yet again. Getting far nearer to its bulk than he felt comfortable with, Romulus slashed down with the iron blade. He made good contact with the trunk, cutting a long wound that made the elephant bugle in pain. Blood sprayed through the air as it went on the attack, lunging at Romulus with its head and tusks. He sensed that it was wary now, though, keeping Sabinus and its trunk raised in the air. Encouraged, he jumped up and hacked a chunk of flesh from the underside of the trunk. There was another deafening trumpet of distress. More blood showered over Romulus, covering him from head to toe. To his surprise, the elephant stopped dead in its tracks, lowering its wounded trunk. Sabinus moaned with fear, but Romulus redoubled his efforts. He had a chance! He chopped back and forth with his *gladius*, no longer watching to see what the beast did. His arm moved in a blur, delivering two, four, six cuts. His ears rang with the thunderous noise of the elephant's pain, but he did not let up for a single heartbeat.

Romulus had never been more grateful for the time he spent carefully sharpening the double-edged blade. The iron was usually sharp enough to shave the hairs off his forearm, and now it proved its worth for evermore. Sabinus dropped to the ground amid a mist of arterial blood and the elephant stepped back. Utterly consumed by the agony of its injuries, it swung around and charged whence it had come.

Romulus grabbed Sabinus, whose face was as white as the fuller's chalk used on togas. "Are you hurt?" he demanded.

Struck mute by terror, Sabinus shook his head.

Grinning like a fool, Romulus helped him up. "It's all right," he muttered. "You're safe now."

When Sabinus' voice returned, it was shaking. "Truly you must be blessed by the gods," he whispered. "Who else could injure a beast like that?"

The enormity of what he had done suddenly hit Romulus. By driving off an elephant with just a *gladius*, he raised the question of what Brennus—who was far stronger than he—might have done with a longsword. At once Romulus' relief at saving Sabinus was washed away beneath a renewed wave of bitterness and guilt.

Was Brennus still alive?

XIX

FOUR TRIUMPHS

The breeze strengthened, billowing the trireme's main sail and increasing its speed, forcing it through the water and raising a decent bow wave. The rate of the pounding drum on the rowing deck did not vary, however. The three banks of oars on each side continued to move in unison at the normal rate—about half the speed of a man's heartbeat. Graceful to look at, it was hot, cramped and backbreaking work for the oarsmen. Standing near the prow in just his belted tunic and *caligae*, Romulus gave thanks once more that he'd never had to serve in the navy. Although the rowers were free men, in his mind their job was far worse than being a legionary. Physically more demanding than the marching and fighting expected of soldiers, the career of a rower also offered the distinct possibility of drowning. Triremes were excellent vessels in the relative calm of waters close to land, but they were death traps in bad weather or on the open ocean. Romulus could still remember the numerous ships lost on his voyage to Asia Minor with Crassus' army. Caesar's fleet had not been immune either.

That was all in the past, though. It was late summer, and the ten triremes had nearly reached Ostia, Rome's port. Joy filled Romulus. He was returning home, and as a citizen! It scarcely seemed possible, but he'd had time to let the reality sink in on the voyage from Africa. Taking a peek at the two gold *phalerae* lying in his pack helped too—after all, they were awards that only a citizen could receive. The second had been awarded after he'd saved Sabinus from the elephant. Romulus grinned at the memory of what Caesar had said as he'd pinned the decoration on his chest. "Trying to win the war all on your own, comrade?"

Of course it hadn't been all Romulus' doing, but the campaign in Africa was over, ended in one day by the victory at Thapsus. After several months of cleaning-up operations, Caesar was returning to the capital to celebrate his conquests with not one, but four triumphs. In a massive propaganda stroke, one was to take place for each of his campaigns in Gaul, Egypt, Asia Minor and Africa. A grateful Senate had declared forty days of public thanksgiving for the dictator's latest victory while pretending that it had been over the Numidian king, not Scipio and a huge number of prominent Republicans. No mention was being made either of Caesar's first success over other Romans: Pharsalus, where his legions had thrashed twice their number under the command of Pompey.

Romulus stared excitedly at the coastline that was running along their starboard side, still amazed that he and Sabinus were accompanying Caesar back to Italy. Yet they were, along with a special century of legionaries. After Thapsus, the legates of all ten legions had each been asked to put forward eight soldiers. The eighty men were to form part of Caesar's honor guard for his triumphs, positions of the highest standing. Throughout the army the competition was fierce to win a place. As battle-hardened, frontline officers, the centurions and senior centurions were best placed to judge, and so the legates had referred the matter to them.

There had been plenty of witnesses to Romulus' incredible rescue of Sabinus and of course the pair had previously taken part in the attack on Petreius. Consequently Atilius fought hard to have both included as part of the Twenty-Eighth's quota. His stubbornness won the day, and along with four other legionaries, an *optio* and a *signifer*, the two friends were ordered to join the ships carrying Caesar back to Italy. Meanwhile, the majority of the army was embarking for Hispania, where Pompey's two sons were reputed to be raising a huge army among the discontented tribes.

That was where the honor guard would be heading after the triumphs. Caesar had told them so himself before they sailed from Africa. This would be a short visit to Italy then, with little free time to search for Fabiola or Gemellus. Romulus tried not to feel bitter about that. There was Sabinus, playing dice on the deck with three others, who would not see his family at all. Their comrades' stories were similar. Few men, if any, had seen their homes in years. *Why should I be any different?* thought Romulus. Catching sight of Caesar's red cloak on the deck of the lead trireme, he thought guiltily of the enormous honor he was being shown to be here. What right had he to expect anything other than a new military campaign when the celebrations were over? He was nothing but an ordinary legionary, and as such had to do what he was told until the day, if he survived, his service came to an end.

Romulus knew that there was more to his discontent than a simple desire to quit the legions. Guilt about his feat against the elephant ruled him entirely. Months had passed, and he still obsessed about it on a daily basis. The realization that he could not only emerge unharmed from an encounter with such a beast, but save Sabinus as well, gnawed at Romulus' insides like a malignant parasite. It could never be proved, but Brennus might have done the same in India as he, Romulus, had at Thapsus. *If only Tarquinius were here,* Romulus wished. He might be able to glean some information from the wind or clouds. Even a hint would help. But who knew where the haruspex was? He sighed, unwilling since Margiana to make an attempt himself. Tarquinius was long gone, which meant that he had to live with the doubt about Brennus. *That* was worse than thinking his big friend was dead.

As always, any thought of the haruspex was tinged with suspicion. Could he have known of Brennus' potential to beat an elephant? Romulus wasn't sure. Any time he and Tarquinius had talked about it, there had been no sense of the haruspex withholding information. Not that that meant a thing. Tarquinius was a master of concealment.

Stop it, Romulus thought. Whatever the haruspex was, he wasn't evil. The look on his face in Alexandria had convinced Romulus that he hadn't actually known how his murder of Rufus Caelius would affect others. With his belief system that a man should decide his own fate, it would not have been for Tarquinius to stop Brennus facing his own death either. While Romulus' guilt remained strong, he felt the same way about destiny.

"Ostia ahoy!" shouted the lookout.

Romulus buried his worries for now.

He was nearly home.

†

Fabiola glared at the dead hen lying before her. Its throat had been cut, and its entrails carefully laid out on the ground for inspection. "Tell me again," she demanded.

"Of course, Mistress," the soothsayer said, his Adam's apple bobbing up and down uneasily in his scrawny neck. Stoop-shouldered in his grubby robe, the soothsayer wore a typical blunt-peaked leather hat. A short knife with a bloody, rust-spotted blade dangled from his right hand. Pointing with it, he repeated his prophecy. "You will find a husband soon. A big man with brown hair. A soldier perhaps?" The soothsayer shot a sly glance at Fabiola, trying to assess her response. "Or maybe he's a noble." He smiled, revealing a mouthful of decay.

"Liar!" Fabiola spat. "Antonius will never marry me. What do you take me for—one of your usual gullible fools?"

Startled, the soothsayer busied himself with the hen's intestines again, poking a dirty fingernail here and there in search of wisdom. This was a consultation he was already wishing was over, but there would be no end to it until he came up with something convincing.

Her nostrils flaring, Fabiola sat drumming her fingers on the arm of her chair. They were alone in the courtyard of the Lupanar. She'd been recommended this idiot by a number of the brothel's clients, and had summoned him here to avoid being seen seeking a divination in public. Her reason was simple, and stark. Her life had changed utterly since the night of Docilosa's death, and it was down to one person. Raw terror filled Fabiola at the mere thought of Marcus Antonius. Why had she got involved with him? Her regular visits to the Mithraeum and to the temple of Jupiter made no difference at all; and, still full of shame over what had happened to Docilosa, she dared not go to Orcus' shrine for fear of seeing Sabina. Fickle as ever, the gods had discarded her. Perhaps forever, thought Fabiola, bitterness coursing through her veins.

She scowled. Brutus' reaction to her affair stung her conscience even now. "Once a whore, always a whore," he'd said. Fabiola's purpose hadn't changed, however. Nothing but death would stop her wanting to kill Caesar, yet her lover's departure had scuppered her best chances of recruiting conspirators. Customers who were willing to profess a hatred of the dictator were proving to be nonexistent. Despite Caesar's leniency toward his former enemies, the fear of reprisal was too great in men's minds. *So here I am,* Fabiola thought angrily, *waiting for a conman to fill my head with false promises, when what I really need is a way back into Brutus' good books. Or a new, powerful lover who hates Caesar. As if this fraudster can tell me how to do that.* "Well?" she snapped.

His face twitching with nerves, the soothsayer looked up. He'd done his homework on Fabiola before coming to the brothel, knew about her affair with Antonius and her breakup with Brutus. If she didn't desire the obvious thing that most women in her situation would want—marriage to Antonius—what did she want? "An old lover comes back to you," he said, taking a desperate guess.

Fabiola's head jerked up, and she fixed him with an icy gaze. "Go on," she demanded harshly.

Pleased by this small advance, the soothsayer decided to wax lyrical. "Once you are reunited, everything will be as it was. Your lover will rise even higher in Caesar's regard, and your future will be secured forever. There will be children . . ."

"Stop!" Fabiola screamed. "Do you think that promising everything *you* think I want will make me happy?"

"Mistress, I . . ." he began.

"Charlatan." Fabiola's voice dripped with contempt. "Get out."

Bowing and scraping, the soothsayer bundled the butchered hen into a dirty leather bag. It would do for his dinner that night. When he'd finished, he risked a glance at Fabiola. "My fee?"

Fabiola laughed. "Benignus," she called.

The massive doorman emerged instantly from his waiting place just behind the door into the house. As always, his metal-studded club hung from one hand. There was also a dagger shoved casually into his wide leather belt. "You require something, Mistress?"

The soothsayer's eyes bulged with fear, but he didn't move. Benignus was blocking the exit.

"Throw this fool out."

Benignus shuffled forward and took a firm hold of the man's arm. "Come quietly and I won't hurt you," he growled. "It's your choice."

The soothsayer nodded. Further protests would result in broken bones, or worse. Meek as a lamb, he disappeared with Benignus.

Brooding, Fabiola looked down at the smears of blood left on the flagstones. The prophecy had clearly been false, but it had still upset her. She wanted no happy reunion with Brutus if she couldn't convert him to her cause. No happy family life unless Caesar paid for his crime. Her mother had to be avenged.

She sat motionless for some time. The shadows grew long in the courtyard as the sun went down. The temperature began to drop, and eventually Fabiola shivered. Feeling sorry for herself would get her nowhere. Perhaps the soothsayer had been partly right. If she stopped seeing Antonius, maybe Brutus would come back to her. A spark of hope lit in Fabiola's tired heart, but her throat closed with fear at what the Master of the Horse might do if she spurned him. Nonetheless, she steeled her resolve. If things continued as they were, her life wasn't worth living. It wasn't as if she hadn't existed under the constant risk of death before and survived to tell the tale.

Her spirits lifted a fraction.

She would go to one of Caesar's triumphs and seek out Brutus. In a public place, he couldn't avoid her and, by begging, she might engineer a reconciliation. Antonius would be there, but with the gods' help, she could avoid him. For the moment, Fabiola did not allow herself to dwell on the matter further. It was time to think happy thoughts. Maybe she'd meet a soldier at the triumph who knew Romulus. It was a pleasing fantasy, and Fabiola took comfort from it.

†

Tarquinius saw the soothsayer being ejected from the brothel. Flying through the doorway in a tangle of limbs, he landed on the hard-packed dirt with a bone-crunching thump.

Smiling, one of the massive doormen emerged after him. "Don't come back," he warned.

Picking up his scuffed leather bag, the lank-haired augur scuttled off.

Tarquinius grimaced, feeling like a fraud too. His visit to the mountain had not achieved nearly as much as he'd hoped for. Still, it had been worthwhile. Moving his parents' bones to a tomb befitting purebred Etruscans had been poignant but satisfying, and spending a day by Olenus' burial mound had eased his reawakened sorrow somewhat. While his old mentor had died violently, he'd walked to meet it with both eyes open, a decision that pained Tarquinius but one he had to respect. In the cave, he'd been dismayed to find the amazing battle chariot smashed into little pieces, probably by the legionaries who had accompanied Caelius. The inspirational paintings of Etruscan life had been defaced too—with the exception of that depicting Charon. Even the Romans respected the demon of the underworld. All the same, the deliberate damage brought home to Tarquinius the utter finality of Etruria's decline into oblivion. His people's civilization was gone forever, which gave him the sensation of being very alone. He longed to see Romulus again, which had brought him back to the purpose of his visit.

The haruspex had dug up the bronze liver and carried it up the mountain, hoping that it would help him with a divination. Yet again, though, he had been frustrated. Not a thing had been revealed in the entrails or the liver of the plump lamb he'd caught on his ascent. In an unusual loss of self-control, Tarquinius had railed and ranted at the cloudy sky and the few vultures hanging in it. Of course his outburst had done nothing except make him feel foolish. It was only when he'd calmed down that the sole revelation of his climb became clear.

The haruspex saw a clear picture of himself in Rome, and of Caesar standing alone. Ominous storm clouds were building overhead. Then, in close succession, he'd seen Romulus and Fabiola. His suspicions about their parentage hardened into certainty. Neither looked happy either, which worried Tarquinius. Were both of them in danger? From Caesar? Why? At once he had known that he still needed to be in the capital. Making the time first to rebury the liver beside Tarquin's ornate *gladius*, he had taken his leave of Caecilius and the *latifundium*. The lump of bronze was too bulky to carry about and the sword would attract too much attention. *What a man like Caesar would do to possess such a weapon,* he thought bitterly. Perhaps Tarquinius would reveal their location to someone in the future. He hoped so. On the road south, he knew that this had been his final visit home.

Reaching Rome, the haruspex had immediately returned to the Lupanar to see if anything had changed. Seeing the soothsayer's dramatic exit on his first morning was more reward than he'd expected. Fabiola was also seeking guidance of some kind, and not just the usual rubbish spouted by such con men. As this realization sank home, Tarquinius got to his feet. Barely remembering to act the simpleton, he hurried after the charlatan. A soothing word in the man's ear and a coin or two would secure some much-needed information about Romulus' sister.

If the gods wouldn't help him, then he'd help himself.

✝

Caesar's first triumph was to celebrate his conquest of Gaul. Although Romulus and the men of the Twenty-Eighth had not taken part in that campaign, they were part of his honor guard and so were to accompany him anyway. The preparations for all four triumphs went on for several weeks after their arrival in Rome. Daily at dawn the honor guard, Caesar's unprecedented seventy-two *lictores* and hundreds of legionaries from various legions assembled on the Campus Martius, the great plain to the northwest of the city. There an officious master of ceremonies drilled them for hours. The soldiers grumbled but did as they were told. Caesar wanted the event to go off well, and it wasn't as if they were risking their lives anymore.

Like his comrades, Romulus was not permitted to leave their camp outside the city, unless it was on official business. This afforded him no opportunity to go off in search of Fabiola or Gemellus.

Part of him was glad. Where would he even begin? Nearly a million people lived in Rome. Who was to say that his sister was here anyway? If Gemellus was ruined, he might no longer be living in the house where Romulus had grown up either. It was odd to feel so helpless now that his dream of returning home had been granted. His guilt about Brennus had eased somewhat, though, for which Romulus was grateful. It wasn't pleasant, berating himself mentally every day.

The frenzied atmosphere in the city also made it easy enough to be absorbed by other things. Everywhere Romulus and his comrades went, they were greeted as heroes. Boys and girls ran alongside them, begging to hold their *gladii* or shields. Fruit, bread and cups of wine were shoved into their hands by grateful housewives while blessings rained down on their heads from old men and women. Romulus had never known anything like it. As a slave growing up in Rome, he'd been practically invisible to most people, a creature to be ordered about or kicked out of the way. Now he was a conquering hero, and it felt very good. Romulus ignored the niggles of unease that kept surfacing at this attitude. After years of hardship and danger, he was going to enjoy himself whenever possible.

Tens of thousands of peasants had flocked to Rome to see the triumphs, and were living in tents in any available open space. Caesar's largesse knew no bounds, and on alternate days he was providing feasts that were open to all. Thousands of tables were set up in the *fora*, each one groaning under the weight of fine food and wine. Each day the public could choose to watch athletic or sporting competitions, chariot racing or fights in Pompey's amphitheater. Hundreds of lions had been procured to appear in large-scale beast hunts. There was even talk of a naval battle taking place on a specially flooded lake that was fed by the River Tiber. Unsurprisingly, Romulus had mixed feelings about the gladiator contests. On the one hand, he felt a burning hatred for the *lanistae* who sent men in to die, and for the crowds who demanded the fighters' blood. On the other, he had some nostalgic memories of his comradeship with Brennus in the *ludus* and of the incredible battles they'd survived in the arena. There was an added complication. When the time came for him to leave the army, he'd have to earn a living, and being a gladiator was all Romulus knew. That, and being a soldier. It hurt his head to think too much, so, like his concerns about finding Fabiola, he put his worries off for another day.

Romulus would remember the first triumph until the day he died. The procession assembled on the Campus Martius early in the morning. Preceded by his *lictores*—twenty-four for each of his three terms as dictator—Caesar rode in a magnificent chariot pulled by a quartet of horses. Wearing a gleaming white toga with a purple edge and with his face painted the red of victory, Caesar had a laurel wreath held over his head by a slave. He looked every part the conquering general. Romulus shouted himself hoarse with his comrades until the fussing master of ceremonies intervened.

Under Caesar's approving gaze, the proud honor guard marched off first, their helmets, mail and shield bosses polished until they glittered like gold. Next were the veterans of Caesar's campaign in Gaul, men who had tramped with him from the Alps to the northern sea, fighting scores of battles against terrible odds. These were the cream of his army, a selection from the soldiers of the Fifth, Tenth, Thirteenth and Fourteenth legions, among others, who loved Caesar as a father and who would follow him to Hades if he asked it.

Then came the captives from the campaign, ten score Gauls picked from the hundreds of thousands captured by Caesar's men. Leading them, with heavy manacles on his wrists and ankles, was Vercingetorix, the valiant chieftain who had led the defense of his land. After six years in captivity, he was a shadow of his former self, a tangle-haired, bearded wretch whose dead eyes spoke volumes about the suffering he'd endured. After the prisoners trundled the wagons of booty from Gaul. They contained swords, axes and shields from the defeated tribes, as well as gold, silver and other precious items. Yet more carts displayed mounted paintings of Caesar's exploits, and placards inscribed with the incredible statistics of his war: the number of enemy killed, the battles won, the size of the territory seized for Rome.

Enjoying the crowd's tumultuous acclaim, Caesar rode at the rear.

It all made for a staggering spectacle.

Yet it didn't entirely go according to plan. Shortly after Caesar had entered the city, an axle broke on his chariot, drawing superstitious cries from the watching throng. Caesar had remained calm, thrown large purses at everyone he could see, and called for a replacement vehicle. Romulus and his comrades had laughed when they heard how easily the crowd's attention was diverted from this bad omen. Their own worries had been allayed by Caesar's humility at the end of the triumphal march, which as always brought the victorious general to the temple of Jupiter on the Capitoline Hill. To avert any ill fortune, Caesar had crawled up the shrine's steps on his knees, with the cheers of his soldiers filling his ears. Once he had performed his devotions, prominent senators and high-ranking nobles had stood forth, heaping accolades upon Caesar in recognition of his stunning achievement in conquering Gaul. Finally, in an offering to the Republic's state god, Vercingetorix had been ritually strangled.

Crazed with bloodlust, the crowd went wild with excitement.

Romulus' stomach had churned at the sight. In his mind, a warrior deserved a better death than that which Vercingetorix had endured. He couldn't put the chieftain's bulging, terrified eyes or his purple face and swollen tongue from his mind. In an effort to forget the ghastly images, that night Romulus got drunker than he had ever been. He, Sabinus and the others from the honor guard took full advantage of Caesar's bounty and commandeered a corner of the Forum Olitorium as their own. There, a score of tables covered with enough bread, meat, olives and drink to satisfy eighty men for one evening awaited them. While the wine was watered down in the Roman fashion, it still got a man drunk if he consumed enough of it. At last able to give in to the relief of being safely back in Italy alive and unharmed, the legionaries let their hair down, tearing into joints of meat with their teeth and quaffing straight from the clay jugs. Romulus did too.

It wasn't just food and drink that were on offer. The women of the city descended on Caesar's men like Furies, giving their bodies freely and unasked for. Nothing was too much for the soldiers who had earned part of the glory for Rome. In a drunken haze, Romulus had taken a good-looking girl of his own age down an alleyway and coupled with her in a sweat-soaked frenzy. Most of his comrades showed less reserve, humping women over the tables to hoots of encouragement from the others. It went on for much of the night, until one by one the legionaries collapsed to sleep it off amid the mess of broken cups, spilled wine and scraps of food.

The next morning every one of the honor guard had a thumping headache. The centurion in charge — a crusty veteran of the Tenth— let them be. Strict army discipline was relaxed at such times. There was also a rest day before the men's services were required again at the next triumph. Romulus was grateful for the breathing space this granted him. Bleary-eyed and nauseous, he could hold down little more than a sip of water at a time. Losing count of the number of times he'd vomited, he slumped miserably on a bench, bitterly regretting the amount of wine he'd downed the night before.

"Cheer up!" Similarly hungover, Sabinus clapped him on the shoulder.

"Why?" Romulus groaned.

"Only another three to go! Think of the food and wine we'll get. And no one to fight for it."

Romulus grimaced, wishing that the celebrations were already over.

"There'll be women to fuck too!" Sabinus thumped him none too gently. "I saw you sneak off with that beauty last night."

An image of his encounter with the brown-skinned girl surfaced in Romulus' foggy mind, and he grinned. Long years of warfare had left precious little time for sex—apart from rape, which he loathed because of what had happened to his mother. In the face of such famine, Romulus' libido often felt like a chained-up, raging beast. Perhaps there were more compliant women to be had in the days ahead. That prospect he could look forward to. Romulus raised his head, willing away the pain. "Is there any wine left?"

Sabinus beamed. "That's the spirit! Nothing like a hair from the dog that bit you."

†

At dawn three days later, Fabiola took Benignus and five other bodyguards and set out for the Capitoline Hill. As she'd hoped, Scaevola and his men were nowhere to be seen. They didn't generally appear near the Lupanar until about midday, the hour when customers began arriving. Mingling with the already heavy crowds, she felt confident of remaining anonymous. The *fugitivarius* didn't even know she'd left the brothel. Returning there might be a different matter, but they could always leave it until dark. Whatever danger that might pose was of less importance than Fabiola's desire to see Brutus again and to regain his favor.

She deliberately hadn't attended Caesar's first triumph, which celebrated his victories in Gaul. Brutus had played a role in many of the battles there, so he would have been taking part in the procession and therefore unable to speak to her—even if he'd wanted to. Fabiola chose the next triumph, which was to mark Caesar's decisive win over Ptolemy, the teenage Egyptian king. Fabiola had been there for part of it, arriving in Alexandria just after the killing of Pompey by the orders of the king's courtiers. Their effort to curry favor with Caesar had failed in spectacular fashion, as he immediately seized power. His bravado had nearly been his undoing, but yet again Caesar had emerged victorious. Much as she despised him, Fabiola had to admit that his feat had been nothing short of incredible. She'd seen the pressure his troops were under in Alexandria's harbor. *Jupiter, grant that Romulus is alive,* she prayed, remembering the bloody stories that had reached Rome shortly after she had. Seven hundred legionaries had died that night, and her twin could easily have been among them. She wasn't the only one to risk mortal danger, Fabiola realized. Romulus' fate was out of her hands, though; she'd done her best to find him. If the gods decided to show her favor once more, he would return home one day. Her efforts to find Gemellus had also failed, leaving Caesar as her sole target.

Annexing Egypt, the Republic's bread basket, was immensely popular, explaining the extra-heavy throngs on the streets. Thanks to her heavies' ability to force a path through, Fabiola still arrived at the base of the Capitoline Hill in good time. The legionaries on duty there were supposed to prevent ordinary citizens from ascending to the temple but she got her little group through with a combination of flirting, flattery and liberal use of the silver in her purse. Plenty of space was available in the open area before the enormous shrine, which was free of the normal crowd of food-sellers, hawkers of trinkets, soothsayers, and prostitutes. The senators and grandees of Rome were just beginning to arrive, bowing reverently to the immense statue of Jupiter that stood before the gold-roofed temple. Following ancient custom for a triumphal day, the god's entire body had just been painted with the blood of a freshly slaughtered bull. It gave Jupiter an even more regal presence, and Fabiola was careful to whisper another prayer. Then she picked a spot near where she thought Brutus might stand. Groups of senior army officers were already in place, joking and laughing with each other in the easy manner of men who'd lived and fought with each other for years.

Fabiola recognized some of them. During her years with Brutus, she'd met countless members of Rome's military class. Raising the hood of her cloak, she was careful not to look in their direction. Like everyone else, the officers would have heard about their split, and she didn't want anyone warning Brutus of her presence before she got a chance to talk to him. There was little need for her to worry, though. Everyone present was far too excited about Caesar's impending arrival. Military messengers arrived regularly, updating the crowd on his progress through the city. Although it would be more than two hours until he reached the hilltop, all eyes were glued to the spot where the road ended.

Anxiety began creeping over Fabiola as the morning dragged by. Was she making a big mistake? Her unease rose sharply when, with his characteristic flair, Antonius arrived in a British war chariot. As his *lictores* cleared a large space for him right at the foot of the temple's steps, he idly scanned the crowd. Her heart racing with fear, Fabiola turned away. She let long moments go by before daring to look at what Antonius was doing. She wasn't surprised to see him chatting to the legionaries on guard. Fabiola's dislike of Antonius intensified. He was a violent bully to her, but the Master of the Horse was a figure of adoration to almost the entire army. It was just another of the reasons why she was powerless before him.

Before she knew it, another hour had passed. There was still no sign of Brutus, and Fabiola's hopes of seeing him began to wane. Her attention faltered as Benignus began asking questions about various security matters to do with the Lupanar. When she next studied the group of military officers, Brutus was in their midst. Fabiola's heart fluttered at the sight of him. Pleasant-looking rather than handsome, Brutus cut a dash in full ceremonial dress. Amused by something one of the others said, he smiled and laughed, increasing Fabiola's sadness even more. Previously, that's how he'd acted toward her. Maybe Brutus wasn't just a means to an end, she thought. What had she done by carrying on with Antonius?

"Wait here," she instructed Benignus. Leaving him protesting in her wake, Fabiola moved purposefully through the waiting throng. To her relief, Antonius was nowhere to be seen. Reaching the group of officers, she faltered. Then a dark-haired tribune with a brightly colored sash around his waist turned to address the man beside him. When he saw Fabiola, his mouth opened. As a rich teenager, he'd been a frequent and enthusiastic client. Her manumission was the only reason that their trysts had stopped.

Fabiola cursed inwardly. This fool could ruin everything. Giving him a withering look, she brushed past to Brutus' side. He was deep in conversation with a comrade and didn't notice her immediately. Fabiola glanced back at the tribune to check he wasn't following her. Thankfully, he wasn't. Trembling, she reached out and tapped Brutus on the shoulder. He didn't respond, so she did it again, harder. "Brutus."

Recognizing her voice, he turned, surprise and anger already twisting his features. "What are you doing here?" He lowered his voice. "Come to fawn over Antonius?"

"No," she protested.

"Or Caesar?" he said suspiciously. "He's been asking for you. Wondering where you were. Why would that be?"

"I don't know," replied Fabiola desperately, the news chilling her to the bone. She wished that she'd told Brutus of her near rape at Caesar's hands three years before. If she mentioned it now of course, he wouldn't believe her. She had to just plow on. "Can we talk?"

Brutus snorted. "Here? Now?"

She touched his arm lightly. "Please, my love. Give me a few moments."

Some of the anger left his face, and he sighed. "Come this way." Beckoning, he led her past the goggling tribune to the back of the crowd. There was some space leading up to the very edge of the Capitoline Hill, and for a moment they stood in silence, looking down over Rome.

"I've missed you so much," Fabiola began. Brutus said nothing, but she knew him well enough to see that he shared the same sentiment. The tiny ember of hope in her heart flared up a little. "Getting involved with Antonius was such a mistake. The man's a brute. He makes me . . ." A sob rose in her throat at the indignities Antonius regularly forced on her. Her distress wasn't acted, and Fabiola was heartened by Brutus' response.

"What does he do?" he demanded, grabbing his sword hilt.

"Pretty much anything and everything," boomed a familiar voice. "And she loves it!"

Blanching, Fabiola spun to find a sneering Antonius not five paces away. To her utter horror, he was accompanied by none other than Scaevola. Dark malice glittered in the *fugitivarius'* deep-set eyes. Terrified, she moved closer to Brutus.

"What did you say?" Brutus stared at Antonius with clear dislike.

"You heard," replied Antonius icily. "Most of the time, it's her who suggests the position. Or the other people."

Scaevola chuckled.

Despite himself, Brutus looked scandalized. Orgies were not his style.

"Men, women, it doesn't really matter," Antonius went on, relishing the effect his words were having on Brutus. "I drew the line at the gladiators, though."

"No," Fabiola cried, looking at Brutus. "He's lying."

Antonius laughed. "Lie about a whore like you? Why would I bother?"

Brutus scowled and Fabiola felt the situation slipping from her grasp.

A loud fanfare from the trumpeters announced Caesar's impending arrival, and Brutus' face changed. "I have to go," he muttered, turning on his heel.

Fabiola reached out to him. "Will I see you later?" she pleaded.

His lip curled. "After what's been said? I don't think so." Without another word, he strode off.

A black tide of despair swamped Fabiola. If Scaevola had stabbed her there and then, she wouldn't have cared. Of course things were never that simple. The instant Brutus was lost to sight, Antonius moved in. She felt his hand caress her throat.

"Getting tired of me?" he demanded.

Fabiola looked from him to Scaevola, who was grinning delightedly. In spite of her fear, her temper flared. "More than that," she hissed. "I hate you. Touch me again, and I'll . . ." Her words were lost in a cacophony of blaring trumpets.

"Shame you feel like that. It's been fun. All good things come to an end, though." Antonius' eyes glinted, reminding Fabiola of a snake that was about to strike. "I'd love to finish this, but Caesar will think it strange if his deputy isn't there to greet him." He stepped away, giving Fabiola an unpleasant stare. "Scaevola can wrap up things for me. Permanently."

The *fugitivarius* pressed forward, his fingers curling around the hilt of his sword. "Now?" he asked eagerly.

"Not here, you fool," Antonius snapped. "Half of Rome is watching. Later."

Scaevola nodded sullenly and stepped back.

Fabiola took the opportunity to dart into the press of people a few steps away.

They let her go, which was even more frightening.

XX

THE SEARCH

S ure you don't want to come with us?" asked Sabinus. He jingled his purse. "We've got money to burn!"

The other legionaries cheered. On the last day of Caesar's celebrations, he had awarded every single one of his foot soldiers the staggering sum of five thousand *denarii*. Even the poor had benefited from the dictator's largesse, receiving wheat, olive oil and one hundred *denarii* each. The legionaries' bonus was more than they'd each earn in a lifetime's service with the legions, and royally repaid their dogged loyalty to him. Suddenly the frequent periods of hardship and death seemed worthwhile, and now, the next day, the men couldn't wait to blow some of their riches. The triumphs had ended the night before, and all legionaries were off duty for a week.

The honor guard had been granted the surprise of an early discharge from the army. This was, Caesar had said, thanks to their outstanding contributions to his cause. Consequently, they were even more eager than the rest of the soldiers to rejoice. Dressed in just their belted tunics and *caligae*, Romulus' comrades were in search of wine, women and song. He felt differently. After all the marching, all the adulation and the excesses of the previous ten days, he wanted a break. While his early release meant that he had all the time in the world, it was time to look for Fabiola, and if he got the chance, Gemellus.

"Well?" demanded the *optio* from the Twenty-Eighth. "Make up your mind."

There was an impatient rumble of agreement from the rest. They had walked together from their camp on the Campus Martius as far as the first major crossroads inside the city walls. Straight ahead lay the Forum, while on each side were streets leading to the Capitoline and Viminal hills. The smell of cooking sausages and garlic filled the afternoon air, and innkeepers shouted to encourage passersby into their dingy, open-fronted establishments. Kohl-eyed prostitutes beckoned from the doorways that led to the cramped *insulae* above the shops. There was temptation everywhere for the newly enriched soldiers and they weren't going to wait long.

Romulus shook his head. "There's some business I need to take care of."

"Come on," Sabinus urged. "Can't it wait until tomorrow?"

"No."

"Why so mysterious?" asked Sabinus, his brow wrinkling.

"I'll tell you another time," replied Romulus tersely. Without realizing it, he touched the sheathed *pugio* on his belt. If his military haircut and russet tunic weren't enough, it was a giveaway sign that he was a soldier.

Sharp-eyed, Sabinus noticed the movement. "Want me to tag along?"

Romulus gave him a brief smile. "No thanks."

"You're your own master." Sabinus stepped away. The group was already drifting off, and he would have difficulty finding them if he got separated. "You know where to look if you need us. That big inn by the Forum Boarium."

Romulus raised his hand in farewell, wondering where he should start his search for Fabiola. He'd put off thinking about it until now. Remembering her in Alexandria helped. She'd been well dressed, and her mere presence there hinted at a relationship with a senior army officer. Romulus had wondered at the time if it was Caesar, but discovered since that, unlike some of his officers, his general didn't take women on campaign. That left a host of other nobles, many of whom might not even live in Rome. Even if they did, how would he find Fabiola among them? Unless he wanted a flogging—or worse—he couldn't as an ordinary soldier go about asking personal questions regarding their mistresses. Romulus began to despair before he'd even started. *Stop it*, he thought. *Think.* He stood for a moment, letting the crowd push by. While Caesar's triumphs might have ended, the festivities had not, and the streets were even more packed than ever. The legionaries weren't the only ones in search of a good time. Unbidden, an image of the brothel outside which the fight had taken place came to mind. What had it been called? Romulus racked his brains. The Lupanar, that was it.

Disgust filled him at the idea that Fabiola might still be a prostitute. Tarquinius had said that she'd left the brothel, though, and he couldn't think of a better place to start. He pulled at the arm of a passing urchin. "Where's the Lupanar?"

The filthy child gaped, then recovered his poise. "No need to go that far, sir." He pointed at the nearest doorway, where a half-naked girl of no more than sixteen stood, touching herself in an attempt to look seductive. "My sister. She's clean. Only costs ten *sestertii*. If she doesn't take your fancy, there are others inside."

Romulus glanced over. In the shadows behind the child-woman lurked an old man in a grubby robe. Seeing Romulus stare, he whispered in her ear. She slipped down the top of her robe and lasciviously caressed her tiny breasts. Romulus felt sick. At least the women he'd had in the previous few days had been willing. "I want the Lupanar," he said, striding off.

Promising every kind of pleasure, the dark-haired boy kept pace with Romulus, doing his best while his master watched.

As soon as the old man was out of sight, Romulus produced a *sestertius*. "Well?" he asked.

The other's thin face lit up. The silver coin was far more than the paltry amount he'd get for guiding customers toward the nearby doorway. "It's up that lane," he offered eagerly. "Take the second right and then the first left."

Romulus flipped him the *sestertius* and walked off, ignoring the urchin's promises of more information. Shrugging, the boy pocketed his reward and returned to his post. His directions were accurate, though, and it didn't take Romulus long to reach a narrow street dominated by an arched doorway with a painted erect penis on either side. Outside stood a number of doormen, their swords and clubs in plain view. The sight stopped Romulus in his tracks. Old memories surged back. His flight from the inn with Brennus. The Gaul offering to pay for a prostitute for him. Their collision at the brothel's entrance with a drunk, red haired noble whose arrogant attitude had sparked the fight. Deciding to make a run for it. Hearing the shouts of "Murder" behind them as they ran. *Gods*, thought Romulus, *how my life has changed since that night. For the better.* A feeling of calm acceptance, which he'd never allowed to emerge before, settled over him. He was back in Rome, a free man. His anger at Tarquinius faded away; his old guilt about Brennus suddenly felt weaker too. The Gaul had walked the path of his destiny willingly, and it was not for Romulus to stand in the way of that.

Romulus took a step toward the Lupanar. Fabiola probably wasn't working there any longer, but someone would know where she'd gone. He'd soon track her down. How might his sister have changed? Romulus wondered excitedly. What would be her reaction to him? Deep in thought and with his reactions slowed by ten days of drinking, he didn't really take in the large party of unshaven heavies strolling along just in front of him.

The doormen in front of the Lupanar did, however. "Look lively, boys," shouted one, an enormous shaven-headed man with gold bands around his wrists. "Trouble!"

Romulus heard the familiar sound of *gladii* leaving their scabbards. Startled, he looked up. Armed with axes and clubs as well as swords, the thugs were charging headlong at the brothel's entrance. Rather than stand back or retreat, the guards drew their own weapons and spread out in a defensive arc around the doorway. His heart pounding, Romulus turned and fled back down the alleyway. Who knew what was going on, but this was not his quarrel. Besides, he had only a *pugio* to defend himself. When he judged it safe, he stopped and looked back. Thanks to the permanent semidarkness that existed in all narrow streets, he could see only a roiling mass of figures moving backward and forward. From the blood-curdling yells and screams, men were being seriously injured or killed.

"Should have fucked my sister," said a piping voice behind him. "You'd be finished by now, and looking for your friends."

Romulus turned to find the skinny urchin who'd given him directions nonchalantly eating an apple. His smug expression spoke volumes. "Did you know there was trouble here?" Romulus demanded, taking a step forward. "Why didn't you tell me? Hades below, I could have been killed."

"I did try," answered the boy, looking scared. "You weren't interested."

Romulus remembered the offers of more information and relaxed. He wasn't going to pick a fight with a scrawny child who owed him nothing. "True enough," he said gruffly, eyeing the brawl again. "So what's going on there?" Silence. Looking down, Romulus saw an outstretched hand.

"Nothing free in this city, sir," said the urchin with a cheeky grin.

Romulus tossed him another *sestertius*.

The response was instant. "It's some kind of feud between the Lupanar and another brothel. Quite a few men have been killed. Although it's been going on for months, things have been quiet recently. Until today, that is."

"What's it about?"

The boy shrugged. "Not sure. Want to try my sister now?"

"No," Romulus snapped, frustrated that his search had ended before it had even begun. Where else could he go? Nothing came to mind, and he decided to rejoin Sabinus and the others. He could always return to the Lupanar in the morning. "I need a drink," he muttered.

"The best inn in Rome is very close," volunteered the urchin. "Want me to take you there?"

Romulus smiled. He liked the boy's spirit. Clad in rags, and no doubt half-starved, he was still obviously resourceful. "No. But I'd say you can take me a shorter way to the Forum Boarium than retracing my steps, eh?"

"Of course! Two *sestertii.*"

Romulus chuckled. "Quite the businessman, aren't you? Don't push your luck, though. I've already paid you five times more than I needed to."

This produced a serious nod. "One *sestertius* it is," said the urchin, proffering a grubby paw.

"When we get there," Romulus warned.

Laughing, they shook hands. At once the boy darted off, leading Romulus through a confusion of alleys that joined the Capitoline Hill to the Palatine. During the recent celebrations, Romulus had had no time to explore the city, and of course the triumphs had taken place on the largest thoroughfares. It made his journey now all the more poignant. These were the type of streets on which he'd grown up. No more than ten paces wide, their unpaved surfaces covered in rubbish and waste, and with three- and four-story buildings on both sides blocking out all light apart from a narrow band of sky high above. Open-fronted shops sold everything from bread to vegetables to wine, their goods sprawling out onto the street. There were potters, smiths, carpenters, barbers and every other profession under the sun. Inns, brothels and money changers' premises were situated side by side, each one with its attendant begging leper or limbless cripple. Rows of shuttered windows overhead belonged to the cramped *insulae*, or tenements, in which most citizens lived.

While he wasn't familiar with their exact location, Romulus could remember running errands for Gemellus through similar quarters. The memory of his former owner brought a stab of anger. Where could he be? Romulus scowled. Was there any point going to the house where he'd grown up? Probably not, but at least it would be a place to start. Right now, though, the thought of meeting Sabinus and his comrades was far more appealing.

It was then that Romulus walked past a nondescript opening between two *cenaculae*, or apartment buildings. Something made him go back to take a second look. About fifty paces in, and surrounded by derelict houses, was a temple he'd never seen before.

Sensing his customer stop, the urchin came scurrying back, his bare feet silent on the dirt. "Nearly there, mister." He tugged at Romulus' arm. "It's not that way."

"Which deity is that dedicated to?"

The boy shivered. "Orcus."

The god of the underworld. Romulus smiled thinly. Where better to make an offering that might help him find Gemellus? It had to be worth a quick visit. He was half a dozen strides into the alleyway before his guide could react.

"Sir! What about the inn?"

"I won't be long," Romulus replied over his shoulder. "Wait outside for me."

Grim-faced, the urchin obeyed. While the stained stone altar in front of the shrine might terrify him, he wasn't going to miss out on the promised *sestertius*.

Romulus walked up the steps to the main entrance, past the usual seedy-looking soothsayers, vendors of food and trinkets and men selling little squares of lead sheet. Stopping by one of these last, he bought a piece of the heavy gray metal. Romulus leaned against a pillar and used his knife tip to scratch on it a curse upon Gemellus. Plenty of other worshippers were doing the same, or paying hovering scribes to do so on their behalf. Once more, Romulus was glad he could write. This matter was deeply private to him and he had no wish to share it with anyone. He looked again at his words. "Gemellus: One day, I will kill you, very slowly." It was what he'd silently mouthed as the merchant had left him in the *ludus*. Satisfied, Romulus folded the square and headed inside.

A robed acolyte guided him to the main chamber, a long, narrow affair filled with devotees. There were separate rooms available for more private visits, but Romulus had no need of them. After so long away from Rome, the chance of being recognized was slim to none. He took his place in the queue that was wending its way toward the large fireplace at the back of the room. Upon reaching it, the supplicants bowed their heads, said a prayer and tossed their offering into the flames. High on the wall above, overlooking all, was a circular depiction of the god similar to the one on the portico outside. Romulus glanced at Orcus' dark-eyed, bearded face, under hair that consisted of a mass of snakes. He shuddered. The image was intended to strike fear into his heart, and it worked.

He continued to shuffle forward to the fire, however. The desire for revenge burned stronger than his dread, just as it did in the hearts of the other people present. Romulus studied the faces he could see, wondering what suffering or wrongdoing had brought them here. There was a good cross-section of society in the large chamber. He could see shopkeepers, plain citizens, slaves and soldiers like himself, even an occasional nobleman or -woman. Romulus smiled, feeling his self-belief grow. No one was unique: They all had a grudge to settle. Reaching the front of the queue, he was stopped by a short, wide-faced priestess with long brown hair tied up behind her head. Like all her companions, she was dressed in a simple gray robe. She was quite plain, but Romulus was struck by her deep green eyes. He watched as she raked the fire using a long iron poker, pushing the heaped metal squares deeper into the blaze.

"You may approach," she said at last.

Romulus bowed and tossed in his piece of lead, along with several *denarii*. *I have few desires in life*, he thought. *Orcus, grant me this one.*

A curt nod from the priestess told him that his audience with the god was over. Romulus obediently moved on, walking behind those who had offered before him. He sighed, wondering if his request would bear fruit. It felt even more of an impossible quest than his search for Fabiola. What chance had he of finding a bankrupt merchant in such a large city? There was always divination, he supposed. After Tarquinius' lessons, he'd attempted it a number of times, but the shock of being accurate had put Romulus off since. Facing death on a daily basis meant that life was better lived in uncertainty. That way, he wouldn't spend his time worrying about things that were essentially beyond his ability to influence. *Not yet,* he thought. *Let's see what Orcus offers first.*

The urchin was still waiting outside the temple. He looked inquiringly at Romulus, who gave away nothing. "The Forum Boarium," he ordered.

"Follow me, sir." Eager to leave the shrine behind, the lad was off like a bolt from a *ballista*.

Owing to the number of devotees clogging the alleyway, their pace slowed as they neared the junction to the street they'd been on previously. Putting Gemellus from his mind, Romulus was already thinking of the inn where he'd meet Sabinus and the others. He was thirsty for a cup of wine. Perhaps there'd be women there too.

A little way ahead, someone stumbled and fell against the person in front. A loud curse was the instant response. Despite a profuse apology, the hapless individual was subjected to a tirade of abuse, which only died down when those who were waiting to exit the alley began to complain. Romulus frowned as the outburst died away and the crowd began to move again. He could not see the speaker, but the voice was familiar. Like a lightning strike from on high, recognition hit. Although he hadn't heard it since his first day in the *ludus*, Romulus recognized Gemellus' sarcastic tone.

Full of awe, and a little terror, he looked back at Orcus' temple. What devilry was at work for this to happen so fast? There was no time to ponder it, just to act. He elbowed the protesting urchin out of the way and muscled his way forward, desperate to catch the merchant. Romulus' efforts earned him a chorus of protests, but no one had the courage to stand up to the vengeance in his eyes. Panting with anger, Romulus reached the street a few moments later. His head turned this way and that, searching, but the crowds here were even denser than in the alley. Gemellus had vanished.

"Damn the whoreson to Hades!" Romulus yelled. "He won't escape forever."

His outburst elicited barely a glance from the passersby. Rome was full of drunk soldiers shouting insults and causing trouble. Prudence was always the best option in such cases.

Worming his skinny frame alongside, the urchin glanced reproachfully at Romulus. "Trying to get away without paying me?"

"What?" Romulus snapped. "No, of course not. I just heard the voice of someone I'd dearly love to meet. I followed him, but he's disappeared into the crowd." Then he smiled. "Want to earn ten *sestertii*?"

It was an enormous sum for a half-starved street child. "Tell me what to do," he clamored.

Romulus made a stirrup of his hands. "Climb up," he ordered. "Look for a short, fat man with a red face. He sweats a lot."

Quickly the urchin obeyed, placing his calloused feet on Romulus' shoulders and balancing by resting one hand against the wall of the nearest building. Raising his other hand to his eyes, he peered up and down the street with quiet intensity.

Romulus could hardly bear the tension. "Well?" he demanded.

"I can't see him," came the disappointed answer.

Romulus bit his lower lip until it bled. *Curse Gemellus for evermore,* he thought. *I'll never get a chance like that again. Gods don't hand out such opportunities twice.*

The other's next words nearly stopped Romulus' heart. "Wait," he said. Then his voice grew shrill. "That way! Sixty paces that way!"

With an urgency he'd never felt before, Romulus helped the boy down.

"Follow me," he cried, heading left.

Romulus charged after him like a raging bull.

Half running, half walking, they pushed and shoved their way into the mass of people moving along the street. Progress was slow, but the urchin was so thin and nimble that he fitted into spaces that Romulus never could. Climbing over amphorae of wine laid on beds of straw or piles of ironmongery, he thumbed his nose at the indignant shopkeepers and soon drew far ahead. His piping voice carried back, however, giving Romulus extra impetus. "Hurry! I can see him!"

Sick with nerves, Romulus plowed on. By the time he'd reached a crossroads, he had closed the gap with the urchin to perhaps twenty paces.

"Left!" came the boy's shout.

Romulus obeyed, using a small gap in the crowd to gain another six steps. He loosened his *pugio* in its sheath, wondering what part of

Gemellus he'd cut off first. An ear? His greasy nose? He grimaced. Maybe he should castrate the bastard first.

A thin hand reached out to stop him.

Startled, Romulus took in the urchin by his side. "What is it?"

"He's gone in there."

Romulus' gaze followed the boy's pointing arm down a narrow lane strewn with rubbish and broken pottery. A few paces in, a huge dung heap steamed gently. His nose wrinkled with disgust. "You're sure?"

He nodded. "Yes, sir. A short, fat man with a red face, like you said. He looks very poor."

He'd have to be, thought Romulus, eyeing the alley with some satisfaction. Any *insulae* down there would be rat-infested, stinking hellholes. "Come on," he said, leading the way.

Eager for his money, the urchin followed.

Keen not to tread in the stinking ooze from the dung heap, Romulus moved slowly at first. By the time he'd passed it, his eyes were acclimatized to the near darkness. The uneven ground was still treacherous underfoot, but all his attention was on the shambling male figure not twenty paces ahead of him. Certainly it was the right height and girth to be Gemellus, Romulus thought. Then the man stubbed a toe on a shard of pottery and cursed loudly. Romulus froze, feeling a childish tremor of fear. It *was* Gemellus. Few things could make him react like this, but the scars left on his soul by the merchant during his childhood were deep. *That was then, this is now,* Romulus told himself. He drew his dagger, causing the urchin to gasp. "Quiet!" Romulus hissed.

In the same instant, the man ahead disappeared through a narrow doorway. There was a quiet click as it shut behind him. With his heart in his mouth, Romulus walked the last few steps. A succession of images flashed before his eyes, and he let them come. Gemellus forcing himself on his mother. Gemellus beating Fabiola. Beating him. Ranting to his bookkeeper about his ailing finances. The merchant's gloating face as he had dragged Romulus away from his screaming mother and twin sister, and in the *ludus*, where he had boasted about how he'd sell them to the salt mines and a brothel respectively. Romulus bared his teeth with rage. Only the last memory gave him any pleasure: Hiero the *bestiarius* telling him how Gemellus had been ruined.

Romulus lifted his *pugio* to eye level, noting that his hand was trembling. *Calm down,* he thought. *My prayers are about to be answered. Vengeance will be mine.* At once the shaking stopped, and he readied himself to end it, once and for all.

Using the dagger's hilt, he hammered on the door. "Open up!"

XXI

DANGER

Since her attempt at reconciliation with Brutus and the following confrontation with Antonius and the *fugitivarius*, Fabiola had hardly been sleeping. Over and over, she cursed her stupidity for taking up with the Master of the Horse. It had proved to be the worst decision she'd ever made. *If only time could be turned back,* she thought, but of course that was impossible. Now she had to live with the consequences of her actions. A bag of nerves compared to her normal calm self, Fabiola had been bad-tempered with everyone. Benignus and Vettius, now her most trusted confidants, could not shift her black mood. Their lessons on defending herself with a sword and knife—which built on the basics that Sextus had taught her—did not help much. Nothing was right. Days dragged by without event and Fabiola grew more irritable, snapping at potential customers and losing good business that the brothel sorely needed. Furious at herself, she then shouted at the prostitutes for not pleasing their few clients enough. Toughest of them all, even Jovina was tiptoeing around her warily.

Fabiola no longer cared. As far as she was concerned, her life was sliding into oblivion. She still had no potential allies for her plot to kill Caesar. The size and grandeur of the dictator's four triumphs had sent any enemies he might have even deeper into the woodwork. So where did owning a brothel get her? thought Fabiola in frustration. Without Brutus, nowhere. There had been no further contact from her former lover either, which meant that he probably believed the lies Antonius had told. For the moment, she dared not try to contact Brutus again. *Let the dust settle,* she thought. He might come around. The other silence she was enduring—from the Master of the Horse—was far more chilling. From visiting Fabiola on average more than once a day, Antonius had cut her off completely.

In contrast, Scaevola's presence had become altogether more threatening. After long months spent in the shadows, it was as if he wanted the pressure on Fabiola to build to an unbearable intensity. It was a clever, and successful, tactic. More of his heavies than ever before appeared to man the blockades around the Lupanar. If spotted, its known customers were beaten up, while ordinary passersby were harassed and intimidated. A small group of Fabiola's men who had gone to buy food were set upon and killed, reducing her forces. The merchants who provided the brothel with food were threatened, and to prevent her supplies from completely running out, Fabiola was forced to pay them extortionate prices. This further depleted the money Brutus had given her, which was already going fast thanks to her extra guards. Benignus had managed to hire an additional four, but Fabiola wanted to hire even more. Thanks to the huge numbers of fighters required for the celebratory games, though, few were available. In one way, it was just as well. While she might need them, she couldn't really afford more men. At her current rates of expenditure, Fabiola knew she'd have to sell the Lupanar in one to two years. Not that she cared about that. She'd be lucky to live that long.

It was the dull ache of expectation that kept Fabiola awake at night. Antonius had decided that she was expendable, but he was no fool. Even if he was not "directly" responsible, it was common knowledge throughout the city that Scaevola was in his employ. A blood-bath during Caesar's riotous celebrations would not go down well with his master. No, she thought, any attack would come after the last of the triumphs had been held. This realization provided only momentary relief. Fabiola did not care that much about herself any longer, but she felt a duty of care for those she owned and employed. Benignus, Vettius, the prostitutes and guards were all innocent victims of her rash behavior. None of them deserved to be injured or killed because of it.

Night after night, Fabiola tossed about on her bed, worrying. Other than walking away from the Lupanar, what could she do? If she left, she would be homeless. In the brothel, at least she had a roof over her head. Gradually, Fabiola became aware that she had not quite given up hope. She could not just abandon her business and those who worked there, despite the grave danger she was placing them all in. She wondered if this was how a general might feel before a battle—worrying whether his cause was worth the price of his soldiers' lives. Naturally, her dilemma brought Romulus to mind. Fabiola couldn't imagine him backing away from a challenge this important. Or was she just being selfish, justifying an arrogant decision?

On the night of Caesar's last triumph, there were hardly any customers. Despite the massive numbers of citizens on the streets, Scaevola's blockade was tightening. Fabiola's terror became all-consuming. Although only the gods knew what would transpire, the waiting would soon be over. She could feel it in her bones. If she died during Scaevola's attack, then all her worries would vanish, in the process denying her both revenge upon Caesar and a meeting with Romulus. Fabiola thought this the most likely outcome. Since Scaevola's attack in Orcus' temple, all the deities she prayed to—Jupiter, Mithras and the god of the underworld—had shown her virtually no favor.

If by some divine chance she was spared, then her purpose would remain the same. She would make another attempt to approach

Brutus. If that didn't work, she decided she would start taking on new clients of her own, using the wiles that had won her such adoration in the past. A mountainous and distasteful task, yet she did not balk at it. To stoke her levels of anger, Fabiola flagellated herself mentally, remembering her mother's story of how she'd been raped by a nobleman while on an evening errand for Gemellus.

The tactic had a dramatic effect. Fabiola found herself clutching the knife she kept under her pillow, imagining the pleasure of plunging it into Caesar's flesh herself while telling him her reason why. She wondered how Romulus might react to the knowledge of their parenthood. No doubt it would be with an even greater fury. How thrilling it would feel to have her twin join her cause, she thought. With Romulus by her side, things would be so much easier. He might even want to kill Caesar himself. With this happy notion, Fabiola fell asleep, slipping into a vivid world in which the dictator was dead, she and Romulus were reunited and Brutus cared for her again.

It was the best night's rest she had had in months.

She finally emerged into the reception area at midday the following day.

Jovina nodded cautiously at her. "Sleep well?"

"Yes, thank you. Morpheus remembered me at last," smiled Fabiola, remembering her dream. "Any customers yet?"

"No," the old madam replied. "We won't see any until much later. They'll all have massive hangovers thanks to Caesar's munificence."

Fabiola scowled. Word had swept through the city about the twenty-two thousand tables of food and wine that were to be supplied by Caesar on the night of his last triumph. His popularity continued to grow with each passing day. *Curse him,* she thought. *The bastard can do no wrong.*

"Don't worry," Jovina chirped, misinterpreting her reaction. "The amount of money he gave away will bring his soldiers through the doors in droves. After all those years on campaign, half of them probably look like Priapus." Chortling, she indicated the painting on the wall. As always, the god of gardens, fields and fertility was depicted with a huge erect penis. "Scaevola's men won't dare try and stop them!"

Despite herself, Fabiola smiled. "Who's outside?"

"Vettius," Jovina replied. "Been out there since dawn. Nothing doing, he said. Scaevola's lot probably joined in the festivities last night. No man likes to fight with a pounding head."

"Hmm." When he picked his moment, the *fugitivarius* would make sure his men were ready, free wine or no. Pursing her lips, Fabiola headed out to see for herself.

Vettius was leaning against the wall by the entrance, dozing in a patch of sunlight that reached down to the street. His club rested by his right hand. Eight or nine of the guards were also present, either playing knucklebones or watching the few passersby. Hearing Fabiola emerge, Vettius opened his eyes. He jerked upright with a start. "Mistress."

"I've told you not to call me that," chided Fabiola.

He bobbed his great shaven head, still awkward around her. "Fabiola."

"Any sign of Scaevola or his lot?"

"Not so much as a whisker."

"Stay on your guard anyway." She beckoned him closer and whispered. "Make sure all the men are ready to fight. Now that Caesar's triumphs are over, I think the danger is even greater."

Vettius picked up his club and slapped it across the palm of his left hand. "If the bastard does arrive, he'd better be ready for a good fight."

Fabiola took some reassurance from his confident manner.

As it turned out, Scaevola came prepared for a war.

Later that day.

†

Fabiola's first inkling that something was up came when she ventured out to check on the guards early in the afternoon. To her surprise, the lane was completely deserted. No noisy children playing; no housewives gossiping over their shopping or dirty washing. The few beggars who plied their trade near the brothel were nowhere to be seen. Even the shutters on the windows of the *insulae* in the building opposite were shut.

"How long's it been like this?" she asked Benignus, who had replaced Vettius.

He rubbed his jaw, thinking. "About an hour or so. I didn't pass much comment, because the streets beyond aren't much busier."

Her nostrils flaring, Fabiola stared at the nearest businesses: a bakery, a potter's workshop and an apothecary's. The bakery was shut, which wasn't surprising. It opened well before sunrise each day, baking the loaves that were a staple of most citizens' diet. The entire stock was usually gone by midmorning, and the baker closed soon afterward to catch up on his sleep. Unusually, the potter's was also boarded up, when in normal circumstances it would have been open until dark. Fabiola frowned as she saw the apothecary, a stout, balding Greek, tidying away his display, a host of jars containing the treatment or cure for every disease and malady known to man. Her prostitutes frequented this shop on a daily basis, buying everything from tinctures and doses that prevented pregnancy and disease to love potions for their favorite clients. In fact, the Greek relied on the Lupanar for most of his business. Why then was he closing early?

Fabiola set off toward him at a brisk pace.

"Where are you going, Mistress?" Benignus called. "Fabiola?"

She didn't answer, prompting the huge doorman to pelt after her, along with a trio of the others. The apothecary's was only twenty paces from the brothel, but Benignus was taking no risks.

As Fabiola reached the open-fronted shop, the proprietor emerged, rubbing his hands on his stained apron. Seeing her, he bowed. "A pleasure to see you in person, lady. Need some more valerian to help you sleep?"

"No, thank you." Fabiola indicated the nearly empty stands and tables. "Shutting up shop already?"

"Yes," he admitted, avoiding her gaze. "My wife's not well," he added hastily.

"How terrible," Fabiola cried, the picture of solicitousness. Inside, the suspicion she'd felt at the other two shops' closure was increasing fast. "Nothing serious, I hope?"

The apothecary looked awkward. "She developed a fever during the night."

"You must have given her something for it," barked Fabiola.

"Of course," he muttered.

"What?"

The apothecary faltered, and Fabiola knew that he was lying. The Greek was a family man, and if his wife had really been ill, he wouldn't have opened at all that day. "What's going on?" she demanded, stepping closer. "The potter's gone too, you know. The whole damn street's like a cemetery."

He swallowed noisily.

"Come now," Fabiola urged, taking his hand. "You can tell me. We're all friends and neighbors here."

He glanced up and down the street, seeming relieved that it was deserted. "You're right. I should have warned you before, but he threatened my family." His voice cracked with emotion. "I'm sorry."

"He?" Fabiola's stomach clenched, but she also felt a sense of relief. "Scaevola, you mean?"

His eyes darted about with fear. "Yes."

"What's the dog planning?" Fabiola wanted her suspicion confirmed by someone independent.

"He didn't say. Nothing good, I'm sure," the apothecary replied, wiping sweat from his forehead. "All the shopkeepers have had the same warning—that it'd be best to disappear this afternoon."

Fabiola nodded. The instruction to remove possible bystanders—and witnesses—from the street had probably originated from Antonius. Merciless beyond belief, Scaevola wouldn't care how many people he killed, but the Master of the Horse would want a clean job done. "You'd best leave then," she said briskly. "Get home to your family."

The apothecary looked embarrassed. Here he was, a man, running away while a woman stayed to fight. "Can I do anything?" he asked.

Fabiola smiled warmly, easing his conscience. "Leave us a few bottles of *acetum* and *papaverum*. They might come in handy later."

"Of course." Scurrying inside his shop, he emerged a few moments later with his arms full. "This is all my stock," he said.

Fabiola began to protest, but the apothecary would have none of it. "It's the least I can do," he insisted. "May the gods protect you all."

"Thank you." Directing her men to carry the vital medicines, Fabiola headed back to the Lupanar.

They did not have long to wait.

†

Sweating, Tarquinius finally reached the top of the Capitoline Hill and the great complex dedicated to Jupiter. His head was throbbing and there was a foul taste in his dry mouth. He'd partaken of Caesar's public feast the night before and was now heartily regretting it. What had been a good idea at the time seemed foolish, he thought, given his tardiness today. The best hour for visiting the great shrine was early in the morning before the crowds got there, or in the evening after they'd left. With the sun nearing its zenith, he would arrive to make a sacrifice just as half of Rome did. Hardly the ideal moment to expect a good divination.

The unfortunate truth was that since his return from the *latifundium* the haruspex had found sitting outside the Lupanar extremely dull. Little of interest happened from one day to the next, and his reasons for hurrying back now seemed unnecessary. Tarquinius could have introduced himself to Fabiola, but he still felt reticent about making such a move. Why would she welcome him—the man responsible for her brother's flight from Rome? If Romulus never returned, she would blame him even more. No, it was better to stay in the background, gather information and pray for guidance. Tarquinius' faith was being tested to the limit.

He'd learned some useful information from the soothsayer, though. Fabiola's former lover was Decimus Brutus, but she was currently involved with Marcus Antonius. This explained what Tarquinius had seen when he followed her to this very spot a few days previously. Despite the thronged streets, he had managed to stay close, watching Fabiola as she tried to speak to Brutus, only to be interrupted by Antonius and the leader of the thugs on the blockades. The two noblemen's hostile body language spoke volumes. He hadn't heard what was said, but Brutus' anger, Antonius' triumph and Fabiola's dejected expression told their own tale. At one stroke, she had been deprived of the men's favor, while the ruffian looked set on doing her harm. Things were not going well for Romulus' sister.

The haruspex felt quite helpless before Fabiola's problems. He had no wealth, political influence or power. Apart from watching over the Lupanar, what could he do? Tempted to walk into the brothel two days before, he had resisted the urge thanks to a flare-up of his gut instinct. It was not the time. Still nothing much happened, and by the final night of Caesar's triumphs, Tarquinius needed a break. Practically every street in the city had been lined with tables groaning under the weight of Caesar's generosity. Everyone was in festive mood, friendly to even the most taciturn and scarred of strangers like Tarquinius. Before he knew it, the haruspex had drunk half a dozen cups of wine pressed on him by other merrymakers. After that, he'd done well to find his miserable rented room in the attic of a run-down *cenacula* by the Tiber.

Tarquinius' intention of visiting the Capitoline Hill was forgotten until it came crashing back late the following morning when he woke in a cold sweat. Hence his hurry now. Although he felt guilty about it, taking a break to visit the huge temple was more appealing than sitting by the Lupanar for yet another day, pretending to be a simpleton.

An hour later, the haruspex felt differently. He'd bought a hen and sacrificed it in the proper manner, but seen nothing in its liver or entrails. Frustrated, Tarquinius had purchased another bird and repeated the process to no avail. Ignoring the curious stares of some worshippers, and the requests for divination from others, he had contemplated the results of his work for long, silent moments. Nothing came to him. Praying to Jupiter's statue and visiting the long, dark *cella* produced nothing more than another memory of his nightmare about a murder at the Lupanar. His senses dulled by his pounding head, the haruspex neglected to take note that this time more than one person had been killed.

He gave up and bought several beakers of fruit juice to quench his raging thirst. Glancing in annoyance at the enormous figure of Jupiter, he decided to return to his post at the Lupanar. There at least he could nurse away his hangover. Tarquinius had to negotiate the usual blockades on his journey. They appeared tighter than normal. It was then that he felt the first tickles of unease. His usual drooling idiot routine worked well, though, getting him past the thugs with just the usual insults and cruel laughter. His pace quickened as soon as he was out of their sight, and he reached the brothel without further event. Easing himself to the ground in his usual spot, he took a long swig from his water gourd. Perhaps now his thumping headache would ease.

A few moments later, the haruspex was alarmed to see a large party of heavies enter the other end of the street. He stiffened, noting the poorly hidden weapons under their cloaks. Striding past the other businesses on the lane, they made a beeline for the Lupanar. Tarquinius counted more than twenty, which was enough proof for him. At long last, his recurrent nightmare made sense. Why hadn't he realized at Jupiter's temple? Cursing his decision to drink the night before, he headed toward the Mithraeum as fast as his shuffling feet would take him. With luck, Secundus and his men could be persuaded to help.

Adrenaline surged through the haruspex when he saw the thugs' leader and another group carrying ladders. He broke into a run. The gods had finally decided to show their hand.

Tarquinius prayed that their revelation had not come too late for Fabiola.

†

Scaevola's attack came about an hour after Fabiola had spoken to the apothecary. She felt an immediate sense of relief, which diluted her fear. Not knowing when it might happen had sapped her energy more than she knew. It was time to end this feud one way or another. She'd already prepared the brothel for a siege. There was enough food for more than a week, while a well supplied their water. Just inside the entrance were all the spare weapons her men possessed: axes, clubs, swords and a few spears. The front door's locking bar was to be augmented by large pieces of heavy furniture once they'd retreated inside, preventing entry by battering ram. Buckets of water had been placed throughout the building in case of fire. The prostitutes were safely in their rooms at the back, but Jovina remained at her post in the reception, a dagger clutched in her frail hands.

Half of her men were outside with Benignus, while Vettius and the others stood ready in the reception. Fabiola was determined to defend the street, at least for a while. Hiding away in the brothel would make Scaevola think she was scared, or already beaten, and she wasn't having that. This was her turf, not his, and it would be defended. Her forces weren't immense, though. Including Benignus and Vettius, she had eighteen men. Most of them were slaves or *collegia* toughs whose quality and courage were uncertain, but five were gladiators, professional fighters who, with the two doormen, would form the heart of her little army. Wearing a selection of armor according to their gladiator class, the quintet were being paid twice as much as any of the others. Although Catus and the kitchen slaves were untrained in the use of weapons, they had also been armed, which brought the potential number of defenders up to twenty-three. Twenty-four, Fabiola thought. Discarding convention, she had strapped on a belt and *gladius* herself. After all, she was a follower of Mithras, the warrior god, so she would fight like one.

Despite her bravado, there was a sinking feeling in Fabiola's gut. Soon after, it began.

"Look lively, boys," shouted Benignus from outside. "Trouble!"

Fabiola rushed to the door, which was ajar. Sauntering up the street came a gang of at least twenty thugs. She could not see Scaevola, but her stomach still clenched into a knot. Wearing cloaks to conceal their weapons, the nonchalant newcomers were acting as if they were on a morning stroll. A short distance to their rear walked a solitary figure, a well-built black-haired man in a soldier's red tunic. Fabiola frowned. Their leader? No, she decided: He looked out of place. She had no time to study him further. Realizing that their cover was blown, the heavies threw back their cloaks and produced a fearsome selection of axes, clubs and swords. Screaming blue murder, they charged straight for the Lupanar.

"You know what to do," Fabiola shouted at Benignus.

"Kill as many of the bastards as possible, and then retreat inside," came the answer.

"Mithras protect you all," she called back, her heart thumping against her ribs in a combination of fear and excitement.

Benignus gave Fabiola a grim nod before joining his men, who had formed a tight defensive arc around the entrance. Preparing to take the brunt of the attack, he and the five gladiators formed the center. Like a line of legionaries, they moved shoulder to shoulder. Neither side was using shields, which meant that casualties would come thick and fast.

First blood went to Fabiola's fighters. A burly man with a long-handled axe who fancied himself against Benignus came screaming in a few steps ahead of his companions with his weapon raised high. Fabiola flinched; the curved blade would fatally injure or remove a limb with ease. She needn't have worried. Holding his club by the ends, Benignus lifted his arms and used it to meet the swingeing blow full on. Sparks flew into the air as the iron axe struck the profusion of metal studs on the club's surface. Instead of cutting Benignus' head in two, it bit two fingers' depth into the wood. Frantic, the axeman tried in vain to pull his weapon loose. With an evil smile, Benignus used his club to yank his struggling opponent closer before delivering a huge kick to the groin. The screaming thug dropped to the ground in a heap, whereupon the doorman ripped the axe free. Grasping his club with both hands, he brought it down with all his strength.

Fabiola had seen joints of meat split open with a cleaver many times before. Until that moment, though, she'd never seen a man's skull opened so easily. When Charon came into the arena to check that all the fallen gladiators were dead, she always looked away. Now, she was rapt. With a sickening crunch, Benignus' club smashed his enemy's head apart. A fine red mist sprayed into the air and small lumps of gelatinous brain matter flew everywhere. A number splattered off the door frame by Fabiola's head. She wished they had been from Scaevola.

The remainder of his heavies crashed into her defenders' line an instant later. The confined space of the laneway magnified the clash of weapons and screams to that of thunder. Swords bit deep into flesh and men tussled with each other, punching, wrestling and even biting if the opportunity presented itself. Fabiola danced from foot to foot, unconsciously mimicking her men's movements. She had already drawn her *gladius*, and only Vettius' restraining arm was preventing her from joining the fray. "You're not to go out there," he muttered firmly. "That's our job." Fabiola obeyed, knowing he was right.

To her horror, things started to go badly almost at once. First to go was the defensive arc around the doorway. Although Fabiola's men had cut down five more of their enemies, they had lost three of their own. No one was left to fill the gaps, and in a heartbeat a pair of thugs had wriggled inside the half circle, throwing themselves straight at the doorway. If that could be taken, the battle was won. Locked in their own struggles for survival, Benignus and his comrades could do nothing about it.

Vettius politely shoved Fabiola to one side. Leading three men outside, he dispatched the first ruffian with a sword thrust to the chest. Unfortunately the second managed to badly hurt one of the doorman's companions before his head was severed from behind by a gladiator. The respite was momentary. Benignus was nursing a flesh wound to his chest, and a *secutor* was down. Roaring for more blood, the thugs pushed in even harder, their weapons licking out hungrily like so many snakes' tongues. Fabiola could see that if she didn't call her men back in, they'd all be killed.

"Pull back," she screamed. "Get inside."

Fabiola's fighters were only a few steps away, but two more were slain before they could gain the safety of the brothel. Standing just inside the entrance, she watched in horror as, pleading for their lives, they were hacked apart. Benignus was last inside, managing somehow to smash a thug's shoulder into smithereens with his club before the door slammed shut. Panting heavily, the doorman slid home the bolts. Quickly the others shoved forward the heavy items of furniture as fists and weapons hammered futile blows on the other side. Colorful insults filled the air as both sides recovered their strength after the brutal encounter. Although brief, it had been energy-sapping.

Fabiola was confident that their enemies' efforts would come to nothing. Unless of course they'd brought a battering ram. Busying herself by attending to the wounded, she tried not to think of that eventuality. To her relief, Benignus was not badly hurt. Once she'd cleaned the gash with some *acetum*, one of the gladiators used a needle and some linen thread to stitch him up. Several of the others also had minor injuries. Only one man was critically hurt, suffering a deep slash on his right thigh that had cut down to the bone. A major blood vessel had been severed which pulsed out bright red blood all over the mosaic floor. Fabiola could not believe he was still alive. There was already a huge pool of it around the semiconscious man. It was only after a tourniquet of rope and pieces of wood had been tied around the top of his leg that the bleeding stopped. Whether he survived was another matter.

By the time everyone had been attended to, the torrent of abuse from outside had almost stopped. Fabiola began to feel uneasy. Surely Scaevola's rabble wouldn't give up this easily? Opening the door would be far too dangerous, so she hurried to one of the bedrooms that had a window on to the street. Like most large houses, the brothel's exterior was almost featureless. Just a few windows— high up and thankfully too small to admit a man—were present in the front wall. While this feature facilitated privacy and security, it was extremely difficult to see what was going on outside.

Standing on a stool, Fabiola peered through the green pane of glass. An expensive luxury, the small pane distorted the world beyond. All she could see was a group of men talking and pointing at the Lupanar. Worryingly, there were now far more of them, so reinforcements had arrived. A central, stocky figure appeared to be ordering the rest about. Fabiola's pulse shot up. Was it Scaevola? She couldn't be sure. Holding her breath, she watched for some time.

There was no mistaking the ladders' shape when they came into view. Fabiola's spirits plunged. This was an eventuality she hadn't thought of. The men carrying them were directed to move up to the brothel's wall, and she cursed bitterly. By lifting the tiles, the thugs would gain access to the roof space and then the whole interior of the Lupanar. With more than twenty men, they could attack in multiple places. She would have to divide her forces among the network of rooms, in the hope of containing their enemies' ingress. Yet Fabiola panicked as she counted the ladders.

There were five.

She jumped to the floor, shouting for Vettius and Benignus.

One option remained. They would have to pull back to the central courtyard, which could only be accessed by two doors. There at least they could give a good account of themselves before they died. Fabiola knew that her fate and that of the prostitutes would not be that easy, though. The thugs would not be able to resist the temptation of so much flesh, and Scaevola wanted to finish what he'd begun years before. Fabiola's skin crawled at the memory and the anticipation of so much horror, but she did not allow her resolve to waver. One of the doormen could be detailed with the job of killing her and the women before they were captured.

Clutching her *gladius*, Fabiola ran to the reception.

All her dreams and hopes had come to this.

To nothing.

XXII

GEMELLUS

For a long time, there was no answer.

Bathed in an icy fury, Romulus pounded on the timbers again.

This time, he heard the sound of shuffling feet inside, and then silence.

"Gemellus! Open up!"

A long pause followed, but Romulus was sure now that the merchant was on the other side of the door. He leaned his shoulder against the flimsy planks, and they immediately started to give. "Don't make me come in the hard way," he warned. "I'm going to count to three. One."

"Who is it?" The voice was querulous, and unmistakably that of Gemellus. "I've paid my rent this week."

"Two," said Romulus, sheathing his dagger on a whim.

"Very well." A bolt was pulled back, and the portal creaked ajar. Blinking warily, Gemellus stood framed in the doorway. Gray-haired, he looked older and wearier than Romulus had ever seen him. His jowls now sagged from his stubble-covered jaw, and his gut was a great deal smaller. Never one for dressing up, the merchant wore a ragged tunic covered in food and wine stains. His sandals were worn-out too. He looked like one of the homeless vagrants who lived around the tombs on the Via Appia, but had lost none of his arrogance. "Who are you?" he demanded. "Do I know you?"

Romulus ignored the question. He couldn't quite believe that this rank-smelling specimen was his former master. "Porcius Gemellus?" he asked, just to make sure.

"Yes," replied the merchant irritably. "What do you want?"

Romulus bit back his instinctive retort. "It's been hard to track you down. I thought you lived on the Aventine. In a big house."

Gemellus scowled. "I did, once."

He had to rub some salt in the other's wounds. "Lost it all, did you?"

Gemellus missed the sarcasm. "The gods turned against me. Every business venture I tried went wrong. Especially the last one," he moaned. "Should have made me as rich as Croesus, but it beggared me instead."

"The wild beasts," said Romulus, beginning to show his hand. "Shame they drowned, eh?"

Gemellus looked stunned. "How could you know about that?" he cried.

"I worked for Hiero for a while," Romulus confided. "Good man, that *bestiarius*."

The merchant relaxed a fraction, but then grew suspicious again. "Hiero's not after any money, is he? Tell him I've got nothing left, nothing. The fucking moneylenders took it all. Even had to sell my villa in Pompeii." His shoulders sagged.

"I'm glad to hear it," sneered Romulus.

"Eh?" The first signs of fear appeared in Gemellus' face. "Who are you? What do you want?" he breathed.

Drawing his *pugio*, Romulus smiled mirthlessly. "Nothing much," he growled.

Gemellus' mouth opened in horror and he tried to slam the door, but Romulus wedged a foot in the frame, stopping him. They glared at each other for a moment before, with a quick movement, Romulus rested his dagger on the edge of Gemellus' left eye socket. "Don't you remember me?"

The petrified merchant let the door fall open. "No," he whispered. "Never seen you in my life."

"Look again," Romulus advised, moving the blade a hairsbreadth closer to Gemellus' eye.

Panting with fear, Gemellus studied the brawny off-duty soldier before him. Black-haired, handsome, with blue eyes and an aquiline nose, he had a Mithraic tattoo on his upper right arm. Still he didn't catch on. "Did you work for me once?"

"Oh, yes!" Romulus laughed. "From dawn till dusk, seven days a week." Confused, Gemellus just stood there and Romulus grew impatient. He pointed the dagger at himself. "Look, you fool! You owned me, and my mother and twin sister."

The merchant gaped with disbelief. "Romulus?"

"Yes," he replied from between clenched jaws. "The very same."

Gemellus' face went gray with terror. He stumbled back a step, looking as if he'd seen a ghost. " 'One day there will be a knock on your door,' " he muttered.

"What did you say?"

The merchant had gone into a daze. " 'Who stands outside? A soldier, perhaps?' "

"You're right there, shitbag. First I was a gladiator, but now I'm a legionary," snarled Romulus, grabbing Gemellus by the front of his tunic and dragging him out into the alley. The merchant wailed with fear as Romulus slammed him up against the wall. "This is just the start," he hissed, carefully drawing his *pugio* along Gemellus' left cheek. The merchant screamed as a thin line of blood ran down his face from the wound. Romulus smiled at him. "Time for you to pay your oldest debts." His voice dripped with sarcasm. "With your miserable stinking life."

Gemellus began to sob. "Please," he said. "Don't hurt me."

Romulus grabbed the merchant's chin, forcing Gemellus to look at him. "I'm going to slice you into little pieces for what you did to Juba and my family," he promised. "But before I do, you'll tell me exactly what happened to my mother and Fabiola."

Fat tears of self-pity welled up in Gemellus' eyes and spilled down his haggard cheeks, mixing with the blood from Romulus' knife cut.

"Speak!" shouted Romulus, spittle flying from his lips. "Where did Fabiola end up?"

"I sold her to the Lupanar," Gemellus finally admitted.

His casual manner stung Romulus to the quick. It was delivered in the same way as if he were selling an ox to the market. Quickly Romulus placed the tip of his *pugio* over the merchant's chest. Whimpering, Gemellus closed his eyes. With great effort, Romulus restrained himself from slipping the blade between Gemellus' ribs and into his cold-blooded heart. *Patience,* he thought. The merchant was going nowhere, and after years of living in the dark about his family, this was his chance to find out so much. "Go on."

His eyes shut tight, Gemellus shook his head. "A few years back, I heard a rumor that she'd been bought by Decimus Brutus, one of Caesar's right-hand men. Turned out later it was true."

Romulus mentally noted the name for future reference. Perhaps that was the man he'd seen with Fabiola in Alexandria. Thanks to Tarquinius, he already knew that his mother was dead, but he wanted to hear it from the merchant himself. "And Velvinna?" He pricked Gemellus with the *pugio.* "Look at me!"

Gemellus' piggy eyes actually looked guilty. "She went to the salt mines."

"How much did you get for her?" Romulus shot back.

The merchant shrugged. "I can't remember."

Another poke with the dagger, harder this time.

Gemellus squawked. "Two, maybe three hundred *sestertii*?"

It was a fraction of what a healthy slave would fetch on the block. Blind fury consumed Romulus. The idea that a living, breathing person—his mother—could be condemned to die in such a miserable way, and for so little, was too much to bear. "You filthy bastard," he hissed, slicing Gemellus' other cheek open from ear to jawbone. "Meant nothing to you, did we? Just pieces of meat to fuck, to buy or to sell."

Gemellus clutched at his ruined face, his chest heaving with loud sobs.

"Answer me!" Romulus roared. "Why did you do it?"

The bleeding merchant fell sobbing to his knees and clung to Romulus' *caligae* like a supplicant at a shrine. "Forgive me," he whimpered. "I am an evil man."

Already Romulus' feet and sandals were covered in blood. Disgusted, he kicked Gemellus away. There would never be a satisfactory reason why the merchant had treated them all so cruelly. "Stand up, you whoreson." There was no response, so he booted Gemellus again. "Up, I said. It's time for you to feel some real pain. Before I send you to Hades."

"No," wailed Gemellus. "Please." A circle of wet appeared on the ground beneath him as he lost control of his bladder. "I'm an old man."

"Sewer rat, more like," spat Romulus. "Don't like the rough treatment yourself, do you?" The merchant did not answer, and Romulus knew he was going to have to stab him in the back. Gemellus was too afraid to face his own death. Yet he—Romulus—was unprepared to kill even a monster like this in such a cowardly way. Catching hold of Gemellus by the scruff of his neck, he forced him to sit up. "There," he said, panting. "You're going to look at me while I cut off your balls."

"No!" Gemellus' voice rose to a cracked scream.

The next door along the alleyway opened and a man's head poked out.

"Get back inside," Romulus shouted furiously. "Or I'll castrate you too!"

The householder vanished, terrified by Romulus' threat. Things like this happened every day in Rome, and the powers that ruled the city couldn't be bothered to employ a force to maintain order. Who was he to intervene?

Romulus set to slicing open the lower part of Gemellus' tunic. Lying like a slab of meat on the butchers' block, the merchant did nothing to stop him. Only the movements of his chest and his piteous sobbing gave the lie that this was not a side of beef or pork. Off came Gemellus' wet, stinking *licium*, his undergarment, revealing his wizened, unwashed manhood. Romulus laughed when he saw it. "Not much to lose, is it?" he taunted. "I bet it'll hurt all the same." Leaning forward, he grasped the shrunken bag below and pulled it tight to make the cut easier.

Gemellus' throat opened and he began to wail anew.

Romulus' *pugio* was a hairsbreadth away when something made him stop. Turning his head, he saw the urchin observing him with an expression of absolute terror. Their eyes met, and Romulus was reminded of himself as a boy, witnessing people being robbed and injured on the streets of Rome. Abruptly he felt his senses return, and a wave of shame swamped him. *What am I doing?* Romulus thought, looking with disgust at Gemellus' sagging flesh. *Torturing an old man while a child watches? What have I become?*

Wiping his dagger clean on Gemellus' tunic, Romulus stood. "You're not worth it," he said, breathing heavily. "Living in this shit-hole is punishment enough."

Gemellus didn't answer. Clutching alternately at his bleeding cheeks and his exposed privates, he lay motionless as Romulus sheathed his *pugio*.

"Come on," Romulus said to the relieved-looking urchin. "Time to find that inn, and pay you."

The boy came alive at the mention of money.

"Are you hungry?" Romulus asked, ushering him toward the street.

There was a vigorous nod.

"Tell you what," Romulus said, keen to show that he wasn't a complete thug. "You've been a great help so far. I'll throw in some food as well as the ten *sestertii*, all right?"

The urchin's face split in a beaming smile. "Thank you, sir."

Romulus grinned, ruffling his hair. Decent meals had been rare in his childhood too.

His little guide gave him a tentative smile in return, but abruptly his expression changed to one of alarm. "Look out!" he cried.

Too late, Romulus began to turn. Something heavy smashed into the back of his head and stars exploded across his vision. His knees buckled and he crumpled to the ground, catching sight of Gemellus right behind him. Still half-naked, the bloody-faced merchant held a large lump of rubble in his hands. "Little bastard!" he spat. "I should have had you crucified alongside the Nubian."

Sprawled on the rough ground, Romulus tried to turn over, or to draw his dagger, but he couldn't. All his strength had gone, and his mind wavered on the very edge of consciousness. His eyes closed, which was a great relief. He was vaguely aware of the urchin rushing at Gemellus, screaming for him to stop, but the cursing merchant slapped him away with ease. When the boy tried again, Gemellus smashed him across the face with the back of his hand. Sobbing, the urchin withdrew. A moment later, Romulus felt someone looming over him. With great effort, he rolled onto his back.

Leering triumphantly, Gemellus raised the piece of brick high. "I'm going to enjoy smashing in your skull," he said. Blood dripped from his wounds onto Romulus' tunic. "Shame your sister's not here to watch. Then I could fuck her afterward."

Impotent rage flooded through Romulus at the insult, but he was helpless to react. A mass of stabbing needles were radiating from the back of his head and he was seeing double. Clumsily he raised a hand, but like his other limbs, it seemed to belong to someone else. Unable to do more, Romulus sagged back down. *After all I've been through,* he thought wearily, *this is the way I'm going to die. Should never have got Juba to teach me how to use a sword. At least he'd still be alive.* Romulus' remorse over the death of his friend triggered sheer resignation. He watched passively as Gemellus swung down with all his might.

This is my punishment, he thought.

Instead of crushing Romulus' head like a rotten egg, though, Gemellus collapsed on top of him. The chunk of rubble fell from his slack fingers with a crash, and he went limp. Confused, Romulus lay there for several heartbeats. Gemellus did not move again, prompting him eventually to try to sit up. The merchant's dead weight on top of him was far more than his nerveless fingers could shift, though. Even the tugging efforts of the urchin made little difference. Romulus closed his eyes. All he wanted to do was sleep anyway.

A moment later, a deep, sonorous voice joined the boy's piping tone. "Let me help."

It sounded familiar, but Romulus didn't know why. He felt Gemellus' body being rolled off him. To his surprise, the back of the merchant's ragged tunic was saturated with blood. Protruding from the middle of the red circle was the bone hilt of a knife. If Gemellus wasn't already dead, he would be soon. A dull relief settled over Romulus, partly because his former master had received his just desserts, and partly because it had not been he who finished the job.

"By all the gods, it is you," said the voice. "Both of you were in danger!"

Romulus looked up. Flanked by the urchin, Tarquinius was stooped over him. Utter amazement mixed with groggy understanding. "What are you doing here?" he croaked with a leaden tongue.

Typically, the haruspex didn't answer. Gently turning Romulus' head so that he could assess his wound, he probed through the matted blood and hair with expert fingers.

Fresh agony flooded outward from the area. "Jupiter, that hurts," Romulus protested.

"Hold still."

He obeyed, using the opportunity to focus on the cloaked haruspex. Apart from a caved-in cheek and a few more gray hairs, his friend had scarcely changed. *Yes,* Romulus thought, pleased by his instinctive reaction. *That is what he is   my friend. I forgive him for what he did.* At once he felt lighter, and his lips turned upward in a pleased smile. "Is that your knife?"

There was a nod.

"Thank you," Romulus muttered.

"I was in a real hurry. Who knows what made me glance down this alleyway," said Tarquinius, pressing down on Romulus' skull here and there. "Thank all the gods I did."

"It's good to see you."

Tarquinius paused for a moment to regard him. "You're sure?"

Romulus nodded, and then wished he hadn't. His head felt like the drum on the rowing deck of a trireme. "Yes," he whispered. "I've missed you."

"Likewise." The haruspex grinned, taking years off his age. He wiped his bloody fingers on his roughly spun tunic. "Mithras and Fortuna are truly smiling on you today. I can't feel any breaks. A day's rest and you should be fine."

Unanswered questions that Romulus had been carrying around for an age started to surface. "Why did you disappear in Alexandria? Who looked after you?" he demanded. "Where have you been since?"

"Later," replied Tarquinius, looking concerned. He got to his feet. "You'll be all right on your own for a while, won't you? This lad can accompany you back to your camp."

Worry was a most uncommon emotion to see on the haruspex' face. "What's going on?" Romulus asked. "Can't it wait?"

"I didn't want to bother you," Tarquinius muttered. "There's trouble at the Lupanar."

Surprised by Tarquinius' awareness, Romulus shrugged. "I know. Nearly got mixed up in it myself. Who cares, though? It's just one lot of thugs fighting another."

"It's far more than that," said Tarquinius quietly.

Uncomprehending, Romulus stared at him.

"Fabiola runs the Lupanar now."

He could have hugged the haruspex. She was there? His sister was found? "You're sure?"

"Yes," Tarquinius replied. "She's inside too, and the ruffians attacking it won't stop until they've killed her."

Horror gripped Romulus. "How do you know?"

"I heard them talking as they came up the street."

Romulus cursed. If only he'd got there before the heavies. At least he'd have been inside then, and able to defend the brothel. He racked his brains to recall who'd been on the street. He'd seen no one else apart from the thugs, but then Tarquinius was a master at remaining inconspicuous. "What were you doing there?"

Romulus had never seen the haruspex look sheepish before either. "Watching over Fabiola."

"Why?"

Now embarrassment wrestled its way onto Tarquinius' face. "Trying to make sense of a dream, and to atone for what I did to you."

Clambering to his feet, Romulus grabbed him in a bear hug. "Thank you."

Never one for physical contact, Tarquinius patted him awkwardly. "This is no time for pleasantries," he said.

Romulus stepped back. "How many of the whoresons are there?"

"I counted at least twenty, but there were more arriving."

At once Romulus thought of his comrades. A dozen veteran legionaries would be the equal of more than twice that number of scum. Then he remembered that his friends were in civilian dress and without their swords. They were probably all drunk by now too. Panic swelled in his chest. "What should we do?"

"I was going for help," Tarquinius revealed. "I know some ex-soldiers who live nearby. Followers of Mithras. They've no love for filth."

"Bring them as fast as you can," said Romulus. He beckoned to the urchin. "Can you take me back to the Lupanar? I'll make it fifteen *sestertii*."

The boy bobbed up and down with excitement. "Of course."

Tarquinius frowned. "You're in no fit state to fight."

"My sister needs me," Romulus replied fiercely. "Cerberus himself couldn't stop me from doing what I can."

The haruspex didn't argue. Shrugging off his cloak, he unslung his double-headed axe. The alleyway's dim light couldn't entirely dampen the shine of its oiled blades. "Take this."

"Thank you." Romulus gripped the well-worn shaft, taking strength from its solidity. If necessary, he could use it as a crutch on the way to the Lupanar.

Standing over Gemellus' body, they looked at each other for a long moment. There was so much they needed to talk about.

"Go," ordered the haruspex. "The brothel's walls are thick, but they had ladders too."

Romulus closed his eyes, imagining the result of the thugs dropping unexpectedly from the roof space. "The gods grant you speed." Letting the urchin lead the way, he headed for the Lupanar.

Tarquinius hurried in the opposite direction, hoping against hope that his delay hadn't cost Fabiola dearly.

XXIII

REUNION

Including herself, Fabiola had sixteen people left who could fight, but only ten of those were hired men. The rest were kitchen slaves, who by now looked terrified. The remainder weren't so badly affected, although Fabiola had no idea how they would fight when it became clear defeat—and death—was imminent. She gave them all a short pep talk, promising more money to the guards, and manumission to the slaves if they fought well. This seemed to lift everyone's spirits. It was all she had time for. The noises from above indicated that Scaevola's thugs were already on the roof. Lifting the red clay tiles and gaining entry wouldn't take long.

Fabiola had her men gather the prostitutes and take them to the courtyard, which was dominated by fruit trees and a fountain. They locked all the rooms as they passed by—anything to slow down their attackers. In the open-aired square, she positioned three gladiators by one exit and the two doormen at the other. A quick head count of the weeping, terrified women revealed that one was missing. Jovina. Before Vettius or Benignus could object, Fabiola darted up the dimly lit corridor. Although she had little love for the old madam, she felt a duty to protect her. She found Jovina by her desk in the reception, grim-faced and with a dagger at the ready.

"Come to the courtyard," Fabiola cried. "It's the best place to defend."

"I'm staying here," Jovina replied, setting her jaw. Along with her usual jewelry and heavy layer of makeup, she was wearing her finest dress. She looked like a tiny, determined sparrow about to defend its nest. "This is where I've spent more than half my life, and no sewer rat is going to make me run away."

"Please," Fabiola pleaded. "They'll kill you."

Jovina laughed knowingly. "And they won't out there?"

Fabiola had no answer to that.

"Go," Jovina ordered her, reversing their positions. "Die with Benignus and Vettius. They're your men—have been since the first day you won them over. Just make sure one of them ends it for you before that brute Scaevola gets too close."

Fabiola nodded. Bizarrely, tears were brimming in her eyes. "Perhaps we'll meet again," she whispered.

"I doubt it," cackled the old madam, showing more life than she had for months. "After all I've done, Hades is the only place for me."

"And me," replied Fabiola, remembering how she'd slain Pompeia, a prostitute who'd tried to murder her. While her motive had been self-preservation, she had done it in cold blood, just as she had ordered the doormen to kill Jovina. Her decision about that had only been reversed because Antonius made their affair public. Surely that was as bad as anything the old madam might have done? Biting back a sob of guilt, Fabiola lifted a hand in farewell.

Jovina did the same.

As she ran down the passageway, Fabiola could hear voices and the sound of breaking plaster emanating from many rooms. Loud thuds followed as the intruders jumped to the floor, and her pace increased to a sprint. She must not get caught here! Steps moved to the doors on either side and then the handles turned. Finding them locked, those within began to rain kicks and blows upon the flimsy timbers, quickly splintering them apart. *Why did we even bother?* thought Fabiola. *It's only delaying the inevitable.* Resignation filled her every pore.

She heard Jovina shout a shrill challenge. Unconsciously, Fabiola slowed down to listen. Scaevola's men laughed contemptuously at the crone, but their attitude soon changed. Screaming at the top of her lungs, Jovina launched herself at the intruders. There was a cry of pain and then the sound of muffled blows carried down the corridor. At once Jovina fell silent. Fabiola closed her eyes. She had heard the sound of swords hacking into flesh before. *Go well,* she thought. For all her faults, Jovina had possessed a warrior's heart. *May the gods reward her courage.*

The two doormen reacted with surprise and respect when Fabiola recounted what had happened. "Who knows, she might have even killed one," muttered Vettius.

For a while after that, Fabiola wondered if she was wrong about losing the battle. It was easy to defend a narrow corridor in which only one man could attack at a time, and her followers performed heroics to deny the *fugitivarius'* heavies access to the courtyard. For the loss of only two men—both gladiators—Fabiola's defenders had killed more than a dozen of the enemy. There were so many corpses piled in the passages that the attackers had a job to clamber over them, which made them easy targets.

Scaevola was no fool, however. At length, he pulled back his thugs and barked a succession of orders, which Fabiola could not make out. Then silence fell.

A new fear filled her: that of uncertainty. "Have they gone?" She looked to Benignus.

"I doubt it."

"What are they doing?" Fabiola demanded, peering into the nearest corridor.

He sighed deeply. "If I were in charge of those bastards, I'd get a few bowmen or spearmen. Attack from above."

Alarmed by his words, Fabiola scanned the roofs around the courtyard. To her relief, no one was visible, but Benignus' words made sense. Soon they would be picked off one by one, unable to defend themselves. Like fish in a barrel, she thought disgustedly. "We're all going to die," she whispered.

"It's not looking good," agreed Benignus. "There's nowhere else I'd rather be, though."

Beside him, Vettius growled in agreement.

Fabiola's mouth opened in surprise.

"You've always treated us like people, not animals. That's more than anyone else ever did." Benignus gave her a gentle smile, which made Fabiola feel twice as bad about what she was going to say next.

"When the end comes . . ." She paused, feeling sick. She realized that, despite everything, she didn't want to die. How foolish it had been to wish such things on herself! Now, with the end fast approaching, Fabiola felt a new humility. "Scaevola came close to raping me once before. I don't want the same to happen again." She looked at them both pleadingly. "I ask you as a friend. Will you kill me before I'm captured?"

The pair's faces twisted with sorrow and pain. They glanced at each other, and then back at Fabiola. She did not speak, could not speak. Incongruously, tears began rolling down the men's cheeks. They were not cowards, though; they would not shirk from their duty. First Benignus, and then Vettius, nodded.

"Thank you," said Fabiola, fighting her own emotions. She wanted to ask the other women if they wanted the same way out, but she never got a chance.

Unseen until that moment, several of Scaevola's men had crawled along the roof to the edge of the tiles overlooking the courtyard. Armed with spears and bows, they launched an immediate attack. They aimed solely at men, and at such close range, they could hardly miss. First, a broad-headed hunting spear struck Vettius in the middle of his broad back, driving down into the lower part of his chest cavity. He staggered to one side with the force of the impact, looking surprised. Fabiola stared in horror, seeing the outline of the spearhead straining against the front of his tunic. Cutting through lungs, diaphragm and his intestines, it had exited the doorman's body over his belly. Vettius' eyes bulged with surprise as his legs gave way beneath him.

"No!" Fabiola screamed.

Vettius tried to speak, but couldn't. With a heavy sigh, he fell onto his side, dropping his club. Gouts of blood soaked his tunic and began to pool beneath him. Clutching weakly at the wooden shaft protruding from his back, he closed his eyes. Even a man as strong as he could not keep fighting with such a wound. It was a case of slowly bleeding to death instead.

Panicking now, Fabiola scanned the courtyard. Scaevola's thugs were wreaking havoc with their spears and arrows, still targeting those who could fight first. Not counting Vettius, three of her men were down, injured or killed. A number of the prostitutes had been hit by stray missiles too. Their screams of agony were adding to the general air of mayhem and terror. While Catus had picked up a spear and hurled it at a bearded ruffian, the other kitchen slaves were huddled together, weeping. Fabiola's shouts of encouragement made no difference, which didn't surprise her. After all, they barely knew how to hold a sword, let alone what to do with it. The courtyard had become a bloodbath, reminding her of the battlefields she'd seen. While it was tiny in resemblance, the heaps of arrow-riddled bodies and the amount of blood bore a horrifying resemblance to Alesia. All that was missing was the flies and the carrion crows. *Give it time,* Fabiola thought bitterly. By tomorrow, they would be here too.

Only she, Benignus and three guards remained to keep up the fight. Yet, other than cower behind the fallen, there was almost nothing they could do against the rain of missiles from above. Occasionally, loose spears could be retrieved and thrown back, but there were never enough. There were already more than a dozen thugs on the roof, and she had lost another man. Fabiola could see the bodies in the corridor being pulled aside too. Soon shapes filled both doorways, quickly emerging into the courtyard.

Directing the others to charge at this new threat, Benignus moved to Fabiola's side. He looked unusually troubled. "Is it time?" he asked.

Fabiola's mouth was bone dry, and she felt really cold. Looking down at Benignus' club, she saw that the end was covered in matted hair, blood and brain matter. When she gave him the word, hers would be added to it. A wave of bile surged up her throat, and Fabiola was sick all over her sandals. Hating her weakness, she was about to speak when a strangled shout drew her attention. She turned toward the nearest doorway. The last of her guards there had just gone down with a sword blade buried in his spine. Scaevola, the man who'd killed him, was staring straight back at her. Before pulling his weapon free, he made a circle with the forefinger and thumb of his right hand. Licking his lips, he shoved the forefinger of his left hand in and out of the space in a clear gesture of what she could expect. "I've promised all my men a turn with you," he shouted. Fabiola couldn't bear the fear any longer. Anything was better than having that monster force himself on her again, never mind his brutish followers. "Yes," she muttered. Her *gladius* dropped to the tiles. "Do it. Now."

Benignus looked at her long and hard, making sure that she was serious. Then he raised his club high. "Turn around, Mistress," he said quietly. "Close your eyes."

Fabiola obeyed, trying to block out what was about to happen. A succession of images flashed before her mind's eye, most of them painful or sad. Her life had been nothing but a waste of time, she thought. Then a solitary picture of Romulus came to mind, her twin grinning proudly as he told her of the important message that Gemellus had entrusted him to deliver to Crassus' house. One of only a few happy memories, it prompted tears to run unchecked down Fabiola's cheeks. *Mithras, grant that Romulus is still alive and well,* she prayed. *Give him a long life, and a better one than mine.*

There was a gasp from behind her and something heavy clattered to the ground. Shocked to be alive, Fabiola looked around. Benignus was still there, but an arrow now protruded from the biceps of his right arm. The noise had been his club falling from his useless fingers. "Sorry, Mistress," he gasped, stooping awkwardly to retrieve it with his left hand. Before he could, two well-aimed shafts hissed through the air, striking him in the legs. Grunting in pain, the doorman managed to pick up his weapon. "Come closer," he muttered. "I can do it."

Wiping away her tears, Fabiola shuffled toward him.

Then things began to happen very fast. Armed figures appeared behind Benignus, raining a flurry of blows on him with their spears and swords. In slow motion, and with an apologetic expression on his broad, unshaven face, he slid to the ground. Defenseless, Fabiola froze as she took in the rest of the scene. All her men were down, and more than fifteen of Scaevola's gang filled the courtyard. While the kitchen slaves watched helplessly, they were ripping the prostitutes' clothes off. The screams and wails this elicited seemed to increase the thugs' frenzy. Cuffing or threatening their captives into submission, most were soon thrusting away between the legs of a shrieking woman. Fabiola's stomach wrenched again, but she had nothing left to bring up. Dimly, she was aware of two men before her, those who had killed Benignus. Lust twisted both their faces and, uselessly, Fabiola raised a hand to push them away. They laughed and stepped closer.

"Don't touch her!" shouted a familiar voice. "She's mine."

In slow motion, they moved aside to reveal Scaevola, who looked delighted with himself. "This time there'll be no escape," he snarled. "You're going to suffer for hours. By the end, you'll be begging me to kill you."

Suddenly light-headed, Fabiola felt her knees fold beneath her. She toppled sideways in a faint, landing on Benignus. The last thing she heard was the *fugitivarius'* voice. "Carry her inside to a bed. Might as well fuck her in comfort."

Then blackness took her.

†

Romulus' journey back to the Lupanar felt longer than any march he'd ever had to make. Struggling with the pain radiating through his head and the press of the crowd, he kept his fuzzy mind focused on just one person. Fabiola. After ten long years of separation, he finally knew where his twin sister was, and she needed him. Urgently. The knowledge gave Romulus the energy he needed, although Tarquinius' axe was a useful crutch. Every time the urchin stopped, Romulus waved him on impatiently. *Mithras, let me get there in time,* he prayed, forcing one leg in front of the other. *Please.* He was even more grateful that he had spared Gemellus' life now. It was an example to the warrior god that he was an honorable man. Whether Mithras chose to help, of course, was another matter, which sent fresh waves of panic coursing through him. *Breathe,* Romulus thought. *Breathe deeply.* Remembering the method taught him by Cotta, his trainer, he slowly filled his chest with air, counting his heartbeat at the same time. One. Two. Three. Four. Hold for a moment. Start to exhale. One. Two. Three. Four. Over and over he repeated the process, using it to restrain the swelling panic in his breast.

Gradually they drew nearer, using tiny alleyways to dodge the thugs' blockades. At last they reached the street in which the Lupanar was situated. Five ladders were placed against the high wall, showing how the attackers had gained entry. Bodies were plainly visible all around the front door, which lay ajar, but there was no sign of anyone living. Romulus' heart sank. Tarquinius and the veterans weren't here yet. Ahead of him, the urchin broke into a run. By sheer force of will, Romulus forced himself into a shambling trot. He took a short breather when he reached the first bloody corpses, knowing that he would need every scrap of strength in his body once they got inside. The brief pause afforded him an opportunity to study the slain. It was hard to tell the difference between the two sides. Apart from a couple of gladiators, they looked like typical lowlifes.

"They're all dead," piped the boy, already rifling for valuables.

"Good," muttered Romulus, heading for the door. He sensed the urchin at his back. "Stay outside," he ordered. "When my friend arrives, tell him to hurry."

The voice behind him rose to a squeak. "You're going in alone?"

"I have to," Romulus replied, gripping the axe's broad shaft with both hands. "My sister's in there."

"They'll kill you."

"Maybe," answered Romulus grimly. "I can't just stand outside like a fool, though." Pushing the door inward, he entered. The reception area was much like those he'd seen in brothels in other parts of the world: garishly decorated, with erotic paintings and statues everywhere. The heavy furniture that had been shoved against the door by the defenders was piled up to one side, and bloodstains covered the mosaic floor. Apart from the bodies of a small thug with a sword and an old woman, which lay entwined by a desk, the room was abandoned. Covered in hack wounds, the crone's hands still reached toward the dagger that protruded from the other's chest. Romulus' eyebrows rose. If everyone in the brothel fought like this, there was still hope.

His fanciful notion was quashed a moment later as he neared the passageway to the back. Instead of the clash of arms, he heard only men's shouts and laughs. Mixed with the ribaldry were the screams of women. Lots of them. Romulus had been a soldier for long enough to know what this meant. The fight was over, and the raping had begun. His knuckles whitened with anger on the axe handle.

Praying that the thugs would all be lost in pleasure, Romulus shuffled down the corridor, carefully checking each bedroom. Gaping holes in the ceilings of many showed where they had entered, but they were all empty. The noise seemed to be emanating from the central courtyard, leading Romulus to the conclusion that Fabiola and the defenders had retreated there. Faced with attackers dropping into every room, it made sense. It hadn't changed the outcome, though, he thought, worry eating his guts.

"Wake up, you bitch!"

He came alive at the angry shout, which had come from the next chamber along. A loud slap and a terrified wail followed in close succession. Ensuring that the passageway was clear, Romulus tiptoed closer, Tarquinius' axe at the ready. Peering around the doorframe, he made out the naked lower half of a woman lying on the bed. Her struggling arms were pinioned by a pair of laughing thugs while a stocky third figure was stripping off his clothes and armor.

"I've waited years for this," he panted. "So I'm really going to enjoy it."

Romulus felt sick. Should he intervene, or proceed to the courtyard? Doubtless this scene was being played out all over the brothel. How could he find Fabiola among all the prostitutes, and save her without also leaving this wretch? Unsure what to do, he watched for a moment.

The woman on the bed was injured or half-conscious, because when her tormentor yanked her legs apart, there was barely any resistance. Just a low, terrified moan, which instantly brought back memories of his mother lying beneath Gemellus. Having just seen the merchant, it was too much to bear. Romulus was moving before he knew it. He went in fast and hard, maximizing his chances against three uninjured men. With his back to the door, the stocky would-be rapist was oblivious to Romulus' desperate charge. The pair of thugs holding the woman's arms spotted him at once, though.

Their warning shouts came too late to stop Romulus bringing the battleaxe down on the rapist's right shoulder, cleanly taking off his arm. A great roar of pain left the man's throat and he staggered away, bright red blood spurting from the wound. Fortunately, he stumbled into one of the thugs, thus preventing him from going on the attack. The other man was so shocked that he was still reaching for his sword when the axe came humming down to split his skull in two halves. Cleft almost to the chin, his visage wore an expression of total astonishment. Bone and gore flew everywhere, and he dropped to the floor without a sound.

Dragging the blade free, Romulus spun around to face the last ruffian, who had managed to extricate himself. With an evil expression, the man shuffled closer, sword at the ready. Romulus took a step toward him. Suddenly the pain in his head was overwhelming. A physical duel was more than his weary body could bear. Then he looked down at the naked figure on the bed and was stunned to recognize Fabiola. A searing fury such as Romulus had never felt before shot through him, sweeping away his exhaustion in a tidal wave of adrenaline. Bellowing an inarticulate scream, he leaped forward to the attack.

Covered in blood from his mutilated comrade, the third thug was already intimidated by the speed of the mad-eyed legionary's entrance. Now his anger unnerved him. Rather than fight, he sprinted for the door. His sandals slapped off the floor as he fled, shouting for his fellows. Romulus knew that any respite would be brief. The ruffian would be back with reinforcements very soon, and then both he and his sister would die. Unless, by some tiny chance, they could escape first. In the meantime, every precious moment had to be wrung from this most unexpected of reunions. Ignoring the moaning one-armed man lying in the corner, he ran to the side of the bed, dropping his axe alongside. Using the shreds of her dress, he gently covered his sister's nakedness as best he could. She flinched at his touch, breaking his heart. "Fabiola," he whispered. "Fabiola."

There was no reaction.

He shook her by the shoulder. "It's me, Romulus. Your brother."

At last Fabiola's eyes opened, revealing a void of terror. Then her pupils widened, and she gasped. "Romulus?"

XXIV

DISCORD

Crying tears that he'd never shed in all the years of their separation, Romulus could only nod.

"It's you. You're alive." Incredulous, Fabiola reached up to stroke his cheek with a shaking hand. "Thank all the gods." A sob of relief shook her. They gazed at one another, scarcely able to believe their eyes. After the years of heartbreak and separation, the gods had finally allowed them to meet. It seemed that the impossible had come true. After a moment, Romulus grinned. Eventually Fabiola did too. They clutched each other's hands, scared to let go.

"Are you alone?" she asked.

"Yes."

Fabiola's face crumpled. "All my men are dead. Now the bastards are raping the prostitutes."

"I know," Romulus replied heavily. "What can just two of us do, though? We should try and get away. Now."

Guilt twisted her pretty features. "I can't just leave the women. They're my responsibility. Help me to sit up."

Romulus pulled her upright.

Fabiola saw the semiconscious bleeding figure in the corner. There was a sharp intake of breath. "The whoreson is still alive!"

"Not for long." Romulus indicated the enormous pool of blood around him, and the bleeding hole in the side of his trunk.

She smiled. "Sextus has been avenged then."

Romulus looked back at the motionless shape. "Who is he?"

"Scaevola," she spat. "He's a *fugitivarius*. Works for Antonius."

"The Master of the Horse ordered this?" cried Romulus. "Why?"

Fabiola had no time to explain. Noise from the corridor stopped their conversation in its tracks. Strangely, it was coming from both ends. Escape was now out of the question. Gripping the axe, Romulus got to his feet.

"Who are you?" a rough voice demanded from near the courtyard. "Antonius' men? Come to check we've done the job properly?"

"No," came the calm reply. "Raise shields!"

Following the order, Romulus heard the familiar clink of *scuta* against each other.

"Quick! Back outside!" shouted the thug to his companions.

Hope flared in Romulus' heart as the tread of *caligae* clashed off the mosaic floor. When a middle-aged veteran in a battered bronze helmet popped his head around the door, Romulus could have cried with relief.

"Secundus!" Fabiola cried delightedly. "You came!"

"Of course we did," he answered. "Couldn't get here quick enough when Tarquinius told us what was happening."

She beamed, and he smiled benevolently.

"You all right in here?"

"Fine," Romulus replied. "Thank you."

With a pleasant nod, Secundus withdrew. From the noise, Romulus judged he had at least twenty companions. Plenty to deal with the situation. As the danger subsided, the pounding in his head became resurgent. Wincing, he sat down on the edge of the bed.

Fabiola noticed the blood in his hair at once. "What happened?"

"Gemellus hit me," he muttered, lifting a hand to the wound. "Not hard enough, though, thank Mithras."

"You met Gemellus?" she gasped.

"I saw the whoreson coming out of a temple and followed him to the hovel he called home."

"*Called*," said Fabiola slowly. "Did you kill him?"

"No," replied Romulus. "I was going to, had sworn it so many times over the years. But I couldn't. He was utterly pathetic. It would have made me as bad as him."

"So you walked away?" Fabiola's voice was incredulous.

Romulus nodded, seeing the fury in his twin's eyes. Clearly she would not have acted with the same restraint. This realization was shocking, but he forced himself to continue. "Then the coward attacked me from behind. Fortunately Tarquinius was at hand. But for his knife throw, I'd be lying in an alleyway with my skull caved in."

"Tarquinius?"

"A friend. You'll meet him later."

"So Gemellus is dead?" Fabiola smiled. "Can't say I'll miss the piece of shit. It would have been good to tell him I own his *latifundium* near Pompeii, though."

Romulus was shocked. She also ran the Lupanar. "How much does a property like that cost?" he asked.

Fabiola's face clouded. "A lover bought it for me. Decimus Brutus."

"Where is he?"

"We argued," she revealed. "He left."

Noise wafted in from the courtyard: the clash of swords off each other, shouted orders from Secundus and the thugs' wails of terror as they realized that there would be no escape.

Romulus was trying to piece things together. "What has Antonius to do with it then?"

She flushed. "Stupidly, I had an affair with him. Brutus found out."

Romulus indicated Scaevola's blood-sodden corpse. "Yet he worked for Antonius?"

Fabiola ignored the question. "It's so good to see you!"

Romulus smiled, acutely aware that she had just changed the subject. Why? *Stop it*, he thought. *Your wildest dream has just come true.* "It's amazing," he agreed. "We were children the last time we saw each other. Now look at us: all grown up. Mother would be so proud."

Fabiola's expression grew sad. "Did Gemellus tell you what happened to her?"

"Yes. I lost it when he did," Romulus answered. "Sliced his cheek right open. It felt good for a moment, but it didn't bring her back."

"Never mind. She's in Elysium now," Fabiola declared robustly. "I'm sure of it."

They sat in silence for a moment, honoring Velvinna's memory. The noise of combat from outside was dying down, to be replaced by the prostitutes' screams of distress. Fabiola could take it no longer. "I've got to help." Getting up, she chose a dress from the selection hanging on the wall. With her modesty restored, she turned to Romulus. "Come on. I'll take you to another room where you can rest, away from him. Bastard." She spat on Scaevola's body.

Struck by her steely will, Romulus followed Fabiola into the corridor. *She must have suffered terribly here,* he thought. *Sold into a brothel at thirteen, and forced to sleep with men for money. It's not much different to rape.* For his part, he was glad that his path had been to fight and kill men. Yet his sister had survived, and grown into a smart, confident woman. Romulus was already proud of her. "You'd make a good legionary," he said.

"Secundus says I fight well," she revealed proudly. "Soldiering is best left to men, though. After all, it's just about brute strength and ignorance, isn't it?"

Romulus laughed at her dig. "There's far more to it than that," he protested. "Look at someone like Caesar. He's the most incredible general." His face lit up. "The man can read a fight like no one else. Turn the tide of combat with a single order. Win against all the odds." He grinned at Fabiola. "I've even met him."

"So have I," she spat back.

Romulus recoiled at her fury. "What did I say?"

"Nothing," Fabiola muttered. She had been burning to tell her brother about Caesar since the moment she'd clapped eyes on him, but had held back. The moment had to be right. Now Romulus' obvious admiration for the dictator filled her with anger and confusion.

"Don't you like him?" asked Romulus. "He's meant to be charming toward women."

Fabiola's rage could no longer be contained. "Don't you see? He tried to rape me," she screamed.

Romulus' eyes bulged with shock. "He did what?"

"Fortunately Brutus came back, so the whoreson couldn't carry through with it," she continued. "But he did enough for me to know."

"Know what?"

"Who he was."

He gave her a confused look.

Fabiola took both of his hands in hers. "Caesar was the one who attacked Mother."

Romulus didn't really take in the words. "Eh?"

She repeated herself. Then, to make it crystal clear, "He raped her."

Shaken, he pulled away. "How do you know?"

"The look in his eyes, and his tone. His words—they . . . I just knew," Fabiola said, her voice shaking with passion.

His mind reeling, Romulus looked away. "You mean . . . you think we are . . ."

"Caesar's children. Yes," she replied.

"Gods," Romulus muttered. The man he idolized—his *father?* Who had raped his mother. *How can that be?* his mind screamed. It went against everything he'd come to believe in. "Did you ask Caesar if he'd done it?"

She looked at him with scorn. "Of course not. As if the bastard would admit to it anyway."

"Then you can't be positive it was he."

"I can," she retorted vehemently. "You weren't there. And you only have to look at yourself ! Look in a mirror! Can't you see it?"

Romulus studied his sister's face, which was contorted with anger. "Steady now. I believe you," he said, reeling at her words. He *did* look like Caesar.

"Good." She relaxed a little. "Then you can help me kill him."

His mouth fell open. "You're joking."

"Do I look as if I am?" she shot back, her eyes blazing.

"Hold on," Romulus protested. "You have no proof."

She tapped over her heart. "I know it here."

"That's not enough. The Republic needs Caesar. Thanks to him, there will soon be peace."

"What do I care about that? Why should you, for that matter? You're a slave," Fabiola shouted. "He raped Mother."

Shaken by his sister's revelation, and feeling guilty that his feelings for Caesar did not match hers, Romulus did not answer.

"Fabiola?" called a voice.

Her eyes opened wide. "Brutus?"

Romulus peered over her shoulder, seeing a brown-haired man in an expensive tunic walking down the corridor. His pleasant face wore a look of deep concern. "Are you hurt?" he cried, breaking into a run. Behind him trotted a group of tough-looking legionaries.

"Oh, Brutus," Fabiola cried. Her bottom lip began to tremble, and a tear ran down her cheek. "I'm fine. No one touched me."

Romulus was confused by his sister's body language. Was this real or affected emotion?

Clearly, Brutus thought it was genuine. Reaching them, he pulled Fabiola into a fierce embrace. "I came as soon as I heard," he whispered, his voice cracking. "Thank all the gods." He muttered an order and his men immediately began checking every room. "Bring me any you find alive," he cried. "I want to know who ordered this."

"It was Antonius," said Fabiola. "I'm certain!"

Brutus looked unsettled. "Not so loud," he murmured, patting her hand. He glanced at Romulus and smiled. "This must be your twin brother."

Fabiola wiped away her tears. "Yes."

Romulus saluted. "Honored to meet you, sir."

Brutus inclined his head in acknowledgment. "The gods are truly smiling today."

"They are," agreed Fabiola, beaming. "How did you know who he was?"

"Apart from the fact that you look like two peas in a pod?" Brutus grinned. "The scarred man who came to warn me about the attack told me. A friend of yours?" he asked Romulus.

"Tarquinius? Yes, sir. He's an old comrade."

"He's waiting outside," said Brutus. The implication was obvious.

"With your permission, then, sir?" Romulus requested politely. It was time to fade into the background. A reconciliation between the two lovers looked possible, so he must not intrude. There was a great deal to reflect on too. Caesar was not just his general, he was—perhaps—his father, and Fabiola wanted to kill him. While Romulus had sworn the same if he ever discovered the rapist's identity, he was shaken to the core by the fact that it was Caesar. This was the man who had freed him from slavery. Whom he'd followed through thick and thin, from Egypt to Asia Minor and Africa. Whom he'd come to love. Romulus felt sick with confusion.

"Of course." Brutus glanced at Fabiola. "We'd best get you back to my *domus*. Romulus can visit later."

"Don't leave it too long." Fabiola reached out a hand. "Bring your friend too."

"We'll be along soon," said Romulus.

"Everyone knows my house," said Brutus. "It's on the Palatine."

"Thank you, sir." Romulus was halfway down the corridor when he heard Brutus ask, "Who raped your mother?"

A sudden tension filled the air.

Romulus stopped.

"What's that, my love?" Fabiola's laugh was brittle and unconvincing, to Romulus at least.

"I heard the tail end of something you were saying when I came in. Something about who had raped your mother. You've never told me about that."

"Of course not," she replied. "It happened a long time ago."

"You sounded furious," said Brutus. "Who was it?"

Romulus waited for Fabiola to say the words "Julius Caesar," but she didn't.

"Well?" prompted Brutus gently.

"I'm not sure. Mother never told us," she said. "What I said was that someone like Scaevola *could* have raped her."

Romulus couldn't believe his ears.

Yet Brutus seemed satisfied. "Is the whoreson here?"

"Yes. In there." She pointed. "He's dead. My brother killed him."

What's going on? Romulus wondered. Fabiola was lying through her teeth. The realization hit him hard. Brutus was a loyal follower of Caesar. She didn't want him to know because she wasn't sure how he would react. *I'm supposed to agree to murder him without batting an eyelid, though. This when Fabiola actually has no definite proof, just the fact that Caesar came on to her a bit forcefully and he and I both have aquiline noses.* She had probably drunk too much wine that night. Romulus knew that he was inventing reasons not to believe Fabiola's story, but couldn't help himself. When he glanced back at his sister, she winked at him. Brutus missed the gesture.

Rather than being reassured, Romulus was infuriated. Fabiola was clearly used to manipulating men, and now she was treating him in the same way. A previously unthinkable idea popped into his mind. Could Fabiola be trusted?

Of course she can, he thought, *she's my sister. My twin. My own flesh and blood.*

His response was instant: *who's trying to work me.* Bridling now, Romulus started down the corridor. They would have to talk about this again: in private.

His happiness soured, Romulus went in search of Tarquinius.

†

Romulus' reunion with the haruspex was all that he had hoped for, and more. Walking to the Mithraeum, which Tarquinius had suggested they do, seemed to take only a moment. The delighted urchin tagged along, awestruck by the twenty-five *denarii* that his expertise had earned him. To Romulus, the extra sum was a trifle for getting him to the Lupanar in time to save Fabiola. As he realized later, he had made a fan for life in the boy, whose name turned out to be Mattius.

Romulus told the haruspex about his experiences in the army, including his exposure as a slave in Asia Minor and Petronius' courage in standing by him. About returning to the *ludus*. Not usually demonstrative, Tarquinius sighed at Petronius' death and gasped to hear how Romulus had killed the rhinoceros. "Gods," he breathed.

"After seeing that beast captured, I wouldn't have given you a chance in Hades."

Romulus shook his head, not quite believing it himself.

"That was when you met Caesar."

"Yes." Romulus related the tale of how he had been freed.

There was a shocked gasp from Mattius at this point.

"Slaves are no different than you or I," Romulus explained, aware that the urchin probably looked down on the only class lower than his own. "They can do anything, given the chance. As you could, if you want to."

"Really?" Mattius whispered.

"Look at me, and what I survived," Romulus replied. "Yet I was a slave once."

Mattius nodded determinedly.

Tarquinius chuckled. "Yet rather than enjoying your freedom, you volunteered to fight in Caesar's army?"

Romulus flushed. "He believed my story. It seemed the honorable thing to do."

"He would have appreciated the gesture," said the haruspex, clapping him on the shoulder. "You fought in the African campaign, then?"

"Yes. Ruspina was like Carrhae," revealed Romulus. "We had almost no cavalry, while the Numidians had thousands. It should have been a massacre, but Caesar never lost his cool." He went on to describe his attack on Petreius, as well as the battle at Thapsus.

"I'd heard that the Pompeians' elephants hadn't had the same success as the Indian ones did against the Forgotten Legion."

Romulus' guilt over Brennus resurfaced with a vengeance and he told the haruspex about how he'd saved Sabinus at Thapsus.

Tarquinius' face grew somber, and when Romulus was finished he did not say anything for a few moments. They walked on in silence until Romulus realized that the haruspex was studying the sky, the air and everything around him. Trying to see if anything would be revealed about Brennus. His heart rate shot up.

"It's too far away. I can see nothing," Tarquinius said at length. He sounded disappointed.

Romulus felt his shoulders slump. He jerked them back forcibly. "If I can drive off an elephant, what could Brennus do?" he demanded. "He could still be alive!"

"Indeed he could," the haruspex admitted.

Romulus grabbed his arm, hard. "Did you have any idea that this might happen?"

Tarquinius met Romulus' gaze squarely. "No. I thought that Brennus would meet his death by the River Hydaspes, avenging his family. I saw nothing beyond that."

Romulus nodded in acceptance. "Did you look further, though?"

"No," Tarquinius replied with an apologetic glance. "Who'd imagine that one man could fight an elephant, and live?"

Romulus could not bear the idea of his beloved comrade and mentor facing torments and dangers without him by his side. Swallowing, he changed the subject. "What happened to you in Alexandria?" he asked. "Why did you disappear?"

Tarquinius looked awkward. "I was ashamed," he said simply. "I thought you'd never forgive me for not telling you before, and that I deserved to die."

The pain in his voice tore at Romulus' heart, and again he thanked Mithras for bringing them together. "It didn't warrant that," he said.

"Well, I'm still here." Tarquinius' lips twisted upward in a wry smile. "The gods haven't finished with me. Of course I never foresaw more than a return to Rome with you. Once we were parted, I was unsure what to do."

"Did you not sacrifice, or attempt to divine?"

"Constantly." He frowned. "But I kept seeing the same confusing images. I could make no sense of them, so I went to study in the library, thinking that something might be revealed."

Romulus was all ears. "Was it?"

"Not really. I saw danger in Rome, but couldn't be sure if it was to you, or Fabiola, or someone else entirely." The haruspex sighed. "I did see Cleopatra, though." He lowered his voice. "When she was pregnant with Caesar's child."

Startled, Romulus jerked around. The Egyptian queen and her son had recently been installed in one of Caesar's residences in the city, provoking much talk among the population. Despite being married, the dictator was publicly honoring his mistress. Romulus hadn't given it much thought before, but what Fabiola had just told him changed things completely. If she was right, they and Cleopatra's child were half-siblings. His mind boggled.

To his alarm, Tarquinius' dark eyes were studying him closely.

Romulus looked away. He wasn't ready to share that information just yet, or Fabiola's demand that they kill Caesar. What he needed was time to think about it all, and to decide what he should do.

The haruspex didn't ask him anything. Instead, his story unfolded, leading right up to his drunken encounter with Fabricius, which had unexpectedly won him a passage back to Italy. "I never thought to return here," Tarquinius said. "Although it has taken this long to know why, it was the right thing to do. Being there to stop Gemellus was a true blessing."

"You also saved Fabiola's life," Romulus added gratefully.

The haruspex smiled. "I should have guessed that both of you could have been in danger."

"You said that Gemellus was your owner once," Mattius piped up.

"Yes," Romulus answered. "He mistreated my mother terribly, and beat us regularly for the most trivial reasons."

"Sounds like my stepfather," said the urchin darkly. "He deserved to die then, surely?"

Romulus' face grew somber. "Perhaps. I'm glad that I spared his life, though. Revenge should not be the only reason for living."

Mattius fell silent, making Romulus wonder what his family situation was like. He'd have to find out. Falling into a reverie about the day's events, he missed Tarquinius' approving look. After all his travails, the gods had shown him their favor once more. His only worry was Fabiola's shocking revelation, which still hadn't fully sunk in. He couldn't stop thinking about it either. After all he'd been through under Caesar—the marching, the fighting and killing—how could it be that the dictator had raped their mother? *Damn it all,* Romulus thought. *I love the man, as does every legionary in his entire army. But I hate the bastard who raped my mother.*

Tarquinius' hand on his arm startled him. "This is it."

Romulus looked up. They were high on the Palatine Hill, a wealthy area, and although plain, the high wall of the house before them was an imposing sight. "The Mithraeum is here?" he asked in surprise, remembering the veterans' ragged look.

"Left to them by a wealthy army officer who'd converted to the religion," Tarquinius disclosed. "It's even more impressive inside." He rapped on the door in a staccato pattern.

"Who goes there?" came the challenge from within.

"Tarquinius, and another friend."

The portal partly opened and a stolid veteran peered out. Seeing Romulus behind the haruspex, his face split into a grin. "This must be Fabiola's brother. Enter."

Romulus bid farewell to Mattius, who promised to come by each morning. Following Tarquinius inside, he was bowled over by the first thing he saw: an immense, brightly painted statue of Mithras crouched over the bull, which dominated the *atrium*. The oil lamps that burned in alcoves all along the hallway gave the figure a most forbidding air. He made a deep bow, remaining in obeisance for several heartbeats to show his respect and awe.

The doorman was watching him when he straightened. "It has that effect on everyone. The atmosphere in the Mithraeum is even more intense."

Self-conscious, Romulus grinned. Already he felt at home.

"You'll want a wash and a good meal first," Tarquinius butted in. "I can take you to the temple later."

Looking down at Scaevola's blood on his arms, Romulus nodded. With his headache and weariness combined, he felt utterly drained. It was a familiar feeling after combat. With luck, though, he was done fighting for a while. How good it would be to take up Sabinus' invitation and visit him on his farm, Romulus thought.

After he'd sorted things out with Fabiola.

†

His stay in the *domus* proved to be a welcome break. Because Romulus was a devotee of Mithras, the veterans received him as another comrade. Knowing that Fabiola would need time to reestablish herself in Brutus' good books, Romulus took the opportunity to catch up on lost sleep, and to think. Accompanied by the limpet-like Mattius, he made a brief visit to the honor guard's camp, seeking out Sabinus and the rest of the unit to let them know he wasn't dead. The legionaries' bleary faces, wine-stained tunics and demands that he join them for more revelry were not hard to refuse. Making his excuses, and promising to visit Sabinus, Romulus headed back to the veterans' house. The previous period of riotous celebrations had left him exhausted. A contemplative life of regular meals, prayer and rest was like manna from heaven. Of course it was more than just a need to take it easy. As Romulus soon realized, what he was doing was trying to decide how he felt about Caesar raping his mother, being the dictator's son, and Fabiola's demand that they kill him.

After three days, Romulus had solved nothing. He was even more confused.

A huge part of him—influenced by the memories of his childhood—still hated the man who had violated his mother, and wanted to plunge a knife into his heart. Another part, having been freed by Caesar and then fighting under him for more than a year, held the general in the highest regard. Romulus could not deny to himself that this devoted feeling bordered on love—*was* love. Like his comrades, he had reveled in it before, but now it threw him into paroxysms of guilt. Could it even be the filial feelings of a son for his father? How could he regard Caesar like that, given the abominable way the dictator had treated his mother?

Yet he did.

Of course Fabiola could be wrong, he told himself. If Caesar hadn't actually admitted to the rape, how could she be so sure? Their father might be any one of a thousand faceless nobles. The longer Romulus thought about it, the more convinced he became that this must be the case. Every time he tried to consider the other option— believing Fabiola, and then possibly agreeing to help her—he grew upset and angry. He also began to compare his decision not to kill Gemellus with his predicament over Caesar. Had the merchant not been a far worse man? After all, he had raped their mother on count- less occasions, rather than just once. If he hadn't wanted to end Gemellus' miserable life, then how could he do the same to Caesar? Romulus was genuinely disturbed by the idea of murdering the gen- eral. Furious at Fabiola for trying to destroy his idolization of Cae- sar, he also felt great anguish at not believing her word completely. He worried at the problem until his head spun, but no solution emerged.

Respecting Romulus' obvious need for silence, Secundus and the other veterans let him be. Tarquinius did not interfere either. He was regularly there for short periods, checking if Romulus needed to talk—which he didn't—but made himself scarce the rest of the time. The young soldier was not so wrapped up in his thoughts that he didn't recognize this. Tarquinius had seen that he was an adult now, who made his own decisions, which made his situation all the harder. Of course the haruspex had his own demons to face; despite his best efforts, he had still not managed to perform an interpretable divination. Rather than disappear, his visions of Rome under storm clouds were visiting him daily, obscuring all else. To his shame, Romulus was somewhat relieved by this. It meant that there was no point asking Tarquinius to seek the truth about his parentage. It was better that way. Romulus wanted to resolve the matter by himself.

On the fourth morning, he resolved to go and see Fabiola. She would be wondering what had happened to him, he told himself. It was difficult to brush away the fact that while his twin knew where he was staying, no messenger had come to find him. Perhaps this could be explained by Fabiola's need to be with her lover, but Romulus felt piqued. Brutus' house was not far.

"Want me to come along?" Tarquinius asked.

"No, thank you." Washed and shaved, Romulus was clad in a brand-new russet military tunic. He'd polished his *phalerae* until they shone, and greased the leather of his belt and *caligae*. He might be a plain legionary, but he could present himself well. There was no question of leaving his decorations behind in case Fabiola was offended by them: They meant the world to Romulus. While Caesar had awarded him the *phalerae*, they stood for far more. "I need to do this on my own."

Understanding, the haruspex nodded.

"What are you planning?"

There was a shrug. "The usual. To try and see something of the future. Ask for information about Brennus."

Pleased by this, Romulus took his leave. On the short walk to Brutus' *domus*, he did not consider his dilemma at all, chatting instead to Mattius. Romulus just wanted a joyous reunion with Fabiola—like the one he'd spent years imagining. That was what would happen this morning, he thought excitedly. It wouldn't take long for everything to be as it was in their childhood. Romulus reveled in the idea of properly seeing Fabiola again, of getting to know her a little. He wanted to learn all about his sister's life over the previous ten years—how she had risen above the degradation of prostitution to become the lover of one of the Republic's most prominent nobles; what she had done to find their mother. Doubtless she would want to hear of his experiences too.

Romulus' pretense did not last any longer than it took to arrive at Brutus' residence. Giving his name to the *optio* in charge of the legionaries outside, he was ushered inside. In the *atrium*, a military messenger was taking receipt of a rolled parchment from an imposing figure in full uniform. "Take this straight to Caesar," ordered the staff officer. "Wait for an answer." Saluting crisply, the soldier brushed past Romulus on his way out. He immediately felt irritated. Did he have to be reminded of the dictator's existence straightaway?

"Who is this man?"

The imperious demand shocked Romulus back to the present, and he found the officer regarding him with downright suspicion. Anger flared in his belly. *Who does the prick think he is?* Wary of the other's rank, he waited for the *optio* to speak.

"Fabiola's brother, sir. A veteran legionary," answered the *optio* hastily. "He has come to visit."

"I see." The officer raised an eyebrow. The tiny gesture was more powerful than a thousand words, clearly conveying his contempt. "Carry on, then."

Romulus was furious. *Arrogant bastard,* he thought as the *optio* guided him through the grand *tablinum*. *Is that what Brutus will think of me too?* Close on the heels of this idea was the uncomfortable fact that he might always face similar receptions from the company Fabiola now kept. Romulus was shocked by his inner voice's instant response. *Unless, of course, I am recognized as a son of Caesar.* It was an incredible thought. If Fabiola was right, they were much closer relations of the dictator than Octavian, his grandnephew and reputed heir. *I'm dreaming*, Romulus told himself. *We're former slaves, not nobility.*

Angered and disquieted, he still noticed the beauty and grandeur of the garden in the house's courtyard. The sound of water was everywhere: flowing gently past him in little channels, pouring from the mouths of nymphs or splashing from delicate fountains. In between rows of vines, he saw fig and lemon trees. Well-sculpted, painted statues of dryads and fauns peeped coyly from behind the lush vegetation. Like the richly decorated rooms Romulus had just passed through, the place oozed wealth.

Feeling even more uneasy, he followed the *optio* to a small open area with a table and chairs. Bread and fruit for breakfast were laid out on glazed red plates, but there was no sign of Fabiola. An amazing mosaic lay underfoot, depicting the exploits of a general on horseback. With an army of hoplites at his back, he faced an enormous host of dark-skinned soldiers, cavalry and elephants. Romulus studied it with complete fascination.

"It's Alexander of Macedon," muttered the *optio*.

"I thought so," replied Romulus, remembering his interest in the Greek general as he and his comrades had marched east from Seleucia. His pleasure at that memory didn't last. Looking at the massive war elephants made his guilt about Brennus surface all over again.

The other knew nothing of his inner turmoil. "What a leader Alexander was. Who knows where he might have got to if his men hadn't refused to carry on?" The *optio* grinned. "But we have our own Alexander in Caesar, and more, eh? Rumor has it that he wants to travel east once the civil war is over. That'd be an adventure worth going on!"

Startled, Romulus was about to ask the *optio* more when Fabiola arrived. Clad in a silk and linen gown that clung to her figure, she had her long black hair tied back. Bracelets and rings adorned with precious stones decorated her wrists and fingers, accentuating the deep blue of her eyes. Around her neck was a string of large pearls, each one of which would feed a family for a year. She was the personification of poise, beauty and wealth. "Brother!" she cried, sweeping toward him in a wave of rosewater perfume. "What took you so long?"

Romulus shuffled forward, acutely aware of his battle scars, his coarse tunic and heavy leather *caligae*. Compared to Fabiola, everything about him was rough and crude. "Sister," he said, pecking her on the cheek. "It's good to see you." He looked pointedly at the *optio*.

Taking the hint, the junior officer bowed toward Fabiola and withdrew.

She indicated the chairs by the rosewood table. "Sit," she commanded. "Share my breakfast."

Romulus waited until they were alone before speaking again. "You needed time to patch up things with Brutus. That's why I delayed visiting until now." He picked up a ripe peach and held it to his nose, enjoying its rich aroma. There had been few luxuries like this in Margiana, he thought, trying to shove away the main reason he'd stayed away. Romulus sank his teeth into the fruit, and busied himself with catching the juice. Uneasily, he realized that he was playing a game with his own sister. Waiting to see what she'd say.

Fabiola bestowed him with a stunning smile. "You are observant. Thank you for giving me some space."

"Is all well now?"

Now she looked like a cat that had got the cream. "Better than that. We're happier than ever. Brutus has also complained to Caesar about Antonius' behavior. He told him about what happened at the Lupanar."

"Really?" Romulus leaned forward, all ears. "What did Antonius say?"

"He denied everything, of course. Said that Scaevola was a rogue character, a lone wolf who acted without authorization." Fabiola pouted. "While Caesar chose to believe Antonius, he decided not to renew his position as Master of the Horse. There has been too much talk of his drunken excesses."

"But nothing more will come of it. Typical."

"One good thing did," retorted Fabiola. "Brutus had a stand-up argument with Antonius, which nearly came to blows. Caesar had to intervene in the end."

Romulus stared at her, not understanding. "So?"

"Brutus is aggrieved that Caesar did not believe his account of what had gone on before the attack on the brothel. Basically, Antonius is being shown favoritism, even though he has committed an outrage." She smiled. "It's helping to bring Brutus around."

Romulus' heart sank. There was to be no easy chat about their childhood or how they'd both survived until now. "To your way of thinking," he said heavily.

"Yes." It was Fabiola's turn to bend forward, her blue eyes dancing. "Brutus isn't convinced yet, but I'll win him over. He'll be able to find all the senators and noblemen we need. There must be plenty who are discontented and unhappy. Caesar's done nothing but ride roughshod over every law in the book since he got back."

Uneasy, Romulus looked over his shoulder. This was treasonous talk.

"Don't worry," advised Fabiola. "Brutus has just left for the Senate, and everyone knows that I like to be left alone here. You can speak without fear."

His sister's blithe assumption that he would agree with her plan irritated Romulus intensely. "So you're still planning to kill him?" he whispered.

"Of course." Seeing his reluctance, Fabiola pursed her lips. "Will you help?"

"How can you be sure that he's the one?" Romulus cried. "That he's our—"

"Don't even say the word," she spat. "Caesar is nothing but a monster who has to pay for what he's done."

"Before you murder a man, you need real proof," Romulus countered. "Not just a hunch."

"He tried to rape me, Romulus."

Romulus' indecision crystallized. "That doesn't mean he did the same to Mother."

They glared at each other, both unwilling to give way.

"Is that it?" demanded Fabiola eventually. "You come back from the dead, and won't even avenge the wrongs done to your own flesh and blood?"

Stung, Romulus got to his feet. "While you may have been upset by Caesar's advances, you weren't hurt. That's hardly a reason to end his life. Find me evidence that he attacked Mother, and I'm all yours," he growled. "But I won't slay someone who might be innocent. I've had to do that too many times before."

"So you think that you're the only one who has suffered?" Fabiola shouted. "Did I whore myself with every man in Rome for nothing? All I wanted was to discover where you might be, and who had raped Mother, and I hated every single moment of it. Knowing Caesar is the one, and having you by my side to kill him, is surely my reward."

Horrified by her words, Romulus looked away. What had happened to him bore no comparison to his sister's ordeal. Yet his opinion remained the same. "Caesar wasn't responsible for selling you into the Lupanar," he said at last. "Gemellus was, and he has paid the ultimate price. Let it go."

"It's Caesar, Romulus, I know it," she said, pleading. "He has to pay."

The raw emotion in Fabiola's words drew Romulus' eyes back.

He was shocked to see that she was crying—sobbing, even. Instinctively he moved to reassure her, and she fell into his arms. "There, there," he said, awkwardly patting her back. "It will be all right."

The tears stopped at once, arousing his suspicions.

"Help me," she whispered.

Romulus' jaw hardened and he pushed her away. "No. I can't."

Unshed tears glittered in Fabiola's icy blue eyes. "Why not?" she demanded.

"I told you," Romulus replied, stunned by her ability to change mood like the wind. "You have no proof."

Again they glowered at each other.

After a few moments, Romulus broke eye contact. "I want no part in it," he said. "I'm going."

At once Fabiola looked distraught, like a lost little girl. "Don't leave. Please."

Romulus stepped away from the table and bowed formally. "If you need me for anything—apart from *that*—you know where I'm staying."

"Yes." Her voice was wobbly, but she didn't try to stop him.

He had walked a dozen steps before Fabiola spoke again. "You won't tell anyone, will you?"

Romulus spun around. "Is that what you think of me? That I'll go running to Caesar?"

Her face went pale. "No, of course not."

"Why ask then?" he shot back. She did not answer.

Disgusted, Romulus stalked from the courtyard.

XXV

CONSPIRACY

More than five months pass . . .

Fabiola sat in the reception area, fondly watching Benignus as he instructed a new doorman in his duties. Despite the horrific injuries he had sustained during the battle with Scaevola's men, he had survived. With a host of new scars and a bad limp in one leg, he had insisted on returning to work a few weeks later. Benignus' recovery was in no small part due to Tarquinius' medical abilities, and the last remnants of dust from a little leather pouch, which the haruspex had scattered over the worst of his wounds. *Mantar*, he called it. Fabiola had no idea what was in the musty-smelling particles, but she would always be grateful to Tarquinius for its power. Without it, Benignus would have died. Without his intervention, so too would Romulus. Furthermore, if the haruspex hadn't warned Secundus and Brutus of the danger she was in, they might never have come to the Lupanar. In turn, this meant that she and her lover might never have been reconciled, a prospect Fabiola dared not think about. For all these reasons, she retained a keen interest in Tarquinius.

Initially, she'd thought that his close friendship with Romulus might provide her with a way of breaking the ice with her brother. After their argument in Brutus' garden, the twins had not seen each other for some time. Fabiola had been so angered by Romulus' refusal to join her that she was not prepared to make the first move. As she had discovered, neither was he. Yet Tarquinius' visits to care for Benignus meant that Fabiola saw the haruspex daily. Long conversations followed, during which she heard much of Romulus' story, which of course she hadn't had the chance to hear from his own lips. While she'd been told about the torturous campaign into Parthia and the horrors of Carrhae, Fabiola had never heard it from someone who had stood by Romulus' side. She wept at Tarquinius' descriptions of the Parthian arrow storms, of the arrow-riddled legionaries and their defeat under the burning desert sun, and sat horror-struck by the details of Crassus' execution, the Forgotten Legion's march to Margiana, and their ordeals against the Sogdians, Scythians and Indians.

The haruspex' account of that last battle was perhaps the most shocking revelation for Fabiola. Interrupting Tarquinius, she told him how she had crept into the underground Mithraeum and drunk a vial of an hallucinogenic liquid. Bizarrely, she had been transformed into a raven. Flying over a strange land, she'd been struck by powerful images of Romulus. Next she had seen an outnumbered Roman army facing a huge host with elephants in its midst. The notion that Mithras had revealed that her brother was alive only to show her the method of his destruction had been overwhelming, driving Fabiola to dive madly at one of the massive beasts.

When she mentioned this, Tarquinius' mouth actually fell open.

"A raven, you say?"

She nodded. "But Secundus woke me up before I could see what happened."

"I saw that bird," the haruspex muttered. "So did Romulus. It dropped like a stone from the sky, aiming straight for the lead elephant. I told the men that the raven was a sign from the gods!"

Goose bumps rose all over Fabiola's body. "It was sent by Mithras himself," she whispered.

"Like my vision in the Parthians' Mithraeum," mused Tarquinius. "I've had perhaps six that clear in my whole life, and the last one was in Margiana. It feels as if I have lost my focus." He sighed.

Despite the haruspex' pessimism, Fabiola's interest was piqued. Unlike the charlatans she'd come across all her life, here was a soothsayer with real ability. If she could take Tarquinius into her confidence, he might be persuaded to divine for the success of her plot against Caesar. Yet it was not quite that simple. Before revealing her hand in such a bald manner, Fabiola wanted to know if she could trust Tarquinius. He might feel the same way about Caesar as her brother. She started by asking him to have a word with Romulus, but to her frustration, he wanted nothing to do with their feud. In fact, he turned her down flat. "I've done enough harm poking my nose in other people's business," he said. "You and your brother have to sort it out yourselves, like adults." The haruspex' refusal prevented Fabiola from taking him into her confidence.

Fabiola wasn't ready to try mending her relationship with her twin either. Stubbornly, she wanted him to come to her first, and when he didn't, she was even more aggrieved. Although Fabiola knew that he was probably feeling the same way, she felt unable to budge from her position. She was right about Caesar being their mother's rapist. Romulus would come to see that one day, she knew it. Nor was Fabiola deterred from her planning by Tarquinius' refusal to help. She would press on regardless, with or without evidence of divine approval. Or her brother's assistance.

Fabiola's first major advancement had been her reconciliation with Brutus. Overwrought by her ordeal and the manner of Romulus' departure, she had still noted the speed of Brutus' arrival in the

Lupanar. Knowing that this was her great chance to win her lover back, Fabiola had used every weapon in her considerable armory. Sobbing like a child, she had thanked Brutus for coming to her aid. After taking up with Antonius, she didn't deserve anything other than contempt from him. Secretly delighted by his magnanimous response, Fabiola had gradually turned kitten-like, telling Brutus how proud she was of him, and how much she'd missed his kindness and attention. Light caresses of his chest had drawn an instant response, giving Fabiola much-needed encouragement to continue. If he was good enough to take her back, she promised, she would lavish all her attention on him for the rest of her days.

Fabiola's ploy was only partly an act. She was hugely relieved to be rid of Antonius and Scaevola, his malevolent sidekick and she had genuinely missed Brutus' pleasant company. However, her main need was still to enroll him in her conspiracy. Naturally, Brutus had no knowledge of this, yet, won over by Fabiola's abject penitence and smoldering sexuality, he had drawn her into a lingering embrace. That night she had used every trick in the book to drive Brutus wild with lust, and their coupling had been nothing short of animal.

She'd kept up the tactic, focusing entirely on him in the days and weeks that followed. In the aftermath of Caesar's triumphs, and with no immediate prospect of fighting anywhere else, Brutus was happy to relax. Years of conflict in Gaul had been replaced by the civil war, and while he hadn't fought in all of its campaigns, he had constantly been performing high-level duties for Caesar. Enjoying each other's company like new lovers, they had vacationed on the coast, visited the theater and circus, and entertained Brutus' friends and allies. Fabiola took extreme care to say nothing but positive things about Caesar. Her rash behavior with Antonius had nearly been the ruin of her, and she needed to be sure of Brutus' complete devotion once more before mentioning such an inflammatory topic. When Brutus was ordered to Hispania, she kept up the pretense, knowing that the right moment would make itself known.

Until then, she would bide her time.

†

For a second time, Romulus walked by the turn-off that would lead him to the Lupanar. Mattius darted back and forth impatiently, but had the sense not to speak. It was not for him to question his sponsor's actions. He knew it was something to do with Romulus' sister, but nothing more. To the urchin, it didn't really matter. Having someone so hero-like to follow and learn from was enough for him. After Romulus' dire threats to his stepfather, Mattius no longer had to worry about spending all his time away from home. His sister was no longer selling her prepubescent body either; instead she sold bread for a local baker, a veteran whom Romulus had approached. Their mother, a scrawny ill-fed woman, was now installed in a clean two-room *cenacula*, along with Mattius and his sister. Her features, which had been pale and gaunt from giving most of her food to her children, were now a more healthy color. Romulus had never seen himself as a sponsor of the poor—after all, he'd been a slave until recently—but once he'd started helping Mattius, it felt wrong not to extend the same gesture to his family. In many ways, they were no different to him a decade previously. It felt good being wealthy enough to help ease their misery, and it almost took his mind off his own predicament.

Romulus had been drawn back to this spot with monotonous regularity ever since his argument with Fabiola, but he never allowed himself to go any closer to the brothel. Today was no different. *Damn her eyes*, he thought. *Can't she reach out first? Why does it have to be me?* By now, he knew that Tarquinius had told Fabiola much of what had happened to him since their parting, that she had wept at the worst parts of it and rejoiced at the best. She obviously cared for him. *Just as I do for her,* he reflected. *Yet I can't go along with her plan to murder the man who freed me from slavery.*

Despite his reservations, Romulus still worried that Fabiola might be correct. Maybe Caesar *had* raped their mother. The idea revolted him. It was so at odds with all his regard for the dictator, and left him feeling guilty about his manumission, which in turn angered him. No matter how he tried, Romulus could not resolve the issue. All he knew was that killing Caesar—guilty or not—would make him as bad as Gemellus, and that was not what he wanted. Fabiola could make her own decision, but he did not want to be part of it.

Romulus couldn't ignore Caesar and his accomplishments either. After a decade of unrest and bloodshed, he had brought peace to the Republic. Without him, the specter of civil war would undoubtedly raise its ugly head again. How many thousands of innocent people would die in that conflict?

The dictator's abilities were proving to be far more than leadership on the battlefield. Rather than rest on his laurels in the newfound calm, Caesar had been very busy. Rafts of far-seeing legislation had been passed, most of which had been universally welcomed. Rome's population of poor had been reduced by tens of thousands—mostly to found new colonies in Gaul, Africa and Hispania. Generous allocations of land there would allow them to provide for their families rather than rely on the state for everything. Large-scale works had been started in the capital too, both on the Campus Martius and on Caesar's massive new Forum complex. These provided employment for a vast number of citizens, allowing the dictator to reduce the number of people who received free grain by more than a hundred thousand.

Caesar's soldiers and supporters had not been forgotten either. At last his veterans were receiving the plots of land that they had been promised for so long. His tribunes and centurions were particularly well looked after. Nothing made a general more popular than these two gestures, as Caesar knew well. Pompey's enormous popularity with his legions had been in no small part due to his generous retirement settlements for his old soldiers. While Romulus and his comrades in the honor guard had not all served for the minimum period required to earn an allocation of land, Caesar still chose to include them with those who had. Furthermore, he'd granted them properties in Italy, naturally the most sought-after location.

Romulus was now the owner of a small farm near Capua, and he'd made a number of visits to it, each time calling in on Sabinus. Naturally, Mattius accompanied him on every trip. Even Tarquinius came along occasionally. Romulus' former comrade was a mine of information about how to run an agricultural enterprise. A pattern soon evolved: They would lie around, talking and drinking too much, while Octavia, Sabinus' wife, muttered in the background and Mattius ran wild with the veteran's children. Once they'd had enough, the men would travel by mule to Romulus' property, which was situated on a south-facing slope fifteen miles from Capua. Mattius would stay behind with Octavia, usually at his request. To him, life on a farm, with playmates and regular meals thrown in, was like heaven on earth.

With Sabinus' help, Romulus employed six local peasants as well as an overseer. Paying wages greatly increased his costs, but it went against everything in his nature to become the owner of servile labor. Next he bought mules and agricultural tools—a plow, scythes, axes, spades and rakes. The men were set to work restoring the half-collapsed farmhouse and sheds, and ripping up the weeds that filled the disused fields. It was too early in the season to expect a crop, but the seeds could be sown. Later in the year, there would be wheat and barley. The vines, however, would take many months longer before they produced a yield. Sabinus stood with his hands on his hips, explaining the intricacies of growing, tending and harvesting. Romulus listened with half an ear, but his mind constantly wandered, making him wonder if he was really suited to being a farmer.

As a boy, he'd dreamed of becoming a new Spartacus, of rising up against the Republic and freeing the countless multitudes whose unpaid toil built its buildings and tended its farms. Returning to Italy had killed that idea, because Romulus now saw the task for what it was: an impossible dream. Slavery was too integral a part of the Republic, and the opposition to any uprising—Caesar's battle-hardened legions—was a far cry from the conscript troops that Spartacus had defeated. They would have little difficulty in defeating whatever motley force of slaves he might muster.

Worrying about the change in his stance, Romulus assuaged his conscience by remembering two things. The first was his favorite of all Caesar's new statutes: that at least one-third of the workforce on every *latifundium* in the south of Italy should be made up of citizens. While this law had been passed to increase employment, it also reduced the need for servile labor. The second was that while he might sympathize with the plight of slaves, he wasn't responsible for their situation. He owed them nothing. His former comrades were a totally different proposition. If one of these needed help, Romulus would move heaven and earth to do so.

Unsurprisingly, the most prominent candidate in his mind was Brennus. Reminded of his friend at regular intervals—by the Pompeians' elephants at Thapsus, his own battle with one, Caesar's use of them in his last triumph and finally their depiction on the mosaic in Brutus' garden—Romulus frequently wondered if the Gaul was still alive. Hearing that Caesar might be taking an army to Parthia was thrilling beyond belief. A hunger to revisit the land where he'd fought and been taken prisoner now gnawed daily at Romulus' belly. Italy had not proved to be all that he'd hoped for. This was his second problem. He didn't want to fight in the arena again, yet farming seemed positively pedestrian. Without the roots that men like Sabinus possessed, Romulus knew he could walk away from it all with ease. Discussing it with Tarquinius made things worse, for he could see the same desire to travel east in the haruspex' eyes. Fabiola was his only reason *not* to leave.

Tarquinius wasn't sure what his reason was but, anxious not to move prematurely, he stayed put.

To Romulus' frustration, he'd heard nothing further about the proposed Parthian campaign since. All the news was of Caesar's struggle in Hispania, where he was attempting to put down the rebellion against Cassius Longinus, his unpopular governor there. In a shrewd move, two of Pompey's sons had used the opportunity to call on the tribes' historic loyalty to their father. Raising a huge army, they were giving Caesar a real run for his money.

Nonetheless, Romulus kept his ear to the ground, keeping in touch with all the veterans he could. The dictator's daring plan to avenge Crassus' defeat was another reason to oppose Fabiola's plan. If Caesar was killed, the invasion would not go ahead, and a huge chance to find out more about Brennus' fate would be lost. Troubled that he was being selfish, Romulus was always brought back to his feud with Fabiola. Somehow he doubted if her position had budged.

Cursing, Romulus walked away from the Lupanar—again. It was infuriating. During his years of exile, he had always imagined that a return to Rome would mean a happy ending—namely a joyful reunion with Fabiola.

Instead, fate kept putting obstacles in his way.

†

Spring moved into early summer, and news arrived in Rome of Caesar's stunning victory at Munda. In a desperate struggle during which his legions had fought uphill against superior numbers, the dictator had prevailed yet again. At one stage in the battle, when his lines had been in real danger of collapsing, Caesar rushed to the spot and rallied his panicking men. Knowing that a heroic gesture was needed, he had charged alone at the enemy, ducking the *pila* and arrows that were being fired in his direction. Stirred by his courage, the nearby officers had joined him, followed by the legionaries, and in one moment of madness, the tide of battle was turned. In the ensuing slaughter, more than thirty thousand Pompeian troops were said to have been slain, for the loss of only a thousand Caesarean soldiers.

The announcements of victory were made for days from every crossroads in Rome. Furious, Fabiola busied herself with running the Lupanar and looking forward to Brutus' return home. As the accolades poured in, a grateful Senate bestowed upon Caesar the extraordinary number of fifty days of thanksgiving. He was also given the title of "Liberator," and the construction of a temple of Liberty was ordered. The honor of being called "Imperator" permanently was also bestowed on the dictator—prior to this it had only been used to hail a victorious general in the aftermath of a triumph. So far Caesar had not returned to receive his awards, occupying himself in Hispania with mopping-up operations, and resettling the province.

Fabiola was bitterly disappointed that Caesar had not been killed or defeated at Munda. She wanted the pleasure of seeing him die a lingering death, but after so long without any success, she would look no gift horse in the mouth. Caesar's victory denied her revenge yet again. To make matters worse, he was now the undisputed ruler of the Republic. There was no one left to fight. From Greece to Asia Minor, Egypt to Africa and Spain, any meaningful resistance had been crushed.

However, as Fabiola found out soon afterward, reward comes from the most unpromising places. Whether it was because the civil war was now truly over, or because Caesar was still away, she would never know. To her absolute joy, murmurs of discontent about the dictator began to surface. First it was the number of thanksgiving days, the greatest amount ever awarded in Rome's history. Then it was the title "Liberator"—after all, who had he liberated? Lastly, it was the permanent designation of "Imperator." As Fabiola heard on the street and from rich clients in the Lupanar, this would give Caesar ideas above his station. Was he not just an excellent general? Why did he need such grandiose titles? Nodding sagely, Fabiola said little, instead noting each person's identity for future reference. The time was not ripe yet.

†

By late autumn, Fabiola's rift with Romulus had been going on for nearly a year. They had met on a number of occasions, and been quite civil to each other, even taking a trip to Pompeii to visit her *latifundium*. In many ways, the twins were the same as they had been as children and their old easy relationship was revived when they spent time in one another's company. However, the unresolved row over Caesar's role in their parentage was always lurking beneath their genuine pleasure in seeing one another, and regularly flared up. They had a second argument, worse than the first, when Caesar returned to Rome from Hispania. Once again, Romulus refused to have any part in Fabiola's plan to murder the dictator. Torn by guilt, he began for the first time to wonder if he should tell anyone. However, the result of that—Fabiola's likely execution—was too awful to contemplate. Convincing himself that she would never have the courage or the ability to actually carry out the threat, Romulus tried to bury his concerns in the recesses of his mind. He wanted to tell Tarquinius, but his worries about what the haruspex might divine in the light of such knowledge kept his lips sealed.

Fabiola's feelings were similar to those of Romulus. Although she fretted that her brother would expose her, she could not bring herself to act against him. Her ruthlessness did not extend that far. Yet she would not give up on her idea, even if it meant that she was never to be friends with Romulus. Not that Fabiola wished for such an outcome—how could she? He was the beloved twin she had so longed to find again. Yet her determination was unshakable. Her need for revenge defined her. Her enthusiasm increased as the details of Caesar's latest triumph were announced. In a notable exception to his previous four victory parades, it was undoubtedly to commemorate his success against a Roman enemy. This was breaking tradition in the boldest of fashions, and guaranteed to anger many senators. Of course no one dared say a word. Remarkably, though, Pontius Aquila, one of the tribunes, refused to stand as Caesar passed by in his chariot. Incensed, the dictator had shouted that Aquila should try to take back the Republic from him. The tribune's gesture was tiny, but spoke volumes to Fabiola.

Her hopes continued to rise as a fawning Senate heaped honors and rights upon Caesar. His dictatorship was extended to ten years, and he was granted the right to the consulship, should he wish it. He was entirely in control of the Republic's army, and the treasury. At formal meetings, Caesar sat on an ivory chair between the two consuls, while his statue was carried among those of the gods to the ceremonial openings of games. Other effigies of him were placed near those of Rome's kings of old, and in the temple of Romulus.

Prominent former Pompeians such as Cicero now felt confident enough to make mildly sarcastic comments about these developments, but the vast majority of nobles and politicians remained quiet, or spoke in private. It didn't matter to Fabiola. To her delight, Brutus was one of those who had begun to grumble. Her lover had realized that Caesar had no intention of returning total power to the Senate. In fact, almost no real debates took place there any longer. Instead the dictator and his advisers met behind closed doors, deciding what should be done about a particular issue. Once the matter had been settled, a decree was issued, purporting to be from the Senate. To Brutus' outrage, it often contained a list of those who were supposed to have attended.

†

"The damn war is over," he ranted to Fabiola one night near the turn of the year. "It's time for the Senate to take control again. The Republic has been ruled well that way for hundreds of years. Who does Caesar think he is?"

Fabiola studied Brutus' face intently. Was this finally her time to speak? She'd planted the first seed in his mind after the battle of Pharsalus, but had been unable to capitalize on it since. She had worried that it had withered away and died, but here was the first sign of growth.

"There's a rumor that his dictatorship is to be made permanent. So is his right to the censorship! And, as if all his titles weren't enough, he is to be called 'Father of the Country.' No ivory chair is good enough either—only a gold one will do now," Brutus sneered. "I should have known when he added the pediment and pillars to the front of his house. For Jupiter's sake! Making it look like a temple doesn't turn him into a god. Neither does creating a damn college of priests in his name."

"Didn't men like Marius, Sulla and Pompey get honored in this manner?" Fabiola asked, probing the depth of Brutus' anger.

Pure scorn twisted his face. "No," he cried. "They were humble in comparison to Caesar! It's all thanks to the lickspittle senators whom he has appointed too. 'Jump,' Caesar says, and they reply, 'How high?' He respects no one any longer. Having exceeded anything ever awarded to a general, he didn't even get to his feet when we came to tell him. It's not right."

Delight filled Fabiola. *He's really unhappy,* she thought. Caesar's recent refusal to stand when the senators arrived to offer him the exceptional honors had offended many. As dictator, Caesar was senior to the two consuls. Technically, therefore, he was not obliged to rise, but by not doing so, he had shown contempt toward the senators in general. This was the second or third time that Brutus had mentioned the incident, and although her stomach was a nervous pool of acid, Fabiola decided to act. If she didn't make a move soon, the chance would be lost. In recent days, Caesar had been talking more and more of his intended campaign to Parthia. While the army of sixteen legions and ten thousand cavalry would take time to assemble, preparations were well in train. "Do you remember what I said to you once?" she asked softly. "After Pharsalus."

Brutus gave her a quizzical look.

"Rome must beware of Caesar."

His eyes widened as the memory returned. "Why did you say that?"

"Because he'd won a battle that no one else could have." Fabiola laughed. "I had no idea! Gone much further than that, hasn't he? Egypt, Asia Minor, Africa and Spain. Now all these extra powers. Where will it stop? On the banks of the Tigris or Euphrates?"

"You said 'Caesar will make himself king,'" Brutus muttered.

"He already is, in all but name," Fabiola retorted. "We are now his humble subjects."

His cheeks suffused with fury, and she knew that her barb had run deep. "You are a wise woman," he sighed.

Little do you know my reasons, thought Fabiola. *I have Mithras to thank for that insight.*

"What would you do about it?"

She looked at him calmly. "There is only one thing to do. Rid Rome of the tyrant before he departs for Parthia."

There was a long silence, during which Fabiola began to worry that she had overstepped the mark. But she had burned her bridges, so, trying to calm her pounding heart, she waited.

"Tyrant? I'd never thought of him like that," Brutus admitted. "Yet that's what he's become. It's not as if we can just ask him to retire either. Caesar's not like Sulla: He lives for war."

Fabiola's hopes slowly began to rise.

There was another pause before Brutus spoke again. "I can't see any other course of action," he said heavily. "It needs to be done in Rome too. No one can touch Caesar in the bosom of his army, and the Parthian campaign will take three years or more."

Thank you, Mithras, thought Fabiola exultantly. *I've convinced him.*

"I'll need help. Not to say that I would be scared of acting alone," he added.

"You don't have to prove your courage to anyone," Fabiola reassured him.

He gave her a grateful smile. "Sadly, I already know whom to approach. Servius Galba and Lucius Basilus are both unhappy at the moment. They feel that they've been overlooked while everyone else gets rewarded for their service to Caesar. Caius Trebonius has been complaining too."

Fabiola felt a thrill of excitement. Two of those mentioned, Galba and Trebonius, had been legates in Caesar's army during the prolonged campaign in Gaul. If they were ready to turn on their master, then it was likely that others would be too. Brutus' next words confirmed this.

"My cousin, Marcus Junius Brutus, would be interested. Not to mention Cassius Longinus."

Fabiola's spirits soared.

"Have you told Romulus about this?"

Fabiola's mouth opened and closed. "Yes . . . I mean . . . no," she stuttered.

Brutus frowned. "Which is it?"

"I might have mentioned it once, in passing," she muttered, unable to meet his stare.

"And what did he say?" he asked, reaching out to clasp her arm. "Tell me!"

Fabiola dragged her gaze up to his. She quailed before the look in his eyes. "He wanted nothing to do with it," she admitted.

"Your own brother won't get involved," Brutus said unhappily. "I can't do it either then. Especially after all Caesar's done for me."

"I'll win him over," Fabiola ventured, lying through her teeth. "Caesar has to be stopped. He's becoming a monster. You know it's true."

It was as if Brutus hadn't heard her. "There must be another way."

Fabiola felt the situation slipping from her grasp.

"I'll pay Caesar a visit," he declared. "Talk some sense into him."

"Have you gone mad?" cried Fabiola, panicking. She didn't want to lose Brutus for a second time. "Caesar's veiled threats to Pontius Aquila went on for days. Who knows how he'd react to the person who crosses him next?"

"True enough." Brutus ran a hand through his short brown hair, thinking. "I must consider the matter further. Make an offering at Mars' temple, asking for guidance."

"There isn't much time," Fabiola warned, frustrated by his indecision. "He's talking about leaving Rome straight after the Ides of March."

Brutus' expression darkened at her pressure. "We're talking about the murder of a man here. It's not a matter to be taken lightly."

"I know, my love," Fabiola murmured reassuringly. "Of course you're right."

To her relief, he relaxed.

Fabiola considered the situation for a moment. *I have enough names to go on,* she realized. Euphoria filled her. While Brutus vacillated, she would press on. Invite the nobles he'd mentioned to the Lupanar one by one. Win them over, by whatever means necessary.

In time, Brutus would come to see that killing Caesar was the only option.

Even if he didn't, the information he'd let slip gave Fabiola enough to act alone. Which was what she'd do. This was too good an opportunity to miss. If she didn't act soon, there wouldn't be another chance for years.

She was prepared to wait no longer.

Whatever the risk.

XXVI

THE PLOT

Just over three months pass . . .

THE CAPITOLINE HILL, ROME, SPRING 44 BC

Romulus glanced sidelong at Tarquinius, trying to judge his mood. With Mattius in tow, they were climbing the Capitoline Hill, intent on visiting the enormous temple to Jupiter there. Numerous attempts by the haruspex to read the future in the Mithraeum had failed, frustrating them both. Something momentous was approaching, Tarquinius said over and over, but he wasn't sure what. Today, no effort would be spared. Still scarred by his own vision in Margiana, Romulus refused to consider the idea that he might try. Yet he needed to know so many things, and it felt as if time was running out. Recently, his suspicions had been roused by the knowledge that a large group of men were holding regular meetings in the Lupanar. Detailing Mattius to sit outside each day, Romulus had soon learned that scores of nobles were involved, including prominent politicians such as Marcus Brutus and Cassius Longinus. Tellingly, the urchin had not seen Decimus Brutus, Fabiola's lover, which told Romulus that he wasn't the only one to have reservations. This knowledge angered him even more.

He hadn't confronted Fabiola over it for two reasons. First was that she probably wouldn't admit any conspiracy, and secondly Romulus wasn't sure he trusted her any longer. If she actually was going through with her plan, then he was but a small obstacle in her path. Fabiola's original heavies had been replaced by brutal-looking men who looked well capable of killing their mistress's twin brother. None had been especially friendly, even when they'd known who he was, leading Romulus to conclude that he wasn't exactly flavor of the month at the Lupanar. Despite this, he felt loath to take the obvious and opposite path—that of betraying Fabiola and the other conspirators. What if he was wrong about her?

Even if he wasn't, Romulus couldn't bear the idea of his only living relation being permanently taken from him, for that would be the only fate awarded Fabiola if she were caught. Yet the consequences— Caesar's murder—were just as bad. It didn't help that Rome was awash with rumors of plans to assassinate the dictator. One moment it was Marcus Brutus, then another it was Dolabela, one of Caesar's long-term allies. Sometimes it was even purported to be Antonius, the dictator's most loyal follower. Riven by uncharacteristic indecision, Romulus had to know if the threat to Caesar was real, and if so, what he should do about it.

Then there was the thorny subject of Fabiola herself. Could he patch up his relationship with her? No matter how much Romulus wanted it, he could not see a reconciliation happening while his sister was planning to kill Caesar. This awareness further lessened his ties to Rome, but made him feel guilty as Hades. There must be a way to renew the intimacy of their childhood, when they each had only the other.

Only the gods knew the answer to this problem—if they could be persuaded to reveal it.

Romulus also burned to know if Brennus was still alive. He did not let the thrilling idea go to his head. Even if the big Gaul had fought off the wounded elephant, there was nothing to say that he hadn't been killed immediately afterward. The Forgotten Legion had been struggling against an overwhelming enemy force when Romulus and Tarquinius had fled, and its fate, like that of Brennus, was unknown. Since Thapsus, though, Romulus had not been able to stop wondering about the Gaul.

His desire to take part in Caesar's forthcoming campaign was fanned by the regular news that swept the city. Thousands of cavalrymen had been recruited from Gaul, Hispania and Germania, and were assembling in Brundisium, the main jumping-off point for voyages to the east. Caesar's legions were gathering too, marching from all over the Republic to the south of Italy, or taking ships there. Romulus knew that he could easily reenlist in the Twenty-Eighth. There would be little difficulty winning Tarquinius a place either. Although he was older now, the haruspex could still fight, and his medical knowledge equaled, or exceeded, that of most army surgeons. There had been no direct statement about Parthia, but Romulus sensed a growing agitation in the haruspex. His own rootless feelings fed from this.

It made the lack of guidance from Mithras even more frustrating.

"Perhaps Tinia will be more forthcoming," said Tarquinius.

Startled, Romulus grinned. "Jupiter, Greatest and Best," he replied, using the commonest title for the greatest god in Rome. As an Etruscan, the haruspex used his people's name for the deity. "Let's hope he's in a good mood today."

Soon after, they reached the vast temple complex that covered the top of the hill. Originally built by the Etruscans, it was the most important religious shrine in Rome. Pilgrims came from far and wide to worship here and to make their pleas of the god. In front of the gold-roofed temple, a huge statue of Jupiter gazed down over the city, looming, protecting and all-seeing.

Romulus muttered a prayer, just as he had as a boy. His daily appeal then had been to kill Gemellus. Although he had not carried through with this wish, he felt as if, aided by Orcus, the god had orchestrated his last confrontation with the cruel merchant. Today his need felt similarly urgent. What should he do about Fabiola and Caesar? Was journeying to Parthia again a good idea? Should he not resolve things with his sister first? From the corner of his eye, Romulus caught Tarquinius also muttering a request.

Both of them were in the same boat.

Shoving past the throngs of citizens, hawkers and entertainers, they climbed the steps to the entrance to the *cellae*, the sacred rooms that formed the main part of the shrine. There were three, one dedicated to each of the deities, Jupiter, Minerva and Juno. As the preeminent god in Rome, Jupiter's was the central chamber. Joining the end of the queue, the trio shuffled forward in silence. Inside, shaven-headed acolytes walked to and fro, swinging bronze vessels from long chains, and releasing the heavy scents of burning incense and myrrh.

Owing to the large numbers of devotees in the long, narrow *cella*, they were not afforded much time for contemplation. It was a case of bending their knees, placing their offerings—a pile of *denarii*, a miniature Etruscan bowl and two bronze *asses* from Mattius—and making a swift request from the forbidding carved stone face above the altar, before withdrawing.

Making their way outside, they blinked as their eyes adjusted to the bright sunlight. At once the *cella*'s calm was replaced by the noise of the crowds filling the open area between the temple and the statue of Jupiter. The cries of food vendors competed with acrobats, street performers and peddlers of trinkets. Here a mother scolded her wayward children, and there a bevy of painted whores stood, doing their best to encourage men down the nearest alley. Cripples, lepers and the diseased filled every available space, presenting a forest of outstretched palms for those kind enough to open their purses.

"What did you ask for?" Romulus asked Mattius.

"Nothing," answered the urchin.

"Yet you wanted to come in with us."

"To give thanks," came the reply. "And to fulfill my vow."

Romulus gave him a quizzical look.

"You took me away from my stepfather. Jupiter *must* be responsible for that," said Mattius seriously. "I had been praying to him every night, asking for his help. Then you came along."

"I see." Romulus smiled indulgently, before realizing that the boy's belief was no different to his. How else could one explain the removal of a huge obstacle from one's life? In his case, it had been the impossibilities of surviving Carrhae and returning to Rome, while in Mattius' it was escaping from the cruelty he suffered daily at home.

When he looked up, Tarquinius was already heading for the men who sold animals for sacrifice. Romulus hurried after him, buying a healthy-looking fawn-colored kid that caught his eye. The haruspex settled for a plump black hen with bright eyes and clean plumage, and together they shouldered past the soothsayers who instantly converged, offering to reveal their wondrous futures. Mattius bobbed in their wake, amazed at the contempt his friends showed toward the robed augurs. He was even more flabbergasted a few moments later when Tarquinius found a spot right between Jupiter's feet.

"He's a soothsayer?" Mattius whispered.

Romulus nodded.

"Hold this." Tarquinius handed the hen to Mattius, who accepted it with a nervous smile.

Clearing away the trinkets and small offerings left there by hopeful citizens, the haruspex eyed the paving slabs, which were covered in dark red smears. Romulus saw them too, and understood Tarquinius' purpose. The bloodstains told their own story.

Although he had never seen it done, other people had sacrificed here before.

Taking a deep breath, Tarquinius drew his dagger. "Give me the bird," he said in a deep voice. "It is time."

As Mattius obeyed, beads of nervous sweat broke out on Romulus' forehead.

Jupiter, Optimus Maximus, *tell me what to do,* he prayed.

✝

"Welcome," said Fabiola, inclining her head graciously at Caius Trebonius. "All the others are here."

"Good." Trebonius smiled. A short, balding man in middle age, he still had the muscular physique of someone much younger. With shrewd brown eyes and high cheekbones, he was not dissimilar in appearance to Caesar. His height was the most noticeable difference, yet it did not detract from his presence. Like most of the Roman nobility, he carried himself with the utmost confidence. "What of Brutus?"

Fabiola shook her head. "He can't bring himself to join us yet."

"A shame." Trebonius sighed. "Such a son of Rome would be a great addition to our number." With a courteous bow, he headed to the largest of the bedchambers, which had been converted to a meeting room.

Fabiola followed, still not quite believing that someone else who had served the dictator so faithfully—Trebonius had been a suffect consul the year before—now wanted to kill him. Yet he had been one of the first to join her conspiracy. Responding promptly to her invitation, Trebonius had arrived at the brothel to be treated to a lingering massage by Fabiola herself. This was before three of her best-looking prostitutes had led him, unprotesting, away. "Do anything he requests," Fabiola had ordered the trio earlier. "Absolutely anything." They all nodded, eagerly eyeing the weighty purses she'd promised them afterward.

A couple of hours later, Trebonius had been in the most affable of moods. Enjoying a cup of fine wine with Fabiola in the brothel's newly refurbished courtyard, he had been quick to offer his condemnation of Caesar. "The man's lost the plot. Wearing those red calf-length boots like he's a king of Alba Longa. As for topping his costume off with a gilded laurel wreath, well . . ." He patted his thinning hair and smiled. "What the gods give, the gods take away. It isn't for us to hide it under fancy headgear."

Laughing at his joke, Fabiola had leaned over to refill his cup, making sure that her cleavage was on full display. "Some of the people think he's a sovereign already," she said, deliberately alluding to the recent episode when Caesar had been hailed with shouts of "king" during a procession into the city. Reports of the incident had swept through Rome like wildfire.

Trebonius had scowled. "So we're supposed to swallow the lie that he's not king, but Caesar. Pah! It's laughable."

He had gone on to describe why Caesar had to be stopped. It wasn't the dictator's manner or treatment of those who voiced their opposition to him, for in these cases Caesar continued to be mild-mannered and forgiving. Even the tribunes who had ordered the arrest of the man who'd first shouted "king" had escaped with light punishments. Sulla would not have been so lenient, Trebonius admitted. Nor would other previous dictators. It was the absolute power that Caesar had gathered unto himself, eliminating virtually all the power of the Senate and elected magistrates. Half a millennium of democracy had been swept away in less than two years.

Fabiola had deployed the same tactic with the other prominent nobles whom Brutus had mentioned. Although she'd been prepared to sleep with all the men if she had to, that had not proved necessary, which helped her feel better about herself and her promise to Brutus. Thankfully, the tide of ill feeling against Caesar was running high, and all the disgruntled needed was the catalyst to bring them together. Fabiola had proved to be this medium, and in less than a week she had enlisted the help of Marcus Brutus, Cassius Longinus, Servius Galba and Lucius Basilus. Marcus Brutus was her lover's cousin, and the son of Servilia, Caesar's long-term lover. Despite this, he had taken the part of the Republicans and had fought with them at Pharsalus. Welcomed back into the fold afterward thanks to Caesar's magnanimity, he had secured the same pardon for Cassius Longinus, who had served Crassus in Parthia. It was no surprise, therefore, that both men joined the conspiracy together. Marcus Brutus' reasons for taking part were simple. Like Trebonius, he felt aggrieved at the manner in which Caesar had assumed total power, reducing able men like himself to impotent bystanders. However, like Decimus Brutus, Fabiola's lover, he was also a member of the family who had reputedly deposed the last king of Rome five centuries before. In addition, he was the nephew of Cato, the Republican orator who, rather than live under Caesar's rule, had committed suicide after Thapsus. This act had turned Cato into the epitome of Roman aristocratic virtue, and driven Marcus Brutus to write a pamphlet in his praise. Now he was showing his true colors and, in his eyes, his Roman honor, by taking part in the conspiracy.

Fabiola wanted more than five eminent men, however. Fame and public recognition did not guarantee success. Moreover, any attempt on the dictator's life risked onlookers coming to his aid. Despite Caesar's disbanding of his loyal Spanish bodyguards at the beginning of the year, the public and most senators still loved him dearly, and might intervene on his behalf. She could see it happening. More recruits were needed.

Fabiola's prayers had been answered nearly four weeks before, during the Lupercalia, the ancient fertility festival. Watched by huge crowds, Antonius had publicly offered Caesar a royal diadem and asked him to become king. Caesar had demurred twice, ordering the crown to be taken instead to the temple of Jupiter. This clumsy attempt by the dictator to allay suspicions about his aspirations to the monarchy had immediately been negated by a soothsayer's prediction that Parthia could only be conquered by a king. Another soon followed it, alleging that the Senate would vote Caesar the kingship of everywhere except Italy.

These new threats were the final straw, and many new conspirators had joined the plotters in the subsequent days. Their arrival made Fabiola confident that she would soon be revenged on her mother's rapist. There were almost sixty men in the large, well-lit room at the end of the corridor, from all parties and factions within the Senate. Former consuls, tribunes and quaestors rubbed shoulders with ordinary politicians. It boded well for the success of their dark venture.

The most prominent absentee was Brutus, her lover, who had taken to spending much of his time at various temples. As well as praying, he consulted the augurs there over the best course of action to take. Typically, he received differing advice from every man whose palm he greased with silver, which increased his confusion. Sleep began to evade him, and he paced the corridors of his *domus* each night, asking Mithras and Mars for guidance. None was forthcoming, and he grew tired and irritable. Fully aware that Fabiola was conducting large meetings in the Lupanar—she had given up subterfuge—Brutus did not ask her purpose. Yet he did not mention this suspicious activity to anyone either, which gave Fabiola hope that she would win him over before the end.

Reaching the meeting chamber a step behind Trebonius, Fabiola realized that despite her resolve to continue without Brutus, she wanted him by her side. With Romulus determined not to help, she keenly felt the need for some psychological support. The enormity of what they were about to do was becoming more real. Despite Fabiola wishing it were so, Caesar was not just her mother's rapist. He was the greatest leader the Republic had ever seen, and his death would shake it to the core.

†

Holding the black hen firmly by the head, Tarquinius laid it down on the stones. Raising his eyes to the statue of Jupiter looming over them, he prayed, "Great Tinia, accept this sacrifice from a humble servant." With a smooth movement of his blade, the haruspex sliced its head clean off. He quickly transferred his grip, holding the stump of the bird's neck and its body as gouts of arterial blood sprayed onto the ground. Its wings flapped to and fro in a frenzy of useless effort, before gradually relaxing. Holding the hen firmly, Tarquinius studied the pooling red fluid with an intense air of concentration.

Romulus watched agog, looking at the runnels of blood with more interest than he'd paid to a sacrifice in years. He made no effort to try to elicit any information. This was a matter best left to an expert. Beside him, Mattius had been struck dumb.

"East," Tarquinius murmured after long moments of silence. "It's flowing east."

The haruspex' tone increased Romulus' interest at once. "A good omen?" he breathed.

A slow smile spread across Tarquinius' face. "Yes. The spirits that favor mankind dwell in the east. My people also came from there."

"Margiana lies in that direction," added Romulus, his nerves twitching with anticipation.

Tarquinius gave him a tiny nod of acknowledgment.

"Where's that?" asked Mattius.

The haruspex did not answer. He was plucking feathers from the hen to expose its belly. Letting each handful go, he watched to see if they would travel anywhere. Most fell to the ground in a disorganized scatter, but others were caught by a light movement of air. Tarquinius' eyes focused on them like a hawk upon a mouse. Tumbling end over end, the black feathers moved a few steps away from the statue. Then a few more. For half a dozen heartbeats, they lay still, but eventually the breeze tugged them upward, off the top of the hill and into the air over Rome. A few moments later, they were lost to sight as they disappeared eastward.

Romulus' pulse rate shot up, but he didn't interrupt.

Tarquinius became even more solemn. Placing the hen on the ground between Jupiter's great feet, he slit open the thin skin of its belly, taking care not to damage the internal organs. Laying down his knife, he eased out the green ribbon-like intestines, examining them with great care. To Romulus' relief, the haruspex seemed pleased by what he saw, but he revealed nothing. His lips moving faintly, he opened the bird's abdomen completely and removed its small dark red liver. Romulus could tell from its rounded lobes and the even color of its flesh that it was healthy and clear of parasites.

Holding up the liver in his left hand, Tarquinius turned his gaze to the sky, studying the cloud patterns and the direction of the wind. "Great Tinia, receive this offering today," he said at length. "Grant two humble devotees the blessing of your wisdom that we may seek out the best path."

"Three," interjected Mattius. "I also believe."

Worried that this might break the spell, Romulus frowned.

Tarquinius reacted differently. "My apologies," he said to Mattius, inclining his head. He looked up at the statue. "Not forgetting our friend here, Great Tinia."

Mattius settled back on his heels, satisfied.

Romulus felt a surge of admiration for the boy's spirit. Few adults would dare to speak in such a situation.

Turning the liver this way and that, Tarquinius studied it for a long time. Looking dissatisfied, he moved on to the bird's heart, slicing it open to look at the blood within. Next he scrutinized the hen's entire body, from its beak to its vent. When he was finished, he sighed heavily.

Romulus could wait no longer. "What did you see?"

"Not much."

"The blood ran east, though. The feathers flew that way too!" Romulus cried, the first fingers of panic clutching at his guts.

"Which is a good omen," replied Tarquinius.

"Does it mean we should travel east?"

Tarquinius met his gaze squarely. "I don't know. I saw nothing of Margiana."

"Anything about Caesar?" muttered Romulus. "Or Fabiola?"

The haruspex shook his head in a resigned manner.

Romulus overcame his reservations and spent a few moments looking at the butchered hen for himself. He saw nothing. Fighting his disappointment, he glanced at Tarquinius again.

"I saw nothing bad, which we should be grateful for."

"Nothing about my stepfather?" Mattius asked nervously.

"No," Tarquinius answered, managing to sound jovial. "But no guidance for me or Romulus either."

Rallying his spirits, Romulus pushed forward the fawn kid. "There's this still," he said.

Without a word, the haruspex cleaned up the mess of feathers and blood, shunting them all away from the statue. "Get rid of it," he ordered Mattius. As the boy scurried off with his hands full, Tarquinius took the kid from Romulus, subjecting it to a close examination. With a satisfied nod, he stood it where the hen had lain until a moment earlier. Scenting the blood, the animal bleated and made to jump off the stone plinth.

"Quickly, before it gets too stressed," Romulus urged. He grabbed the kid and extended its neck forward. *Jupiter*, he begged silently. *Hear our plea. We need your help.*

Tarquinius wiped his knife clean on his tunic and muttered a quick prayer. Holding the animal's neck to keep it steady, he drew the iron blade across the underside of its throat. "We thank you for your life," he whispered as a crimson tide gushed over his fingers and onto the ground. This time, the blood pooled rather than running away from him. "Shouldn't matter," Tarquinius declared confidently as he flipped the kid onto its back. Following the same procedure as he had with the hen, he cut open the abdomen first.

"Those look healthy," said Romulus as the first loops of pinkish intestine slithered out.

Tarquinius grunted. Silently, he sifted through the whole length from the back passage right up to the small set of stomachs. "Nothing," he announced. Catching Romulus' worried look, he chuckled. "Courage. The liver and heart are usually far more revealing."

Swallowing down the acid that kept climbing his throat, Romulus forced himself to calm down.

Using the point of the knife, Tarquinius freed the kid's liver from its snug position against the diaphragm. A more purple color than the hen's, it was clear of blemishes or visible parasites. Again the haruspex held it skyward in his left hand and made a fervent appeal to Tinia. Romulus added his own request and waited with bated breath as Tarquinius prepared to begin his divination.

It only took a moment for the haruspex' body language to change. Stiffening with surprise, he sucked in a sharp breath. "This is why you and Fabiola are always caught up in the storm," he muttered. "The rumors are true."

Horrified, Romulus was peering over Tarquinius' shoulder before he realized it. "About Caesar?" he said in a whisper. Few things caused more of a stir in Rome than an augur or a witness to a divination relating what he'd seen. The recent notion of Caesar moving the Republic's capital to Alexandria had probably originated like that. Romulus had no wish to be responsible for potentially harmful gossip—but he had to know. "Tell me!"

"They really are planning to kill him. Caesar is not a god after all," Tarquinius said. He gave Romulus a penetrating look. It mattered little to him if Caesar died, but his protégé was different. In more ways than one.

Romulus' nausea grew worse, and he clenched his fists. "Who?"

The haruspex' eyes gazed into the distance. "Olenus knew what he was talking about yet again. It's incredible."

"Your mentor had a vision about Caesar?" Romulus cried, amazed. "That was half a lifetime ago."

Tarquinius fell back to examining the liver.

Romulus did not press his friend further. It was far more important that every last detail was gleaned from the dead kid.

"A lot of men are involved," the haruspex said a moment later. "High-ranking nobles of all backgrounds—former Pompeians and some of Caesar's oldest followers. More than fifty of them."

Romulus' heart sank. This would explain the meetings in the Lupanar that Mattius had reported. There was no mention of a woman, which gave him some hope. Was it possible that Fabiola didn't know? How could it be, given the location? He bit a nail and tried to compose his emotions. "When will they strike?" According to most reports, Caesar would leave for Dacia and Parthia within the week.

Tarquinius prodded the liver with a reddened forefinger before he answered. "Tomorrow, I think," he said at last. "The Ides of March."

Romulus could feel waves of blood pounding in his ears. "So soon?" he repeated. "Are you certain?"

Tarquinius looked again. "Yes."

Romulus' response was instant. "I have to warn him."

"You're sure about that?"

Tarquinius' dark eyes felt all-seeing and, not for the first time, Romulus wondered if Fabiola had told him of her conviction that

Caesar was their father. Or had he seen it at another time? Indecision battered his resolve. Did the haruspex also know the truth of what had happened to his mother? Maybe Caesar *was* guilty of rape. Romulus couldn't bring himself to ask this question. If the answer wasn't what he expected, it might sway him from what his instinct was shouting. He *had* to act, or a gang of nobles would murder Caesar for their own ends. "Yes," he said simply. "I am."

Tarquinius blinked, accepting his decision. "Go to Caesar's house tomorrow morning, then. Before he goes to the Senate."

"That's where it will happen?"

The haruspex nodded.

Romulus' fingers automatically fell to the dagger on his belt. He would need to dig out his *gladius* too. If necessary, he'd defend Caesar with his own life. He owed him no less.

"There is more," said Tarquinius abruptly, sounding troubled. "A woman is involved."

Stricken, Romulus stared down at his friend. His lips framed the name Fabiola.

"I'm sorry." The haruspex looked genuinely sad.

Romulus swallowed hard. Whether his sister would actually take part in the murder was uncertain, but all he could think of was her stabbing Caesar. Aghast, he took a step backward.

At that moment, Mattius came skidding to a halt by their side. "What have I missed?" he cried excitedly.

Romulus turned away, feeling worse than he ever had in his life. "Nothing of importance," he mumbled. Ignoring Tarquinius' cries, he stumbled off into the crowd.

†

As usual, Fabiola played very little part in the discussions. In most, if not all, the conspirators' minds, she was just a woman, albeit a clever and beautiful one. Killing was man's work, one had whispered kindly to Fabiola once. *Little do you know,* she had thought. Nothing could quite remove the stain of former slavery either, especially when it came to murdering the foremost man in Rome. By this stage, though, Fabiola was content to take a back seat and watch as the plot developed.

A pleased murmur went up as Trebonius entered. Surrounded by nearly two dozen chairs, a long table occupied the center of the crowded room. Jugs of watered-down wine and plates of bread, fruit and olives covered much of its polished surface. The seating wasn't sufficient for all those present, so the most important members sat while the rest stood behind. Naturally, a chair had been reserved for Trebonius.

"At last," said Marcus Brutus, tapping his fingers on the table top. "A word, if you will?"

Making his apologies to those he passed, Trebonius sat down beside Marcus Brutus, who immediately began muttering in his ear.

Fabiola turned away to hide her amusement. Although he had been one of the last to join, Brutus was now one of the main leaders and acted as if he had been all along. Nodding to Benignus, who would remain outside the door to ensure no one eavesdropped, Fabiola quietly shut the door. Glad of her discreet position, she scanned the assembled men. Servius Galba, a short man with protruding eyes, was sitting beside his main crony, Lucius Basilus, a broad-shouldered figure with a bull neck. Both men bore grudges against the dictator, which was why they'd been so quick to join up. Thanks to his association with Caesar, Galba had failed in his attempt to become consul just before the general had crossed the Rubicon, and Basilus had rightfully been denied a provincial command because of his murky business dealings. Fabiola liked neither of them, but their anger at Caesar justified their presence.

She'd first met Cassius Longinus, one of Crassus' former deputies, at a banquet five years before. Fabiola had spoken with him about Carrhae, and heard the true horrors of what had befallen Crassus' army. Hearing of Romulus' involvement, the grizzled soldier had tried to soften the blow, which endeared him to Fabiola still. Catching Longinus' eye, she smiled, and was rewarded with a courteous nod. *I must introduce him to Romulus,* she reflected. A pang of guilt clawed at her. *If we ever make up.* Fabiola shoved the disquieting thought away. *Deal with that later. Concentrate on the moment.*

The conspirators were now so numerous that Fabiola had high hopes of success. While few had the courage to strike the first blow, they would follow where others led. *Like a pack of dogs turning on the weakest,* she thought. *Ugly, but effective.* Fortunately, Caesar would be defenseless. In public, members of the nobility wore the toga and carried no weapons. The dictator was no exception. Alarmed by the dark rumors, Antonius and other close associates had asked Caesar to re-form his Spanish bodyguards, but he had refused, stating that he had no wish to live in fear or under constant protection.

Contempt filled Fabiola. Whether Caesar's refusal was driven by his arrogance, or his belief that, thanks to his restoration of the peace and raft of new reforms, no ill feeling against him remained, she did not know. Whatever the dictator's reasons, he was now easy prey to a band of determined assassins.

"Gentlemen." Marcus Brutus rapped on the table with his knuckles. "If we could begin?"

His words brought all the conversations to an end, and an expectant hush fell. Pent-up with tension, Fabiola waited. None of the nobles knew it, but she was more eager than any of them for Caesar's death.

"During our last meeting, we agreed that the best date would be the Ides of March," Marcus Brutus began.

"The Ides? That's tomorrow," said a portly senator, looking nervous.

"Congratulations," replied Marcus Brutus in an acid tone. He glared around the table. "Time has moved fast, but we've committed ourselves now."

A titter of nervous laughter moved around the room.

Satisfied, Marcus Brutus sat back in his chair. No one was trying to back out.

"Caesar hasn't been well for the last few days," another man chipped in. "He might not attend the Senate tomorrow."

"There are many important issues to be addressed before he departs for Dacia," Longinus demurred. "Caesar won't want to miss those debates."

"The man is a demon for work," agreed Trebonius. "He'd need to be half dead not to come."

"Why not send someone to his house first thing to make sure?" suggested Basilus.

"Good idea," cried Marcus Brutus. "Any volunteers?"

Before anyone could answer, a familiar voice spoke in the corridor. "Where's Fabiola?"

Fabiola's stomach turned over.

She wasn't the only one to recognize Brutus' deep tones. Like small boys caught thieving, the nobles waited to see what would happen next.

Benignus cleared his throat uneasily. "Sir?"

"Is she in there?" Brutus demanded. "Answer me!"

"Yes, sir," mumbled the huge slave, crumbling before Brutus' temper.

"Stand aside."

Fabiola moved away from the door, which opened a heartbeat later. Brutus entered, scowling. Fabiola and he locked eyes. "Dearest," she said lamely, unsure what else to say. "What a surprise."

Without answering, Brutus looked around the room. His mouth opened with astonishment at the number of men present, and their identity. Many would not meet his gaze, but Marcus Brutus, Longinus and Trebonius did.

"Well met, cousin," said Marcus Brutus. "We have missed your company."

"What's all this about?" cried Brutus, looking at Fabiola.

"I think you know," said Trebonius, intervening.

Brutus flushed. "You're intending to murder Caesar?"

"Rid the Republic of a despot, more like," Longinus butted in. "And make things how they were again."

There was a loud rumble of agreement.

Brutus scanned the nobles' faces for several heartbeats. "I see," he said heavily.

"Look how many men are present, cousin," said Marcus Brutus gently. "This is not just a collection of lunatics. All shades of opinion are represented here. What unites us is our hatred of tyranny."

Brutus stared into his cousin's eyes. "Tyranny?" he whispered.

The conflict in his voice made Fabiola's heart bleed. Much as she wanted him to join them, the pain he was suffering tore at her conscience.

"Yes," Marcus Brutus replied emphatically. "That is how Caesar rules the Republic. What is the Senate but an empty vessel? What are we now but his puppets?"

Angry mutters met this comment.

Brutus sighed.

Mithras above, Fabiola thought. *Convince him, please.* She moved to her lover's side. "You know it's true," she said. "All that power has gone to Caesar's head."

"The augurs are giving bad omens for tomorrow, while on every corner the people are calling him king," he whispered. "King of Rome."

"Will you join us?" asked Trebonius.

Brutus chewed his lip. Beside him, Fabiola scarcely dared breathe.

Marcus Brutus pushed back his chair and stood. "Our ancestors rid this city of its last tyrant. Now the time has come to repeat that painful task. It is our duty to be part of it," he declared.

There was a long silence.

Fabiola burned to say something, to persuade Brutus of their righteousness, but she held back. Much as she wanted him on board, this was his decision alone. The others knew that too—she could feel it—but would her lover's strong moral sense win out over his fierce loyalty to Caesar?

Marcus Brutus extended his right hand. "What do you say?"

There was the slightest pause, and then Brutus took his cousin's grip. "Count me in. For the good of the Republic."

A combined sigh of relief filled the air. Fabiola's was loudest of all. At this late stage, the conspirators could not allow their cover to be blown. If he'd refused, Brutus would have signed his own death warrant.

"When is it to happen?" Brutus inquired.

"Tomorrow," replied Marcus Brutus. "Where the Senate meets."

To his credit, Brutus barely blinked. "I see," he said. "Caesar is ill, though. Are you sure he'll attend?"

"He might need some convincing," admitted Longinus. "We were just wondering who could visit him in the morning."

"I'll do it," Brutus offered.

"You're sure?"

He nodded firmly.

"Good," said Marcus Brutus with a smile. "The rest of us will assemble at the Senate early. We've got a good reason too—Longinus' son is to assume the toga tomorrow."

"Should we attack him the moment he arrives?" mused Basilus.

"I think not. We don't want members of the public to see it happen," interjected Longinus. "Let the tyrant descend from his litter and make his way inside."

"I'll go in close," volunteered Cimber, a former Republican. "Request he allow my brother back to Italy."

"We can surround him, all pleading the same case," added Marcus Brutus. "Allay any suspicions he might have."

"Then produce our weapons," said Longinus with an evil grin. Opening the long wooden case for his stylus, he produced an ivory-handled dagger and thrust it forward viciously. "Finish the job."

Everyone's gaze was drawn to the oiled blade, but not one man spoke against their intended course.

"What about Antonius?" asked Brutus a moment later. "He's not likely to stand by while Caesar is slaughtered. Should we kill him too?"

Longinus' eyes narrowed. "Why not? He's such an arrogant bastard."

"Good idea," agreed Galba. "Gods know how he'll respond if we don't." Antonius' fierce temper was renowned throughout Italy.

Thank you, Mithras, thought Fabiola, delight filling her. *I will be rid of two monsters at one stroke.*

"No," declared Marcus Brutus loudly. "We are not a band of common thieves. This is being done for the Republic. Once Caesar is dead, free elections can be held and the Senate will be able to run matters as it always has. Antonius will not argue with that." He glanced around the room, daring anyone to challenge him. Few had the willpower to hold his gaze for long.

"If you're sure," said Longinus, looking doubtful.

"I am," growled Marcus Brutus. "So we need someone to distract Antonius—detain him outside maybe."

"I can do that too," Brutus offered.

"You don't want to be in on the act itself?" asked Marcus Brutus.

"Killing Caesar might be the best thing to do, but that doesn't mean I actually want to stick a knife in him," said Brutus.

"No," his cousin agreed. "Fair enough."

"Hold on," frowned Trebonius. "You and Antonius hate each other's guts."

"Exactly," Brutus retorted with a smug look. "It's time to kiss and make up."

Longinus swore. "Antonius will never forgive you when he discovers why you did it."

Brutus laughed sourly. "Do I care? He'll have to live knowing that he might have saved Caesar if I hadn't stopped him."

Fabiola suddenly realized the damage that her dalliance with Antonius had done to her lover. He was good at hiding it, except at moments like this. She moved her hand to touch his. "I'm sorry," she whispered.

Brutus gave her a small nod, which eased Fabiola's pain a fraction. Expert at reading his emotions, she could see that he was still torn by his decision to join the conspirators. His anger at Antonius was in part a knee-jerk reaction to this. Things were moving too fast for him to stop and think, though.

"It is agreed then. My cousin will persuade Caesar to attend the Senate, and then he'll also distract Antonius," said Marcus Brutus, pressing on. "When the tyrant enters, Cimber will approach him first, imploring clemency for his brother. The rest of us will close in, adding to the clamor."

"What signal should we use for it to begin?" asked Longinus. "A special word, perhaps?"

"I'll pull his toga off his shoulder," announced Casca, a stout man with a red face. "To give us more of a target."

Growls of approval left the nobles' throats. Euphoric that her long-held dream was about to be realized, Fabiola closed her eyes and thanked Mithras and Jupiter from the bottom of her heart. *Mother will be avenged. Tomorrow.*

What of Romulus? her inner voice suddenly asked. *What if he's right and you're not?*

Ruthlessly, Fabiola shoved the thought away. She would countenance only one possibility: Caesar was the guilty one, and tomorrow he would pay.

XXVII

THE IDES OF MARCH

At first Romulus thought he would go straight to the Lupanar to have it out with Fabiola. After his initial shock had abated, a cold fury had swept his soul at her boldness. He had to admit that it was unsurprising that his sister had the courage to carry on with her plan. Their mother had to have been immensely strong to survive the life of torment she'd led, and her blood flowed in Fabiola's veins just as it did in his. Velvinna had been trying to do her best for them, and Romulus doubted that he could have endured what she had. Yet his twin had done so for years by constantly having sex with men against her will. Fabiola had eventually done well from prostitution, but that didn't mean that it hadn't caused her irreparable damage. Maybe that was where her ruthless streak came from. Plotting her revenge must have been the only way Fabiola had managed to survive, Romulus concluded.

In his mind, it still didn't excuse planning to murder the Republic's leader. Without Caesar admitting to Velvinna's rape, how could Fabiola *really* know? She couldn't, and Romulus simply wasn't prepared to murder a man on a hunch, especially when it was the person who had granted him manumission. If at all possible, he wasn't going to let his sister and a gang of disgruntled nobles do so either.

Romulus decided that it was too risky approaching Fabiola at this late stage. If she was prepared to take the final step of killing Caesar, then she wouldn't let him stop her. The heavies outside the Lupanar didn't give a damn who he was. He didn't want to end up with his throat slit. Damping down his anger, Romulus resolved to take Tarquinius' advice and visit Caesar's palatial *domus* early the next morning. He would make no mention of Fabiola. Romulus didn't want his twin executed. He would deal with her later himself.

Returning to the veterans' residence, he went looking for Secundus. The one-armed ex-soldier was the *Pater* of the Mithraeum, which meant that he was the leader of more than fifty hardbitten men who'd served in the legions for many years. In his brief time there, Romulus had come to like the pensive, middle-aged figure who often listened rather than spoke. When Secundus did open his mouth, his words were invariably wise, which reminded him of Tarquinius. Romulus had not been surprised to find that the two knew each other from the past. He found Secundus in the large courtyard, enjoying the watery spring sunshine.

"Well met." Secundus smiled. "Is Tarquinius with you?"

"No," Romulus replied awkwardly. "I left him at the temple on the Capitoline."

Secundus raised an eyebrow.

Romulus let it all out. Seeing the hen's blood and feathers moving east, but learning little else from it. The kid he'd bought. Tarquinius' alarm at what he saw in its liver.

Secundus sat bolt upright. "The danger to Caesar is real?"

"Tarquinius thinks so. It is to happen at the Senate tomorrow," Romulus muttered. "I'm not going to stand by and let it happen. Caesar has to be warned."

"He needs protection too," growled Secundus. "What was he thinking to disband those Spanish bodyguards?"

"That's why I came to you," said Romulus. "I thought perhaps your men could help."

"Of course."

Greatly relieved, Romulus sat for some time, discussing with Secundus the best ways to deploy the ex-soldiers the next morning. Finally they decided that surrounding the dictator's litter the moment he arrived would be the safest option. Their mere presence and determination would unsettle, or even put off, the conspirators. If they attacked regardless, they would pay a bloody price with little chance of success. Politicians could not fight army veterans.

Tarquinius returned some time later, prompting Romulus to wonder if he'd seen anything else in the kid's organs. A monumental wave of shame struck him as he thought of Brennus, whom he'd forgotten during the drama. A muttered conversation with the haruspex revealed that he had discerned no more of interest. This did little to ease Romulus' guilt about neglecting to ask about the big Gaul, but he had to put it aside. What was going to happen tomorrow outweighed all else.

"Are you all right?" Tarquinius' scarred face was concerned.

Romulus didn't want to talk. "I need a good night's sleep, that's all."

"You're still going to warn Caesar?"

"Of course," he snapped. "Wouldn't you?"

Tarquinius shook his head. "It is not for me to interfere with another's destiny. Besides, Rome did too many terrible things to my people for me to help it now."

"That was hundreds of years ago."

"I have a direct link with the past," said Tarquinius sadly. "It is thanks to the Romans that I am the last haruspex."

"Of course. I apologize," Romulus muttered, his understanding of his friend's hatred of Rome deepening. Yet, despite his strong feelings, the haruspex was making no effort to stop him warning Caesar, which proved he was staying true to his beliefs. In turn, this strengthened Romulus' desire to do the same. Thinking of Caesar, Fabiola and his relationship with them both, he was startled by Tarquinius' next words.

"You could use your own powers to divine the matter."

"No," said Romulus, hating the fact that his refusal would cause Tarquinius pain. "I'm sorry. Predicting the future is not for me."

Tarquinius smiled in acceptance. "A man can only be what he is meant to be. Kind. Loyal and courageous. A true soldier. That is more than enough."

Embarrassed but proud, Romulus threw him a grateful look. He would follow his heart then. Tomorrow he would warn Caesar, and prevent his murder. Then he would have it out with Fabiola. Despite her actions, Romulus did not want the bad blood between them to continue.

What if she's right, though? his inner voice asked. *If Caesar raped your mother, does he not deserve to die?*

He didn't do it, thought Romulus fiercely. *He's not that type of man.*

Keeping this uppermost in his mind, he took his leave of Tarquinius and Secundus. Finding Mattius outside the door of the *domus* like a faithful puppy, Romulus asked him to return at dawn the next day. The urchin clearly knew nothing of what the haruspex had seen, so Romulus glossed over the matter, saying that he had left because he was feeling unwell. The revelation needed to remain top secret, and while Mattius was loyal, he was still only a boy.

After a brief and uneventful visit to the Mithraeum, Romulus retired to his small room. Afternoon had passed, and night was falling. It was time to get what rest he could before the morning.

The Ides of March.

†

Romulus' dreams were vivid and disquieting. Caesar, Fabiola and Tarquinius featured in a variety of violent and distorted sequences that had him tossing and turning all night. Drenched in sweat when he awoke, Romulus could not remember a single detail, just the identities of those he'd encountered. Normally, he would have asked Tarquinius about the nightmares, but not today. Thoroughly unsettled, he went outside to see what time it was. It was still dark, but the cobbled courtyard was already full of Secundus' men, readying themselves for combat. Wearing mail for protection under their cloaks, they had discarded their bronze-bowl crested helmets and heavy *scuta* in favor of remaining inconspicuous.

Taking heart from their determined faces, Romulus headed back to his room. He strapped on his *gladius* as well as his dagger, but chose not to wear armor or carry a shield. His weapons alone would arouse the suspicions of Caesar's guards, and he could not afford the risk of failure. Last of all, Romulus pinned his two gold *phalerae* to his tunic. These, his proudest possessions, would hopefully gain him an audience with the dictator, and also trigger his memory of their three meetings. If Caesar remembered him, he would be more likely to believe Romulus' warning. He was not surprised to find the haruspex waiting by the entrance, his battleaxe hanging from his back. Romulus was touched by this loyalty. Whatever his feelings about Caesar and Rome, Tarquinius would stand by his comrade.

"Good luck."

"Thank you," Romulus replied. "Hopefully I won't need it."

"Fabiola?" It was the first time the haruspex had mentioned his sister since the divination.

"I won't say a word about her. Who knows what will happen once the conspirators are arrested, though?" Romulus gave a resigned shrug. "That's up to the gods. With luck, I'll get to settle things with her afterward."

Tarquinius' dark eyes were unreadable. "See you at Pompey's complex."

Quickly they gripped forearms and then Romulus drew wide the door. Stepping outside into the predawn cool, he found Mattius waiting. They set off in silence, but it wasn't long before the boy's curiosity got the better of him.

"Where are we going?"

"Caesar's *domus*."

Mattius' eyes widened. "Why? Did Tarquinius see something important yesterday?"

"Yes." Romulus didn't elaborate further.

He didn't need to. Rome was chock-full of rumors and, while young, Mattius was streetwise. "Someone wants to kill Caesar. That's it, isn't it?" he piped. "Why else would you be going to his house at this hour, wearing a *gladius*?"

Despite his grim mood, Romulus grinned. "No flies on you," he admitted.

"I knew it!" Mattius crowed. There was a short pause. "Is it just you and me?"

Romulus heard the tremor in his voice and looked down. Despite his obvious fear, Mattius was clutching a rusty kitchen knife, which must have been hidden under his tunic. His heart filled at the boy's courage. It did not matter to him who ruled Rome, or whether Caesar lived or died. He was here for one reason: to show solidarity with his friend. Romulus stopped in his tracks. "You've got real guts, lad, but you won't have to do any fighting," he said, patting Mattius' bony shoulder. "The veterans are coming along. Tarquinius too."

"Good," Mattius replied, relieved. "I'll be ready just in case."

Thinking of himself as a youngster, Romulus hid his smile.

A short time later, they reached Caesar's current *domus*, a palatial affair on the Palatine Hill. The sun was rising now, revealing the construction of a new high-pointed exterior intended to make it resemble a temple. Building had only just started, so almost the entire front of the building was obscured by scaffolding, which concealed the pair until they had reached the entrance.

"Halt!" shouted one of four soldiers before the massive iron-studded doors. "Declare yourselves."

"Romulus, veteran legionary of the Twenty-Eighth, and Mattius, a boy from the Caelian Hill," Romulus answered, stepping out of the shadows.

The sentry's lip curled. "Your business?"

Romulus half turned, so his *phalerae* glittered in the torchlight. He was pleased to see the soldiers' eyes widen. Few men earned two gold medals. "I seek an audience with Caesar," he said.

"Now?" scoffed a second guard. "It's not even *hora prima*."

"It's very urgent."

"I don't give a shit," replied the first man. "On your way. Come back this afternoon, and you might be lucky."

"I can't wait that long."

The sentries exchanged an incredulous look before the first lowered his *pilum* to point at Romulus' chest. "I suggest you and your little friend fuck off," he growled. "Now."

Romulus didn't move a step. "Tell Caesar that it's the slave who killed the Ethiopian bull. The one he granted manumission to."

Romulus' extraordinary calm and outlandish claim were off-putting, and more than ordinary soldiers were used to dealing with. Scowling, the first guard went inside to confer with his *optio*. The junior officer emerged a moment later, pulling on his helmet. Bleary-eyed and irritable, he listened to Romulus' request in silence. "And your purpose?" he demanded.

"That's for Caesar's ears only, sir," Romulus answered, careful to keep his voice neutral. If he didn't play this just right, his mission would fail, and he couldn't let that happen.

The *optio* looked at him long and hard. "Where did you win those?" He pointed at Romulus' *phalerae*.

"One at Ruspina, the other at Thapsus, sir."

"What for?"

Romulus briefly described his efforts, and the officer's face soon changed. "Stay put," he ordered, disappearing inside.

Ignoring the legionaries' glowers, Romulus leaned against the scaffolding. Mattius stayed close, more intimidated than his big friend. They waited for perhaps half an hour before the *optio* reappeared.

"Caesar will see you," he said. "Leave your weapons here."

The guards goggled at this unexpected outcome.

Bending his head to conceal his grin, Romulus unbuckled his belt and handed it to Mattius. "I'll be back shortly," he said. "Don't say a word to these fools," he added under his breath.

The boy nodded, delighted with the responsibility.

Following the *optio*, Romulus entered the *atrium*. Few torches were burning, but there was sufficient light to see that the house was decorated in opulent fashion. Richly patterned, well-laid mosaic covered the floors, and the stuccoed walls were painted with striking scenes. Beautiful Greek statues filled every alcove, and through the open doors of the *tablinum* Romulus heard the patter of water from a fountain in the garden.

The *optio* led him to one of the many rooms around the central courtyard. Compared to the rest of the house, this was decorated in Spartan fashion. Apart from a striking bust of Caesar, the only other furniture was a crowded desk, a leather-backed chair and a pair of tables groaning under rolls of parchment and papyrus. A young slave was placing oil lamps here and there, lending the chamber a warm golden glow.

Indicating that Romulus should stand before the desk, the *optio* retreated to the door. They waited in silence for some moments, and Romulus began to wonder what Fabiola was doing at that exact instant. Making her last preparations, no doubt. Would she be present at the Senate later? Sudden panic overtook him at the thought of defending Caesar from his sister. *Jupiter, don't let that happen,* Romulus prayed. That would be too much to bear. *How would you react?* his inner voice asked.

"Legionary Romulus," said a voice from behind him. "You rise early."

He spun around. Wearing a plain white toga, Caesar stood framed in the doorway. Beside him, the *optio* had snapped to rigid attention. Romulus did likewise. "My apologies, sir," he said.

Rubbing a hand through his thinning hair, Caesar walked to the desk and sat down. "I hope your reason's good," he said dryly. "Dawn is only just breaking."

Romulus flushed, but did not apologize. "It is, sir." Studying the dictator with a new interest, he was startled by the strong resemblance Caesar's features bore to his own. Coincidence, Romulus told himself. It had to be coincidence.

"Well, get on with it, man," said Caesar, staring at him. Lines of exhaustion had drawn gray bags under his eyes. Covering his mouth with his hand, he began to cough. "This damn chest of mine. Tell me."

Romulus looked pointedly at the *optio,* and the slave, who was now tidying the tables. "I'd rather you were the only one to hear it, sir."

"Would you, by Jupiter?" Caesar rubbed his chin, considering. "Very well," he said. "Leave us." He jerked his head.

The slave obeyed at once, but the *optio* started forward. "Don't trust him, sir!"

Caesar laughed. "My enemies are many, but I don't think they include this man. I freed him from slavery for killing an Ethiopian bull, *optio,* and have twice decorated him on the field of battle since. A more loyal soldier doesn't exist in the Republic. Go, and shut the door behind you."

With a beetroot face, the officer did as he was told.

"He's steadfast, but suspicious," said Caesar. "I should be grateful, I suppose."

"Sir." Romulus didn't dare agree or disagree.

To his surprise, the dictator didn't launch straight into a barrage of questions about his reasons for being here. "How's life treating you since your discharge?"

"Very well, thank you, sir."

"Your farm satisfactory?"

"Yes, sir," said Romulus with as much enthusiasm as he could muster.

Eagle-eyed, Caesar chuckled. "Tilling the fields isn't quite so exciting as standing in a shield wall, is it?"

Romulus grinned. "No, sir."

"A healthier occupation, though, if you can stick it," said Caesar.

"Funny you should say so, sir," Romulus blurted. "I was thinking of volunteering for your new campaign."

"Soldiers like you are always welcome," Caesar replied, clearly pleased. A thoughtful look crossed his long, thin face. "Didn't you serve at Carrhae?"

"Yes, sir," Romulus answered, vivid memories filling his brain. "I wouldn't mind another lick at the Parthians either."

"That's the spirit. Why don't you come along to the Senate this morning," Caesar suggested brightly. "The senators would benefit from hearing what it's like to face them in battle."

"I'd be honored, sir," said Romulus. "Except I'm here to ask you not to attend the debates today."

"My wife has been unhappy too." Caesar frowned. "Why shouldn't I go?"

"It's too dangerous, sir," Romulus cried. "There's a plot to kill you!"

The dictator grew very calm. "Where did you hear about this?"

"From a friend, sir."

"Who is?"

Romulus paused, worried how the other would react. "A haruspex, sir."

"One of those?" Caesar scoffed. "They're liars and cheats to a man. If I'd lived my life by what augurs say, I'd never have conquered Gaul, or the Republic. Anywhere, for that matter."

"This man is no charlatan, sir," Romulus protested. "He served with me under Crassus, and predicted the defeat at Carrhae and many other things that came to pass. His abilities are second to none."

"Hmm." Caesar regarded him steadily. "So what did he see?"

"A plot to kill you at the Senate House, sir. Scores of men are involved."

"And they are to strike today?"

Romulus swallowed the lump in his throat. "Yes, sir. Beware the Ides of March."

"Has your friend ever been wrong in his prophecies? Are they sometimes of uncertain meaning?"

"Of course, sir. That's the nature of haruspicy."

Caesar barked a contemptuous laugh. "I love it! It's the same damn reason that soothsayers give to explain the fact that they make up every damn detail that comes out of their mouths. There has been talk of assassination for months, and it's all hot air. Why would anyone kill me? After decades of infighting, the Republic is at peace. Your friend is imagining things. Believe what you will, Romulus, but don't ask me to do the same. There are important matters that need to be discussed in the Senate today. I have to be there, and I see no reason not to attend."

Undeterred, Romulus fell back on his reserve tactic. "I've taken the liberty of rounding up some loyal veterans, sir. About fifty of them. They'll be at the Senate by now."

"One of my ex-soldiers sees fit to gather a motley crew of body-guards, eh?" Caesar shook his head in amazement.

Romulus realized his boldness. "Sorry, sir," he faltered. "I didn't mean to act out of turn."

"From the humblest origins spring the finest virtues," murmured Caesar. He smiled. "On the contrary, you did well, and I thank you."

Relief flooded through Romulus. "So the veterans can come into the Senate with you, sir?"

Caesar's eyes flashed with anger. "No, they may not."

"I don't understand, sir," Romulus stammered.

"Your motives were noble," said Caesar with a nod of gratitude. "But do not forget who I am. As the best general in the history of the Republic, I cannot arrive at the Senate accompanied by a ragtag selection of retired soldiers. It's beneath my dignity."

"Just this once, sir," Romulus pleaded. "If there's no danger, you can laugh it off as a spontaneous demonstration of your men's love for you. If trouble does occur, you'll be safe."

Caesar considered his request for a moment, giving Romulus some hope. Then he shook his head. "No. I will not live in fear when there is no need."

Romulus' spirits plummeted, before he had a brainwave. Secundus and the veterans could wait outside the Senate regardless. At the first sign of trouble, they could rush inside. It was more risky for the dictator than if they accompanied him, but it was better than nothing. "Very well, sir," he said. "May I still come?" *One decent soldier is worth more than twenty fat senators*, he thought. *Perhaps I can hold them off until Secundus and the others storm in.*

Romulus hadn't counted on Caesar's incisive mind. "You can, but your comrades are to go home," he ordered. "No hanging around in case there's trouble. Clear?"

Romulus gave him a despairing glance. "Yes, sir."

"Give me your word that you'll tell them to disappear." Caesar stuck out his right hand in the soldier's fashion.

"How do you know I'll keep it?" asked Romulus.

"Because you're a good man. I can see that," Caesar replied. "You're also a soldier of mine."

"Very well, sir." Cursing the dictator's perception, Romulus accepted the grip.

"Good," Caesar muttered. "I need some time now to prepare for the day ahead. Have a think about what to say regarding Carrhae. Get yourself to Pompey's complex for *hora sexta*. That's when I'll arrive."

"Sir." Helpless before Caesar's power, Romulus felt sick to his stomach. Tarquinius wouldn't make up something like an assassination. The dictator didn't know that, of course, and was taking him for a loyal but superstitious soldier. He had to make one more attempt. "I—"

"Not another word," said Caesar firmly. "I appreciate your concern." He raised a hand to his mouth. "*Optio!*"

To Romulus' dismay, the junior officer appeared at once. "Sir?"

"Accompany this soldier to the door," Caesar ordered. "Tell the majordomo to count out twenty *aurei* for him."

"That's not necessary, sir." Romulus protested. "I didn't do it for money."

"Nonetheless, your fealty will be rewarded." Caesar waved his dismissal. "I'll see you later."

"Sir!" Giving the dictator his best possible salute, Romulus marched to the door.

The bemused *optio* took him back to the entrance hall, and a few moments later, Romulus emerged into the street, clutching a heavy leather purse.

The sentries had changed, but Mattius was still there. He focused on the clinking pouch like a vulture on carrion. "Caesar believed you then?" he cried.

"No," Romulus replied grimly. "He wouldn't listen. This is just for being loyal."

Mattius' face fell. "What are we going to do?"

Romulus thought for a moment. "Go to the Lupanar," he declared. If she was there, perhaps Fabiola could be persuaded to call off the assassination. He doubted it, and his fear that her men would knife him to death resurfaced. Romulus scowled and set out anyway. It was clutching at straws, but what else could he do?

He was somewhat consoled by the sight of Decimus Brutus peering from an approaching litter Romulus hoped that Fabiola's lover, as a man who had not been at any of the meetings in the Lupanar was also a man of principle. Maybe Brutus' purpose was the same as his.

Romulus muttered a prayer to Jupiter that this was the case.

✝

Fabiola's final preparations began when Brutus left for Caesar's house. Her lover's resolve still seemed firm, which relieved and terrified her at the same time. Concerned that he would reconsider his position and back out of the conspiracy, she had not let him out of her sight since the meeting the previous evening. Fabiola had also made a concerted effort to divert Brutus' attention from the matter at hand. She had commanded the kitchen slaves to prepare a sumptuous feast, and ordered in the best entertainers available. Between courses of pork, fish and various types of fowl, they watched Greek athletes covered in oil wrestle naked on the floor and poets recite their latest satires. Actors had performed short comedy pieces, and acrobats amazed them with their skills. On the surface, Fabiola's ploy had appeared to be a success. Brutus had laughed and smiled, appearing to enjoy the performers' efforts, yet she knew him well enough to see that he was preoccupied. Naturally, the only thought in his mind had been Caesar's murder. Behind her vivacious exterior, Fabiola had been able to think of little else herself, but she hadn't dared to bring it up in conversation. For his part, Brutus had been content not to mention it either.

Although Fabiola did not like admitting it, Brutus' considerable qualms about joining their number had forced her to recognize the previously unacknowledged doubt that lurked in the furthest recesses of her own heart. Whether it had been present before Romulus' refusal to join her, she wasn't sure, but her brother's steadfast support for the dictator was hard to disregard completely. He had always been full of honorable ideas, such as wanting to free the Republic's slaves. Despite his traumatic experiences in the arena and Crassus' army, this quality seemed to have strengthened. Fabiola could see it in Romulus' upright bearing, and in the way Tarquinius spoke about him. Even the way he'd been able to walk away from Gemellus spoke volumes about his moral fiber.

What, on the other hand, had she become? The question had kept Fabiola awake all night long. She'd done her best to rise above the degradation of her former profession but now Fabiola had to face up to the fact that it had tainted her. The most obvious result was her total distrust of men. Her years in the Lupanar had taught her that they were not to be trusted in any shape or form. Brutus was the sole exception to the rule, his unswervingly honorable conduct earning him the exemption. Was it any surprise, therefore, Fabiola asked herself, that she presumed Caesar to be her father when he'd tried to rape her? Had she been overreacting?

No, her heart screamed. It hadn't just been the look in the dictator's eyes, but his voice, his words, that had convinced her of his guilt. But when Fabiola forced her mind to reexamine what had happened that winter's night, she came to a different conclusion. Caesar had admitted nothing. The fact that he had attacked her did not *prove* that he was the rapist. Romulus was right about that much. Her conscience stung by this idea, Fabiola had lain staring at the ceiling, knowing that the plans she had fostered could not be stopped now. Too many angry, powerful men were involved.

When Brutus woke, fresh-faced and still set on his course, Fabiola had put on her best mask to disguise her mixed feelings. Her lover must have sensed something was wrong. "What we're going to do is the best thing, my love," he'd murmured. "For Rome. For all of us."

Fabiola hadn't dared to talk about it. Part of her was exultant, and part terrified. Shoring up her belief that Brutus was right, she had wished him luck and kissed him good-bye. Now, sitting alone by her dressing table, she was again plagued by doubt. If only she could verify, or discount, Caesar's guilt, and discover whether his actions really signified the death of the Republic. A thought struck her. Tarquinius might be able to answer these questions.

Would he do it, though?

Harsh reality sank in at once. It was far too late for such measures. Even if Tarquinius were to discover that Caesar was innocent of all charges, the conspirators would not be swayed from their course. Too many of them stood to profit from the dictator's death, not least Marcus Brutus. Her role in the assassination might have been influential, but Fabiola realized that it would probably have happened eventually anyway.

Telling herself that her gut reaction to Caesar had been correct, Fabiola headed to the Lupanar. Best to keep to her ordinary daily routine for as long as possible. While she intended to be at the Forum when Caesar arrived, she did not want to attract any attention to herself either. What she needed was to take her mind off it, Fabiola decided, and the best way to do that was to relax in a hot bath. Entering the brothel, she ordered Benignus to admit no one.

She had no idea of the impact that the casual order would have.

†

Arriving outside the brothel a short time later, Romulus marched straight up to the entrance. A trio of men were on guard, led by a shaven-headed brute who was covered in recently healed scars. Romulus recognized him as Benignus, the doorman who'd nearly died after Scaevola's attack, but had survived thanks to Tarquinius. He nodded at him in a friendly manner. "I'd like to speak to Fabiola."

"She's not receiving visitors," said Benignus civilly enough.

Romulus laughed. "I'm her brother!"

"I know who you are," Benignus replied, moving right in front of the door.

"Let me in, then!"

Benignus' voice hardened. "No visitors, I said."

Leering, his companions moved to stand by his side.

Romulus considered his options. He was a skilled professional soldier, but Benignus alone was as strong as an ox. The other two looked tough too. There was no guarantee that he'd emerge unscathed from a fight with them. Even if he did, would Fabiola listen to him?

"I don't want to fight you," he said. There was too much at stake.

"Good," said Benignus.

While his comrades sneered, Romulus was pleased to see a hint of relief flash across the doorman's eyes. Benignus was only doing his job. Cursing the luck that had pitted him against his own sister, Romulus beckoned to Mattius and together they headed for the Campus Martius. Situated on a plain to the northwest of the city, it was at least a quarter of an hour's walk away. It was some time until Caesar would arrive at Pompey's complex there, but Romulus didn't know where else to go. The time for prayers was past, he thought, taking comfort from the hard grip of his *gladius*. Another battle loomed. Even as a free citizen, in Rome, it could find him. Romulus set his jaw. Very well. It didn't matter whether five men attacked Caesar, or five hundred. He'd made his decision, and would stick to it.

Looking down at Mattius, Romulus was struck by a pang of conscience. It wasn't just about him any more. *If I die defending Caesar, the boy will be back where he was within a week.* Even though she worked in a fuller's workshop, Mattius' mother was incapable of providing for her two children, or seeing off her cruel second husband, who had only retreated thanks to Romulus' threats.

He'd have a word with Secundus, make the veteran aware of his wishes. That would have to suffice for now. Wanting to prepare the boy for the worst, Romulus decided to broach the subject. "It's hard to understand, but there are some things in life that a man can't back away from," he said. "If there are men who want to kill Caesar at the Senate this morning, I will try to stop them. Whatever the cost."

Mattius looked unhappy. "You'll be all right, won't you?"

"Only the gods know the answer to that question."

"I'll fight them too," muttered Mattius.

"No, you won't," replied Romulus seriously. "I have a far more important job for you."

†

Secundus and his veterans were waiting for them outside the large temple to Venus in which the Senate occasionally met. Situated in the middle of a magnificent park full of exotic plants, the shrine was part of Pompey's immense complex, which had been finished nine years before. Its most popular part was Rome's first stone-built theater, the place where Romulus had faced the Ethiopian bull. Even though it was hours until midday, the day's entertainment had already started. Romulus shivered at the familiar bloodthirsty roar that went up at regular intervals. After his last experience, he never wanted to set foot in an arena again.

Secundus didn't seem that surprised when told of the dictator's order to disband his group. "Caesar's a strong character," he said.

Devastating Romulus, he was also unprepared to remain in the nearby streets in case his men were needed. "Each person's destiny is his own. You offered our assistance, and Caesar turned it down flat. That's his prerogative, and we should not interfere with it."

"He might be killed, though!" cried Romulus.

"His choice," replied Secundus somberly, whistling an order.

"What are you doing?"

"Returning to the Mithraeum," came the simple answer. "We'll make an offering to Mithras for Caesar's safekeeping."

There was nothing Romulus could do. After he'd muttered in Secundus' ear about looking after Mattius, Romulus watched, utterly disconsolate, as the veterans filed past him in neat ranks. Many nodded farewell in friendly fashion, but none offered to stay. Their belief in Secundus' authority was total, even stronger than that which Romulus had seen in the army. He found it impossible to be angry with them. Their philosophy of respecting a man's destiny came from the same belief system that Tarquinius subscribed to, and had taught to Romulus. Today, though, he found it impossible to put into practice.

The realization brought a sardonic smile to Romulus' face, and he glanced at the tattoo on his upper right arm. *Maybe I'm not such a good follower of Mithras after all,* he thought. Yet there was no way he was going to reconsider his decision. Backing out would feel too much like leaving Brennus to face an elephant alone.

For some time, Romulus watched senators arriving for the morning's session. Eager to know what his task would be, Mattius never left his side. Suspiciously, Romulus studied each toga-clad man in turn, trying to determine any glimmer of evil intent. To his frustration, he could see none. Clutching their long stylus boxes, the politicians alighted from their litters, calling greetings to those they knew. Romulus recognized few of them. Strolling to and fro, he did his best to listen to their conversations, but it was difficult to do so without being obvious. Most of what he heard was idle gossip or concerned Longinus' son, who was to assume the toga of a man that morning. Despite himself, Romulus relaxed a fraction.

It was interesting to see the man who had served Crassus once more. He had only seen Longinus from a distance on the Parthian campaign, but he'd been grilled by the grizzled former soldier just before he'd received his manumission from Caesar. He felt a degree of kinship with Longinus, and seeing him unsettled Romulus. Why would he keep being reminded of Parthia if it wasn't something to do with Caesar's upcoming campaign? This fueled Romulus' slim hope that Tarquinius might be wrong about the assassination.

†

By late morning, Romulus was growing optimistic that Decimus Brutus had succeeded where he'd failed, convincing Caesar to stay away. Within the temple, the morning's proceedings had started. Despite the blustery weather, which threatened rain, there were still plenty of senators outside. None of that mattered if Caesar didn't turn up, thought Romulus.

His heart sank, therefore, when a richly decorated litter approached through the inevitable crowd of citizens, who gathered to see the rich and famous, or to plead for their intervention in a business deal gone wrong. Borne by four strapping slaves in loincloths, it was preceded by another bearing a long stick with which to clear the way. Romulus could see no sign of guards or soldiers. Hearing the lead slave crying Caesar's name, he jumped to his feet.

"It's time," he muttered to Mattius. "The *lictores* would never let me past, but you might be able to worm your way inside. Can you manage that?"

His face filled with childish determination, Mattius nodded. "What should I do then?"

"Don't take your eyes off Caesar for a single moment," Romulus warned. "At the slightest sign of trouble, call me. I'll stay as near to the entrance as I can."

"It might be too late by then," said the boy solemnly. "Especially if the *lictores* try to stop you entering."

"What else can I do?" asked Romulus, raising his hands in a helpless gesture.

A moment later, the haruspex appeared from the crowd. "Fabiola is here," he said quietly.

"Where?" Romulus demanded, simultaneously shocked and unsurprised.

Tarquinius pointed to a hooded and cloaked figure standing half concealed by a pillar near the temple's entrance. It was slight enough to be a woman.

"You're sure?" Romulus didn't want to believe his eyes.

Tarquinius' smile was mirthless. "Do you think she'd miss this?"

Romulus' mouth filled with a harsh, dry feeling. Tarquinius' divination was about to come true. Why else would Fabiola be here? A strong urge to confront his sister took hold, and his eyes darted from her to Caesar's litter, which had stopped by the bottom of the steps. A large party of senators was waiting for the dictator, and Romulus began to panic. He saw Longinus there, and Marcus Brutus. Although Marcus Antonius, Caesar's most loyal supporter, was also present, the assassins might still strike immediately.

He wouldn't have time to run up to Fabiola and then back down before Caesar alighted. Cursing, he shouldered his way through the eager crowd, toward the dictator's litter. Mattius made to follow him, but Romulus jerked his head and the boy remembered. With a grin, he darted up the huge carved staircase, coming to a halt right beside the entrance. The guards ignored him, just another excited spectator trying to get the best view. They were doing the same themselves. Acting with casual aplomb, Mattius sloped inside and out of sight. Romulus' lips twitched with satisfaction. At least one thing

was going according to plan. It remained doubtful whether anything else would. Loosening his *gladius* in its sheath, he muttered
maybe his last prayer to Jupiter and Mithras, asking for their protection and help.

There was a loud cheer as Caesar clambered down from his litter.
Despite the unhappiness of some politicians, his popularity with the
ordinary citizens was huge. The dictator's piercing gaze scanned the
throng and, seeing no danger, he acknowledged the acclaim with
nods and smiles. Behind him, a brown-haired man emerged. To
Romulus' astonishment, it was Decimus Brutus. Did this mean that
Fabiola's lover was also one of the conspirators? Or, like Romulus,
had he failed to persuade Caesar to stay away? He couldn't be sure.
Edging to the front of the crowd, Romulus saw that the waiting
senators had formed up in two lines, offering Caesar a clear path up
to the shrine. Effusive greetings filled the air. He could take the tension no longer, and darted forward to the dictator's side.

"Legionary Romulus. Good to see you again." Caesar placed his
foot on the first step. "I'll call on you shortly."

"Thank you, sir." Romulus saluted, before muttering from the
side of his mouth, "Please let me accompany you inside."

Caesar smiled. "That won't be necessary." Raising his arms, he
indicated the senators. "I have these good men to guide me in."

"But, sir," Romulus objected. "My friend said—"

"That'll be all, soldier," Caesar said curtly.

His protest dying in his throat, Romulus stood back. He was
aware of the senators giving him disapproving looks, but he didn't
care. A combination of terror and sheer adrenaline was in control.
Seeing no immediate threat, Romulus came to the decision that the
attack would take place inside. Working his way to the side of the
gathering, he pounded up the steps to the entrance. To have any
chance of saving Caesar, he had to be as close as possible. Behind
him, he was vaguely aware of Decimus Brutus greeting Antonius in

a jovial fashion. His suspicions aroused by this, Romulus glanced back. Fabiola had told him that the two men hated each other, yet here was Brutus throwing his arm over Antonius' shoulders. The former Master of the Horse looked annoyed at first, but as Brutus kept talking, a slow smile spread over his broad, handsome face.

Caesar began to climb the staircase, leaving Antonius and Brutus behind, deep in conversation. Realization struck Romulus like a blow from Vulcan's hammer. It was all part of the plan. The conspirators only wanted to kill Caesar, so they would delay his greatest supporter outside. Romulus wanted to scream out loud. Could no one else see it? *Stay calm*, he thought. All was not lost—yet. How would they kill Caesar? Togas were not the kind of garment that facilitated the concealment of weapons. Was there a secret stash inside? He discounted that theory at once. Too many other people— priests, acolytes and devotees—had access to the temple.

Then Romulus' eyes were drawn to the stylus cases in each senator's hand, and his stomach lurched. The elegant wooden boxes were just the right size to hold a knife. His mind reeled at the simplicity, and the lethality, of it. Despairing, Romulus let his gaze drift from the ascending group. There, across the width of the steps, at his level he saw Fabiola. They locked eyes, staring at each other with an unbearable intensity. After a moment that seemed to last forever but in reality was probably no more than several heartbeats, Fabiola's mouth opened.

Before she could speak, though, Caesar had reached them. Surrounded by the mass of senators, he was talking about Longinus' son's great day. Assuming the toga of a man was one of life's most important events. Antonius was still at the bottom of the steps talking to Decimus Brutus. Romulus felt more weary than he had in his life. He was just a helpless observer.

"I am here," said Tarquinius from behind him.

Romulus could have almost cried with relief. "Will you come with me?"

"Of course. That's what comrades are for," the haruspex replied, unslinging his double-headed battleaxe.

"We might be killed," said Romulus, eyeing the six guards, all of whose attention was on Caesar.

"How many times have I heard that?" Tarquinius smiled. "Still doesn't mean I can leave you to go in alone."

Romulus turned away from the crowd and drew his *gladius*. He shot a glance at Fabiola, but she was too busy watching the dictator. A mixture of emotions twisted her beautiful face, and Romulus thought of their mother. What if his twin was correct? he asked himself again, despairingly. His gut instinct answered at once. Even if she was, Caesar did not deserve to be killed like a sheep surrounded by a pack of starving wolves. So he wasn't going to back away now.

Romulus watched tensely as the dictator passed out of view. To his delight, four of the guards also entered, leaving only two at the doors, which remained open.

Now it was up to Mattius.

He took a couple of steps toward the entrance, and Tarquinius followed suit. Talking to each other, with half an eye on the proceedings within, neither guard noticed for a moment. Romulus slid his *caligae* across the stone, getting a few paces nearer.

"Romulus!"

Fabiola's shout was like the crack of a whip in a confined space.

Romulus stared at her, aware that the guards had seen him.

"What are you going to do?" she screamed.

An image of Velvinna's suffering burned every part of Romulus' mind. It was followed by one of Caesar smiling as he granted him his manumission in the arena not three hundred paces away. Torn, he glanced at Tarquinius.

"Your path is your own," whispered the haruspex. "Only you can decide it."

"You two!" yelled one of the guards. "Drop your weapons!" Calling for help, he and his comrade advanced with lowered *pila*.

They were stopped by an animal cry of pain from inside the temple.

"Casca, you idiot, what are you doing?" Caesar demanded.

"Help me," shouted a voice. "Kill the tyrant!"

"Romulus!" screamed Mattius. "Come quickly!"

A baying sound of anger rose and Romulus heard the muffled sound of blows landing. Fury consumed him. Raising his *gladius*, he leaped forward at the two guards.

The gods were smiling down at that moment. Distracted by the commotion inside, both their heads were half turned away. Romulus was grateful for this—he had no desire to hurt them unnecessarily. Reversing his *gladius*, he brought down the hilt hard on the back of the nearest man's skull. From the corner of his eye, he saw Tarquinius using the metal-tipped butt of his axe to do the same with the other sentry. Jumping over the falling men, they sprinted inside.

Fortunately, the remaining guards had been totally distracted by what was going on, so their path was clear. Romulus' eyes opened wide at the splendor of the long, high-roofed chamber, which was well lit thanks to the number of small glass-paned windows high on the walls. Of course his attention did not remain on the decor, or the ranks of toga-clad senators who were on their feet, shouting and pointing. Clearly most of the six hundred had known nothing about the attempted assassination. Romulus felt disgust that none had tried to intervene. On he ran, to the central area where the consuls' chairs and that of Caesar stood. He could make out a cluster of men there. All were carrying knives, and many already had bloody robes. Their faces had the empty, shocked look of those who have just grasped the enormity of what they've done.

I'm too late, Romulus thought, anguish tearing at him like the claws of a ravening beast. *As I thought I would be.* Screaming his fiercest battle cry, he charged straight at the assassins. Tarquinius loped alongside, lean and gray-haired but terrifying-looking with his raised axe. Romulus was dimly aware of Mattius pelting along to his rear, adding his childish voice to the clamor. To his surprise, their cries had the most dramatic effect. Scattering like a flock of birds attacked by a cat, the assassins broke and ran, stampeding up into the tiers of seating. Their fear was infectious, and within a few heartbeats, the entire body of senators was fleeing along the sides of the chamber and out of the doors. Their departure revealed the most bloody of scenes.

Beneath a large statue of Pompey, Caesar lay in an expanding pool of his own blood. His entire toga was covered in damning red stains, each one the mark of a knife's entry point. His chest, belly, groin and legs had all been wounded. The white woolen garment had been ripped off his left shoulder, and there too Romulus could see multiple stab and slash marks. Caesar resembled a badly butchered side of pork. No one could survive that many injuries. Skidding to a halt, Romulus dropped to his knees by the dictator's side. His eyelids were closed. Shallow, shuddering breaths shook his chest and his skin had already assumed the gray pallor of those near death.

"What have they done?" Romulus wailed. An all-consuming grief flooded him that Caesar's life should end like this.

Shocked by the bloodshed, Mattius hung back.

"Romulus?"

Startled, he looked down at Caesar, whose eyes had opened. "Sir?"

"It *is* you . . ." Caesar's breath rattled in his chest.

Romulus found himself clutching one of the dictator's bloody hands. "Don't say anything, sir," he said frantically. "We'll soon get a surgeon to fix you up."

Caesar's lips turned upward. "You're a poor liar, legionary," he whispered. "I should have listened to you about coming here."

Romulus hung his head, trying to hide his tears. All his efforts had been in vain. A moment later, he felt his hand being squeezed.

"You're a fine soldier, Romulus," Caesar gasped. "Remind me . . . of myself when I was younger."

Romulus' instant feeling of pride at this enormous compliment lasted no longer than two heartbeats. Beads of clammy sweat broke out on his forehead, and he pulled away his hand. Raging doubt filled his mind.

Caesar looked confused. Trying to sit up, he started off a fresh bout of bleeding from his wounds. It was too much for him, and he sagged back onto the marble floor. His eyes took on the distant stare of those who can see Elysium, or Hades.

Romulus thought of Fabiola, and the reason she wanted Caesar dead. Stemming his grief, he took a deep breath. Only moments remained before it was too late. "Twenty-six years ago, a pretty slave girl was raped by a noble one night near the Forum," he whispered in Caesar's ear. Checking the dictator's expression, Romulus was satisfied that his words had been heard. He let them sink in for a moment, and then leaned in close for a second time. "Was it you?" He watched closely to judge Caesar's reaction.

There was none. A moment later, Romulus had to place a dampened fingertip over Caesar's mouth and nostrils to feel any movement of air. The faintest chill on his wet skin told him that there was still some life in the slashed and blood-spattered body beside him. *Jupiter,* Romulus prayed with all his might. *Don't let him die, leaving me ignorant of the truth.* He bent over the dictator, willing him to look up once more. Nothing happened. "Are you my father?" he said, forcing the words out.

Caesar's eyelids jerked open and his body went rigid.

Romulus gazed deep into the other's eyes, and saw the naked

truth. "By all the gods, you did rape my mother," he breathed, feeling the weight of the revelation come crashing down on his shoulders. Fabiola had been right all along. Looking like Caesar was no coincidence—he was his son.

Where did that leave him? Had his love for Caesar been more than that of a devoted soldier? Romulus didn't know. In his mind, all was confusion. A moment later, he saw that the dictator was dead. Romulus felt an immediate sense of grief, which he tried to reject. How could he feel sad? The bastard had violated his mother. New tears flowed as this old wound was reopened.

"He was not all bad," said Tarquinius suddenly. "Granting your manumission proved that."

Romulus felt the haruspex' hand on his shoulder. The human touch was most welcome. "Did you know?" he asked.

"I suspected for a long time," Tarquinius replied. "More recently, my feelings grew stronger."

"Why didn't you say?" Romulus cried.

Tarquinius sighed. "I've harmed you too much before, and I couldn't see the benefit of telling you. Caesar's children will be in danger in the days to come too. In any case, would you have joined Fabiola if you'd known?"

Looking down at Caesar's supine form, Romulus considered his friend's question long and hard. Years of his life had been spent wondering what he'd do if he ever met his father. His ideas had usually involved long torture sessions like those he'd planned for Gemellus. Yet when he'd had the merchant at his mercy, things had seemed very different. "No," he said eventually.

"Why not?"

"Rape is a terrible crime, but it doesn't warrant this," Romulus answered sorrowfully. He touched Caesar's mutilated corpse. "Taking part in his killing wouldn't bring Mother back either."

"Unfortunately," said Fabiola.

He turned to find his sister beside him. They exchanged a wary glance, before Romulus took the plunge. He had to. "You were right," he admitted.

Fabiola's face lit up, and she touched his arm. "He confessed to raping Mother?"

"I asked him," Romulus revealed, "and the look in his eyes when he heard the question . . . he was guilty. I'm sure of it."

"I knew it," Fabiola crowed. She looked down at Caesar's bloodied body and laughed. "The whoreson has paid the price. Praise all the gods!"

Romulus hung his head, feeling guilt that his emotions didn't mirror Fabiola's.

It was as if she sensed his confusion. "Aren't you glad?"

Romulus didn't know how to answer her. "Partly," he muttered at last.

"What more proof do you need?" Fabiola spat. "Mother to rise from her grave and identify him for you?"

"Of course not," answered Romulus defensively. "But it's complicated, sister. He freed me from slavery. If you'd killed him a few years ago, I wouldn't be standing here now." He imagined someone else as the *editor* of the games that day. Killing the rhinoceros would have merely delayed his death. "I ended up as a *noxius*, you know. But for Caesar, my bones would be lying on the Esquiline Hill."

Fabiola did not respond.

Mattius came hurtling back from the entrance. "A crowd is starting to gather," he announced.

Romulus came alive. "They'll want blood when they see what's been done. Let's go."

Leaving Caesar lying beneath the statue of his great rival, they made their way to the entrance. Romulus and Fabiola did not speak. Each was reeling from the enormity of what had happened and the gravity of what lay unsaid between them. Tarquinius' dark eyes were on them both, but he did not interfere. For his lot, Mattius was too young to notice the strained atmosphere.

The guards had also fled in the panic, leaving the unconscious bodies of their companions sprawled by the massive doors. No doubt they and the innocent senators had spread the word that Caesar had been murdered, thought Romulus. His hunch was correct. At the foot of the steps, a large rabble had already gathered. Still too fearful to climb the steps and see for themselves, they were shouting and wailing, egging each other on. Romulus had seen the frenzy of an uncontrolled mob before. It developed rapidly and was terrifying to behold. No one would stop to hear that he had been attempting to save Caesar's life, and even Mattius would not be spared.

"Walk right behind me. Do not look at anyone," he ordered. "Tarquinius, you take the rear." Raising his sword menacingly, Romulus walked down the steps. The others followed.

Members of the crowd soon saw them. Angry shouts rose at once. "Is it true?" shouted a bearded man in a workman's tunic. "Has Caesar been murdered?"

"He has," Romulus replied, still descending.

An inarticulate sound of anger rose from the gathered citizens, and Romulus sensed Fabiola flinch. "Keep moving," he hissed.

"Who did it?" shouted the workman.

"A group of senators," answered Romulus. "You'll have seen them running off with their clothes covered in blood."

"I saw some," yelled a voice.

"So did I!" howled another.

The workman's face twisted with fury. "Which way did they go?"

"Down there," came the answering cry.

In an instant, the rabble's attention had switched from Romulus and his companions to a side street that led off toward Pompey's exotic gardens and then the city. "After them," bellowed the work-man. Responding to his shout, the mass of citizens moved off at speed, with a sea of fists and weapons waving above it.

"Gods help whoever they catch," said Tarquinius.

Fabiola shuddered, remembering the mob that had swept her away after Clodius Pulcher's murder.

Romulus ignored her obvious distress. Now was not the time to settle their differences either. "We'll head that way," he said, point-ing at the arena. "Then we can enter the city by a different gate."

They had only covered a short distance before a small group of figures emerged from a door in the wall of the amphitheater. Squinting to make them out, Romulus stiffened. The men were gladiators. Instinctively he increased his pace to get away.

It was pointless. Seeing them, the party broke into a sprint, an-gling to cut them off from the street toward the city. "Stop," Romulus ordered. He and Tarquinius moved protectively in front of Fabiola and Mattius, and they waited. Soon they could make out four fight-ers: two *murmillones* and a pair of Thracians. All were helmeted and carrying swords and shields. *Who the hell are they?* Romulus wondered, wishing he had more than just a *gladius*. Behind the fighters trotted a man in a fine white toga. It was Decimus Brutus. Romulus shot a glance at Fabiola. She seemed delighted, which pleased him. Fighting four fully armed gladiators was not what he wanted to think about right now.

"I thought it was you, my love," Brutus cried as he drew near. "Thanks be to Jupiter you're safe. Where did you go?"

She looked surprised. "Inside, to make sure Caesar was dead."

Brutus winced. "I've come with these fighters of mine to carry his body away. Treat it with the dignity it deserves."

Romulus' blood began to boil. "It's a bit late for that," he growled. "Might have been better if you'd stood by his side instead of keeping Antonius outside."

"How dare you?" Brutus snapped. "It's not that simple."

Romulus was so angry that he forgot the difference in their status. "Really? Perhaps you'd care to explain how it's possible to swear service to someone and then plan their murder."

Brutus' lips pinched with fury. "I answer you only because Fabiola is your sister. He'd become a tyrant who treated the Republic with contempt."

"Caesar ended decades of strife and civil war," Romulus retorted, contemptuous that the noble had succumbed to Fabiola's charms when he had had the strength not to. "He was the best future for this country and you know it. Not forgetting that you were his sworn follower."

"Romulus," Fabiola said, stepping forward. "Please."

Uncaring, Romulus let all of his fury out. Subconsciously, he knew he was transferring some of his anger at Fabiola—and himself—but he didn't care. "Call yourself a soldier? Fucking coward, more like."

"Scum," Brutus shouted. "You're nothing but a freed slave!"

"Scum, eh?" screamed Romulus. "At least I stood up for Caesar, while you didn't even have the balls to stick a knife in him."

Apoplectic now, Brutus stabbed a finger toward Romulus. "Kill that whoreson! And his friend."

With malevolent grins, his gladiators shuffled forward. They didn't care who the young soldier and his companion were.

"He's my brother!" Fabiola cried.

"I don't care who he is," Brutus replied, the veins on his neck bulging. "No lowlife speaks to a nobleman in that way and lives to tell the tale."

"Get out of the way, Fabiola," said Romulus urgently.

"No." Fabiola raised her hands in supplication toward Brutus. "Please calm down, my love. The tyrant is dead. That's what matters. There's no need for further bloodshed."

"Listen to you," Romulus snarled, his rage boiling over at his sister now. "The 'tyrant,' was he? What did you care about that? All you wanted was revenge on the man who raped our mother."

Brutus' face went white. "That was your motive?"

Fabiola lifted her shoulders proudly. "It was. That's why I picked you rather than any of the other fools who visited the Lupanar."

Brutus looked stunned. "I chose you first."

"Maybe so," Fabiola replied. "After that, though, it was all my making. You were my path to Caesar, and I did absolutely everything to make sure that you preferred me above all others."

Brutus raised a hand, trying to push away the words. "No," he muttered. "You're lying."

"Why would I do that?" Fabiola spat. Spittle flecked her lips. "Revenge is the only thing that kept me sane while I whored myself with you and a thousand others. I was right all along about the bastard too."

Her distress pierced Romulus to the core.

Brutus reeled away, overcome by Fabiola's confession.

Things started to happen very fast.

The gladiators made a rush for Romulus and Tarquinius. Four against two, and better armed, they had an excellent chance of ending the fight before it had even begun. Drawn forward by her outburst, Fabiola was standing between the two sets of adversaries. Romulus darted in desperately, trying to shove her out of harm's way. He succeeded, but in doing so left himself open to attack. Tarquinius swept in alongside, wielding his axe in a blur of motion that slowed three of the fighters down. The last, however, saw a golden opportunity and struck Romulus in the chest with his metal shield boss. Delivered with the force of a running man, it knocked him in a heap to the ground. Winded, Romulus could do nothing more than look up dully at the *murmillo*.

With a satisfied growl, the gladiator swept back his right arm to deliver the death blow.

"NO!" Fabiola screamed, throwing herself into the blade's path.

To the end of his days, Romulus would remember the sight of his sister's body arcing through the air above him, and in slow motion, the sword tip come shoving through the side of her rib cage. Spatters of blood covered his face, and then Fabiola landed on him, a warm, immobile heap. For a moment, Romulus couldn't comprehend what had happened. Then the terrible truth hit him. He wrapped his arms around Fabiola, and an inchoate bellow of pain left his lips. It went on and on, until his throat was raw. Lost in a sea of grief, he was vaguely aware that the *murmillo* hadn't finished him off, and that people were shouting.

"Romulus." Tarquinius' voice was very gentle. "Let her go. Sit up."

Like a sleepwalker, Romulus obeyed, feeling Fabiola being rolled off him. Pulling himself upright, he saw that his tunic was totally saturated in his sister's blood. She lay across his knees now, as beautiful as ever, but her mouth hung open slackly, and her piercing blue eyes had already gone dull. She was dead. "Why?" Romulus whispered. "Why did you do it?"

"You were her only family," Tarquinius replied. "Wouldn't you have done the same for her?"

"Of course," Romulus sobbed.

"Well, then." Tarquinius put his arm around his shoulders. "She was a woman, but possessed the heart of a lion."

"Fabiola?"

Romulus looked up to see Brutus standing over them. He took in the rest of the scene too: One Thracian was down, screaming, clutching at the stump of his right arm, which must have been removed by Tarquinius' axe. Two of the others were ministering to him, while the *murmillo* who'd killed Fabiola lay nearby with Brutus' dagger buried to the hilt in his back. Steadfast to the last, Mattius was beside him, his kitchen knife ready. "She's dead," Romulus snarled at Brutus. "Thanks to you."

This time, Brutus didn't react to his taunt. His face contorted with grief, he knelt down and lifted Fabiola's bloody corpse off Romulus' legs. Rocking her to and fro, he began to keen.

Romulus' anger faded when he saw the depth of Brutus' grief. Clearly he had loved Fabiola, which made him easy prey to her wiles. After all, manipulation had been her main weapon. Romulus' sorrow grew even greater. His sister had not been like that as a child. Before, he had not really appreciated what Fabiola had been forced to become, but her confession had brought it all home. To endure the Hades of men using her body day after day, she had focused all her energy on imagining revenge upon Caesar. It was all that had kept his twin sane.

While his life experience had also been brutal, Romulus knew that he'd made the right decision not to join Fabiola. He'd killed men in cold blood at the behest of others before, but would do it no more. Furthermore, while Caesar's crime had been great, his grant of manumission rivaled it as an act of kindness. Fabiola had not received such a gift, though—instead, the dictator had tried to rape her, his own daughter. Was it any surprise that she had become twisted and bitter?

Then Romulus remembered how Fabiola had freely given her life for his, which proved that she'd had another motive to survive the hell of prostitution. Him. At this example of simple family loyalty, he broke down and wept again. The thought of Fabiola was what had carried him through the horrors of Carrhae and beyond. How alike they had been without even knowing it.

Tarquinius stood over the two sobbing men and Fabiola's body for long moments. When he spoke, his voice was low and urgent. "The crowd is coming back."

Romulus lifted his head and listened. Sure enough, angry shouts could be heard approaching from the main way that led to the city. He looked down at himself, covered in blood. Brutus did likewise.

"They'll kill us for sure," said the noble. He called over the two unhurt gladiators. "Carry her back to the arena," he ordered.

Romulus knew it was time to leave. In more ways than one. With Caesar dead, he owed the Republic nothing. Octavian was reputed to be the dictator's heir, but that didn't mean Romulus wanted to fight a civil war for him, or anyone else. Standing, he stared at Brutus.

The noble sensed his question. "Her funeral will be in eight days."

Romulus nodded once. Despite his earlier fury, he could tell that Brutus would tolerate his presence as Fabiola was buried. The noble owed him that much.

Brutus gathered his men and was gone. Having lost too much blood, the injured Thracian was left to die.

Without further ado, Romulus and his companions headed for the nearest alley. It would be easy enough to work their way past the crowd and back into the city. Tarquinius handed over his cloak. "Best not to advertise where you've been."

His mind spinning, Romulus donned the garment. Eight days afforded enough time to tidy up his affairs. What would he do after that? With Caesar dead, there would be no campaign to Dacia and Parthia. Yet the thought of going back to his farm was wholly unappealing. The bugle of an elephant in the nearby arena carried through the air, and suddenly Romulus knew that he could never be happy in Italy while the slightest chance of Brennus being alive remained. He caught Tarquinius' eye and saw that the haruspex had read his mind. What about Mattius, though? There was no need to break it to him immediately, thought Romulus.

"Mattius, I have another job for you."

"What is it?"

"Go to the Mithraeum and tell Secundus what has happened," said Romulus. "Caesar's heir may need some muscle in the coming days."

Mattius repeated his words perfectly; nodding determinedly, the boy turned and ran off.

Romulus watched Mattius until he was lost to sight. *Great Mithras, watch over his path,* he prayed. *Jupiter,* Optimus Maximus, *keep him from harm.* He'd need to see the lawyer whom Sabinus had recommended and have his will made out in favor of the boy and his mother. Romulus' heart ached that he would have to be left behind, but Parthia and Margiana were no places for a child. Here in Rome, under the guidance of Secundus, Mattius had a chance of a future—which was more than life had offered him and Fabiola.

The haruspex looked up at the banks of scudding cloud overhead. Within a few heartbeats, a smile worked its way across his scarred face. "I *am* destined to travel east again," he announced.

Romulus looked sadly at the gladiators carrying Fabiola, and then toward the temple where Caesar's body still lay. He had lost his sister and father in the space of an hour. It was a devastating blow, yet his mother had been avenged. What had happened turned Tarquinius, and Brennus, if he was still alive, into his only family. In a strange way, that set him completely free.

At a stroke, Rome had lost its position as the center of his world.

It mattered less than Romulus thought.

"I'll come too," he said.

AUTHOR'S NOTE

No doubt many readers will be familiar with the civil war and the events that led to Caesar's death. Where possible, I have stuck to the historical record. I would feel remiss in not doing so: The rich detail of the time lends itself so well to a novel. The night battle in Alexandria and Caesar's dramatic swim to safety, holding his documents in the air, is recorded. While he had the depleted Twenty-Seventh Legion with him, not the Twenty-Eighth, I needed Romulus to be a part of a legion that was at Ruspina too (and the Twenty-Eighth was); therefore I changed the one present in Egypt. Pharnaces' soldiers are noted to have castrated Roman citizens whom they captured. Although the use of scythed chariots at Zela is accurate, we do not know the composition of the rest of the Pontic army. I have therefore used troops common to the area and the time. Typically, peltasts and *thureophoroi* were skirmishers, not soldiers who would have tackled legionaries head on. Given Pharnaces' troops' overwhelming numerical superiority, however, I have taken the liberty of having them attack en masse. The manner of Caesar's victory was as rapid as I described.

Rome in the late Republic was not the clean and tidy city depicted in many modern films and TV programs. Few houses had indoor sanitation. Instead most people used public toilets, or flung the contents of their "waste" pots on open-air dung heaps. All but two main avenues were less than 3.1 m (10 ft) wide, and most were unpaved. Buildings of three, four and even five stories would have produced a dim twilight at street level for much of the day. Unlike Imperial times, when the city quarters were somewhat divided by social class, the rich and poor in Republican Rome lived cheek by jowl with each other. Inscribing a curse upon an enemy on a lead square and offering it to a god was commonplace, as anyone who has visited the amazing Roman baths in Bath, England, will know. Dozens of the metal squares have been retrieved and translated, opening a vivid window on the past.

Contrary to popular opinion, most of Alexandria's massive library survived the night battle in the port, thanks mostly to its two sites in the city. Unfortunately, a zealous Christian mob succeeded four centuries later in razing the lot to the ground. By doing so, they destroyed the most incredible collection of information ever seen in ancient times.

To my knowledge, the Sixth Legion did not accompany Caesar back to Italy after Zela, nor were there large games in celebration so soon after his victory in Asia Minor, but the astonishing manner in which the general dealt with the mutinous legionaries is accurate. Rhinoceroses were captured and transported to Rome at that time, and were referred to as "Ethiopian bulls." *Noxii* often died by being thrown in with such creatures. It's difficult to assess how a rhino might be killed with only a spear, and my efforts in trying to find out naturally did not go far. Try typing "kill rhino spear" into Google and not very much comes up! Even a book by a big game hunter wasn't much use. Eventually I decided to rely on my veterinary training: Virtually all mammals' hearts lie behind the left elbow, so it is a place where a spear blade can be shoved in. Whether a man can actually kill a rhino in such circumstances is a moot point, of course, but I think it is *possible!*

Having read about the Antikythera mechanism (the boxlike object that Tarquinius nearly sees in Rhodes), I felt obliged to mention it in *The Road to Rome*. Although it was found over a hundred years ago, its immense significance has only become apparent in the last decade, thanks in the main to an eight-ton X-ray machine that has taken images that give incredibly fine "slice" pictures. Built in approximately 150–100 BC, possibly in the region of Syracuse, the device was able to do all the things mentioned. Remarkably, the technology to replicate its intricate gears was not rediscovered for more than 1,500 years. If the Greeks were building things like this, what else were they able to do? How incredible that the chance discovery of a sponge diver should reveal so much. We do not know where it was being transported to at the time of its loss at sea. One popular theory, which I have used, is that it had been taken from the famous Greek Stoic school on Rhodes by Caesarean troops, who were known to have plundered the region for treasures to display at his triumphs.

My account of Ruspina largely follows the historical record, including a storm scattering Caesar's fleet, his cavalrymen feeding their horses dried seaweed, Scipio's concealment of his mounted forces until the last minute, Caesar's rebuke of the *signifer* and his remarkable retrieval of the situation. Labienus was attacked by a veteran legionary, not a senior centurion. Marcus Petreius, who appeared in *The Silver Eagle*, fought at Ruspina, and was probably injured. It is my construct that this occurred during the last action of the day, and at Romulus' hands. Before Thapsus, several Caesarean cohorts were trained specifically to fight the Pompeian elephants. Remarkably, his veteran legions were so eager to close with the enemy at the outset of the encounter that they charged before being ordered to do so. One of my favorite discoveries during the research for *The Road to Rome* was that during this final battle in Africa, a legionary of the Fifth "Alaudae" Legion had successfully attacked an elephant that had picked up a camp follower, forcing it to drop its victim. I felt I had to include this sequence in the novel, even though it changed what I thought might (or might not) have happened to Brennus.

Caesar did indeed celebrate four triumphs in the autumn of 46 BC, and the staggering scale of each parade can only be imagined. The dictator's generosity to his soldiers and the Roman public in general is recorded. His honor guard composed of soldiers from all ten legions is my invention, so that I could have Romulus return to Rome. It was during these parades rather than at Ruspina that his men were recorded as singing of the "baldheaded lecher." Evidence for the victorious general's face being painted red is limited, as is the custom of smearing the statue of Jupiter with blood (or the red pigment cinnabar), but I felt it added to the sense of drama. The battle of Munda was just as remarkable as I've described, however, as were the staggering awards Caesar was granted upon his return to Rome.

Marcus Antonius was indeed the larger-than-life character depicted in *The Road to Rome*. A wild-living natural soldier, he was famous for his drinking, philandering and womanizing. He is recorded as having vomited in front of the entire Senate, and liked to travel in a British war chariot. While his response to the unrest during Caesar's absence in Egypt was heavy-handed, there is no evidence to my knowledge of his being involved with a *fugitivarius* or organizing dirty work on Caesar's behalf. Of course, Fabiola being the catalyst for the conspirators to meet is pure fiction, as is the use of the Lupanar as the location for their meetings. Marcus Junius Brutus was indeed one of the last to join the plot, although he quickly became one of the leaders. As I explained in the note at the end of *The Silver Eagle*, his compatriot Gaius Cassius Longinus is an amalgam of two historical characters, one of the same name, and his brother (or cousin) Quintus Cassius Longinus.

All kinds of signs were supposed to have occurred in the run-up to the Ides of March. Soothsayers predicted unfavorable omens and

Calpurnia, Caesar's wife, had a nightmare about him being murdered. Apparently, the dictator chose to stay at home that morning, but whether it was because of her warning, or because he really was unwell, we do not know. The size of his new army, and his planned campaign to Parthia, are documented. Romulus' dawn visit is fictional, but Decimus Brutus did call in that morning and succeed in persuading Caesar to attend the Senate. Although his Spanish bodyguards really had been disbanded, there is no evidence to suggest that any veterans tried to protect the dictator on that last fateful day.

Two senators did try to help Caesar when his assassins struck, but the press was so great that they were unable to reach him. Obviously, Romulus and Fabiola's encounter over his body is made up, but the presence of Decimus Brutus' gladiators in the nearby arena is not. Who knows if this is coincidence or not? Rather than fleeing immediately, the conspirators placed the cap traditionally worn by a freed slave on a pole and carried it to the Capitoline Hill, showing the public how they had freed the Republic from slavery. The rioting I described actually happened a few days later, after Caesar's funeral. During it, many of the conspirators' houses were attacked, and a loyal supporter of the dictator was murdered when he was wrongly identified as one of Caesar's enemies.

Thanks to the many holes in our knowledge, much has to be left open to interpretation when describing the ancient world. While I have changed details here and there, many of which are explained above, I have also tried to portray the time as accurately as possible. Hopefully this has been done in an entertaining and informative manner, without too many errors. For those that might be present, I apologize.

I must offer some appreciation to the multitude of authors without whose works I would be lost. First among these is *A History of Rome* by M. Cary and H. H. Scullard; closely following are *The Complete Roman Army* and *Caesar*, both by Adrian Goldsworthy; *Armies of the*

Macedonian and Punic Wars by Duncan Head; and *The Roman Triumph* by Mary Beard, as well as numerous fantastic volumes from Osprey Publishing. Thanks once again to the members of www.romanarmy .com, whose rapid responses to my questions often help so much. It is quite simply one of the best Roman reference resources there is. I would also like to express real gratitude to my old friend Arthur O'Connor, for all his constructive criticism and help with this and my previous two books. Also a veterinary surgeon, he is blessed with an incisive and insightful mind when it comes to novel-writing, and he frequently helps me to see "the wood for the trees." Many thanks too to another old friend and vet, Killian Ó Móráin, for similar services rendered.

Last, but definitely not least, I want to thank my top-class agent, Charlie Viney, for his untiring work on my behalf. To Rosie de Courcy, my wonderful editor, I owe so much: Without her razor-sharp input I would be lost. Thanks too to Nicola Taplin, my managing editor, and to Richenda Todd, my excellent copy editor, two people whose efforts on my behalf I appreciate immensely. I am extremely grateful to Keith Kahla and Kathleen Conn, my editors at St. Martin's Press, who fight the good fight in the USA on my behalf so well. I am also greatly indebted to Claire Wheller, my physiotherapist, for keeping at bay the various RSIs I have acquired while writing. To my wife, Sarah, and children, Ferdia and Pippa, I owe the deepest debt, for they provide me with all the love I could need.

GLOSSARY

acetum: sour wine, the universal beverage served to Roman soldiers. Also the word for vinegar, the most common disinfectant used by Roman doctors. Vinegar is excellent at killing bacteria, and its widespread use in western medicine continued until late in the nineteenth century.

Aesculapius: son of Apollo, the god of health and the protector of doctors.

amphora (pl. *amphorae*): a large, two-handled clay vessel with a narrow neck used to store wine, olive oil and other produce. It was also a unit of measurement, equivalent to 80 pounds of wine.

aquilifer (pl. *aquiliferi*): the standard-bearer for the *aquila*, or eagle, of a legion. To carry the symbol that meant everything to Roman soldiers was a position of immense importance. Casualty rates among *aquiliferi* were high, as they were often positioned near or in the front rank during a battle. The only images surviving today show the *aquilifer* bare-headed, leading some to suppose that this was always the case. In combat, however, this would have been incredibly dangerous and we can reasonably assume that the *aquilifer* did wear a helmet. We do not definitely know if he wore an animal skin, as the *signifer* did, so to have him do so is my interpretation. His armor was often scale, and his shield probably a small one, which could be carried easily without using the hands. During the late Republic, the *aquila* itself was silver and clutched a gold thunderbolt. The wooden staff it was mounted on had a spike at its base, allowing it to be shoved into the ground, and sometimes it had arms, which permitted it to be carried more easily. Even when damaged, the *aquila* was not destroyed, but lovingly repaired time and again. If it was lost in battle, the Romans would do virtually anything to get the standard back. The recovery of Crassus' eagles by Augustus in 20 BC was thus regarded as a major achievement.

as (pl. *asses*): a small bronze coin, originally worth one-fifth of a *sestertius*. In 23 BC, its makeup was changed to copper.

atrium: the large chamber immediately beyond the entrance hall in a Roman house or *domus*. Frequently built on a grand scale, this was the social and devotional center of the house. It had an opening in the roof and a pool, the *impluvium*, to catch the rainwater that entered.

aureus (pl. *aurei*): a small gold coin worth twenty-five *denarii*. Until the time of the early Empire, it was minted infrequently.

ballista (pl. *ballistae*): a two-armed Roman catapult that looked like a big crossbow on a stand. It operated via a different principle, however, utilizing the force from the tightly coiled sinew rope holding the arms rather than the tension in the arms themselves. *Ballistae* varied in size, from those portable by soldiers to enormous engines that required wagons and mules to move them around. They fired either bolts or stones with great force and precision. Favorite types had nicknames like "onager," the wild ass, named for its kick; and "scorpion," called such because of its sting.

basilicae: huge covered markets in the Roman Forum; also where judicial, commercial and governmental activities took place. Public trials were conducted here, while lawyers, scribes and moneylenders worked side by side from little stalls. Many official announcements were made in the *basilicae*.

bestiarius (pl. *bestiarii*): men who hunted and captured animals for the arena in Rome. A highly dangerous occupation, it was also very lucrative. The more exotic the animals—for example elephants, hippopotami, giraffes and rhinoceroses—the higher the premium commanded. The mind boggles at the labor and hazards involved in bringing such animals many hundreds of miles from their natural habitat to Rome.

bucina (pl. *bucinae*): a military trumpet. The Romans used a number of types of instruments, among them the *tuba*, the *cornu* and the *bucina*. These were used for many purposes, from waking the troops each morning to sounding the charge, the halt or the retreat. We are uncertain how the different instruments were played—whether in unison or one after another, for example. To simplify matters, I have used just one of them: the *bucina*.

caldarium: an intensely hot room in Roman bath complexes. Used like a modern-day sauna, most also had a hot plunge pool. The *caldarium* was heated by hot air that flowed through hollow bricks in the walls and under the raised floor. The source of the piped heat was the *hypocaustum*, a furnace kept constantly stoked by slaves.

caligae: heavy leather sandals worn by the Roman soldier. Sturdily constructed in three layers—a sole, insole and upper—*caligae* resembled an open-toed boot. The straps could be tightened to make them fit more closely. Dozens of metal studs on the sole gave the sandals good grip; these could also be replaced when necessary. In colder climes, such as Britain, socks were often worn as well.

cella (pl. *cellae*): the windowless, rectangular central room in a temple dedicated to a god. It usually had a statue of the relevant deity, and often an altar for offerings as well.

cenacula (pl. *cenaculae*): see *insula*.

Cerberus: the monstrous three-headed hound that guarded the entrance to Hades. It allowed the spirits of the dead to enter, but none to leave.

consul: one of two annually elected chief magistrates, appointed by the people and ratified by the Senate. Effective rulers of Rome for twelve months, they were in charge of civil and military matters and led the Republic's armies into war. Each could countermand the other and both were supposed to heed the wishes of the Senate. No man was supposed to serve as consul more than once. But by the end of the second century BC, powerful nobles such as Marius, Cinna and Sulla were holding on to the position for years on end. This dangerously weakened Rome's democracy, a situation made worse by the triumvirate of Caesar, Pompey and Crassus. From then on, the end of the Republic was in sight.

contubernium (pl. *contubernia*): a group of eight legionaries who shared a tent or barracks room and who cooked and ate together.

denarius (pl. *denarii*): the staple coin of the Roman Republic. Made from silver, it was worth four *sestertii*, or ten *asses* (later sixteen). The less common gold *aureus* was worth twenty-five *denarii*.

domus: a wealthy Roman's home. Typically it faced inward, presenting a blank wall to the outside world. Built in a long, rectangular shape, the *domus* possessed two inner light sources, the *atrium* at the front and the colonnaded garden to the rear. These were separated by the large reception area of the *tablinum*. Around the *atrium* were bedrooms, offices, storerooms and shrines to a family's ancestors, while the chambers around the garden were often banqueting halls and further reception areas.

editor (pl. *editores*): the sponsor of a *munus*, a gladiatorial contest. Once part of the obligatory rituals to honor the dead, such *munera* had by the late Republic become a way of winning favor with the Roman people. The lavishness of the spectacle reflected the depth of the *editor*'s desire to please.

Felicitas: the goddess of good luck and success.

Fortuna: the goddess of luck and good fortune. Like all deities, she was notoriously fickle.

fossae (sing. *fossa*): defensive ditches, which were dug out around all Roman camps, whether temporary or permanent. They varied in number, width and depth depending on the type of camp and the degree of danger to the legion.

fugitivarius (pl. *fugitivarii*): slave-catchers, men who made a living from tracking down and capturing runaways.

Gallicinium **watch:** the Romans divided nighttime into eight watches, four before midnight, and four after it. The *Gallicinium* watch is the second of these latter four, so approximately 2 a.m. to 4 a.m.

gladius (pl. *gladii*): little information remains about the "Spanish" sword of the Republican army, the *gladius hispaniensis*, with its waisted blade. I have therefore used the "Pompeii" variation of the *gladius* as it is the shape most people are familiar with. This was a short—420–500 mm (16.5–20 in)—straight-edged sword with a V-shaped point. About 42–55 mm (1.6–2.2 in) wide, it was an extremely well-balanced weapon ideal for both cutting and thrusting. The shaped hilt was made of bone and protected by a pommel and guard of wood. The *gladius* was worn on the right, except by centurions and other senior officers, who wore it on the left. It was actually quite easy to draw with the right hand, and was probably positioned like this to avoid entanglement with the *scutum* while being unsheathed.

haruspex (pl. **haruspices**): a soothsayer. A man trained to divine in many ways, from the inspection of animal entrails to the shapes of clouds and the way birds fly. As the perceived source of blood, and therefore life itself, the liver was particularly valued for its divinatory possibilities. In addition, many natural phenomena— thunder, lightning, wind—could be used to interpret the present, past and future. The bronze liver mentioned in the book really exists; it was found in a field at Piacenza, Italy, in 1877.

hora prima: Roman time was divided into two periods, that of daylight (twelve hours) and of nighttime (eight watches). The first hour of the day, *hora prima,* started at sunrise. Great inaccuracies were present in the Romans' methods of measuring time. The main instrument used was a sundial, which meant that the latitude of the location defined day length. Thus the time in Rome was quite different to Sicily, far to the south. In addition, varying day length throughout the year meant that daylight hours in the winter were shorter than in the summer. We must therefore assume that time was more elastic in ancient times. The Romans also devised the clepsydra, or water clock. By using a transparent water vessel with a regular intake, it was possible to mark the level of water for each daylight hour, and then to use it at night or during fog.

Imperator: a Latin word that meant "commander" in Republican times. Later it came to be one of the emperor's titles, and of course gave rise to the English word.

insula (pl. *insulae*): high-rise (three-, four, or even five-story) tenements in which most Roman citizens lived. As early as 218 BC, Livy recorded the tale of an ox that escaped from the market and scaled the stairs of an *insula* before hurling itself to its death from the third floor. The ground level of each *insula* often comprised a *taberna,* or shop, which opened right onto the street via a large arched doorway. The shopkeeper and his family lived and slept in the room above. Built on top of this was floor after floor of *cenaculae,* the plebeians' apartments. Cramped, poorly lit, heated only by braziers, and often dangerously constructed, the *cenaculae* had no running water or sanitation. Access to the flats was made via staircases built on the outside of the building.

intervallum: the wide, flat area inside the walls of a Roman camp or fort. As well as serving to protect the barrack buildings from enemy missiles, it could when necessary allow the massing of troops before battle.

Juno: sister and wife of Jupiter, she was the goddess of marriage and women.

Jupiter: often referred to as *Optimus Maximus*—"Greatest and Best." Most powerful of the Roman gods, he was responsible for weather, especially storms. Jupiter was the brother as well as the husband of Juno.

lanista (pl. *lanistae*): a gladiator trainer, often the owner of a *ludus*, a gladiator school.

latifundium (pl. *latifundia*): a large estate, usually owned by Roman nobility, and utilizing large numbers of slaves as labor. *Latifundia* date back to the second century bc, when vast areas of land were confiscated from Italian peoples defeated by Rome, such as the Samnites.

legate: the officer in command of a legion, and a man of senatorial rank. In the late Roman Republic, legates were still appointed by generals such as Caesar from the ranks of their family, friends and political allies.

lictum: linen loincloth worn by nobles. It is likely that all classes wore a variant of this; unlike the Greeks, the Romans did not believe in unnecessary public nudity.

lictor (pl. *lictores*): a magistrate's enforcer. Only strongly built citizens could apply for this job. *Lictores* were essentially the bodyguards for the consuls, praetors and other senior Roman magistrates. Such officials were accompanied at all times in public by set numbers of *lictores* (the number depended on their rank). Each *lictor* carried a *fasces*, the symbol of justice: a bundle of rods enclosing an axe. Other duties included the arresting and punishment of wrongdoers.

ludus (pl. *ludi*): a gladiator school.

manica (pl. *manicae*): an arm guard used by gladiators. It was usually made of layered materials such as durable linen and leather, or metal.

mantar: a Turkish word meaning "mold." I have taken advantage of its exotic sound to use it as a word for the penicillin powder that Tarquinius uses on Benignus.

manumissio: during the Republic, the act of freeing a slave was actually quite complex. It was usually done in one of three ways: by claim to the praetor, during the sacrifices of the five yearly *lustrum,* or by a testamentary clause in a will. A slave could not be freed until at least the age of thirty and continued to owe formal duties to his or her former master after manumission. During the Empire, the process was made much more simple. It became possible to verbally grant manumission at a feast, using the guests as witnesses.

Mars: the god of war. All spoils of war were consecrated to him, and no Roman commander would go on campaign without having visited the temple of Mars to ask for the god's protection and blessing.

Minerva: the goddess of war and also of wisdom.

Mithraeum (pl. **Mithraea**): the underground temples built by devotees of Mithras. Examples can be found from Rome (there is one in the basement of a church just five minutes' walk from the Coliseum) to Hadrian's Wall (Carrawburgh, among others).

Mithras: originally a Persian god, he was born on the winter solstice, in a cave. He wore a Phrygian blunt-peaked hat and was associated with the sun, hence the name *Sol Invictus:* "Unconquered Sun." With the help of various creatures, he sacrificed a bull, which gave rise to life on earth: a creation myth. The sharing of wine and bread as well as the shaking of hands were possibly initially Mithraic rituals. Unfortunately we know little about the religion, except that there were various levels of devotion, with rites of passage being required between them. A mosaic in a mithraeum at Ostia reveals fascinating snippets about the seven levels of initiate. With its tenets of courage, strength and endurance, Mithraicism was very popular among the Roman military, especially during the Empire. Latterly the secretive religion came into conflict with Christianity, and it was being actively suppressed by the fourth century AD.

modius (pl. *modii*): an official Roman dry measure of approximately 8.6 l (just over 15 pts). To prevent malpractice, all weights and measures (wet and dry) were standardized.

murmillo (pl. *murmillones*): one of the most familiar types of gladiator. The bronze, crested helmet was very distinctive, with a broad brim, a bulging faceplate and grillwork eyeholes. The crest was often fitted with groups of feathers, and may also have been fashioned in a fish shape. The *murmillo* wore a *manica* on the right arm and a greave on the left leg; like the legionary, he carried a heavy rectangular shield and was armed with a *gladius*. His only garments were the *subligaria*, an intricately folded linen under-cloth, and the *balteus*, a wide, protective belt. In Republican times, the most common opponent for the *murmillo* was the *secutor*, although later on this became the *retiarius*.

noxii (sing. *noxius*). criminals convicted of the worst offenses, prisoners of war, slaves, traitors or deserters. Their punishment was to be condemned to execution in the arena by the most extreme of methods. These included crucifixion, being pitted against wild beasts, or burned to death. To our modern sensibilities, these methods seem monstrous, but in the Romans' minds, the punishment had to fit the crime.

optio (pl. *optiones*): the officer who ranked immediately below a centurion; the second in command of a century.

Orcus: the god of the underworld. Also known as Pluto or Hades, he was believed to be Jupiter's brother, and was greatly feared.

pali (sing. *palus*): 1.82-m (6-ft) wooden posts buried in the ground. Trainee gladiators and legionaries were taught swordsmanship by aiming blows at them.

papaverum: the drug morphine, made from the flowers of the opium plant. Its use has been documented from at least 1000 BC. Roman doctors used it to allow them to perform prolonged operations on patients.

peltast: a light infantryman of Greek and Anatolian origin. Apart from a shield, they fought unarmored and, depending on their nationality, carried *rhomphaiai* or javelins and sometimes spears or knives. Their primary use was as skirmishers.

phalera (pl. *phalerae*): a sculpted disc-like decoration for bravery that was worn on a chest harness, over a Roman soldier's armor. *Phalerae* were commonly made of bronze, but could be made of more precious metals as well. Torques, arm rings and bracelets were also awarded.

pilum (pl. *pila*): the Roman javelin. It consisted of a wooden shaft approximately 1.2 m (4 ft) long, joined to a thin iron shank approximately 0.6 m (2 ft) long, and was topped by a small pyramidal point. The javelin was heavy and, when launched, all of its weight was concentrated behind the head, giving it tremendous penetrative force. It could strike through a shield to injure the man carrying it, or lodge in the shield, making it impossible for the man to continue using it. The range of the *pilum* was about 30 m (100 ft), although the effective range was probably about half this distance.

Priapus: the god of gardens and fields, a symbol of fertility. Often pictured with a huge erect penis.

primus pilus: the senior centurion of the whole legion, and possibly—probably—the senior centurion of the first cohort. A position of immense importance, it would have been held by a veteran soldier, typically in his forties or fifties. On retiring, the *primus pilus* was entitled to admission to the equestrian class.

principia: the headquarters of a legion, to be found on the Via Praetoria. This was the beating heart of the legion in a marching camp or fort; it was where all the administration was carried out and where the unit's standards, in particular the *aquila*, or eagle, were kept. Its massive entrance opened onto a colonnaded and paved courtyard which was bordered on each side by offices. Behind this was a huge forehall with a high roof, which contained statues, the shrine for the standards, a vault for the legion's pay and possibly more offices. It is likely that parades took place here, and that senior officers addressed their men in the hall.

pugio: a dagger. Some Roman soldiers carried these, an extra weapon. They were probably as useful in daily life (for eating and preparing food, etc.) as when on campaign.

retiarius (pl. *retiarii*): the fisherman, or net and trident fighter, named after the *rete*, or net. Also an easily recognizable class of gladiator, the *retiarius* merely wore a *subligaria*. His only protection consisted of the *galerus*, a metal shoulder-guard, which was attached to the top edge of a *manica* on his left arm. His weapons were the weighted net, a trident and a dagger. With less equipment to weigh him down, the *retiarius* was far more mobile than many other gladiators and, lacking a helmet, was also instantly recognizable. This may have accounted for the low status of this class of fighter.

rhomphaia (pl. *rhomphaiai*): essentially a polearm. This fearsome weapon had a straight or slightly curved single cutting edge attached to a pole which was considerably longer than the blade. While primarily used by the Thracians, a variant called the *falx* was also used by the Dacians. The design of both gave tremendous cutting force. After encountering the *falx* in Dacia, the Romans' response was to make the only known documented change to their armor in response to an enemy's weapon, that of strengthening their helmets with reinforcing bars.

rudis: the wooden *gladius* that symbolized the freedom that could be granted to a gladiator who pleased a sponsor sufficiently, or who had earned enough victories in the arena to qualify for it.

Not all gladiators were condemned to die in combat: far from it. Prisoners of war and criminals usually were, but slaves who had committed a crime were granted the *rudis* if they survived for three years as a gladiator. After a further two years, they could be set free.

scutum (pl. *scuta*): an elongated oval Roman army shield, about 1.2 m (4 ft) tall and 0.75 m (2 ft 6 in) wide. It was made from two layers of wood, the pieces laid at right angles to each other; it was then covered with linen or canvas, and leather. The *scutum* was heavy, weighing between 6 and 10 kg (13–22 lb). A large metal boss decorated its center, with the horizontal grip placed behind this. Decorative designs were often painted on the front, and a leather cover was used to protect the shield when not in use, e.g., while marching.

secutor (pl. *secutores*): the pursuer, or hunter class of gladiator. Also called the *contraretiarius*, the *secutor* fought the fisherman, the *retiarius*. Virtually the only difference between the *secutor* and the *murmillo* was the smooth-surfaced helmet, which was without a brim and had a small, plain crest, probably to make it more difficult for the *retiarius'* net to catch and hold. Unlike other gladiators' helmets, the *secutor's* had small eyeholes, making it very difficult to see. This was possibly to reduce the chances of the heavily armored fighter quickly overcoming the *retiarius*.

sestertius (pl. *sestertii*): a silver coin, it was worth four *asses*; or a quarter of a *denarius*; or one hundredth of an *aureus*. Its name, "two units and a half third one," comes from its original value, two and a half *asses*. By the time of the late Roman Republic, its use was becoming more common.

signifer (pl. *signiferi*): a standard-bearer and junior officer. This was a position of high esteem, with one for every century in a legion. Not much definite information survives about the uniform worn by *signiferi* at this time. Following later examples, I have made the *signifer* wear scale armor and an animal skin over his helmet, and carry a small round shield rather than a *scutum*. His *signum*, or standard, consisted of a wooden pole bearing a raised hand, or a spear tip surrounded by palm leaves. Below this was a crossbar from which hung metal decorations, or a piece of colored cloth. The standard's shaft was decorated with discs, half-moons, ships' prows and crowns, which were records of the unit's achievements and may have distinguished one century from another.

stade (pl. *stadia*): a Greek word. It was the distance of the original foot race in the ancient Olympic games of 776 BC, and was approximately 192 m (630 ft) in length. The word "stadium" derives from it.

stola: a long, loose tunic, with or without sleeves, worn by married women. Those who were unmarried wore other types of tunic, but to simplify things, I have mentioned only one garment, worn by all.

tablinum: the office or reception area beyond the *atrium*. The *tablinum* usually opened onto an enclosed colonnaded garden.

tesserarius: one of the junior officers in a century, whose duties included commanding the guard. The name originates from the *tessera* tablet on which was written the password for the day.

testudo: the famous Roman square formation, formed by legionaries in the middle raising their *scuta* over their heads while those at the sides formed a shield wall. The *testudo*, or tortoise, was used to resist missile attack or to protect soldiers while they undermined the walls of towns under siege. The formation's strength was reputedly tested during military training by driving a cart pulled by mules over the top of it.

Thracian: like most gladiators, this class had its origins with one of Rome's enemies—Thrace (modern-day Bulgaria). Armed with a small square shield with a convex surface, this fighter wore greaves on both legs and, occasionally, *fasciae*—protectors on the thighs.

The right arm was covered by a *manica*. A Hellenistic-type helmet was worn, with a broad curving brim and cheek guards.

thureophoros (pl. *thureophoroi*): an infantryman very similar to the peltast. The *thurephoroi* succeeded the peltasts as one of the most common types of mercenary in the eastern Mediterranean from the third century BC onward. Grave paintings for *thureophoroi* have been found in Greece, Anatolia, Bithynia and Egypt. Carrying oval or rectangular shields rather than round ones, they wore Macedonian-style helmets and a variety of colored tunics, and were armed with a long spear, javelins and a sword.

tribune: senior staff officer within a legion; also one of ten political positions in Rome, where they served as "tribunes of the people," defending the rights of the plebeians. The tribunes could also veto measures taken by the Senate or consuls, except in times of war. To assault a tribune was a crime of the highest order.

trierarch: the captain of a trireme. Originally a Greek rank, the term persisted in the Roman navy.

triplex acies: the standard deployment of a legion for battle. Three lines were formed some distance apart, with four cohorts in the front line and three in the middle and rear lines. The gaps between the cohorts and between the lines themselves are unclear, but the legionaries would have been accustomed to different variations, and to changing these quickly when ordered.

trireme: the classic Roman warship, which was powered by a single sail and three banks of oars. Each oar was rowed by one man, who was freeborn, not a slave. Exceptionally maneuverable, and capable of up to 8 knots under sail or for short bursts when rowed, the trireme also had a bronze ram at the prow. This was used to damage or even sink enemy ships. Small catapults were also mounted on the deck. Each trireme was crewed by around 30 men and had approximately 200 rowers; it also carried up to 60 marines (in a reduced century), giving it a very large crew in proportion to its size. This limited the triremes' range, so they were mainly used as troop transports and to protect coastlines.

valetudinarium: the hospital in a legionary fort. These were usually rectangular buildings with a central courtyard. They contained up to sixty-four wards, each similar to the rooms in the legionary barracks that held a *contubernium* of soldiers.

velarium: a cloth awning positioned over the seats of the rich at the arena. It protected them from the worst of the sun's heat and allowed Roman women to remain fair-skinned, a most important quality.

venatores (sing. *venator*): a trained beast-fighter. They hunted animals like antelope, wild goats and giraffe, and more dangerous ones such as lions, tigers, bears and elephants. Typically the lowest class of gladiator, the *venatores* provided the warm-up acts in the morning, before the main attraction of man-to-man combats later in the day.

Venus: the Roman goddess of motherhood and domesticity.

vexillum (pl. *vexilla*): a distinctive, usually red, flag that was used to denote the commander's position in camp or in battle. *Vexilla* were also used by detachments serving away from their units.

vilicus: slave foreman or farm manager. Commonly a slave, the *vilicus* was sometimes a paid worker, whose job it was to make sure that the returns on a farm were as large as possible. This was most commonly done by treating the slaves brutally.

Now read a chapter from

SOLDIER OF CARTHAGE

The first book in Ben Kane's thrilling new trilogy

I

HANNO

Hanno!" His father's voice echoed off the painted stucco walls.

"It's time to go."

Stepping carefully over the gutter which carried liquid waste out to the soakaway in the street, Hanno looked back. He was torn between his duty and the urgent gestures of his friend, Suniaton. The political meetings which his father had recently insisted he attend bored him to tears. Each one he'd been to followed exactly the same path. A group of self-important, bearded elders, clearly fond of the sound of their own voices, made interminable speeches about how Hannibal Barca's actions in Iberia were exceeding the remit granted to him. Malchus—his father—and his closest allies, who supported Hannibal, would say little or nothing until the graybeards had fallen silent, when they stood forth one by one. Invariably, Malchus spoke last of all. His words seldom varied. Hannibal, who had only been commander in Iberia for a year, was doing an incredible job in cementing Carthage's hold over the wild native tribes, forming a disciplined army, and, most importantly, filling the city's coffers with the silver from his mines. Who else was performing such heroic and worthy endeavors, while simultaneously enriching Carthage? On these grounds, the young Barca should be left to his own purposes.

Hanno knew that the first, and particularly the second, reasons were what motivated Malchus, but it was his last point which elicited the loudest reaction, the most nods of approval. The majority of Carthage's leaders were, first and foremost, traders, whose primary interest was profit. According to Malchus though, their financial acuity—and greed—did not grant them the gift of political or military foresight. His carefully chosen words therefore normally swayed the Senate in favor, which was why Hanno didn't want to waste yet another day which could be spent fishing. The interminable politicking in the hallowed but airless debating chamber made him want to shout and scream, and to tell the old fools what he really thought of them. Of course he would never shame his father in that manner, but the hour of final reckoning so often predicted by Malchus wouldn't come to pass today, Hanno was sure of that.

One of Hannibal's messengers regularly visited to bring his father news from Iberia, and had been not a week since. The nighttime rendezvous were supposed to be a secret, but Hanno had soon come to recognize the cloaked, sallow-skinned officer. Before Sapho and Bostar, his older brothers, had joined the army, they'd been allowed to stand in on the meetings. Swearing Hanno to secrecy, they had filled him in afterward. Now the pair were gone, he simply eavesdropped. To his knowledge, there had been no mention so far of attacking Saguntum, a Greek city in Iberia which was allied to Rome. Yet the tension was rising. Saguntum had recently accused a tribe supported by Carthage of raiding its territory, and claimed substantial recompense. Hannibal had answered in his allies' stead, dismissing Saguntum's demands out of hand. His gesture possessed far more intent than just the defense of an ally: It was intended to

offend Rome. Malchus and his allies had been charged by Hannibal's messenger with the task of ensuring that the Carthaginian
Senate continued to back his actions.

The deep, gravelly voice called out again, echoing down the corridor which led to the central courtyard. There was a hint of annoyance in it now. "Hanno? Where are you? We'll be late."

Hanno froze. He wasn't afraid of the dressing-down his father
would deliver later, more of the disappointed look in his eyes. A
scion of one of Carthage's oldest families, Malchus led by example,
and expected his sons to do the same. At seventeen, Hanno was the
youngest. He was also the one who most often failed to meet these
exacting standards. Farming, the traditional source of their wealth,
interested him little. Warfare, his father's preferred vocation, and
Hanno's great fascination, was barred to him still, thanks to his
youth. Frustration, and resentment, filled him. All he could do was
practice his riding and weapons skills. Life according to his father
was so boring, Hanno thought, choosing to ignore Malchus' oft-
repeated statement: "Be patient. All good things come to those who
wait."

"Come on!" urged Suniaton, thumping Hanno on the arm. His
gold earrings jingled as he jerked his head in the direction of the
harbor. "The fishermen found huge shoals of tunny in the bay at
dawn. With Melqart's blessing, the fish won't have moved far. We'll
catch dozens. Think of the money we'll make!" His voice dropped
to a whisper. "I've taken an amphora of wine from Father's cellar.
We can share it on the boat."

Unable to resist his friend's offer, Hanno blocked his ears to Malchus' voice, which was coming closer. Tunny was one of the most
prized fish in the Mediterranean. If the shoals were close to shore,
this was an opportunity too good to miss. Stepping into the rutted
street, he glanced once more at the symbol etched into the stone
slab before the flat-roofed house's entrance. An inverted triangle

topped by a flat line and then a circle, it represented his people's preeminent deity. Few dwellings were without it. Hanno asked Tanit's forgiveness for disobeying his father's wishes, but his excitement was such that he forgot to ask for the mother goddess's protection.

"Hanno!" His father's voice was very near now.

Eager to avoid Malchus, the two young men darted off into the crowd. Both their families lived near the top of Byrsa Hill. At the summit, reached by a monumental staircase of sixty steps, was an immense temple dedicated to Eshmoun, the god of health and well-being. Suniaton lived with his family in the sprawling complex behind the shrine, where his father served as a priest. Named in honor of the deity, Eshmuniaton—abbreviated to Suniaton or simply Suni—was Hanno's oldest and closest friend. The pair had scarcely spent a day out of each other's company since they were old enough to walk.

The rest of the neighborhood was primarily residential. Byrsa was one of the richer quarters, as its wide, straight thoroughfares and right-angled intersections proved. The majority of the city's winding streets were no more than ten paces across, but here they averaged more than twice this width. In addition to wealthy merchants and senior army officers, the *suffetes*, judges and many senators also called the area home. For this reason, Hanno ran with his gaze directed at the packed earth and the regular soakaway holes beneath his feet. Plenty of people knew who he was. Having just reached manhood, he was supposed to attend most of the meetings that his father did. The last thing he wanted was to be stopped and challenged by one of Malchus' numerous political opponents. To be dragged back home by the ear would be embarrassing and bring dishonor to his family.

As long as he didn't catch anyone's eye, he and his friend would pass unnoticed. Bare-headed, and wearing tight-fitting red woolen singlets with a central white stripe and a distinctive wide neck band, and breeches that reached to the knee, the pair looked no different to other well-to-do youths. Their garb was far more practical than the long straight wool tunics and conical felt hats favored by most adult men, and more comfortable than the ornate jacket and pleated apron worn by those of Cypriot extraction. Sheathed daggers hung from simple leather straps thrown over their shoulders. Suniaton carried a bulging leather pack on his back. Although people said that they could pass for brothers, Hanno couldn't see it most of the time. While he was tall and athletic, Suniaton was short and squat. Naturally, they both had tightly curled black hair and a dark complexion, but there the resemblance ended. His face was thin, with a straight nose and high cheekbones, while his friend's round visage and snub nose were complemented by a jutting chin. They did both have green eyes, Hanno conceded. That feature, unusual among the brown-eyed Carthaginians, was probably why they were thought to be siblings.

A step ahead of him, Suniaton nearly collided with a carpenter carrying several long cypress planks. Rather than apologize, he thumbed his nose and sprinted toward the citadel walls, now only a hundred paces away. Stifling his desire to finish the job by tipping over the angry tradesman, Hanno dodged past too, a grin splitting his face. Another similarity he and Suniaton shared was an impudent nature, quite at odds with the serious manner of most of their countrymen. It frequently got both of them in trouble, and was a constant source of irritation to their fathers.

A moment later, they passed under the immense ramparts, which were thirty paces deep and taller than eight men standing on each other's shoulders. Like the outer defenses, the wall was constructed from great quadrilateral blocks of sandstone. Regular coats of whitewash ensured that the sunlight bounced off the stone, magnifying its size. Topped by a wide walkway and with towers every fifty steps, the fortifications were truly awe-inspiring. And the citadel was only a small part of the whole. Hanno never tired of looking down on the expanse of the sea wall which came into view as he emerged from under the shadow of the gateway. Running down from the north along the city's perimeter, it swept southeast to the twin harbors, curling protectively around them before heading west. On the steep northern and eastern sides, and to the south, where the sea gave its added protection, one wall was deemed sufficient, but on the western, landward side of the peninsula, three defenses had been constructed: a wide trench backed by an earthen bank, and then a huge rampart. The quarters within the walls, which were in total over a hundred and eighty *stades* in length, could hold twenty thousand troops, four thousand cavalry and their mounts, and hundreds of war elephants.

Home to nearly a quarter of a million people, the city was also worthy of a second look. Directly below them lay the Agora, the large open space which was bordered by the Senate, government buildings and countless shops. It was the area where residents gathered to do business, demonstrate, take the evening air, and vote. Beyond it lay the unique ports—the huge outer, rectangular merchant harbor, and the inner, circular naval docks with their small, central island. The first contained hundreds of berths for trading ships, while the second could hold more than ten score triremes and quinqueremes in specially constructed covered sheds. To the west of the ports was the old shrine of Ba'al Hammon, no longer as important as it had previously been, but still venerated by most. To the east lay the *choma*, the huge man-made landing stage where fishing smacks and small vessels tied up. It was also their destination.

Hanno was immensely proud of his home. He had no idea what Rome, Carthage's old enemy, looked like, but he doubted it matched his city's grandeur. He had no desire to compare Carthage with the Republic's capital though. The only way he ever wanted to see Rome was humbled—by a victorious Carthaginian army—and then burned to the ground. As Hamilcar Barca, Hannibal's father, had inculcated a hatred of all things Roman in his son, so had Malchus in Hanno. Like Hamilcar, Malchus had served in the first war against the Republic, fighting in Sicily for ten long, thankless years.

Unsurprisingly, Hanno knew the details of every land skirmish and naval battle in the conflict, which had actually lasted for more than a generation. The cost to Carthage in loss of life, territory and wealth had been huge, but the city's wounds ran far deeper. Her pride had been trampled in the mud by the defeat, and this ignominy was repeated only four years after the war's conclusion. Carthage had been unilaterally forced by Rome to give up Sardinia, as well as paying more indemnities. The shabby act proved beyond doubt, Malchus would regularly rant, that all Romans were treacherous dogs, without honor. Hanno agreed, and looked forward to the day hostilities were reopened once more. Given the depth of anger still present in Carthage toward Rome, conflict was inevitable. That didn't mean Hanno wanted to spend all his time listening to boring speeches though.

Suniaton turned. "Have you eaten?"

Hanno shrugged. "Some bread and honey when I got up."

"Me too. That was hours ago though." Suniaton grinned and patted his belly. "We could be gone all day. Best get some supplies."

"Good idea," Hanno replied. They kept clay gourds of water in their little boat with their fishing gear, but no food. Sunset, when they would return, was a long way off.

The streets descending Byrsa Hill did not follow the regular layout of the summit, instead radiating out like so many tributaries of a meandering river. There were far more shops and businesses visible now: bakers, butchers and stalls selling freshly caught fish, fruit and vegetables stood beside silver and coppersmiths, perfume merchants, and glass blowers. Women sat outside their doors, working at their looms, or gossiping over their purchases. Slaves carried rich men past in litters or swept the ground in front of shops. Dye-makers' premises were everywhere, their abundance due to the Carthaginian skill of harvesting the local *murex* shellfish and pounding its flesh to yield a purple dye which commanded premium prices all over the Mediterranean. Children ran hither and thither, playing catch and chasing each other up and down the regular sets of stairs which broke the street's steep descent. A group of Libyan soldiers clattered past, a richly dressed Carthaginian officer in their midst. He was wearing a bell-shaped helmet with a thick rim and a yellow horsehair crest, scale armor, and bronze greaves. An expensive-looking cloak was fastened at his right shoulder by a gold brooch wrought in the shape of a horse's head alongside a palm tree, two of Carthage's sacred symbols. Recognizing the officer, who was probably on his way to the very meeting he was supposed to be attending, Hanno quickly pretended to study the nearest array of terracotta outside a potter's workshop.

Dozens of figures—large and small—were ranked on low tables. Hanno recognized every god and goddess in the Carthaginian pantheon. There sat a regal, crowned Ba'al Hammon, the protector of Carthage, on his throne; beside him Tanit was depicted in the Egyptian manner—a shapely woman's body in a well-cut dress, but with the head of a lioness. A smiling Astarte clutched a tambourine. Her consort, Melqart, known as the "King of the City," was, among other things, the god of the sea. Various brightly colored figures depicted him emerging from crashing waves riding a fearful-looking monster and clutching a trident in one fist. Ba'al Safon, the god of storm and war, sat astride a fine charger, wearing a helmet with a long, flowing crest. Also on display were a selection of hideous, grinning painted masks—tattooed, bejeweled demons and spirits of the underworld—tomb offerings designed to ward off evil.

Hanno shivered, remembering his mother's funeral only three

years before. Since her death—of a fever—his father, never the most warm of men, had become a grim and forbidding presence who only lived to gain his revenge on Rome. For all his youth, Hanno knew that Malchus was portraying a controlled mask to the world. He must still be grieving, as surely as he and his brothers were. Arishat, Hanno's mother, had been the light to Malchus' dark, the laughter to his gravitas, the softness to his strength. The center to the family, she had been taken from them in two horrific days and nights. Harangued by an inconsolable Malchus, the best surgeons in Carthage had toiled over her to no avail. Every last detail of her final hours was engraved in Hanno's memory. The cups of blood drained from her in a vain attempt to cool her raging temperature. Her gaunt, fevered face. The sweat-soaked sheets. His brothers trying not to cry, and failing. And lastly, her still form on the bed, smaller than she had ever been in life. Malchus kneeling alongside, great sobs wracking his muscular frame. That was the only time Hanno had ever seen his father weep. The incident had never been mentioned since, nor had his mother. He swallowed hard, and checking that the patrol had passed by, moved on. It hurt too much to think about such things.

A moment later, Suniaton, who had not noticed Hanno's distress, paused to buy some bread, almonds and figs. Keen to lift his somber mood, Hanno had eyes only for the blacksmith's forge off to one side. Wisps of smoke rose from its roughly built chimney, and the air was rich with the smells of charcoal, burning wood and oil. Harsh metallic sounds reached his ears too. In the recesses of the open-fronted establishment, he glimpsed a figure in a leather apron carefully lifting a piece of glowing metal from the anvil with a pair of tongs. There was a loud hiss as the sword blade was plunged into a vat of cold water. Hanno felt his feet move toward the forge. He knew the smith, had spent long hours in his company, learning something of his craft. Much of the weaponry for

Carthaginian officers was made in places like this. He'd even helped to make his own iron sword there. A typical example of the blade wielded by his race, it was straight—the length of his extended hand and forearm—and double-edged. The simple pommel and hilt were made of carved wood and bone. It was Hanno's most prized possession.

"Hey! We've got better things to do. Like making money," cried Suniaton, blocking his path. He shoved a bulging bag of almonds at Hanno. "Carry that."

"No! You'll eat them all anyway." Hanno pushed his friend out of the way and ran off, laughing. It was a standing joke between them that his favorite pastime was getting covered in ash and grime while Suniaton would rather plan his next meal.

Soon they had reached the Agora. Its four sides, each a *stade* in length, were made up of grand porticoes and covered walkways. The beating heart of the city, it was home to the Senate, government buildings, a library, numerous temples and shops. It was also where, on summer evenings, the better-off young men and women would gather in groups, a safe distance apart, to eye each other up. Socializing with the opposite sex was frowned upon, and chaperones for the girls were never far away. Despite this, inventive methods to approach the object of one's desire were constantly being invented. Of recent months, this had become one of the friends' favorite pastimes. Fishing beat it still, but not by much, thought Hanno wistfully, scanning the crowds for any sign of attractive female flesh.

Instead of gaggles of coy young beauties though, the Agora was full of serious-looking politicians, merchants and high-ranking soldiers heading for one place. The Senate. Within its hallowed walls, in a grand pillared debating chamber, more than three hundred senators met on a regular basis, as, for more than half a millennium, their predecessors had done. Overseen by the two *suffetes*—the yearly elected rulers—they, the most important men in Carthage, decided everything from trading policy to negotiations with foreign states. Their range of powers did not end there. The Senate was also where declarations of war and peace were made—yet they did not appoint the army's generals any longer. Since the war with Rome, that had been left to the people. The only prerequisites for candidature for the Senate were citizenship, wealth, an age of thirty or more, and the demonstration of ability, whether that be in the agricultural, mercantile, or military fields.

Ordinary citizens could participate in politics via the Assembly of the People, which congregated once a year, by the order of the *suffetes*, in the Agora. During times of great crisis, it was permitted to gather spontaneously and debate the issues of the day. While its powers were limited, they included electing the *suffetes*, and the generals. Hanno was looking forward to the next meeting, which would be the first he'd attend as an adult, entitled to vote. Although Hannibal's enormous public popularity guaranteed his reappointment as the commander-in-chief of Carthage's armies in Iberia, Hanno wanted to show his support for the Barca clan. It was the only way he could at the moment. Despite his requests, Malchus would not let him join Hannibal's army, as Sapho and Bostar had done after their mother's death. Instead, he had to finish his education. Hanno did not fight his father on this: There was no point. Once Malchus had spoken, he never went back on a decision.

Following Carthaginian tradition, Hanno had continued to sleep at home from the age of fourteen, but he had largely fended for himself, working in the forge among other places. In this way, he'd earned enough to live on without committing any crimes or shameful acts. This was similar to, but not as harsh, as the Spartan way. He had also had taken classes in Greek, Iberian and Latin. Hanno did not especially enjoy languages, but he had come to accept that such a skill would prove useful among the polyglot of nationalities which formed the Carthaginian army. His people did not take naturally to war, so they hired mercenaries, or enlisted their subjects, to fight on their behalf. Libyans, Spaniards, Gauls and Balearic tribesmen each brought their own qualities to Carthage's forces.

Naturally, Hanno's favorite part of his instruction was that dedicated to military matters. Malchus himself taught him the history of war, from the battles of Xenophon and Thermopylae to the victories won by Alexander of Macedon. Central to his father's lessons were the intricate details of tactics and planning. Particular attention was paid to Carthaginian defeats in the war with Rome, and the reasons for them. "We lost because of our leaders' lack of determination. All they thought about was how to contain the conflict, not win it. How to minimize cost, not disregard it in the total pursuit of victory," Malchus thundered during one memorable lesson. "The Romans are motherless curs, but by all the gods, they possess strength of purpose. Whenever they lost a battle, they did not give up. No, they recruited more men, and rebuilt their ships. When the public purse was empty, their leaders willingly spent their own wealth. Their damn Republic means everything to them. Yet who in Carthage offered to send us the supplies and soldiers we needed so badly in Sicily? My father, the Barcas, and a handful of others. No one else." He barked a short, angry laugh. "Why should I be surprised? Our ancestors were traders, not soldiers." He fixed his dark, deep-set eyes on Hanno. "To gain our rightful revenge, we must follow Hannibal. He's a natural soldier, a born leader—as his father was. Carthage never gave Hamilcar the chance to beat Rome, but we can offer it to his son. When the time is right."

A red-faced, portly senator shoved past with a curse. Startled, Hanno recognized Hostus, one of his father's most implacable enemies in the Senate. The self-important politician was in such a hurry that he didn't even notice who he'd collided with. Hanno hawked and spat, although he was careful not to do it in Hostus' direction.

Hostus and his windbag friends complained endlessly about Hannibal, yet were content to accept the shiploads of silver sent from his mines in Iberia. Lining their own pockets with a proportion of this wealth, they had no desire to confront Rome again. Hanno, on the other hand, was more than prepared to lay down his life fighting their old enemy, but the time wasn't ripe. Hannibal was preparing himself in Iberia, and that was good enough. For now, they had to wait, but Hanno was damned if he'd listen to Hostus and his ilk any longer. It was time to enjoy himself.

Carefully the pair skirted the edge of the Agora, avoiding the worst of the crowds. Around the back of the Senate, the buildings soon lost their grandeur, returning to the shabby aspect one would expect close to a port. Nonetheless, the slum stood in stark contrast to the splendor just a short walk away. There were few businesses, and the single- or twin-roomed houses were miserable affairs made of mud bricks, which looked ready to tumble at any moment. The iron-hard ruts in the street were more than a hand span deep, threatening to break their ankles if they tripped. No work parties to fill in the holes with sand here, thought Hanno, thinking of Byrsa Hill. He felt even more grateful for his elevated position in life.

Snot-nosed, scrawny children wearing little more than rags swarmed in, clamoring for a coin or a crust, while their lank-haired, pregnant mothers gazed at them with eyes deadened by a life of misery. Half-dressed girls posed provocatively in some doorways, their rouged cheeks and lips unable to conceal the fact that they were barely out of childhood. Unshaven, ill-clad men lounged around, rolling sheep tailbones in the dirt for a few worn coins. They stared suspiciously, but none dared hinder the friends' progress. At night it might be a different matter, but already they were under the shadow of the great wall, with its smartly turned-out sentries marching to and fro along the battlements. Although common, lawlessness was punished where possible by the authorities, and a shout of distress would bring help clattering down one of the many sets of stairs. It was a shame, thought Hanno with a backward glance at the pitiable specimens, that such men weren't expected to fight for their country, as ordinary Roman citizens were. Given a purpose, their lot would improve infinitely, as would that of Carthage.

The tang of salt grew strong in the air. Gulls keened overheard, and the shouts of sailors could be heard from the ports. Feeling his excitement grow, Hanno charged down a narrow alleyway, and up the stone steps at the end of it. Suniaton was right behind him. It was a steep climb, but they were both extremely fit, and reached the top without breaking a sweat. A red concrete walkway extended the entire width of the wall—thirty paces—just as it did for the entire length of the defensive perimeter. Strongly built towers were positioned every fifty steps or so. The soldiers visible were garrisoned in the barracks which were built at regular intervals below the ramparts.

The nearest sentries, a quartet of Libyan spearmen, glanced idly at the pair, but seeing nothing of concern, looked away. In peacetime, citizens were allowed on the wall during the hours of daylight. Perfunctorily checking the turquoise sea below their section, the junior officer fell back to gossiping with his men. Hanno trotted past, admiring the Libyans' massive round shields, which were even larger than those used by the Greeks. Although made of wood, they were covered in goatskin, and rimmed with bronze. The same demonic face was painted on each, and denoted their unit. He didn't envy them their heavy bronze helmets and padded linen cuirasses, though. Despite the fact that they were doing nothing, the Libyans' sallow faces were covered with sweat. Hanno wasn't naive: He had trained with similar armor and weapons. In spite of his dreams, the idea of marching long distances and fighting under the hot sun was intimidating. He was glad that diversions like fishing were still an option.

Trumpets blared one after another from the naval port, and Suniaton jostled past, outstripping him. "Quick," he shouted. "They might be launching a quinquereme!"

Hanno chased eagerly after his friend. The view from the walkway into the circular harbor was second to none. In a masterful feat of engineering, the Carthaginian warships were invisible from all other positions. Protected from unfriendly eyes on the seaward side by the city wall, they were concealed from the moored merchant vessels by the naval port's slender entrance, which was only just wider than a quinquereme, the largest type of warship.

Hanno scowled as they reached a good vantage point. Instead of the imposing sight of a warship sliding backward into the water, he saw only a purple-cloaked admiral strutting along the jetty which led from the periphery of the circular docks to the central island, where the navy's headquarters were. Another fanfare of trumpets sounded, making sure that every man in the place knew who was arriving. "What has he got to swagger about," Hanno muttered angrily. Malchus reserved much of his anger for the incompetent Carthaginian fleet, so he had learned to feel the same way. Carthage's days as a superpower of the sea were long gone, smashed into so much driftwood by Rome during the two nations' bitter struggle over Sicily. Remarkably, the Romans had been a non-seafaring race before the conflict. Undeterred by this major disadvantage, they had learned the skills of naval warfare, adding a few tricks of their own in the process.

Since her defeat, Carthage had done little to reclaim the waves. Hanno sighed.

Truly all their hopes lay on the land, with Hannibal.

†

Some time later, Hanno had forgotten all his worries. Nearly a mile offshore, their little boat was positioned directly over a mass of tunny. The shoal's location had not been hard to determine, thanks to the roiling water created by the large silver fish as they hunted sardines. Fishing boats dotted the location and clouds of seabirds swooped and dived overhead, attracted by the prospect of food. Suniaton's source had been telling the truth, and neither youth had been able to stop grinning since their arrival. Their task was simple. While one rowed, the other lowered their small net into the sea. Although they had seen better days, the plaited strands were still capable of landing a good catch. Small pieces of wood along the top of the net helped it to float, while tiny lumps of lead pulled its lower edge down into the water. Their first throw had netted nearly two dozen tunny, each one longer than a man's forearm. Subsequent attempts were just as successful, and now the bottom of the boat was calf deep in fish. Any more, and they would risk overloading their craft.

"A good morning's work," Suniaton declared.

"Morning?" challenged Hanno, squinting at the sun. "We've been here less than an hour. It couldn't have been easier, eh?"

Suniaton regarded him solemnly. "Don't put yourself down. Think of the money we'll make selling this lot. I think our efforts deserve a toast." He reached into his pack and with a flourish, produced a small amphora.

Amused by his friend's irrepressible character, Hannibal laughed, which encouraged Suniaton to continue talking as if he were serving guests at an important banquet.

"Not the most expensive wine in Father's collection, I recall, but a palatable one nonetheless." Using his knife, he pried off the wax seal. Raising the amphora to his lips, he gulped a large mouthful. "Very tasty," he declared, handing over the clay vessel.

"Philistine. Taste it slowly." Hanno took a small sip and rolled it around his mouth as Malchus had taught him. The red wine had a light and fruity flavor, but possessed little undertone. "It needs a few more years, I think."

"Now who's being pompous?" Suniaton kicked a tunny at him. "Shut up and drink!"

Grinning, Hanno obeyed, taking more this time.

"Don't finish it," cried Suniaton.

Despite his protest, the amphora was quickly drained. At once the ravenous pair launched into the bread, nuts and fruit which Suniaton had bought. With their bellies full, and their work done, it was the most natural thing in the world to lie back and close their eyes. Unaccustomed to consuming much alcohol, they were both snoring before long.

†

It was the cold wind on his face which woke Hanno. Why was the boat moving so much, he wondered vaguely. He shivered, feeling quite chilled. Opening gummy eyes, he took in a prone Suniaton opposite, still clutching the empty amphora. At his feet, the heaps of blank-eyed fish, their bodies already rigid. Looking up, Hanno felt a pang of fear. Instead of the usual clear blue sky, all he could see were towering banks of blue-black clouds pouring in from the northwest. He blinked, refusing to believe what he was seeing. How could the weather have changed so fast? Mockingly, the first spatters of rain hit Hanno's upturned cheeks a moment later. Scanning the choppy waters around them, he could see no sign of the fishing craft which had surrounded theirs earlier. Nor could he see the land. Real alarm seized him.

He leaned over and shook Suniaton. "Wake up!"

The only response was an irritated grunt.

"Suni!" This time, Hanno slapped his friend across the face.

"Hey!" Suniaton cried, sitting up. "What's that for?"

Hanno didn't answer. "Where in the name of all the gods are we?" he shouted.

All semblance of drunkenness fell away as Suniaton turned his head from side to side. "Sacred Tanit above," he breathed. "How long were we asleep?"

"It had to be two hours or more," Hanno growled. He pointed to the west, where the sun's light was just visible behind the storm clouds. Its position told them that it was late in the afternoon. He stood, taking great care not to capsize the boat. Focusing on the horizon, where the sky met the threatening sea, he spent long moments trying to make out the familiar walls of Carthage, or the craggy promontory which lay to the north of the city.

"Well?" Suniaton could not keep the fear from his voice.

Hanno sat down heavily. "I can't see a thing. We have to be fifteen or twenty *stades* from shore. Maybe more."

What little color there had been in Suniaton's face drained away. Instinctively he clutched at the hollow gold tube which hung from a thong around his neck. Decorated with a lion's head at one end, it contained tiny parchments covered with protective spells and prayers to the gods. Hanno wore a similar one. With great effort, he refrained from copying his friend. "We'll row back," he announced.

"In these seas?" screeched Suniaton. "Are you mad?"

Hanno glared back. "What other choice have we? To jump in?"

His friend looked down. Both were more confident in the water than most, but they had never swum long distances, especially in conditions as bad as these.

Seizing the short oars from the floor, Hanno placed them in the iron locks. He turned the boat's rounded prow toward the west and began to row. Instantly he knew that his attempt was doomed to fail. The power surging at him was more powerful than anything he'd ever felt in his life. It felt like a raging, out-of-control beast, with the howling wind providing its terrifying voice. Ignoring his gut feeling, Hanno concentrated on each stroke with fierce intensity. Lean back. Drag the oars through the water. Lift them free. Bend forward, pushing the handles between his knees. Over and over he repeated the process, ignoring his pounding head and dry mouth, all the while cursing their foolishness in drinking so much wine. *If I had listened to my father, I'd still be at home,* he thought bitterly. *Safe on dry land.*

Finally, when the muscles in his arms were trembling with exhaustion, Hanno stopped. At least a quarter of an hour had gone by. Without looking up, though, he knew that their position would have changed little. For every three strokes he made, the current carried them at least two further out to sea. "Well?" he shouted. "Can you see anything?"

"No," Suniaton replied grimly. "Move over. It's my turn, and this is our best chance."

Our only chance, Hanno thought, gazing at the darkening sky.

Gingerly they exchanged places on the little wooden benches which were the boat's only fittings. Thanks to the mass of slippery fish underfoot, it was even more difficult than usual. While his friend labored at the oars, Hanno strained for a glimpse of land over the waves. Neither spoke. There was little point. The rain was now drumming down on their backs, combining with the wind's noise to form a shrieking cacophony that made normal speech impossible. Only the sturdy construction of their boat had prevented them from capsizing thus far.

At length, his energy spent, Suniaton shipped the oars. He looked at Hanno. There was still some hope in his eyes.

Hanno shook his head once.

Suniaton cursed. "It's supposed to be the middle of summer! Wind like this shouldn't happen without warning. The Scylla must be angry." He shuddered.

Hanno tried not to think of the winged demon which dwelled in the strait between Carthage and Sicily. Their plight was bad enough already. "There would have been signs," he barked. "Why do you think there are no other boats out here? No doubt they all headed back to shore when the wind began to rise."

Suniaton flushed and hung his head. "I'm sorry," he muttered. "It's my fault. I should never have taken Father's wine."

Hanno leaned forward and gripped his friend's knee. "Don't blame yourself. You didn't force me to drink it. That was my choice."

Suniaton managed to crack a smile. That was, until he looked down. "No!"

Hanno was horrified to see some of the tunny floating around his feet. They were shipping water, and enough of it to warrant immediate attention. Uncaring, he began throwing the precious fish overboard. Survival was now his aim, not earning money. With the floor clear, he soon found a loose nail on one of the planks. Removing one of his sandals, he used the iron-studded sole to hammer the nail partially home, thereby reducing the influx of seawater. Fortunately, there was a small bucket on board, containing spare pieces of lead for the net. Grabbing it, Hanno began bailing hard. To his immense relief, it didn't take long before he'd reduced the level of water to an acceptable level.

A loud rumble of thunder overhead nearly deafened him.

Suniaton moaned with fear, and Hanno jerked upright.

The sky overhead was now a menacing black, and in the depths of the clouds a flickering yellow-white color presaged lightning. The waves were being whipped into a frenzy by the wind, which was growing stronger by the moment. The storm was only just beginning to break. More water slopped into the boat, and Hanno redoubled his efforts with the bucket. Any chance of rowing back to Carthage was long gone. They were going only one direction. East. Into the middle of the Mediterranean. He tried not to let his panic show.

"What's going to happen to us?" Suniaton asked plaintively.

Realizing that his friend was looking for reassurance, Hanno tried to think of an optimistic answer, but couldn't. The only outcome possible was an early meeting for them both with Melqart, the god of the sea.

In his palace at the bottom of the sea.

ABOUT THE AUTHOR

Ben Kane was born in Kenya and raised there and in Ireland. He studied veterinary medicine at University College Dublin, and after that he traveled the world extensively, indulging his passion for ancient history. He now lives in North Somerset with his wife and family.